PENGUIN BOOKS
LADIES COUPÉ

Anita Nair is the author of *The Better Man*. She lives in Bangalore.

D0645855

Ladies Coupé

A NOVEL IN PARTS

Anita Nair

PENGUIN BOOKS

PENGUIN BOOKS
Published by the Penguin Group
Penguin Books India Pvt Ltd, 11 Community Centre, Panchsheel Park, New
Delhi 110 017, India
Penguin Group (USA) Inc., 375 Hudson Street, New York, New York 10014, USA
Penguin Group (Canada), 90 Eglinton Avenue East, Suite 700, Toronto, Ontario,
M4P 2Y3, Canada (a division of Pearson Penguin Canada Inc.)
Penguin Books Ltd, 80 Strand, London WC2R 0RL, England
Penguin Ireland, 25 St Stephen's Green, Dublin 2, Ireland (a division of Penguin
Books Ltd)
Penguin Group (Australia), 250 Camberwell Road, Camberwell, Victoria 3124,
Australia (a division of Pearson Australia Group Pty Ltd)
Penguin Group (NZ), cnr Airborne and Rosedale Roads, Albany, Auckland
1310, New Zealand (a division of Pearson New Zealand Ltd)
Penguin Group (South Africa) (Pty) Ltd, 24 Sturdee Avenue, Rosebank,
Johannesburg 2196, South Africa

Penguin Books Ltd, Registered Offices: 80 Strand, London WC2R 0RL, England

First published by Penguin Books India 2001

For sale in the Indian Subcontinent and Singapore only

Typeset in Sabon by Mantra Virtual Services, New Delhi
Printed at Chaman Offset Printers, New Delhi

For Soumini, my mother
who taught me all there is to know and then let me
make my own way

Acknowledgements

Rohini Kumar, Rhoda Stamell, Gita Krishnankutty, Nalini Suryavanshi, Prema Divakaran, and my beloved Rajeshwari Amma—were it not for these women, whose strength, courage and aptitude for joy have often inspired me, this novel about ordinary women and their indomitable spirit would have remained a mere thought.

As always, I owe much to:

Laura Susijn, my literary agent, for constant encouragement and her total faith in my writing.

Karthika V.K. of Penguin India whose belief in this book bolstered mine. For valuable inputs which took the sting out of re-writes and for being the finest editor I could hope for.

Namas Bhojani who let himself be persuaded into spending many hours waiting for the right train and when it arrived, captured the mood of this book with his camera.

Jayanth Kodkani, whose confidence in my writing far outweighs mine and who continues to be my first reader and sounding board.

Jayapriya Vasudevan of Jacaranda Press who gave me the run of her home and heart and continues to be there for me—a veritable rock.

Amy Eshoo whose affection and friendship I treasure. For

her depth of understanding and her willingness to share in both my triumphs and failures.

For advice, camaraderie and laughs, I have always had Sumentha and Franklin Bell, George Blecher, Anand, Amrita Chak, Antonio E Costa & Tania Mendonca, and Bala Sethi.

Andrew Nash who taught me the all-important and magical lesson of the rightness of now. And to 'pluck the day' even if it is from a window.

Uncle Mani in New York for cheering me on. And Uncle Mani in Mundakotukurissi, Kerala for opening the doors of the village library and the world of Malayalam literature for me.

To hold my hand, as always, there were my parents Soumini and Bhaskaran. And Sunil, Rajani and Unni.

And Maitreya, mother's little helper and writer's best friend.

*Were it possible for us to wait for ourselves to come into
the room, not many of us would find our hearts
breaking into flower as we heard the door handle turn.
But we fight for our rights, we will not let anybody take
our breath away from us and we resist all attempts to
prevent us from using our wills.*

—Rebecca West

1

This is the way it has always been: the smell of a railway platform at night fills Akhila with a sense of escape.

The long concrete corridor that stretches into the night segmented by signboards and the light and shadow of station lights. The moving hands of a clock beating an urgent rhythm to the din of mounted TV screens and the creak of trolleys laden with baskets and sacks. The crackling of the public address system as it hisses into life, announcing arrivals and departures. Jasmine wound in the hair, sweat and hair-oil, talcum powder and stale food, moist gunny bags and the raw green-tinged reek of bamboo baskets. Akhila breathed it all in and thought again of escape. A swell of people all escaping into aspects of richness of which she has no notion.

Akhila has often dreamt of this. Of being part of such a wave that pours into compartments and settles on seats, stowing baggage and clutching tickets. Of sitting with her back to her world, with her eyes looking ahead. Of leaving. Of running away. Of pulling out. Of escaping.

But the truth is, Akhila has never bought an express train ticket until now. She has never climbed into an overnight train to a place she has never been before.

Akhila is that sort of a woman. She does what is expected of her; she dreams about the rest. Which is why she collects epithets of hope like children collect ticket stubs. To her, hope is enmeshed with unrequited desires.

Blue skies, silver linings, a break in the clouds, Akhila knows these to be mere illusions caused by putting on rose-coloured spectacles. She has long ago trodden to shards her rose-glassed spectacles and switched to metal-framed glasses that remain plain indoors and turn photo-chromatic outdoors. Even the sun ceases to shine when Akhila's glasses turn a dusky brown.

So this then is Akhila. Forty-five years old. Sans rose-coloured spectacles. Sans husband, children, home and family. Dreaming of escape and space. Hungry for life and experience. Aching to connect.

✝

Akhila dreams: a train that trundles, truckles and troops into a station. Akhila is seated by a window. Everything but the train is still. The moon hangs at her shoulder and rides with her. She travels through a gallery of nightscapes, each framed by the window. A light in a house. A family huddled around a fire. A howling dog. A distant town. Black oily waters of a river. A menacing hill. A curling road. A railway-crossing with the streetlight glinting on the glasses of a man on a static scooter, hands dangling at his side, heel on the ground, head cocked, watching, waiting for the train to hurtle past.

At the station, portraits replace impressions. Reunions. Farewells. A smile. Tears. Anger. Irritation. Anxiety. Boredom. Stillness. Akhila sees them all. The train begins to move.

Akhila dreams of being there. And not there. Of adding a memory by the moment.

✝

Akhila was not a creature of impulse. She took time over every decision. She pondered, deliberated, slept over it and only when she had examined every single nuance and point of view did she make up her mind.

Even the saris she wore revealed this. Starched cotton saris that demand much planning and thinking ahead. Not like gauzy chiffons and ready-to-wear poly-silks. Those were for people who changed their minds at least six times every morning before they settled on what to wear. Those were for the fickle and feckless. Starched saris need orderly minds and Akhila prided herself on being an organized person.

But when she woke up that morning, stirred out of sleep by a tiny housefly with gauzy wings and a pert black body, hopelessly lost, vagrant and restless, humming and hovering above her face, Akhila felt within her a queer itinerant sensation. An aftermath of her dream the night before, she thought.

The fly settled on her brow for a fleeting second and rubbed its legs briskly. Flies did it all the time; loading and unloading disease and despair. But this one, new adult, had nothing to unburden but germs of disquiet. Akhila flicked the fly off with a sweep of her arm but the fly had accomplished what it had set out to do. A snarl of maggot-like notions swam through the redness of blood and thought till Akhila felt a great desire to board a train. To leave. To go somewhere. Land's end, perhaps. Kanyakumari.

At Kanyakumari, the three seas meet. The Bay of Bengal, the Indian Ocean and the Arabian Sea. A quiet male ocean flanked by two restless female seas. Akhila had heard of how it was at Kanyakumari, only then it was called Cape Comorin, that Vivekananda flung himself into the churning waters and the salts of the three seas and swam to a rock upon which he sat resolutely, waiting for answers that had eluded him all his life. She had read that at Kanyakumari, the goddess, like her, had put her life on hold. And that the beach there was made up of multi-coloured sand; the fossilized remnants of a wedding feast that was never served or eaten.

Akhila lay on her bed staring out of the window and decided that she would go. Tonight.

Padma wouldn't like it, Akhila knew. These days her sister

was suspicious of everything she did or said. Akhila felt her mouth draw into a line. Padma called it the spinster mouth, Akka's mouth: grim, determined and brooking no interference.

She rose and went to look at the calendar hanging on her wall. She skimmed the dates. December 19, 1997. The year would soon be over, Akhila thought, and then not knowing why, she searched the end of the calendar for the needle she kept pierced through the paper. Threaded with a white thread and kept in readiness for an emergency—a loose hook, an unravelling hem...The needle was gone. One of the girls must have taken it and forgotten to put it back. They did it all the time, no matter how often she told them that it was to be put back. That and the mirror by the washbasin dotted with maroon circles of felt—stick-on bindis which they peeled from their grimy foreheads and stuck back on the mirror for another day—made up her mind for her. She would go. She had to, or she would go mad confined within the walls of the house and the life she was expected to live.

Akhila opened her cupboard and drew out a black and red Madurai chungdi sari. It was cotton and starched but the colours and gold zari made Padma look up in surprise. Akhila had long ago ceased to wear bright colours, choosing to hide herself in drab moth tones. Yet, this morning Akhila was a butterfly. With magical hues and gay abandon. Where is the moth? Why aren't your wings folded? Why aren't you trying to pretend that you and the wood are one? Why aren't you hiding yourself among the curtains, Padma's eyes asked.

Padma will know then that this day will be unlike any other, Akhila thought when she saw astonishment swim across her face. Let it not be said that I gave her no warning.

'But you've never had to travel on work before,' Padma said when Akhila told her about her trip at breakfast time. Akhila waited till she had eaten her breakfast—three idlies, a small bowl of sambar, and a piping hot cup of coffee—and only then did she mention the journey. Padma was certain to object; to fuss and even make a scene, all of which would make Akhila lose her appetite. Akhila knew that as well as she had known how Padma's eyes would narrow suspiciously.

When Akhila didn't reply, Padma persisted, 'Isn't this rather sudden?'

For a moment, a lie crept into Akhila's mouth: it's official work. I was informed only yesterday.

But why? she asked herself. I owe her no explanations. 'Yes, it is sudden,' she said.

'How long will you be gone?' Padma's eyes glinted with doubts as she watched Akhila pack. Akhila knew what Padma was thinking. Is she travelling alone or is someone going with her? A man, perhaps. Padma's nostrils flared as if she could smell the stench of illicit liaisons.

'A few days,' she said. There was a certain pleasure in being ambiguous, Akhila decided when she saw the look on Padma's face.

†

All cargo offices smell alike. Akhila pursed her nostrils in readiness. In a moment she would allow herself to inhale slowly. After twenty years of travelling by suburban trains to work and back, she was used to what made everyone else's face screw up in disgust. She drew the line at fish, though. She waited as the cargo handlers dragged a basket of fish to the far end of the station. When they were gone, she walked towards the edge of the platform and stared down at the tracks. Long metal lines that ran into the horizon. She needn't have come into the station but she felt she had to see by daylight what was to be the beginning of her escape route. The platform was deserted. Yet, she felt a hollowness in the pit of her stomach as though any minute the train she was to board would pull into the station and it would be time for her to leave. Akhila smiled at her own foolishness. She walked to the reservation counter where Niloufer was waiting for her.

There was a long line at the far end of the counter. A long line of women mostly. Husbands, brothers and sometimes fathers stood guard, hovering in the periphery while their womenfolk stood, hands knotting the ends of their saree pallus, shifting their weight from one leg to the other, waiting their turn.

Akhila read the board above the line. 'Ladies, Senior Citizens and Handicapped Persons.' She did not know if she should feel angry or venerated. There was a certain old-fashioned charm, a rare chivalry in this gesture by the Railway Board that pronounced a woman shouldn't be subject to the hustle and bustle, lecherous looks and groping hands, sweaty armpits and swear words that were part of the experience of standing in the General Queue. But why spoil it all by clubbing women with senior citizens and handicapped persons? Akhila stifled a sigh and looked for Niloufer.

In some previous birth, Niloufer must have been a bee. She was always in the middle of some project. For a while, it was Chinese cooking; then it was tufting; the last one was the Anchor Stitch-kit. All this meant that she was never out of topics for conversation. All one had to do was listen, and she would do the talking. But in spite of her garrulousness, she was one of the few people Akhila liked and respected. She didn't pry. She didn't gossip and she was very hard-working and efficient. She wasn't Katherine. But then, Akhila wasn't looking for another Katherine.

'Niloufer,' Akhila had said as soon as she walked into the income-tax office, 'can you get me a ticket on tonight's train to Kanyakumari?'

'Why? What's happening there?' Niloufer's kohl-rimmed eyes widened. Niloufer liked dressing up. She wore a lot of jewellery, made up her face and chose her saris to match her jewellery.

'Does anything have to happen there for me to want to go to a place?' Akhila retorted.

'It's going to be difficult. This is peak season with everyone wanting to go to Kerala on holiday, and there are hordes of devotees on their way to Sabarimala,' Niloufer said as she leafed through a sheaf of papers. 'But my friend at the reservation counter will help. Particularly when I tell her it is for you. I'll call her right away.'

A few minutes later, Niloufer had come to her table smiling. 'It's all arranged. I'll go there half an hour before the lunch break. You can come a little later.'

Akhila spotted Niloufer. She was standing alongside the reservation clerk, talking. They stood oblivious to the crowd and the furious looks darted at them. Akhila lifted her hand furtively. She didn't want to draw attention to herself, she thought, as she waved her hand. Niloufer's eyes met hers through the glass counter. Her face was beaming and she waved a ticket.

'She did her best but the train is full. There are no second AC sleeper or first-class tickets. What she has got you is a berth in a second-class compartment, but in the ladies coupé. Is that all right? You'll be stuck with five other women who will all want to know the story of your life.' The gold bells in her ears jangled.

Akhila smiled. 'That's exactly what I need,' she murmured, pulling out her chequebook from her bag.

Akhila was at the Cantonment station by half past eight at night. It was only a few minutes away from where she lived. But she was in a hurry to leave home. It was as if once she had made up her mind, she wanted to shake the dust of home off her feet.

'How can you go by yourself to the railway station?' Padma had asked when Akhila reached home in the evening.

'I'm travelling alone, aren't I?'

'But it will be late when you leave home.'

Akhila reined in the irritation she felt and said, 'Don't worry. There are plenty of autorickshaws and they are very safe. Besides, the station is not all that far away.'

But Padma wouldn't give up and so the last words Akhila heard as she left home were veined with petulance. 'I don't know what Narayan Anna and Narsi Anna will say when they know of your going away suddenly, and all by yourself too...'

But Akhila had already ceased to listen. 'Cantonment Railway Station,' she told the autorickshaw driver with a lilt in her voice.

Ten minutes later, she stood at the entrance of the railway station, skimming the faces in the crowd.

I am here, her heart galloped. A tiny foam-edged wave of pure emotion rushed through her. She felt her lips stretch into a smile. I am part of a ripple that will escape this city tonight. I will board a train and allow it to lead me into a horizon I will not recognize.

✝

Akhila walked towards the stationmaster's office. Outside on the wall, she searched the noticeboard for the list of passengers. The sight of her name reassured her. Beneath her name were five others. Sheela Vasudevan, Prabha Devi, Janaki Prabhakar, Margaret Paulraj and Marikolanthu. They must be the other passengers in the coupé. Who were these women, Akhila wondered for a brief instant. Where were they going? What were their lives like?

Akhila moved away from the reservation chart to locate her compartment on the position chart. Eleventh from the engine. She shifted her suitcase to her other hand and began to walk towards the signboard marked eleven. All the benches were taken, so she went to stand by a dripping water faucet. She bit her lip uncertainly. Was this the right place? She turned towards an elderly couple who stood a little distance away and asked, 'Is this where the S7 compartment of the Kanyakumari Express stops?'

The man nodded. 'I think so. We are in the same compartment too.'

There was something about them that made her eyes return to them again and again. The elderly couple radiated a particular calm; an island of unhurried waiting in that sea of fidgety humans. As though they knew that sooner or later the train would arrive and it would be their turn to climb the three steps into the compartment that would take them to their destination. That there was no point in craning their necks, shuffling their feet or manifesting other signs of dissatisfaction until then.

The pong of urine rose and settled with the breeze. Red-shirted silver-armbanded porters stood alongside the piled suitcases. A beggar with maimed limbs thrust his tin cup this way and that. An urchin and a dog ran busily from one end of the platform to the other. A bored policeman stared at the TV screen.

The Udayan Express was late. The platform was crowded with people. Alongside Akhila stood a whole family of uncles, aunts, cousins and grandparents who had come to see a lone man off. He was headed for Bombay from where he would catch a plane to a Middle-Eastern country.

She wondered what it must be like to be the wife of a man who was away for many years and when he came home was claimed for their own by parents, siblings, cousins, relatives, friends...Akhila looked at the man who carried on his shoulders the burden of other people's dreams. That she knew all about. That she could understand.

She turned away from the man and watched the elderly couple. The woman wore a pale pink sari with a narrow gold border, a slim gold chain around her neck, and metal-rimmed spectacles. Her hair lay gathered in a little bun at the nape of her neck. A gold bracelet watch gleamed at her wrist. One hand held a water bottle while the other clutched a narrow leather purse. In a few years' time I will look like her, Akhila told herself. Except that I won't have a man like him beside me.

He seemed a nice enough man. The well-tailored clothes, the horn-rimmed spectacles, the still muscular body, the pleasant features, the manner in which his hair had receded, the way he stood at his wife's side, they all seemed to suggest a non-aggressive confidence. They looked like they belonged together.

What is it about marriage that makes it possible for a man and a woman to mesh their lives, dreams and even their thoughts in such a complete fashion? Her parents used to be like that. They even resembled each other with broad high foreheads, a slight hook to their noses and a cleft in their chins. They liked their coffee sweetened with two spoons of sugar and their curds set just so. It had to taste almost milk-like.

Often her mother only had to think about something, and her father would voice exactly the same sentiment within the fraction of a second and her mother would say, 'I was about to say that.'

He would beam at her then and guffaw with pleasure, 'That's because we are so well suited. We are two bodies and one soul.' And her mother would smile back coyly.

✝

When she was a teenager, Akhila remembered reading a novel about a couple who were passionately in love with each other even after many years of being married. Years later, she could recall neither the name of the book nor its plot. All she remembered was a line: The children of lovers are no better than orphans.

As a child, her parents' togetherness did not vex her. She was part of that enchanted circle as well. But as she grew up, their playfulness, their affection, the obvious pleasure they found in each other's presence made her feel excluded. Later, it embarrassed her. But they remained completely oblivious to her mortification. And even if they sensed it, nothing would deter or diminish what was practically a life-long love affair.

When her father died, her parents had been married for almost twenty-two years. Every year thereafter, on the date of their wedding day, her mother wept. 'For our twenty-fifth wedding anniversary, your father had promised to buy me a diamond nose-ring. A diamond for the queen of my heart, he said. He loved me so much,' she would moan. With every passing year, her mother's grief seemed only to increase.

She had lost more than a husband. He had been part of her life from the moment she was born. As her uncle, he had carried her in his arms, pointing out butterflies and crows, the moon and the rainbow, the wonders of nature. In many ways, it was only natural that he should be the one to show her the wonder of being a woman.

Akhila's mother married her father when she was fifteen years old. He was twenty-four. Akhila was born two years and eight months later.

'But Amma, how could you have agreed to marry your uncle?' Akhila asked her mother once. 'It's so unnatural.'

'What's unnatural about it?' she had demanded angrily. 'It is a perfectly accepted norm in our community. Who do you think you are to question it?'

Akhila was only fourteen. But even so, she heaved a sigh of relief that there was no uncle waiting in the wings for her to grow up.

Her mother threw her a dirty look and suggested that she go out and bring in the washing. 'An idle brain causes idle thoughts. Dangerous thoughts,' Amma said darkly.

'When you have finished folding and sorting the clothes, iron them. But leave your Appa's shirts for me. He is satisfied only if I do it,' she added.

Akhila grimaced because she knew that it wasn't so. Her father didn't care who ironed his shirts as long as they were done. But Amma liked to perpetuate this myth about a tyrant husband who was easily annoyed and could be placated only by her complete devotion. Unlike other husbands in the neighbourhood who let their wives rule them. Like Karpagam's mother.

Karpagam's mother taught dancing. Every evening between four and six, she gave lessons to the children in the neighbourhood. At the end of a year of lessons, her students knew enough to participate in school dancing competitions and win a few prizes. So she had plenty of girls coming in for dance

lessons. Besides, she only charged thirty-five rupees a month
per student. She made enough money to be able to buy little
trinkets for Karpagam and herself. Maybe that's why Amma
kept her distance from Karpagam's mother. Amma didn't like
anyone who was different from her.

One morning, when Akhila was about nine years old,
Karpagam brought to school a foot-long pencil with a cunning
little pink plastic hand attached to its end. Akhila immediately
wanted one like it.

'Where did you get it?' she whispered when Karpagam
showed her how she could scratch her back with it.

'My mother bought it for me,' she said, giving her back
another long drawn out scratch.

'What does it cost?'

'Six rupees. But Mother bought it at Moore Market. She
bargained with the shopkeepers and got it for three rupees. Its
real value is six rupees,' Karpagam said, giving Akhila the
pencil to hold and scratch her back with.

'Doesn't it feel lovely?' she asked, seeing the pleasure on
Akhila's face.

'It's beautiful. Can I take it home with me for a day? I'll show
it to my mother and ask her to buy me one as well,' Akhila said,
caressing the lines of the pencil hand as if it were a real hand. To
have and to hold.

Karpagam hesitated. 'I have to ask my mother...' she began.

'I promise to bring it back tomorrow. Look, if I get a pencil
like this, then we can scratch our backs together,' Akhila said in
earnest.

'You are quite silly,' Karpagam giggled, tickled by the
thought of the two of them going at their backs with their
pencils. Perhaps that was why she let Akhila take the pencil
home.

Amma was annoyed and then furious. 'Karpagam's mother
can buy her all kinds of things. Karpagam's mother has an
income of her own. I can't afford to buy you such useless things.
Do you realize that Appa works so hard and in spite of it, we

find it difficult to make ends meet? And I do not want you bringing other people's things into our home. What if you break or lose the pencil? Where will I find the money to replace it?'

The next day Akhila returned the pencil to Karpagam. 'What happened?' she asked. 'When will your mother buy one for you?'

'She said she can't afford to buy me things like your mother does,' Akhila said.

But all day and later all night, Akhila thought about it. If Amma had a job, she too would have money of her own and she would be able to buy her the things she needed without troubling Appa about it. But what could Amma do to earn some money?

The next morning, Akhila heard her mother singing under her breath as she went about her chores. It was a holiday and so she had all day to bide her time before she approached her with what she considered was a master move.

'Amma,' Akhila said when she thought Amma seemed in a receptive enough mood. Amma was combing her hair and singing softly. 'Why don't you give music lessons?'

Amma looked up in surprise.

Akhila hastened to explain. 'You sing so well and Appa always says that you have one of the best singing voices he has ever heard. Why don't you teach music like Karpagam's mother teaches dance? Then you would have some money of your own...' she finished lamely wondering if she had said too much.

'I don't approve of what Karpagam's mother is doing. All kinds of people come into their house. Brahmins and non-brahmins. Do you think your father would allow such comings and goings on here? Don't you know how strict he is? Anyway, do you think your father would let me? "If I wanted a working wife, then I would have married someone like that," he told me when we were first married. "I want my wife to take care of my children and me. I don't want her so caught up with her job that she has no time for the house or for taking care of my needs." And that's all I wanted to be as well. A good wife.'

Amma had her own theories on what a good wife ought to be like. First of all, no good wife could serve two masters—the masters being her father and her husband. A good wife learnt to put her husband's interests before anyone else's, even her father's. A good wife listened to her husband and did as he said. 'There is no such thing as an equal marriage,' Amma said. 'It is best to accept that the wife is inferior to the husband. That way, there can be no strife, no disharmony. It is when one wants to prove one's equality that there is warring and sparring all the time. It is so much easier and simpler to accept one's station in life and live accordingly. A woman is not meant to take on a man's role. Or the gods would have made her so. So what is all this about two equals in a marriage?'

Amma left all decisions to Appa. 'He knows best,' she said. 'We have never had to regret any decision that he has taken, even when it was on my behalf.'

Which is why when they had been married a few years and Amma inherited a small piece of land in her village, he thought it fit to sell it rather than keep it. 'The same piece of land was sold at ten times its price a month ago,' she said, reading a letter a cousin had written her. 'If we had kept it, we would have been able to buy a small house of our own,' she sighed.

When Akhila sighed along with her, she changed her expression and said, 'Mind you, I'm not saying that your father made a hasty decision. Who would have known that the land prices would soar so high and that too in a place like Mettupalayam?'

Amma's family was quite rich. But she was the daughter of a first wife who had died when she was eleven years old. Her mother had died trying to give birth to a baby boy who didn't survive either. A year later, her father married again. He was too smitten by his second wife and the sons she produced easily and regularly at eighteen-month intervals to bother too much about a daughter. When Amma was of marriageable age, he arranged for her wedding. A very austere one with Appa. After all, it had been arranged and settled many years ago. In fact, the moment she was born.

There was enough of everything, so no one had any reason to find fault, but there wasn't too much money or jewellery or anything that was of any enduring value. The piece of land had been her only inheritance from a father who left everything else to his sons.

But Appa had been adamant that she have nothing more to do with her family that had treated her so shabbily. 'From now on, I am all you have,' he had said. And Amma had accepted that happily. After her mother's death, no one had loved her as much. And this was to her another declaration of how much she meant to him.

Many years later, Akhila mentioned to a colleague and perhaps her only woman friend, Katherine, that her mother was also her father's niece. Katherine had stared in shock. 'But how can anyone marry their uncle? It is incest!' she had cried, her mouth a round 'O'.

'I suppose it is incest,' Akhila agreed. 'Maybe that's what made them so comfortable with each other.'

'I can't understand what your religion is all about.' Katherine shook her head. 'You consider eating an egg a sin. But it is perfectly acceptable to marry your uncle!'

Akhila could see Katherine's point of view but for some strange reason, she felt she had to defend her parents. Explain what their marriage had been like. 'They were very happy together. The happiest when they were together. Sometimes I think it's because they had always known each other. Imagine, my mother must have dribbled down my father's back when she was a baby. Perhaps even peed all over him. She must have heard his voice crack and seen the first hairs on his upper lip.'

'All that's fine. But you don't have to marry your uncle to be close to your husband,' Katherine had argued. 'In that case, you might as well marry your brother.'

'No, that's not what I mean. But you know what, a few years ago when I still wanted to be someone's wife, I would have agreed to marry anyone. Even an uncle,' Akhila had said, only half in jest.

✝

Akhila glanced at her watch, impatient for the first bell to ring. The Udayan Express had come and gone and now the platform was filled with passengers for the Kanyakumari Express. The elderly couple had moved a few paces ahead. She wondered how long they had been waiting there.

The man was beginning to look restless now. He asked the woman a question. She nodded her head. He edged out of the crowd and went up to the kiosk at the entrance of the station. He returned with a soft drink for her. She took a sip and offered it to him. He shook his head.

Why am I wasting my time watching them? Akhila pursed her lips. Here is proof of everything that my family has told me. A woman can't live alone. A woman can't cope alone. She was saved from further rumination when the signal changed. The headlight of the train moved towards the station and the PA system announced its arrival. Akhila picked up her suitcase and gripped its handle in readiness to board.

The swell of passengers surged forward as the train drew to a halt. Akhila felt fear propel her. How would all of them board the train at the same time? She elbowed her way through the crowd and found her way into her compartment. When she was seated, Akhila found the elderly lady was seated opposite. Her husband pushed a suitcase beneath the seat and blew into an air pillow. When it was puffed and plump, he patted it and put it on the seat beside her. He raised the window and adjusted the catch so that it wouldn't slam down on her hand. 'Do you want help with your window?' he asked, turning to Akhila.

She smiled and refused.

'You will be alright, won't you?' he asked, turning to his wife. 'When you are ready to sleep, pull down the wooden shutters. That way you'll get a good breeze and you don't have to worry about anyone snatching your chain or earrings. Don't forget to take your medicine. I am in the same compartment, so don't worry, I'll check on you often.'

When he was gone, the older woman gave Akhila a wry look and explained, 'We reserved our tickets only two days ago and this is all we could get. He doesn't even have a berth.'

'Looks like there is one empty berth,' Akhila said. 'The TTR might give it to him after all. They don't mind elderly men in the ladies coupé.'

'The berth is already taken. She is boarding at the next station or the one after that, they said.'

The train began to move and Akhila looked around her. There was a woman of her age and two younger women in the coupé.

She thought of what Niloufer had said and smiled to herself. 'Five women. Incessant chatter. Can you handle that?' Niloufer had teased.

'Where are you going?' The woman next to her asked.

A good-looking woman with a light complexion and a trim figure, and dressed in a manner that suggested money. Akhila wondered what she was doing in a second-class compartment.

'I'm going to Kanyakumari. What about you?' Akhila asked.

'Kottayam. There is a wedding there. I was supposed to have driven down with my husband but he had to go on business to Bombay and he will be flying in from there to Kochi.' And this is all I could get at short notice, her expression said, even though the words remained unspoken.

'What about you?' the elderly lady asked the woman seated next to her. A slim pretty creature with bobbed hair and eyes like shards of onyx.

'I'll be getting off at Coimbatore,' she said. Her voice was as sweet as her face and yet something about her made Akhila feel uneasy. 'And you?'

'Ernakulam.'

The woman at the farthest end sat curled towards the door of the coupé. She seemed completely oblivious to the rest of them in the enclosed space.

They stared at her. She wasn't one of them. She didn't look like one of them. It wasn't that she was dressed poorly or that there was about her the stink of poverty. It was simply the expression on her face. As if she had seen it all, human fickleness and fallibility, and there was very little that could happen that would take her by surprise. In contrast, their faces, though much older than hers, were unmarked by experience or suffering.

Besides, they were sure that she didn't speak English as they all did. That was enough to put a distance between them and her.

†

The woman next to Akhila opened a small basket and took out a few oranges. 'I didn't want to leave them behind at home to rot. Here, have one,' she said, holding out the fruit.

'My name is Prabha Devi. What is yours?' she asked no one in particular.

Prabha Devi. The elderly lady was Janaki. The pretty one was Margaret. And she, Akhila, Akhilandeswari.

The woman by the door had waited for the ticket collector and then she had climbed to the top berth and gone off to sleep. For some reason, Akhila knew it made them all feel better that they didn't have to include her in their conversation. That they didn't have to pretend they had something in common with her. That because they were all women they had to group themselves with her.

The scent of oranges filled the coupé. And with it a quiet camaraderie sprung between them. Prabha Devi began to talk to Margaret.

Akhila kicked her sandals off, curled her feet under her and leaned against the window. The breeze ruffled her hair. The moon hung by her shoulder.

'My grandchild gave me a bar of chocolate. To nibble at

during the night,' the elderly lady said smiling. 'Would you like some?' She offered the bar around.

Akhila took a piece of the Kit Kat and tore off the silver foil. Margaret shook her head. 'I used to like chocolate once upon a time. Not any more.'

'I don't eat chocolate either. My son is seventeen years old but he is still like a three-year-old when it comes to chocolate,' Prabha Devi said, passing the chocolate back to Janaki.

Akhila felt her heart lurch as it always did when someone mentioned a seventeen-year-old son. A boy. A teenage boy. An attractive man. Then she would remember that she was forty-five years old. Old enough to be the boy's mother.

'Each time my husband goes abroad on business, he brings back chocolate for my son,' Prabha Devi continued. 'My daughter stopped eating chocolate when she discovered it was chocolate that was causing her skin to erupt. Sometimes I think she spends all her time in front of the mirror checking her face for a pimple or a blemish. Now she demands that my husband bring her back make-up from a store called Body Shop.'

'What does he do?' Janaki asked.

'We have a jewellery business,' Prabha Devi said. 'I shouldn't be saying "we". He has a jewellery business. I am a housewife.'

'Nothing wrong with that. I'm a housewife too,' Janaki said. 'What about you?' she said, turning to Margaret.

'My husband is the principal of a school. I teach chemistry in the same school,' she said.

'Doesn't it get difficult when the two of you work together?' Akhila asked. What must it feel like to share more than a bed with a man? To share his dreams and his day. To be part of his every hour, every minute. Would it foster togetherness or only disdain, Akhila wondered.

'Do you find yourselves arguing about everything?' Prabha Devi giggled and then suddenly, as if conscious of what she had said, she covered her mouth with her hand and tried to explain, 'It's not just the house; you share a workplace too.'

'We had our problems at first but now we know enough to

deflect tension when it occurs. To separate the school life from our home life. It took us a long time but we manage pretty well now. Guess what? My daughter studies in the same school too!' Margaret said with a chuckle.

'What does your husband do?' the elderly lady asked, cocking her head at Akhila.

'I am not married,' Akhila said.

'Oh.' Janaki lapsed into silence. Akhila knew she thought she had offended her. She took a deep breath.

'I am forty-five years old and I have always lived with my family,' she said.

Prabha Devi turned towards her. But it was Margaret who spoke first. 'Do you have a job?'

She nodded. 'I work for the income-tax department,' Akhila said.

'If you don't mind me asking you, why is it that you didn't marry?' Prabha Devi asked, leaning towards Akhila. 'Did you choose to remain unmarried?'

What am I going to tell her? Akhila wondered.

Suddenly it didn't matter. Akhila knew she could tell these women whatever she chose to. Her secrets, desires, and fears. In turn, she could ask them whatever she wanted. They would never see each other again.

'I didn't choose to remain single. It happened that way,' she said. When she saw the curiosity in their eyes, she elaborated, 'My father died and I had to look after the family. By the time they were all settled in their lives, I was much too old to marry.'

'You are not all that old,' Janaki said. 'You can still find yourself a good man. The matrimonial columns are full of advertisements by men in their mid- and late-forties seeking a suitable mature woman to spend their lives with.'

'If you ask me, those men are looking for a housekeeper—someone to cook, clean and fetch for them. If she is happy the way she is, why should she marry?' Margaret asked.

'Are you happy?' Prabha Devi asked.

'Is anyone happy?' Akhila retorted.

'It depends,' Prabha Devi said, tucking a strand of hair behind her ear. 'It depends on what you define happiness to be.'

Akhila leaned toward her and said, 'As far as I am concerned, marriage is unimportant. Companionship, yes, I would like that. The problem is, I wish to live by myself but everyone tells me that a woman can't live alone. What do you think? Can a woman live by herself?'

'Why should a woman live by herself? There is always a man who is willing to be with her,' Janaki said, taking her glasses off and rubbing the bridge of her nose. 'Didn't you ever meet anyone you wanted to marry?'

'I did,' Akhila said and a faint shadow settled on her face. 'But it was not meant to be.'

'Why?' Prabha Devi asked. 'Why was it not meant to be?'

'We were not right for each other. Besides, these days, getting married is hardly on my mind. All I am trying to do is convince myself that a woman can live alone.'

'You should trust your instincts,' Margaret said. 'You have to find your own answers. No one can help you do that.'

Akhila paused for a moment, then began again, 'At first, I thought I would pretend to my family that I had talked to several people before I decided that I could live by myself. But one night, I woke up with a start. My heart was hammering in my chest and I was paralysed by a nameless fear. How can I? I asked myself. How can I who have never spent a week away from my family survive a future alone? What do I know of running a household? I mean, I have never been responsible for the everyday running of one. How am I to manage a home? When I fall ill, what will I do? Who will I turn to? What do I know of life? How am I going to cope? Then I thought that maybe if I met other women who were single, or just...any women...if I talked to them...maybe it could help me make up my mind...'

Prabha Devi and Margaret looked at each other in amusement. 'So are we the ones who are going to do that for you?'

'Don't mock her,' Janaki said. Janaki, who could very well have been her mother and theirs. How easily they slipped into familiar roles. Mother and three daughters. Two siblings ganging up against one.

'She is serious. Can't you two see that?'

Akhila shrugged. 'I don't know if you will be able to help me. But you must tell me what you really think. Can a woman cope alone?'

'Is it advice you are looking for?' Janaki asked.

'I don't want advice. I just want you to tell me if you think a woman can manage alone,' Akhila said in a low voice.

Janaki peered at her face, searching her eyes. Akhila sat there saying nothing. Janaki sighed. 'They are,' she said gesturing to the other two, 'closer in age to you. You should speak to them. Their opinion will mean much more than mine. I am the wrong person to talk to. My husband and I have been married for forty years. That's a long time for a couple to stay together. How can I tell you what it means for a woman to live alone?'

There was silence in the coupé. For a moment, Akhila had thought they had established a connection. Foetuses jostling within the walls of a womb, drawing sustenance from each other's lives, aided by the darkness outside and the fact that what was shared within the walls wouldn't go beyond this night or the contained space.

'I don't know enough about the world or you to offer advice. All I can do is tell you about myself, about my marriage and what it means to me,' Janaki began suddenly, slowly, as if every word had to be chosen with great care. 'I am a woman who has always been looked after. First there was my father and my brothers; then my husband. When my husband is gone, there will be my son. Waiting to take off from where his father left off. Women like me end up being fragile. Our men treat us like princesses. And because of that we look down upon women who are strong and who can cope by themselves. Do you understand what I am saying?

'Perhaps because of the way I was brought up, perhaps because of all that was instilled in me, I believed that a woman's duty was to get married. To be a good wife and mother. I believed in that tired old cliché that a home was a woman's kingdom. I worked very hard to preserve mine. And then suddenly, one day, it didn't matter any more. My home ceased to interest me; none of the beliefs I had built my life around had any meaning. I thought if I were to lose it all, I would cope. If I ever became alone, I would manage perfectly. I was quite confident about that. I think I was tired of being this fragile creature.'

Akhila searched Janaki's face. What did she mean by 'was'?

'But you have changed your mind now. Why?' Akhila asked.

Janaki patted the air pillow as if it were her husband's hand and said, 'Now I know that even if I can cope, it wouldn't be the same if he wasn't there with me.'

2

A CERTAIN AGE

Feathers. Soft wispy down. The swish of satin on the skin of the inner arm. Every night Janaki lay on her side, cradling her face in the crook of her elbow, and thought of all the nice and soft things in life. Anything to drown the noises that seeped through the walls of the bathroom. Noises that she had heard almost every night for the past forty years.

The gurgling of the cistern when he flushed. The splash of water on the floor as the shower spat out fifty-two jets of tepid water. He was that kind of a person; extremes of any sort worried him. His tuneless humming as he soaped himself vigorously, allowing the fragrant white lather to coat his body. Make-believe amniotic fluid before he curled up into a foetal ball beside her. More splashes. The tinkle of his teeth in a china cup. He brushed his dentures and his remaining teeth faithfully every night. Gargling. Spitting. The tuneless humming again and again.

Do I really hear these noises? Or, is it just what I know? Janaki asked herself. Have we really lived together for thirty years?

Janaki married Prabhakar when she was eighteen and he was twenty-seven. Theirs was an arranged marriage; the horoscopes matched, the families liked each other and they were considered perfectly suited for each other. Janaki didn't know what to expect of marriage. All through her girlhood, marriage was a destination she was being groomed for. Her mother and aunts took great care to perfect what they called the skills of marriage—cooking and cleaning, sewing and pickling...she wasn't expected to know what it really meant to be married, and neither was she curious about it. It would come to her as it had to her mother, she thought.

On her wedding night, when he touched her lips with his, all she felt was a stiffening within. It wasn't just shyness. It was perhaps the strangeness. She had never been alone with a man in a room, with the door locked. The company of men had always been frowned upon and suddenly because she was married they said it was all right for her to be with him, let him touch her and even undress her.

'He is your husband and you must accept whatever he does,' Janaki's aunts had whispered as they led her to the bedroom adorned with jasmine and scented with incense sticks.

He lay down next to her and drew her palms to his chest. 'Touch me,' he said and all she could think was how coarse the hair on his chest was.

He nuzzled his chin against her neck and again that wave of repulsion washed over her: What am I doing here? What have I let myself in for?

He touched. He stroked. He caressed and fondled and yet all Janaki felt was a locking within.

Their marriage remained unconsummated for more than two months. He didn't force himself upon her. It wasn't as if he didn't try to make her more receptive. He coaxed, cajoled and even pleaded. He tried very hard to make her accept him into her body. But each time, she flinched at the slightest twinge of pain, and he withdrew and left her alone. She began to wish that he would stop being so gentle and would force himself to close his eyes to her reluctance. She was afraid, you see. That if she didn't give him what he wanted, he would go looking for it elsewhere.

So Janaki learnt to conquer her revulsion, match his caresses, open her arms and part her legs and grind the pain when it came between her teeth, and swallow it down with the cry that threw itself up her throat. That night, he held her close and whispered against her hair again and again, 'You are my wife. You are my wife.'

Nothing else mattered then, she thought, but the knowledge that she was his wife and that she had pleased him.

In the weeks after she had allowed him access to her body, she began to discover the pleasure hidden in rituals of togetherness. Wearing his old shirts to bed, feeling the fabric slither on her skin. Sharing a cup of tea, tasting his mouth in hers. Bathing together. Splashing each other, the loofah a living creature as their fingers teased and caressed skin. The fluffy white cotton towel was a device that said 'Look how much I love you' as it gently wrapped them in a cocoon of warmth, sucking moisture with a thousand lips.

When did they stop going into the bathroom hand in hand? Before the baby came or after?

When you have been married long, bathing becomes simply a means to cleanse yourself. The rest of it is over with the honeymoon.

Janaki turned on her back and drew the quilt up to her chin.

Every night, Janaki lay awake until she heard the bedsprings creak and groan as they accepted his weight. Only when he had settled for the night, arranging his body so as to not intrude into her space, did she allow herself to drift into sleep. He knew that she didn't like the sheet rucked or the blanket tangled around her legs. So he kept his distance with a separate blanket. He tossed and turned. She didn't. In the morning, when they woke up, it was as if they had slept in separate rooms in separate beds.

Some nights they talked. Random pieces of conversation. About their son. A neighbour. Or, perhaps a film they had seen earlier that night. Sometimes they slipped into reminiscences. Memories that were dicephalous. He didn't remember it the way she did. But what did it matter? In retrospect, it was the sharing that counted.

Some nights his body sought hers. His shape moulded hers. Some nights she welcomed him and other nights bore with patience the warmth his skin, lips, hands and thighs inflicted on her so benignly. Later, when spent, they would arrange themselves into separate entities and fall asleep.

After forty years, there were no more surprises, no jarring notes, no peek-a-boos from behind doors. There was just this friendly love advertising liked to capitalize on.

Take out an insurance policy so that the retirement years are spent blissfully walking the dog on the beach, building sandcastles with grandchildren and sipping coconut water. None of those wind-in-the-hair bike rides. Or rolling down a mountainside. You drank your Horlicks and reaped the benefits of your insurance policy.

Why do they make these years seem like a waiting period for death? Janaki thought. She switched channels each time a life insurance commercial appeared.

But wasn't that the way they lived? Borrowing moments from television commercials. The jokes, the laughter, the nostalgia as they looked at photo albums together. Friendly love. The curve of the rainbow before the clouds shrouded them in a haze of down.

Janaki groped for her glasses on the bedside table. What time was it?

Every night for the past ten years, he had laid out a single tablet of Trika with a glass of water for her. Somehow when he did it, it didn't seem so bad, her inability to fall asleep naturally.

The doctor had helped her lift her legs out of the stirrups slung over the examination table and had smoothened the aqua-green hospital smock over her thighs. He had smiled and assured her, 'You are absolutely alright. As for your not being able to sleep...' he had shrugged casually. 'When you get to a certain age, sleep does become difficult.'

A certain age. She was a woman of a certain age. But what about him? He was a restless sleeper but he had no trouble falling asleep. Like a baby. Baby blue. Bonny, bonny baby.

When they had been married for about seven months, in those days when every day had brought with it a delicious tinge of discovery that made love seem like a whole new theory he and she had infused with meaning, they had fallen into the habit of baby talking each other.

Goo goo, juju mani, she would croon. Lu lu, he'd murmur nibbling at her ear lobe. Nonsensical sounds only they knew how to decipher.

Then one day Janaki discovered she was pregnant. She craved the taste of tobacco and smoked the butts he left behind in the ashtrays. When he put his arm around her, she lifted it off with barely concealed rage. She hated him, god knows why, but the doctor explained that it was natural for her to feel that way. Blame it all on the hormones, he said with a laugh.

When the baby began kicking, the hate went as her craving had. She increasingly baby talked him, ruffled his hair fondly and began work on a patchwork quilt for the baby's bed. And like all fathers-to-be, he pressed his ear to her stomach that rippled. A water diviner waiting for the inner forces to tug and draw him closer.

When the baby came, they made it smile with rattles and monkeys that beat on drums when wound with a key. They counted its tiny toes, held it close to their hearts and mouthed gibberish.

In bed, their conversations dwindled to—Is the nappy wet? Did you check the teddy lamp? I thought I heard a cry. Did you?

They stopped doing little quizzes on 'How much do you understand your partner?' or 'Is your marriage still romantic?' Instead they ticked boxes to find out if they were good parents and if their child was growing up right.

It didn't bother them, this invasion of their privacy. They looked at the child and saw themselves in him. He was an extension of their images. When he came home with a silver cup, the prize for a school tennis match, their hearts sparkled. Can you believe it, he came from within us, they signalled to each other in telepathic ecstasy.

There was no stopping this wonder child they fed on cornflakes and milk, toast and butter, soft-boiled eggs and multivitamins for breakfast. He made their lives so full. Report cards, band-aids, summer vacations, birthdays...this child of theirs made their marriage so much more complete.

At parties, they were the golden couple. When she was ready to leave, he knew it and would rise from his chair, setting aside the drink he had been nursing all evening. She would smile and murmur polite words of farewell while he pumped various hands and laughed through his leave-taking. In this marriage, he was the partner with bonhomie and verve.

When they reached home cruising through the city roads, keeping an eye out for meandering drunks and speeding trucks, it would never be later than half past ten. He would park the scooter while she fumbled with the house keys. Together, they would go into their son's room. She would give the boy a glass of warm milk to drink and he would watch from the door.

Half asleep, she would feel his presence next to her as his arm snaked around her waist. She would sigh drowsily. Even in that semi-comatose state, she would utter a silent prayer to God. This man made her forget what the mirror and the daylight reminded her about so annoyingly. The lines on her neck, the droop of her breasts, the sag of her puckered and scarred belly that had never quite recovered from having held captive another live being. Those days, she hadn't got to be a woman of a certain age.

When did the certain age creep up on Janaki? Did she realize it first when she no longer liked his arm around her waist? Or was it when there began a tightness in her temples that grew worse when he laughed as he always did, loudly? Or was it one evening when they took their son, their almost grown-up six-foot tall, broad-shouldered Siddharth shoe shopping and she watched

Prabhakar try and steer their son towards his preferences? Supple leather shoes with well-fitted soles. Middle-aged men's shoes. Janaki saw her son's face tighten in rebellion. He didn't like the shoes. 'Not this,' he said. 'Not this, either.'

Prabhakar threw up his arms and let his vexation show. 'What are you looking for? This is the fourth shop we have been to this evening and nothing seems to suit your fancy. What is it you want? Do you know what you want?'

And she felt this queer rage uncoil within her. 'Let him choose what he wants. I don't understand why we should be here. Siddharth is old enough to be trusted to buy a pair of shoes on his own,' she hissed.

'I was just trying to help,' he said.

'That's not helping. You just want to control him. You want to control everybody. You want everyone to do your bidding,' she said, not caring who overheard.

'Janu,' he said. 'What's wrong? Are you feeling alright?'

'Oh, leave me alone,' Janaki snapped and walked out of the shoe shop leaving father and son together.

Or was it the day when Siddharth brought home with him six other boys from his class for lunch and Janaki stood at the door, smiling a welcome, trying to curb her panic? There was barely enough food to stretch to four. Flustered, anxious, Janaki rushed into the kitchen to cook some more and discovered the gas cylinder was empty and that she had forgotten to call the gas agency and book in advance for another one. Janaki stood by the stove that refused to burn, looked at the washed and soaking rice, the chopped vegetables, and burst into tears. What am I going to do? What will Siddharth's friends think of me?

When Prabhakar came home for lunch, he found her huddled in the kitchen blubbering while Siddharth and his friends sat at the dining table making conversation, pretending that nothing was wrong and that the sobbing they could hear quite clearly was perhaps coming from the TV in the living room.

The certain age. Maybe it came upon her when she saw the

fond indulgence in her adult son's eyes replaced by an irritation bordering on disdain. Or maybe it hit her when she stopped marking the calendar on the day her periods began and instead her husband took to the hospital pharmacist every month a prescription for thirty tablets of Trika.

Thirty days hath September, April, June and November...

'What about the rest of the year?' Janaki grumbled.

But he had a solution, like he always did. He was a good provider. So he remembered the months with the extra day and reminded the doctor about it.

What about him? What had happened to him in those years?

Men don't really change that much. Or so women like to think. They bald a little, their eyes grow dim, but they still insist on checking the door after their wives have locked up.

He was no different. The beating of his heart slowed him down, sometimes it crashed in his ears, but he didn't forget his place as a husband, father and provider.

She didn't think he loved her any less because of her mood swings. He just understood—an understanding person always suffers.

Not that it was true of him. He didn't suffer. She had tried very hard to be a good wife and mother. It was only now, this certain age, that had made her so, well, sensitive.

'Tell me, do you know of any other couple like us? Our son is well settled. We are secure and healthy. We live in our own house. After forty years together, what more can one ask for?'

They had it all, didn't they? They even had sex (how she detested that word) once in a while.

'When my parents got to be our age, they stopped living. I don't mean they died. They breathed, ate, slept. Yes, that's all they did with their lives,' she told this foe who lived in her mind and questioned her marriage.

There was a certain something that he and she shared. A tensile connection that is there between most couples who have been married a long time. She didn't know how to describe it. As companionship? As friendship? Or a mere complicity that springs between people who share a bed, a child and a life? Whatever it may be, she didn't see it between her son and his wife.

Janaki pitied the girl and she wished she could take her son's chin in her palm, like she used to when he was a little boy and being fractious, and tell him sternly—You'll drive her away from you with your callousness, with your cold sullen expression. Is this how your Dad is with me? So who taught you to be like this?

Then it occurred to Janaki that perhaps it was her he was emulating. That the selfish streak had been her contribution to his gene pool. That she was to blame and no one else.

When they had guests, when they had family visiting, when the house was echoing with sounds and laughter and she was in the kitchen, dishing up a meal, Prabhakar would hover alongside wanting to help, unwilling to leave her alone. And even if there was nothing for him to do, he would stand leaning against the kitchen counter, clinking the ice in his rum and soda and wait.

'Go on, I'll join you soon,' Janaki would say, but he wouldn't budge.

Sometimes if it was a couple who they enjoyed having over or a cousin whom Janaki had adored as a child, he would whisper in her ear, 'Happy?'

And she would smile. At that moment she felt truly happy.

Janaki placed the Trika on her tongue and quickly sipped from the glass of water. Then reaching out, she switched off the lamp.

She didn't know why this room made her feel uneasy. The strangeness bothered her. They had only come in this morning from Madras where they had been visiting friends, and were supposed to stay with Siddharth for a week. A week seemed forever in this room.

This bed, she thought fingering the quilt, was out of a

magazine advertisement, with its frilled bedspread, sheets patterned with cabbage roses and pillow slips in muted pink. Even the quilt had pink satin piping. The bedside lamp was a cloud of rose on a terracotta base. It overpowered her, this room.

Jaya, their daughter-in-law, in her gay, affluent child voice had prattled, 'We call it our pink room. It's Suchi's room, which is why we have done it up in pink. But I have removed all her toys and games so it doesn't look like a child's room. I hope you will be comfortable in it.'

Sometimes her daughter-in-law got on her nerves. But she deflected any antagonism between them with the composure she had worked hard to acquire. When you get to a certain age, nothing matters. You only want to cling to your serenity and leave the dreaming and storming for those with steaming blood in their veins. Emotions are for the young; the elderly have no use for them. It doesn't become them either, she had decided a long time ago.

Janaki thought of her mother. Distraught at how her children took her for granted. Unable to accept the senility forced upon her, so that all they had to do was humour her. She had vowed never to be like her mother, eyes streaked with tears, voice cracked with sorrow. When you get to a certain age, nothing matters but your serenity.

After the wedding and honeymoon, Siddharth and Jaya came visiting. All day, Janaki felt Jaya's eyes follow them, Prabhakar and her, as they went through the ballet of household chores. A synchronized performance that years of practice had fine-tuned to perfection. He chopped. She cooked. He washed the dishes. She dried and stacked them. She hung out the clothes to dry. He brought them in. She turned down the bedclothes. He switched off the lights.

A couple of mornings later, as Janaki made dosas in the kitchen and he sat at the dining table chopping vegetables for the sambar, Jaya sipped her tea and said, 'Mummy, you are so lucky to have a man like Uncle for your husband. He helps you in just about every way he can, doesn't he?'

Janaki watched him beam and thought to herself that it was true. She couldn't do a single thing around the house without his help.

'Ever since Papa died, Mamma has had to do everything by herself. But she says that has made her a stronger woman than most.' The pride in her voice caught at Janaki's throat. For some reason, it made her feel inadequate. Are you saying that I am a weak, helpless creature, she wanted to demand.

Prabhakar looked up from the cutting board. He paused in the middle of slicing an onion and said, 'Just because she needs me to open the mixer jar or chop onions for her, you mustn't think Mummy is a weak woman.

'When we were just married and I was stationed in a small town near Hyderabad, one afternoon, our neighbour Mrs Bhatt who was eight months pregnant went into labour. There was no one Mummy could call for help. There were no telephones then, no autorickshaws or taxis at every street corner. And the nearest hospital was five kilometres away. You know what she did...Mummy went to the main road and waved down a truck. The truck driver and Mummy took Mrs Bhatt to the hospital. If Mummy hadn't done that, Mrs Bhatt would have died...

'She might seem delicate and cosseted to you, but she is a strong woman. Mummy is very capable when she wants to be.'

He told that story to everyone. He told that story with such pride that it made Janaki grit her teeth. He told that story as if it was the only worthwhile deed of her life. She wanted to fling down the spatula, upturn the bowl that held the dosa batter and slap his face till the pride crumbled in his eyes and scattered in the air. She wanted to scream, 'Don't call me Mummy. I'm not your mummy. I am your wife. Remember, you used to call me Janu once. Wife. Darling. Sweetheart. And if you find it hard saying those, call me woman, but don't call me Mummy!'

Janaki felt her daughter-in-law's eyes on her and turned her face away. She didn't want her to see the fury in her eyes. Janaki wanted Jaya to think of her as a composed and contented woman.

Janaki switched on the bedside lamp. He had been in the bathroom for more than fifteen minutes. Where was he? She couldn't hear the familiar comforting noises. Had he slipped and fallen? Had he felt a strange weakness overtake him as he slumped on the floor? She would wait for a few minutes more before she got up and went looking for him. She had never fussed over him. He would think it strange if she started doing so now.

What did her mother feel when her father died? What would it be like when he was no more?

Janaki refused to think of it. Siddharth brought it up in conversation every now and then:

'Mummy, when Daddy is gone, how will you stay by yourself in that huge house?'

'You will have to make your home with us one day or the other.'

'My friend deals in real estate. When the times comes, I'll mention it to him.'

Janaki changed the subject every time Siddharth mentioned it. But there was no turning away in this room. What would it be like when every night stretched into the horizon?

You could be the one to die first, a little voice said. But I won't, I know. Janaki felt a tear slide down into her hair. It would be her lot to endure. Souls like his savoured life. They swept their way through births and deaths, not once but a million times.

What would it be like to sleep alone in a bed and to wake up in a room all by herself? Early mornings, nights. Alone, alone. Please god, Janaki prayed, let me fall asleep so that I don't have to think.

When it was time for Jaya to be admitted to hospital for the Caesarean, Siddharth called his parents. 'Please Ma, will you two come? Jaya's mother is here and she is perfectly capable of managing, but if you were around I would feel a lot more secure.'

'Do you want to go?' Prabhakar asked Janaki.

'How can we not go?' Janaki said as she began to pull out saris from the cupboard and arranged them in little stacks on the bed for Prabhakar to pack. 'He is our son. We have to be there for him when he needs us.'

By the third day, the squabbles began. Prabhakar had known they would. Ever since Siddharth got married, almost everything his mother said or did infuriated him. It was as if he had begun to measure his mother with a new yardstick and each time she fell short of what he expected of her. Janu was the same, he thought. She complained that her son had changed and she no longer knew this man whose voice, when it was directed towards her, was heavy with a suppressed dislike. A suppressed dislike for what? What have I done wrong? she asked Prabhakar again and again.

There were no real reasons for them to snipe at each other but they always did. She and Siddharth tossed veiled insults at each other as if it were a ball while Prabhakar stood in the middle, unwilling to take sides.

Then one day, as Prabhakar lay on the bed in the guest room, he heard Siddharth say, 'You are spoilt. Everyone you know has spoilt you. Your family and then Dad. You are such a princess. You want everything done your way, your selfish way. And if someone doesn't do it the way you want it done, you know how to sulk and get them to do it. I can't help but compare you to Jaya's mother. I see how generous she is; how she is willing to give all of herself to her children. You don't do that. When have you ever thought of anyone but yourself?'

As Janaki watched, Prabhakar had stormed into the dining room where they were and said in an ice-cold voice, 'Janaki, pack your things. We are leaving right now. You don't have to take any of this nonsense from him. How dare he talk to you in that tone of voice!'

'Dad, stop being so melodramatic. You always take her side no matter who is at fault. Listen to what I have to say as well. You are the reason why Mom is the way she is,' Siddharth said, flinging his arms out in a gesture of helplessness.

'You,' Prabhakar said, wagging an angry finger, 'shut up. I will have nothing to do with you until you apologize to your mother first. And if I don't take her side, who will? I'm her husband, goddamn it, and I bloody well will take her side.'

Janaki began to cry. Contrite, Siddharth had gone on his knees and pleaded with his mother to stop crying while Prabhakar watched, anger making his face pale and drawn.

Later in the night, he had said, 'We will leave in a couple of days. There is no point in staying on if there is this air of unease all the time. But more than anything else, what bothers me is that if this is how he is with you when I am alive, what will he do to you when I'm dead and no longer around to take care of you.'

But Janaki had put her hand on his arm and tried to breach the cracks as well as she could, for that was what mothers were meant to do. 'Don't let it upset you. He is not a bad son. I know he is tense about the baby being born ill; I know that his work pressure is high; it's the stress that's making him nasty. He is not a bad son. I know that.'

The shaft of light from the bathroom door widened. She turned her head towards him and watched as he padded to his side of the bed.

'Let me ask them for another blanket,' he murmured. 'There is just this one quilt for us.'

She felt her heart lilt. 'No, no, don't,' she said softly.

'Are you sure?'

'Yes, I'm sure. Get into bed. I feel cold watching you stand there.'

Janaki could feel herself blushing in the dark. She didn't understand this warming of her senses. Women her age were not supposed to feel this way. She turned towards him and watched him put the usual distance between them.

'Can we go home tomorrow?' she asked.

'What?' he said.

'Can we go home tomorrow? I'm tired of all the travelling we have been doing these past few weeks. I'd like to go home.'

'They have booked our tickets for the twenty-fourth. Siddharth said that he had to use a great deal of clout to get even that. There are no first-class tickets available before that.'

'I don't mind travelling second-class,' she said.

'Are you sure? It won't be all that clean and the berths are not very wide or soft. You will be tired by the time you reach home.' He lay on his back and cleared his throat.

'That's alright.'

'Siddharth won't like it. He is sure to make a fuss.'

'Let him. I just want to go home,' she said.

Then slowly, because she had never ever said these words before, she whispered, 'I am tired of sharing you with everyone. I want you to myself.'

She moved closer and fitted the length of her body to his side. She felt him hold his breath and then gradually, in wonder, exhale.

She adjusted her breathing to his, inhaling the combination of moisture, toothpaste and soap that was his fragrance. He gathered her in his arms and she lay there with her head nestling on his shoulder.

Friendly love. Under one blanket everything was possible, she thought as her eyes closed and his warmth slipped into her.

3

Panic fans the flames of fear. Panic dulls. Panic stills. Panic tugs at soaring dreams and hurls them down to earth. Panic destroys.

Akhila felt panic dot her face. She had escaped. But from what to what?

Quo vadis. Akhila remembered the strapped Bata sandals her father had bought just before he died.

'*Quo vadis.* Do you know what that means? It's Latin for "Whither goest thou?" I like the conceit of a pair of sandals that dares ask this question. Something I haven't asked myself for a long time.' He justified the expense of buying an expensive pair of footwear, of allowing himself to be inveigled into buying a brand from a shoe showroom rather than picking up a pair from the usual shoe shop.

Quo vadis? Akhila asked herself. Then in Sanskrit: *Kim gacchami.* Then in Tamil: *Nee yenga selgirai.*

Akhila didn't know any more languages but the question dribbled through the boundaries of her mind in tongues known and unknown. Kicked by a creature in a yellow-and-red striped jersey and spike-studded boots called panic.

Akhila saw herself as a serpent that had lain curled and dormant for years. She saw life as a thousand-petalled lotus she would have to find before she knew fulfilment. She panicked. How and where was she to begin the search?

She rested her forehead on the peeling brownish-red window

bars. For the rest of her life, the smell of orange peel and rust would be for her the odour of panic.

†

The train pitched and heaved through the night. The window bars felt cold against Akhila's skin. Janaki's soft voice continued to echo in her head. It occurred to Akhila suddenly that she was doing it all wrong. She was treating other people's lives as though they were how-to books that would help her find clear-cut answers to what she needed to do next. She let the thought loose on her tongue. She hadn't done this for a long time, she thought. Air her feelings, her thoughts, without having to worry that it would be used against her someday.

'You are right.' Akhila slowly turned towards Margaret, feeling the words form in her mouth with relish, 'I can't ask other people to make up my mind for me. If I were to make up my mind based on what Janaki had to say of her life, then I should continue to live with my family. I might not love them, but at least they are there.'

'You've only heard Janaki's story. How can you give up so easily?' Prabha Devi said. The disappointment in her voice was palpable.

'I didn't say I'm giving up. But now I know what I must do,' Akhila said.

'What do you mean?'

'When I worked in Madras, I had a friend. A young Anglo-Indian girl. Her name was Katherine Webber. I used to visit Katherine's home every week and some days her Mummy would chat with me. One time, she said something about finding sermons even in stones. I don't remember why she said it nor did I understand what she meant. But I do now. Your lives are different from mine. And it is silly of me to think that if you told me about yourselves, your lives, that would guide me in my decision. And yet...' Akhila shrugged, unable to continue, her thoughts suddenly in a tangle.

Janaki paused in the middle of combing her hair and smiled.

'Why are you smiling?' Akhila asked.

'I can already see a change in you. For the first time this evening, I can see life in your eyes. I can almost feel the excitement that is within you. Earlier in the night, when I saw you standing on the platform, I thought to myself, what a rigid looking woman, with capable hands and a stern face. I thought you were a school headmistress or a nursing superintendent.'

'I didn't know school headmistresses had a certain look,' Margaret said, not bothering to hide her annoyance.

'Oh, they do,' Prabha Devi butted in. 'They have this air about them as though the whole world is a bunch of unruly school kids who have to be put in their place. But you don't look like that...you look like someone working in a multinational company, you know, successful, confident...'

'Alright, alright, I get your point,' Margaret said with a smile. A radiant smile that made her eyes sparkle and took everyone by surprise.

'I'm not who everyone thinks I am,' Akhila said slowly.

'I know that now. But you hide behind such a stiff armour of control that most people must be in awe of you,' Janaki said.

When Akhila remained silent, she said gently, 'I didn't mean to hurt your feelings.'

'You didn't hurt my feelings. Not at all,' Akhila said. 'But I was thinking about what you said. I wasn't always like this; so stiff and restrained. I had to grow a shell around myself. To protect myself. To deflect hurt and pain. If I hadn't, I would have gone insane.'

Janaki reached over and touched her arm. 'I'm sorry if I made you think of something painful from your past. Forget it. Forget this conversation.'

She briskly plaited her hair and then turning to the others said, 'Isn't it time we thought about settling in for the night?'

One by one, they opened their bags and took out sheets and pillows. Janaki had the lower berth. She stood up so that the others could raise the berth and fix it to the top-most one.

'Which one do you want? The middle one or the top one?'
Prabha Devi asked Margaret.

She shrugged. 'I don't mind either.'

'In that case, I'll take the top one.'

Janaki filled a glass with water from a bottle, unscrewed a
small vial and took out a tablet. When she caught Akhila's eye,
she let a wry smile flutter on her lips. There were no more
secrets, it seemed to suggest. And suddenly, the awkwardness
that had crept in between them seemed to dissipate.

Prabha Devi hovered by the door of the coupé. 'Shall I latch
it?' she asked.

'No, don't worry. I will latch the door once the last passenger
comes in. I'm not sleepy yet,' Akhila said.

'Goodnight' floated from berth to berth; woman to woman.

'Sweet dreams,' Prabha Devi giggled.

'I don't dream, ever,' Janaki said wistfully.

'I do, I think. But I never remember what I dream,' Margaret
said.

Akhila heard their voices drift somewhere in the distance.
She was back to staring out of the window.

Akhila shut her eyes and tried to let the rhythm of the train
lull her to sleep. And into the past...

✝

Appa was a quiet man with bowed shoulders and a grizzly head
of greying hair. An income-tax office clerk who counted the
passage of time by the number of brown files that crowded the
'in' tray on Monday and moved to the 'out' tray by Saturday
From morning to evening, he shuffled through the hours
demanding little from them or anyone, except that they leave
him alone for a day.

To Appa, Sundays were a full-fledged weekly dress rehearsal
for that day when he would retire and could live life on his own
terms again. He should have been a scholar; someone whose
job it was to pore over ancient texts, blowing the dust from

stacks of palm leaf on which a sharp writing tool had imprinted the tenets of life and religion. Mumbling, memorizing, devising corollaries that allowed him to travel through the inner alleys of his mind while life wrapped itself silently around him.

Instead of which he was thrust into the middle of an office where someone always had something to say to him: a taunt, a jibe, an insult, a titbit of trivia that in some convoluted fashion was a reflection of him. He was the butt of jokes and much laughter. They laughed about the way he walked, the clothes he wore, the food he ate...why, they even laughed at the way he suffered their mockery. He stomached his humiliation silently in the misguided belief that if he didn't react, they would finally leave him alone. Instead, it merely incited his tormentors and provoked them to subject him to greater ridicule.

Besides, there was the matter of bribes. A file moved from one table to the other in that office only when its passage was aided by the greasing of palms, a little lubrication to smoothen its transit. Except, Appa did not take any bribes. Which meant the files on Appa's table took longer to leave. He put his signature on a file only when he had read every word and checked every figure until he was satisfied that everything was the way it was meant to be. Some of the clerks grumbled that he was doing it wilfully; that while he might not want to accept bribes, what business did he have preventing them from taking any. 'If he keeps delaying every file, who do you think is going to pay up?' they demanded.

The others—crafty ward officers and sometimes taxpayers with incorrect figures—scorned Appa for his foolish integrity and said, 'It is not as if you have to do anything. Just do as we all do. Turn your head the other way and don't ask any awkward questions. For this you will be paid handsomely. What kind of a man are you? You don't know how to milk an opportunity.'

But Appa always did what his conscience asked him to. So he bowed his head, hunched his shoulders and said, 'I have to live with myself and this is the only way I can do it.'

Appa often talked about his superior, a man called Koshy. 'How does that Koshy sleep at night?' he would say. 'He is so corrupt that he'll ask for a bribe if you ask his permission to sneeze in his cubicle. Even the files that I have verified and signed, he will set aside on his table pretending that I have found a major discrepancy in the computation and that the only way to clear the file would be to pay me a bribe. Only this afternoon, I heard him tell someone—I don't take any bribes, I don't know about the people outside. Who does he mean by that? Me. And all those people go away thinking that I am the reason they have to come back to the tax office again and again. And as if that weren't enough, since he knows that I won't accept any bribes, he has instructed the peon to route the bribes through that Jain fellow who has no scruples about accepting them, for himself or anyone else.'

The unscrupulous Jain, Babu the peon, Dorai the clerk who sat next to him, these names were part of their lives but it was Koshy they had learnt to hate. They didn't know what Koshy looked like but in their minds, he was a demon. A Narakasura, a Hiranyakashyapu, a Ravana, all rolled into one vile monster with poison for blood and sharpened quills for words. Koshy who tormented Appa and tested his goodness. Koshy who hated Appa and every year ensured that Appa's confidential files bore no relation to what Appa actually did in that office.

Every year, Akhila and her mother would wait for Appa to be promoted, for his increment plus benefits to grow so that Appa's face would finally be wreathed in a smile and Amma would have more spending money. But every year Appa knew only disappointment. 'As long as that Koshy is my superior officer, I am destined to work like a mule without any rewards,' Appa would say, anger cresting his voice. And they would turn away, knowing that nothing would change in the way they lived their lives as long as Koshy reigned.

On a Sunday, the first act of pleasure for Appa was the walk to the corner shop to buy the *Hindu*. At the income-tax office, by the time the newspaper reached him, it was stained with tea spills and ink blots, and tattered at the edges. A sheet or two was always missing. On a Sunday, Appa read the newspaper end to end, beginning with the Art Buchwald column on the back page and working his way to the front page, wading through miles of classified advertisements. Sometimes Akhila thought he read every word of those as well. Only when he had finished with it was anyone else allowed to even touch it.

At quarter past ten, Amma would stand at the kitchen door wiping her hands on a rag. He would glance up from the newspaper and stare at her appraisingly. When her lips parted, it was with an invitation that excluded everyone else. 'Aren't you hungry? You must be. You have had nothing to eat since you woke up.'

Akhila and the other children knew that they had to wait till Amma had attended to him first. If their stomachs rumbled, they were expected to stay out of hearing distance so that he didn't hurry through his meal. Sometimes Akhila wondered if Appa would have preferred for all of them to dine together but she never found out. Amma liked it this way.

He would sit on a little wooden platform and she would lay the green plantain leaf before him. The mound of white rice glistened whiter than ever. On Sundays, Amma cooked Appa's favourite dishes. Piping hot, fragrant with the alchemy of steam, spices and Amma's devotion to this man who for her sake and the children's sake lunched on rice and curd and a slice of lime pickle six days a week and never complained.

When Appa had belched to signal that he was replete, he would walk to the broad wooden plank that hung from thick iron chains fastened to the ceiling. He would lie on it with his legs crossed at the knees and allow the swing to lull him into a stupor where all his worries and fears had no place to roam.

The rest of them—Amma, the boys Narayan and Narsimhan, the baby of the family Padma, and Akhila would lie on the grass mats. Outside the sun scaled the skies but the cold stone floors kept them cool. They would lie there, with full bellies, with sleep weighing down their eyelids, languishing in individual pools of want.

What did her brothers seek to complete the circle of their lives? A toy? A book? Some money to buy a ticket for a matinée show at the cinema theatre?

What did her mother need? A house of her own? A piece of jewellery? Akhila knew Padma's dreams. She wanted a silk skirt and a blouse. Akhila didn't know what it was she wanted, though. All she knew was that she felt a strange restlessness echoed by the long-drawn out moan of the swing as it moved this way and that.

For an hour, the house remained in a trance. Around midday, it was Akhila's duty to switch on the radio. On Sunday afternoon, they listened to several programmes. Appa wanted the boys to listen carefully to the Bournvita Quiz Show. Amma and Akhila waited for the Horlicks family show—*Suchitravin Kudumbam*. To Amma and Akhila, Suchitra and her family were the relatives they didn't have. They waited week after week to hear about the happenings in Suchitra's life, chuckling at the escapades of the children, Raju and Sujatha. There was a husband, Shankar, and the family's best friend, Bhaskar. But it was Suchitra whom they loved. Capable, funny, warm Suchitra, solving problems, distributing largesse and love. The perfect mother and wife. She was the woman Akhila wanted to be.

When the various programmes drew to a close and the two o' clock news beep sounded, Amma would put off the radio and rouse Appa by gently sliding his head onto the cushion of her lap. She would hum under her breath some of the kirtanas she knew he liked to hear. *Chelmela ra saketh Rama, chelmele ra*...why are you so obstinate, my lord, why are you obstinate?

When he was awake, she would begin shelling peanuts in time to the music, to the motion of the swing, to the rhythm of their lives. Crack the shell into two halves. When the nuts rolled into her palm, she would slide them between his lips. Occasionally she would toss one into her mouth. With each offering, Amma restored a little of the self-worth that had drained out of him at the end of a week's humiliation at the income-tax office.

Akhila would read with her back to them; an unwilling witness to this Sunday noon ritual of loving, giving and healing.

Just occasionally, only occasionally, a sour thought like the aftertaste of a particularly oily masala dosa would rise into her mouth: when will they realize that I am no longer a child? When will they see that inside me flutter desires that I don't understand? This ache, this wetness, this flooding of nerve ends, what does it all mean?

But just as soon as the thought filled her mouth, she would swallow it down and rush to the kitchen seeking to still her ugly thoughts. But all Amma would allow Akhila to do was hover and watch. On Sundays, Amma insisted on cooking every meal herself and brushed aside all offers of help.

Amma would slice aubergines into half moons, dip them in a batter speckled with finely chopped onions, green chillies and curry leaves and drop them into a pan of hot oil smoking over the kerosene stove. The aubergines, coated with Amma's need to prove her esteem for Appa, would hiss, splutter and then settle to becoming golden brown relics of devotion. Succulent quivering insides, with just a crunch of spice to tantalize his appetite. Feast, feast, my husband, my lord and master. On my flesh, my soul, my kathrika-bhajis.

But wait, Amma never mixed the filter coffee decoction with milk till she had made the sweet. Semolina toasted a golden brown. Cooked in double the quantity of water, equal portions of sugar, plenty of ghee and a hint of cardamom. Stirred till the grains glistened, separate and whole. Coloured with saffron. Garnished with raisins and roasted cashewnuts. They would sip the coffee, bite on the bhajis, sink their teeth into the richness of the sweet kesari and watch Appa as Amma piled his plate with double helpings he would leave untouched while the boys and Padma hungered for a wee bit more.

Later the boys would run out to play under the mango tree and Amma would fetch the dice for a game. The dice that had been part of Amma's dowry.

The tinkle of the brass dice as it fell from their hands. The screech of the chalk on the slate as Padma practised her alphabets. The crackle of the radio that sang in the background. The hum of voices as they talked. Appa had this to sustain him through a whole week of anguish at the income-tax office.

Later when their lives fell apart, Akhila thought of those Sundays when Appa was alive as a time when nothing ever went wrong. And everything was the way it was meant to be.

†

The day Appa died dawned as usual. Days later, Amma would claim that she had a certain foreboding. All night a lone dog had howled. She woke up to a twitching right eyelid. The milk curdled when she boiled it; the vessel with the dosa batter had slipped out of her hands and fallen to the floor, splashing it with a thick white rivulet of fermented fear. At the doorstep as she had bid farewell to Appa, she had seen a mangy cat cross his path...

'I should have stopped him then. I should have read the signs that his life was in danger and kept him at home beside me. Instead I stood there and watched him walk away to his death,' Amma wailed again and again to the women who huddled around her as she kept vigil at his cold rigid side.

If the gods had thought it fit to warn Amma of the impending change in her destiny, they decided that Akhila needed no such signals. On the contrary, she woke up that morning to a quickening of her senses. An exhilaration that got her out of bed with a leap and had her rushing through the morning ablutions.

Akhila hated mornings. Now that she had finished her pre-university course, her parents considered her education complete and she was expected to fine-tune all her housekeeping abilities in preparation for the day she would be married.

Amma insisted that she draw the kolam just outside the front doorstep every morning. 'That's how a home is judged,' she never tired of telling Akhila. 'Do you know what Thiruvalluvar said? A true wife is she whose virtues match her home.'

Akhila sighed. The bearded and matted-haired poet-saint had tormented her school years with his prolific verses. The teacher who taught her class Tamil found it abominable that she faltered when asked to recite from memory Thiruvalluvar's poetry while she was always word-perfect in the English recitations. 'Who is this fellow Wordsworth? A pipsqueak if you compare his poetry to the immortal Thiruvalluvar's. Does he teach you how to be a good wife or a mother? Do his words give you an insight into what is expected of a son or a pupil? And yet, you would rather memorize his verse. What was it you recited in the assembly the other day?' He cocked an eyebrow at her.

'"Daffodils", sir,' Akhila mumbled.

'"Daffodils." And what is that? Have you seen one? Do you think you'll ever see one in your life?' he sneered. 'Can it match the fragrance of our jasmine or the colour of our marigolds?'

'I don't know, sir.'

'Sit down. Don't stand there like a great big bird,' he said, leaning against the blackboard, quite overcome by emotion. 'Tamil is the oldest living language but do we consider it important? We'd rather learn about daffodils and nightingales. I tell you, India might have got its independence but we are still slaves to the English language...Class, turn to page sixteen.'

The spectre of Thiruvalluvar didn't stop there. Every time Akhila got into a bus, there he was, seated on its side. Almost all buses that plied through the roads of Madras and its suburbs had a dark brown metal board mounted above the driver's head with an illustration and a quote.

Akhila's Tamil teacher knew that she travelled by bus to school and devised new and unique ways of making her memorize at least a few hundred stanzas of everything Thiruvalluvar ever had to say. Every morning in the Tamil class, she was expected to recite aloud the verse that rode with her in the bus. The Tamil teacher didn't care whether the stanza was about ideal passengers or drivers or journeys...as long as Thiruvalluvar had authored it. And now here he was. Dancing on the tip of Amma's tongue, heaping coals and housewifely hints on her nineteen-year-old head.

'A sloppily drawn kolam suggests that the woman of the house is careless, indifferent and incapable. And an elaborately drawn one indicates self-absorption, a lavish hand and an inability to put others' needs before yours. Intricate and complicated kolams are something you reserve for special occasions. But your everyday kolam has to show that while you are thrifty, you are not mean. It should speak of your love for beauty and your eye for detail. A restraint, a certain elegance and most importantly, an understanding of your role in life. Your kolam should reflect who you are: a good housewife,' Amma said in those first few days after Akhila had put aside her college textbooks for good.

Amma had a scrapbook of kolam designs put together from the pages of the Tamil magazines she read. There was a kolam there to match every occasion conceivable in a brahmin household and a few more. Then there was a selection of everyday kolams. Good housewifely kolams brimming with all the housewifely virtues that made mothers-in-law refer to their daughters-in-law as the 'guiding light of the family'.

What to most households was a mere ritual was to Amma a science. And the everyday kolam that Akhila drew was a scientific experiment that she assessed every morning. First Akhila had to sweep the ground, then sprinkle water to settle the dust. Living in a town ensured that she didn't have to mix cow-dung with the water. Then she took the bowl of coarse stone dust that Amma bought by the bag every month and set about creating a kolam. Eight dots in a row. Four on top and four beneath. When the dots were done, she circled them with interconnecting lines. When she had finished, Amma would come out and look at it. 'Not bad, but next time see that the dots are equidistant and don't break the lines between two dots. The trick is to let a steady stream of dust trickle out of your fingers. Now come and watch me while I do the inside kolam.'

Amma did the kolam in the puja room herself. And for that she used fine rice flour and the designs came out of the scrapbook of her memories. Akhila hated it. Akhila hated all kolams: the outer and inner ones. She hated this preparation, this waiting, and this not knowing what her real life would be like.

But that morning, Akhila actually wanted to draw a beautiful kolam that would make Amma mouth rare words of praise. Akhila wanted to hear her say, 'Akhilandeswari, that is a beautiful kolam befitting a good brahmin home.' And Amma did. Perhaps that was the omen the gods sent Akhila's way to tell her all was not right about that day.

Later in the afternoon when Akhila had finished all the chores, she went to her mother who lay on the swing reading a magazine. 'Amma, I'm going to Sarasa Mami's house. She's asked me to come and help her with some vadaam.'

Amma looked up from the magazine and mumbled, 'Isn't it rather late in the day to begin making vadaam?'

'Jaya and I are just going to clean the sago and soak it. Sarasa Mami said she'll grind it and season the batter. So all I have to do is go there early in the morning before the sun gets too hot and help her pour tablespoonfuls of it on to the cloth pieces. Oh, and Amma, she asked if you have any of Appa's old dhotis lying around the house for her to use...'

Amma sat up with a sigh. 'Sarasa is a wily creature. For so many years I have asked her what she uses to season her vadaam and she's never revealed all the ingredients. Maybe she'll share it with you. Tell her that you'll bring the old dhotis tomorrow and also tell her that I don't want you standing in the sun. I don't want you burnt black. You need to look after your complexion. All men want fair-skinned wives even if they are black as coal themselves!'

That was Amma's way of granting permission for her to step

out. Padma and the boys had friends of their own in the same street. But Sarasa Mami lived two streets away. And each time, Akhila had to ask her mother if she could go visiting. According to Amma, the streets were fraught with all kinds of dangers that would rob her of her hymen before it was legally perforated by the man who would be her husband. Thereby bringing disgrace to her father, their family, and the whole brahmin community.

Outside, the sun blazed. May was the hottest month in a year constituted of hot months and a few hot and wet months. The Kathiri star had been spotted and nobody in their right senses stepped out during the day. The heat scorched the scalp and parched the throat. Even at three o'clock in the afternoon, shadows remained knee-high. The leaves of the giant ficus tree at the end of the street shivered in the heat, bleached and grey. Dogs crouched beside culverts that ran on one side of the road. Mirages swam before one's eyes in a matter of minutes. Akhila hurried towards Sarasa Mami's house. She didn't care about the heat or that the roads were deserted, but the neighbours did. If someone spotted her, they would find a way to point out to her mother the evils of letting a young girl like Akhila out in the streets by herself.

Sarasa Mami had a trunk full of books. Novels that her brother-in-law had bought during his college years and had no use for any more. It had lain there till one day she asked Akhila to help her clean the trunk. 'Every few months I take it out, dust it, kill the silver fish that seem to breed within the pages and put it back,' she said, opening the lid of the trunk. 'I keep telling my brother-in-law that he must take it with him but each time he has a fresh excuse.'

Akhila let her hand slide over the books. There were James Hadley Chases and Perry Masons; Harold Robbins and Irving Wallace and the odd classic or two. Dog-eared, yellowed with age and sweet-smelling racy books that made the blood hammer in her heart and unfurled forbidden thoughts. Sarasa Mami let her borrow one book at a time. 'Are you sure your mother won't disapprove of these books?' she asked the first time.

'They are not bad books. They just have covers like these to attract attention,' Akhila hastened to explain before Sarasa Mami changed her mind about letting her borrow the books.

'I suppose you are right. But if your mother makes a fuss, don't tell her I gave it to you. She'll give me hell.'

'Sarasa Mami,' Akhila called as she knocked at her door.

Subramani Iyer's face split into a wide grin. 'Look who's here,' he said. It was rare to see him without a smile on his face. 'All dressed up as a princess, I see.'

Akhila looked down at her davani self-consciously. Her skirt and blouse were not new. But the purple-coloured georgette half-sari was almost new. No one but Subramani Iyer would have noticed it.

Akhila knew no one quite like him. She had seen him saunter towards Sarasa Mami and fling his arms around her while she blushed and squirmed to escape from the circle of his embrace. He called her his queen and his children their treasure. Akhila had heard him weep large wet tears, moved by the tragedy of a film they had all gone together to watch at the cinema one afternoon. Every month on the day he was paid, he brought home a large box of sweets from the big sweet shop on Broadway—Ramakrishna Lunch Home. During Deepavali, he bought enough firecrackers to keep ten boys happy. He gifted them to Akhila's brothers and then joined them at the street corner as they sparkled, whizzed and exploded the fire-crackers, filling the air with smoke and the acrid stench of gun powder. All he asked was that every now and then they give blind Srini a lit sparkler to hold, so that he didn't feel left out. 'He can't see but all his other senses are intact and probably work better than ours,' Subramani Iyer would say, ruffling his son's hair affectionately.

His forehead was high and marked with a scar like a half moon right above the bridge of his nose. 'Aren't I lucky? Even if I have forgotten to smear vibuthi on my head, everyone thinks I have...' He giggled, fingering the scar. His eyes popped out of his face, bearing in them a perennial expression of wonder. A child taken for the first time to a fun-fair ground.

His clothes were always scruffy and hung on him as if they belonged to someone else. His shirtsleeves flapped and his trouser bottoms stood three inches above his ankles. He worked as a peon in an office where he had to fetch cups of tea and coffee, carry files from one table to another, empty the wastepaper bins and clean the office every morning, apart from doing an endless number of chores and yet, there was none of that aura of suffering that Appa with his superior clerical job wore around him.

'He's a happy-go-lucky sort of a chap,' Akhila's morose father was fond of saying. 'Though how he can be with a grown-up daughter, a blind son and two young daughters, I wonder.'

But when the ambulance came screeching down the road early in the evening, its shrill siren wailing, and when someone rushed to Sarasa Mami's house with a message for Akhila to come home immediately, there had been an accident, it was Subramani Iyer who hurried out with her murmuring, 'Don't worry, it won't be anything serious. Pattabhi Iyer is a good man. Nothing bad could ever happen to him.'

Who were these people? Where did they come from? Why were they all here? Questions pounded as they hurried towards Akhila's house. They were greeted by the sight of Akhila's father's balding scalp, a steady murmur of voices and Amma's wails: How could this happen? How could he do this to me?

Appa lay on a reed-mat on the floor. A white sheet was drawn up to his chin, beneath which his limbs were tidily arranged. His eyes were closed and there was cotton wool stuffed up his nose. He looked as though he were fast asleep. There was none of that harried exhaustion, the frustration and the bitterness that had marked his waking face. In death, he seemed completely content and relieved.

'It happened just outside the station. At that turning between Central Station and Ripon Building...God knows what he was thinking of when he stepped on to the road. The bus driver claims that he had right of way...There will be an enquiry and all that. But I have some influence with the police department so they gave back the body an hour ago. They have performed a post-mortem so please don't let the family hug and embrace the body too much. Everything was done in a hurry, you see, so the stitches might not hold too well...' Someone from Appa's office spoke quietly to Subramani Iyer. Akhila tried to fit a face to that voice but through the haze of tears all she could see was a miasma of features.

Was he one of her father's tormentors? Was he one of those they had learned to hate for causing their father so much anguish that he lost all ability to draw pleasure from any of their little triumphs?

So that when Narayan or Akhila won a prize at school, the only way he knew how to respond was by sinking low into himself and sighing, 'All this is well but will it help you in real life? What use is getting a certificate for English recitation or for the best handwriting? They ought to give you lessons on how to hurt those who hurt you; on how to trample upon other people's hopes; that will help you survive and not all this. I'm not saying I'm not happy...' he would conclude and wipe his brow with a little gesture of weary defeat they had come to recognize so well as a prelude to a headache.

That was the other thing about Appa. His headaches. It didn't need much to set one off. A hot day. An overcast sky. A loudspeaker that blared forth Tamil devotional songs from the next street. The fragrance of incense sticks. A stomach upset. Padma's chatter. Narsi scraping his knee on the street. A flickering light. A clattering plate. A howling dog. A motorbike revving up outside. A bad day at work. The crowded trains. A memory of some past hurt. A disquieting letter from a relative...

They had learnt to shelter Appa from most things that gave him a headache but in spite of it, he often had an attack. And then Appa would retire to the dark inner room and slam the door shut. A couple of hours later, he would emerge reeking of

Amrutanjan balm, his eyes crinkling in the light after having being in the dark so long. Even after the headache had vanished, he would open a jar of the balm, curl his forefinger into its innards and scoop out a dollop of slick yellow salve that reeked of lemongrass oil and rub it into his temples in a long drawn out movement, filling the house with its unmistakable and completely indelible stench. Then he would rub the remnants that clung to the finger against his thumb and sniff at it. Once. Twice. And a final drawn-in breath that perhaps would carry the sting of the balm to the inside of his skull. He finished off by wiping his fingers on his nostrils.

And now Appa would never be troubled by a headache again. He lay there completely oblivious to the noise of strangers weeping, vehicles stopping and starting as fresh batches of people came in to condole and commiserate, the swirls of sickening sweet smoke from a whole packet of incense sticks lit and placed close to his ear...Appa was finally at peace.

Amma lay curled up on the floor. A heap of lacerated emotions. When she saw Akhila, she rose. The women huddled by her side put their arms around her. One had to keep a close guard on a widow. Grief made even otherwise sensible people do rash and stupid things. Amma shook them off and raised her face to Akhila's. 'How could he do this to us? How could this happen to us?'

Akhila looked at her helplessly. What was she to say? 'Where are the children?' she murmured, sitting down beside Amma.

'They are somewhere around,' she said, laying her head on Akhila's shoulder. After a while, Akhila eased Amma's head off her shoulder and went looking for her brothers and sister. Narsi and Padma were sitting on the veranda playing some complicated game involving vehicle licence plates. They seemed rather excited by all the commotion and the comings and goings. That their father was dead seemed not to have registered yet. Or, if it had, they were quite untouched by its implications. But then Narsi was only eight and Padma six.

Akhila found Narayan crouched in a corner, his arms

wrapped around his knees. His face was clenched with the effort of not giving way to tears. He was fifteen; the fragile age caught between man and boy. He didn't know what he was supposed to be. A man strong enough to accept death, even an untimely one such as this. Or a boy, frightened by 'death and the void caused. Akhila put her arm around him. His shoulder muscles were taut. 'Akka,' he asked the floor, 'why do you think he did it?'

'Did what?'

'Why did he try and cross the road when the traffic was moving? He knows how treacherous that road is...' Narayan's voice cracked.

For the first time, it dawned on Akhila that this perhaps was not an accident. Akhila remembered the note of suspicion that had underlined Appa's colleague's words. And now this: Narayan's question was innocent enough on the surface but she could read the doubt there.

Had Appa stood at the pedestrian crossing that morning and decided to end it all? Had it seemed to him to be the cure for his increasingly frequent headaches? Had the pressures of being the father of a grown-up daughter and three other children been too much for him to take? Had Appa thought he could take no more of Koshy and the torture he piled upon him? What was Appa thinking of when he stepped into the river of traffic? *Quo vadis.* Whither goest thou? *Kim gacchami. Nee yenga selgirai.*

Had he closed his eyes and plunged into it? Or had he walked to his death unaware of where his feet were leading him?

Oh, Appa, why? What was so intolerable that you had to end your life to escape it?

'Akka,' Narayan asked, 'what are we going to do?'

'Cremate him and then...and then, we'll find some way to keep ourselves afloat and alive.' The harshness in her voice astonished her as much as it did Narayan. The tears that had risen in her eyes quelled abruptly. Anger had replaced grief and this Akhila could handle better. Tears made one look around a room wildly searching for someone to cling to and unburden one's sorrow. Tears made you vulnerable and distorted your focus. But anger made one stronger. Anger made one inviolable. Anger prepared one to face things better.

'Where have these people come from? Who brought them here?' Narayan's perplexity cracked the thoughts that wound around Akhila like a coil of steel.

Appa had always kept their relatives at a distance. They saw them rarely, perhaps at a wedding or some other family function. During the school holidays when other people went away to their family homes, they stayed in their house in Ambattur. Once Appa availed of his Leave Travel Allowance and took them to a few pilgrim centres. That was how Akhila went to Rameswaram, Madurai and Palani. There never was enough money for them to go to any tourist spot. Appa's office paid for travel to any part of the country once every four years; but the other things had to be paid for. If you had a family home to go to, nothing would have to be paid for. You stayed with your relatives, and they took care of everything. So one year Narayan and Akhila hit upon the idea of asking their father to take them to the village he was born in.

'There is nothing left there in the village for us,' Appa said, when Narayan and Akhila approached him.

'But couldn't we go there just once? Only to see where you grew up,' Narayan persisted.

'Leave your father alone. Can't you see he is tired?' Amma yelled at them. And sure enough, Appa was already wrinkling his forehead and rubbing his temples.

But Appa's death had brought into their home relatives they didn't know of even by name. And with them came the professional criers. Who had sent for them? And how had they come so quickly?

Narayan and Akhila watched as the family and the criers congregated around Appa's body and lamented. What did they know of Appa to grieve for him? And yet, their grief seemed so real...

Amma who had been too spent by emotion and had subsided into silence began weeping again. Subramani Iyer came towards them. 'Pattabhi Iyer's relatives. They are all from Poonamallee. Go to your mother,' he said to the two of them. 'You two have to be responsible now.'

Amma stared at Akhila's dry eyes in disbelief. 'How can you not cry? Cry, cry, damn you. Shed a few tears for that man lying there. You'll never weep for him again. Weep, at least for decency's sake!'

And so, Akhila cried. For the next ten days as they went through the rituals of death and mourning, Akhila shed all the tears that she had been allocated for a lifetime. She cried when she watched her brothers perform the funeral rites. They looked so young and frail. How could she burden them with any kind of responsibility?

Akhila cried every night when she cooked a bowl of rice and placed it with a jug of water so that Appa's soul still hovering in their house wouldn't be hungry or thirsty. Appa, Akhila cried, as I provide for you tonight, I will have to provide for the family you abandoned so callously. How am I to do it?

When Amma dressed as a bride before dawn broke on the tenth day and the other widows gathered around her and stripped her of her marks of marriage, Akhila cried because she knew that this was what it meant to be a woman.

And then, she never cried again.

✝

The train ground to a halt. The station was veiled in darkness. Akhila looked at her watch. It was almost midnight. She craned her neck and tried to read the station's name but the letters were barely visible. It was a small station; the train would halt there for barely a minute and a half.

Akhila heard the compartment door clang open. She peered through the window to catch a glimpse of who it was. The trains were not as safe as they used to be. All sorts of people got in and committed all kinds of crimes. This was a safe sector, but even then one had to be careful.

A girl stood by the door of the coupé. She must be the passenger Janaki had mentioned, Akhila thought. The girl came inside and stowed her bag under the seat. She looked around the coupé and then at Akhila.

On one side, all the berths were occupied. The girl's was the middle berth.

'Do you want to go to sleep?' Akhila asked. 'You can pull up the berth if you want to.'

'No, no,' the girl said. 'I'm fine. I'm not sleepy.'

Akhila waited for her to bring out a Walkman or a romance novel. But she sat there hugging a bag to her chest, staring at the floor.

She must have been about fourteen or fifteen. A child, in fact. Something about the way she sat reminded Akhila of her brother Narayan, on the day their father died. The same clenching within. The same urge not to give way to tears and disgrace herself. The same dignity. Neither a child, nor a woman. In blue jeans and a red-and-white striped top.

'Are you alright?' Akhila asked softly.

She looked at Akhila, startled. 'I'm fine,' she said. 'Thank you for asking.'

Akhila sensed something was wrong.

'What is your name?' she asked.

'Sheela,' the girl said.

'Which class are you in?' Akhila asked, surprised by her own garrulousness. She seldom made small talk and never began conversations with strangers. But this evening, she had behaved so unlike herself. Eager to spill her secrets. Anxious to probe into lives. Willing to talk.

'I'm in ninth grade at the Holy Angels Convent,' the girl said.

'Are you travelling alone?' Akhila asked.

The girl shook her head. 'My father is in the next compartment.'

'What about your mother?'

She looked at her feet and scuffed the sneaker-shod toes of her right foot. 'My mother left early this afternoon with...' her voice cracked, '...my grandmother.'

'My grandmother...' she said, fumbling for words to explain, 'my grandmother was very ill. She was dying. She died on the way to her home.'

Akhila touched the girl's elbow. 'I'm sorry to hear that.'

'She was very ill and I'm glad she died. I think she would have been glad to die, too. She was just a living corpse anyway,' Sheela said.

4

Go Grandmother, Go

Exactly four months after Sheela turned fourteen, her grandmother wrote a letter saying that she intended to pay them a visit. For as long as Sheela could remember, her grandmother had never come to visit them. They always had to go to her, loyal subjects bearing gifts of fragrant chewing tobacco and packets of Marie biscuits. She would greet them regally, demanding total homage. Nothing less would satisfy her.

When Sheela was born and it was time to name her, her grandmother decided on the name. She had chanced upon it in a magazine. 'I like the sound of it,' she said. 'Besides, it is my right to choose a name for my grandchild.'

So Sheela was named Sheela and not Mini or Girija or Nita or Sharmila or Asha or Vidya as per the list Sheela's parents had drawn up when she was born.

Sheela had no memories of cuddling up in her grandmother's lap or of going to sleep in the crook of her arm. Though her mother insisted that when Sheela was a baby, her grandmother carried her everywhere. Affection for her grandmother meant a squeeze of the arm, a hundred-rupee note slipped into Sheela's hand at the end of the holidays and a meal at the best restaurant in town. But then, she was unlike most grandmothers.

Sheela had another grandmother. Achamma. Her father's mother. She visited them every few months and stayed for many weeks each time. Achamma was small and thin; a little grey sparrow with a tiny mouth and hair she coiled into a little bun at the nape of her neck. When she came to stay, there was no need for extra preparations. Achamma asked for little. She pecked at her food and lay curled under a blanket reading most of the time. In the evenings, she said her prayers and retreated early to bed. Sometimes the only sign of her presence were her dentures that she kept in a little plastic jar by the wash basin in the bathroom.

Achamma blended in with their lives. Sheela thought she blended in so well that she forgot Achamma even existed. She could never do that with her mother's mother.

Sheela called her Ammumma rather than ammama. Her grandmother preferred it so, for she hated any kind of reminders that she was getting old. Ammumma was ambiguous whereas ammama meant only one thing—Grandmother. The logic eluded everyone else but Sheela knew that replacing the vowel made all the difference to her grandmother.

Ammumma was sixty-nine years old, owned several houses in Alwaye, an acre of teak trees and several paddy fields. She also had six grey strands growing on her chin that she meticulously plucked out every few days.

Sheela's home was a flat in a block of four. It had two bedrooms and a squarish balcony in the front that overlooked a park dense with mango trees. Ammumma liked to stand in the balcony lined with pots of crotons, begonias, and a gnarled jasmine bush. She would stare at the trees silently moving this way and that, the blue-grey cylindrical pieces of wood wedged between the parapet and the balustrade. Sometimes she would sniff the air longingly and say, 'The smell of home, mm...'

Sheela's parents would look at each other in delight and agree. They thought it a sort of triumph that she was beginning to feel at home in the flat. But Sheela knew that the only thing Ammumma found bearable about their home was the profusion of mango blossoms around it.

Sheela knew this as she knew everything. Sheela knew her grandmother was there because she was dying. Not that Ammumma knew she was dying. After all, a growth in her womb was not a new occurrence. Seven times her womb had flowered and spat out the fruit when it was time. Why would this one be any different? But this time the baby in her womb was an evil gnome intent on malice. Its angry red face and grasping tentacle hands reached greedily within her, feeding on her life for its sustenance. A parasite child that would never leave the sanctuary of her body until death did them part.

Sheela knew why Ammumma was in their flat and not in the mammoth house Ammumma owned. Sheela knew why Ammumma insisted that the doctors at the hospital near their home were better qualified than anywhere else. Ammumma wanted her sons to know that they had driven her away from her own house. She wanted them to squirm in guilt when they thought of her. She was angry with them for preferring their wives to her. For letting those soft-faced, hard-hearted women addle their minds and blemish their love for her.

Sheela knew Ammumma realized that Mummy, after being ignored for most of her adult life, would be grateful for any crumbs of affection Ammumma threw her way. For being the chosen one among her siblings. Sheela knew Ammumma was playing on Mummy's insecurity. She knew how delighted Mummy would be to be back in Ammumma's favour after a year of estrangement. The previous summer, they had had a bitter disagreement about the writing of Ammumma's will. And for the rest of the year, they had been distant with each other. Eyes didn't meet, hands didn't clasp, and hearts didn't merge. Letters when written were cold and polite. For the first time ever, Mummy stayed away from Ammumma's home during the school holidays.

Sheela knew why Ammumma was reluctant to write her will, to divide her property and bequeath it to her various children. It must seem so tinged with treachery and betrayal to her. Her children waiting and wanting to go on with their lives even after her death. This desire to build their future on her ashes. How dare they even contemplate happiness when she was not around? How could they dispense with her so easily? And anyway, once she wrote her will, what was left for her to do, except die?

And so Sheela knew why Ammumma waited for a moment when her parents were in the room before she drew out a gold necklace and clasped it around Sheela's throat. She was just ensuring that Mummy's loyalty, unlike that of her brothers, didn't shift.

For a week, Ammumma ruled and reigned. She insisted that Sheela be asked to stay at home after she came back from school. 'She's a grown-up girl. You shouldn't let her wander around. And who are all these men she plays badminton with? She may call them "Uncle" but they are not her uncles and how dare that man Naazar put his arm around her? She's not a little girl. And I saw the look in his eyes...If you don't take care, you'll regret it one day.'

'Amma,' Mummy said, 'they are her father's friends. She is like a daughter to them.'

'I have heard that one before. Don't you remember what happened to the girl who was your neighbour? That tall creature called Celine.'

Mummy coughed to prevent Ammumma from talking any further. She had spotted Sheela listening.

But Sheela knew all about the Celine incident even though it had happened about the time Sheela was five years old. Everyone in the housing colony knew about Celine. Of how she'd go to play in her friend's house and of how the friend's father did things to her that friend's fathers are not supposed to do. So Celine became pregnant and both the families left the colony and the town in disgrace. Celine and her parents moved to a place where no one would know about her abortion. And the friend's father went to a far-away town where he would find plenty of young girls to ruin, everyone said.

Sheela knew how easy it would be to be another Celine. To succumb to an older man's attentions. Naazar was her friend's father and her father's friend. His daughter Hasina was her classmate. One Sunday afternoon when Sheela went to their house, rushing in from the heat with a line of sweat beading her upper lip, Naazar had reached forward and wiped it with his forefinger. The touch of his finger tingled on her skin for a long time. Thereafter, Sheela mopped her face with a hanky each time she entered Hasina's home. Another time, the bows on the sleeves of her blouse had came undone and as Hasina and her mother watched, Naazar knotted the bows. Slowly, meticulously. Sheela felt her breath lodge in her throat and when she saw the hurt in Hasina and her mother's eyes, shame wrapped itself around her. Sheela never wore that blouse again.

Sheela knew why Ammumma said what she did about Daddy's friends. Mummy she thought was too trusting, too naïve. But Ammumma knew better and Sheela decided that she would never go to Hasina's house again.

Then came the day before Ammumma was to be admitted to the hospital. Ammumma couldn't stop eating. It began right after breakfast with a basket of jade green grapes. She ate them one by one, spitting the pips into the palm of her hand. When they were nearly over, she went onto the balcony and hailed a fruit vendor on the road. She bought most of the fruit he had with him. Sapodillas so lusciously plump that you could smell the ripeness on her breath. She scooped the flesh out with a teaspoon and wolfed it down. By lunchtime, there was just a heap of languid skins and glistening black seeds. Then she ate everything that had been cooked for lunch for all four of them. A mountain of rice, a whole chicken chopped and fried with onions and spices, a tin of papad, a whole bowl of thick creamy yoghurt, all of the vegetable dish and the prawn curry Sheela had waited for all morning. When she finished what was on the table, she went into the kitchen looking for the pots and pans the food had been cooked in. She tore chunks off a loaf of bread, mopped up the leftovers and crammed the bread into her mouth. She continued to eat until all the food in the house was gone. Mummy looked at her plundered kitchen and sobbed a sigh. Daddy slunk out quietly to buy some lunch and Ammumma fell asleep. All afternoon, through the evening and till the night fell, she continued to snore while Mummy kept shaking her head and mumbling, 'Why? Why is she behaving so strangely? What's wrong with her?'

Sheela could have told her mother but she knew that she wouldn't be taken seriously. That day was Ammumma's last day as a whole woman and this was her way of forgetting what lay ahead. The next day they would take away a part of Ammumma and she knew she would never be the same again.

Ammumma was a great one for manifestations of femininity. She appraised carefully every new woman she saw and most of them were found wanting. 'You call that a woman! A proper woman has a good head of hair and a chest full of breasts.' And a womb that blossomed readily. Tomorrow Ammumma's femininity would be at stake.

Ammumma hated imperfections of any kind. In her home there was no room for a cracked plate, a blotched towel or a faded cushion. And now she was going into a hospital that would in all probability decree that a part of her be removed and thus condemn her to be flawed for life. Sheela knew that Ammumma felt repulsed by her own body.

Late in the night she wanted Sheela to pluck the straggly strands on the underside of her chin. Mummy laughed, 'Who do you think is going to look at you?'

Ammumma gave her a cold look and said, 'That's not the point.'

As Sheela sat there on the balcony with the tweezers and a small hand mirror Ammumma could examine herself in, Ammumma said, 'You mustn't become one of those women who groom themselves to please others. The only person you need to please is yourself. When you look into a mirror, your reflection should make you feel happy. I tried to teach this to your mother and aunt. But they are silly women. They don't understand what I have been trying to tell them. You...you, I hope won't be such a fool.'

When Sheela nodded, Ammumma stroked Sheela's hair and said, 'You remind me of myself when I was your age. Except that I was more buxom and womanly. You don't eat enough. You are so skinny. No man will want you for a wife. Men don't like bones in bed. Men like curves.'

But you told Mummy that you didn't like the look in Naazar Uncle's eyes. And if I was skinny and ugly, why would he look at me like that? Sheila wanted to ask. Except that Mummy got there ahead of her.

'Don't fill her head with nonsense,' Mummy said from the doorway.

'You call this nonsense. You forget I am her grandmother and am entitled to tell her whatever I choose to,' Ammumma snapped.

Mummy hovered around for a minute and then went away and Sheela resumed searching Ammumma's chin for any stray hair that had escaped the tweezers.

Sheela knew Ammumma wanted to feel perfect this one last night. Every night before Ammumma went to bed, she stood by the mirror in her room and splashed her face and neck with calamine lotion. Then she dusted her still smooth face, her lined throat, her plump shoulders and her huge pendulous breasts with talc that smelt of lavender. Finally she opened her jewellery box, caressed the gold and gleaming gems, put on her favourite piece and went to sleep with the weight of her jewellery on her naked skin; a warm surrogate fist nestling between her breasts that covered most of her chest. Sheela knew Ammumma did it so that even if she were to die in her sleep, she would do so looking her best. Her children, of course, dismissed it as a sign of age and its concurrent eccentricity.

Daddy came back from the hospital two weeks later and said,

'The cancer's inoperable. They want to try radiation.'

Mummy's sister and brothers descended on them. A swarm of locusts who devastated the smooth fabric of their lives.

Mummy, Sheela's capable Mummy, became a little vague. The family GP said it was stress taking its toll. He said it was depression caused by the illness of a loved one. He said it was nothing that time, rest and a course of anti-depressants wouldn't cure.

Only Sheela knew different. Mummy depended on Ammumma to provide a sense of continuity in her life. Mummy wanted to bask in the secure knowledge that there was someone who could tell her what to do and never be wrong. Someone who had all the answers for the one million doubts that swam into her mind from the farthest corner of her troubled soul. And suddenly it seemed that someone would no longer be around. Sheela knew Mummy felt lost and helpless. Sheela knew that for the first time Mummy felt the burden of the responsibility that would come to rest with her now that Ammumma was dying. Her sister and brothers would seek in her the wisdom and strength Ammumma had. While all she wished to do was to continue in a state of forever daughterhood. Petted, cosseted, and absolved of all motherly virtues for the rest of her life.

Daddy, Sheela's otherwise kind Daddy, turned into a hideous beast. Nothing Sheela did was right. He picked on her and found fault incessantly: You don't help your mother enough. Your friends are not our kind of people, they're riff-raff! You watch too much TV. You wander around all the time. Who taught you to say 'shit' in every sentence? Who is that boy I saw you talking to near the park gates?

The list was endless and mostly contradictory. Sheela didn't try to reason, as she would have once. 'How can I watch TV all day and still be wandering around as you claim?' She would have demanded when she was younger.

But Sheela didn't talk to her Daddy like that any more. These days, when she thought she was being witty, he scolded her for being rude.

'But I thought you wanted me to be witty. That you were proud of my sense of humour,' Sheela wanted to cry. When she was a little girl, he had encouraged her to speak like an adult. With a razor-edged wit and a finely developed skill of repartee. But now that she was grown, when he saw her, he saw a woman and not his little girl any more and he only felt anger at what he thought was her questioning his authority.

Sometimes when friends came calling and there would be a little girl whose father beamed proudly at his daughter's quick answers, Sheela would want to butt in and plead, 'Don't do this to her. My father was the same. He thought it funny when I was cheeky. Only now he calls it back chat and it makes him furious. Please, don't do this to your daughter. She is going to grow up thinking this is the way to be. Instead, teach her to swallow her words, make her mouth nice and pleasant, innocuous things. Kill her spirit and tame her tongue. So that when she grows up, she won't be like me, wondering what it is I said wrong and what blunder I am going to commit next by opening my mouth.'

Sheela heard Daddy out and waited for him to leave the room. When he was angry, he always left the room as if he couldn't trust himself to remain there and cause no harm. Sheela didn't mind. Daddy was the same when he went to Ammumma's house. Sheela was very often the butt of his ire.

She knew why he was being so abominable. He resented being relieved of his position as head of the household, man of the family. The rich brothers had taken over the running of the house—bills, shopping, they handled everything. The food he provided was not satisfactory. They craved for rare and delicate foods, which only they could afford to pay for. When Daddy produced a bottle of army rum, they ignored it for the duty-free Scotch they had brought with them.

The house was swamped with the fragrance of airline interiors and foreign lands. And the rich sister took over their lives, handing out advice that was both self-congratulatory and insulting. Sheela was the only one Daddy could exercise his power over. And Sheela knew there was no escaping the beast's wrath until Ammumma left or died.

Sheela's grandmother lost her mind. Ammumma sat up in bed, shrugging aside the thin cotton cloth that Mummy's eldest brother and her favourite son had covered her with. She stared at the faded pink walls and began addressing the corner of the wall closest to her bed. 'Mother,' she said. And Sheela's mother and aunt looked at each other in surprise. Why was their mother talking to their dead grandmother?

Women turn to their mothers when they have no one else to turn to. Women know that a mother alone will find it possible to unearth some shred of compassion and love that in everyone else has become ashes. Sheela knew why Ammumma sought her mother.

'Mother,' Ammumma said with a note of urgency in her voice. 'Look at that bitch striding into the bedroom with her long legs. He sees the pale skin of her inner thighs, her milk and water complexion and falls deeper in love with her. The besotted fool!' She was referring to Sheela's eldest uncle's wife; her pet hate and target of constant venom. According to Ammumma, she was the cause of all problems, real and imaginary.

Mummy pacified her distraught brother, 'You shouldn't be so upset. It is just the heat. The radiation causes unimaginable heat in her system, making her talk nonsense. Just turn the air-conditioning up.' And later, she told her sister, 'The heat has let loose all the demons that were slumbering inside our mother.'

Sheela knew it had nothing to do with the heat. Ammumma had finally realized her time was up and she wasn't going to die without having spoken her mind. But Sheela still went to the hospital canteen and ordered a tumbler of pepper rasam. The waiter there gave her a curious look. She was the only one there that day, on that hot day, asking for a fiery hot dish instead of something cold—a badaam kheer or basundi—like everyone else.

Sheela sat there steaming, sweat running off her brow, and sipped the hot pepper rasam, trying to see if it would unleash the demons in her. Give her the courage to tell her father, 'Why don't you get off my back? Quit being a beast, will you? All you do these days is frown and snap at me. I didn't make my grandmother ill. I'm not responsible. Do you understand?'

Make her tell her grimalkin aunt, 'Shut up fat face, go bully someone else—your husband, your children, your half-a-dozen servants, and leave my poor mother alone.'

And make her glare at her uncles saying, 'If you want to show your largesse, your wealth, hire a cook for my overworked mother, and a man to run between home and hospital and on your innumerable chores, instead of treating my father like your resident errand boy.'

The flames raged but the demons stayed locked. So she ordered a double scoop of rum 'n' raisin and doused the fire. She knew she had been right all the time.

Six weeks later, they brought Ammumma back home. The brothers and sister had left after a few days. Mummy and Daddy took turns to nurse Ammumma. But the cancer wouldn't relinquish its hold. Besides, everything that could go wrong did—her blood pressure soared, her kidneys failed and all the while the gnome in her womb kept growing. Once again, the brothers and sister were summoned to her bedside.

Sheela stood on the balcony, watching the road, waiting for Ammumma to arrive from the hospital. Suddenly the world seemed tired. The mango trees looked weary. The hedges were covered in a film of dust and even the colours of the crotons in the pots had turned dull and lifeless. Inside the house, Mummy and her sister wept, hugging each other as they wailed, 'Mother, don't leave us.'

Once when Sheela peeped, she saw them wiping each other's tears until the next burst of anguish caused another stream of brine to flow. To look at them, one would never believe that these women were constantly warring, scoring points off each other all the time. But Sheela knew this was just for now. Their newly found sisterhood would soon come to an end.

When the green van stopped at the block of flats, Sheela knew Ammumma was in it. She saw them park the van in the slender shade of the Ashoka tree. She waited for Ammumma to step out after the men. But there was no sign of her. For the first time, Sheela didn't know what was happening.

'Where is she?' she wanted to scream. She felt Daddy touch her elbow. When she turned to him, he said quietly, 'Go sit with her. She is in the van.'

A helpless creature, a giant mound of flesh smelling of urine and eau de cologne, lay in the back of the van. Its mouth was half-open, its lips cracked and dry. Its skin had creased into multiple folds of coarse parchment and its hair resembled fronds of steel wool. It lay there sucking in air with rasping breaths. Sheela looked at it and knew for certain that her grandmother had already escaped her body. She was, Sheela knew, in some celestial realm, sitting on a four-poster cloud and decking herself with a thousand stars.

Nevertheless, this was Ammumma's abandoned body and Sheela knew how much she would have hated to see herself as she was now. Once when Sheela was spending a summer with her, Ammumma had come back from a relative's funeral looking tormented. Much later she had explained to Sheela the reason. 'Lakshmi was such a well groomed woman when she was alive. But you should have seen what they did to her today. They laid her out stark naked on a banana leaf; every mole, vein and blemish exposed. Her hair was unkempt, her body looked unwashed and there wasn't a grain of gold on her. How could they rob her of her dignity, of her grace? And I realized this is what I too will end up looking like when I'm dead. And there will be nothing I can do to prevent it.'

Sheela fanned the creature's face, spooned water into its mouth and spoke to it. 'Don't worry, I'm not going to let the world see you like this.' She plucked the wiry strands from her chin, carefully brushed the almost brittle hair on her head and braided it into a plait that she fixed in place with a glittering rubber band. Sheela rubbed her aunt's foundation into her grandmother's face, shoulders and chest. And dusted her aunt's expensive talc just the way Ammumma liked to do it. On her face, neck, over her shoulders, and under her breasts that hung limply like empty pouches. When she was covered in a patina of fragrant chalky grey, Sheela rimmed her eyes with a kohl pencil and touched her eyebrows with feathery strokes in the manner her make-up book advocated. Sheela's aunt had already confiscated all of Ammumma's jewellery. So Sheela adorned her with costume jewellery. A crescent moon rested on her flaccid bosom. A waterfall of crystals cascaded from her ears.

When they came down, there were gasps of horror. 'You dreadful girl,' Mummy cried, 'how could you?'

Sheela saw Daddy's face tighten ominously and felt his fingers bite into the flesh of her upper arm in mute anger. Sheela knew they thought that she had committed sacrilege. She knew they thought that she had turned Ammumma into an obnoxious creature—a garish, dressed-up dying harlot. But Sheela knew Ammumma would have preferred this to looking diseased and decaying.

There was no time to clean her up. She had always wanted to die in her own bed and they had a long drive ahead before they reached home. Her home. Through a haze of pain and humiliation, Sheela watched the brothers and sisters get into the van and huddle around their mother's dying body. Daddy stood by Sheela's side, stern with disapproval and disappointment. She didn't care. She knew Ammumma would have been pleased.

5

When Akhila's father died, two things happened: Sundays became just another day of the week and Akhila became the man of the family.

Since Appa had 'died in harness', and Akhila had passed her pre-university examinations with a first-class, she was offered a job in the income-tax department on 'compassionate grounds' and with it the responsibility of keeping her family's bodies and souls together. Akhila was nineteen but she wasn't unsure of what she had to do or overwhelmed by what was expected of her.

Narayan, the oldest of her younger siblings, was to go to the polytechnic college next year. Narsi, who was only eleven, was to continue at the school. He still had four years left and by that time, Akhila thought, they could afford to put him through college. She said, 'Think of it, he will be the first graduate in our family. A Bachelor of Arts or Science, whichever stream he chooses. As for Padma, we needn't worry about her right now. She is content as long as I buy her satin ribbons for her hair and glass bangles for her wrist.'

That left just Amma, who wore a pleat of worry in the middle of her forehead and had taken to twisting and wringing her hands as if they were tangled in the intricate folds of the voluminous nine-yard sari she swathed herself in.

'I don't care what anyone says,' Akhila told her. 'But I won't let you shave your head or exchange your pretty madisars for a saffron sari. Just because Appa is no more, you don't have to turn yourself into a hideous monster.'

Akhila saw the relief in Amma's eyes and felt what at first was pride. Only later it turned to a sense of heaviness that caused muscles to knot into tight hard lumps in her shoulders. To Amma, Akhila had become the head of the household. Someone who would chart and steer the course of the family's destiny to safe shores.

The next few years went by without much incident. Their lives were led with military precision. That was the only way Akhila knew how to preserve order and keep her family from floating away from its moorings. Dawns diminished to dusk and Sundays dwindled to be the day when she washed, starched, dried and ironed the six cotton saris that comprised her entire office-going wardrobe.

Akhila thought of her father every morning when, heavy with starch and sunlight, the sari rustled around her as though someone were turning the sheets of a newspaper. When she tucked the last pleat in at the waist and flung the pallu over her left shoulder, the bottom of the sari hiked up her legs playfully, so that the last thing Padma did before Akhila left home was to crouch at her feet and teach the sari the laws of gravity. Tug, tug...what goes up has to come down and stay there. By evening, the sari had neither the vitality nor the starch to resist the pull of the earth. The humid air and the dripping heat corroded even the staunchest human spirit, so what hope did a blob of starch have? It was perhaps in those years that the starch entered Akhila's soul. Imbuing her every action and word with a delicate film of stiffness that soon became her natural way to talk and be.

Sometimes on a Sunday afternoon, Akhila lay on the swing like her father had. The iron chains moaned as always, only now they were the echoes of her grief, for what had been and would never be again.

Amma would comb Akhila's hair. Tugging at the knots and

disentangling them with a gentleness that almost made Akhila want to cry. It was the only time she felt as though she could close her eyes and life would take care of itself without her having to plot and plan.

Narayan joined the tank factory as a machinist. Narsi became the first graduate in the family and then, the first postgraduate. He found a teaching job. Akhila felt the iron bands around her chest begin to loosen: Dare I breathe again? Dare I dream again? Now that the boys are men, can I start feeling like a woman again?

Narsi decided he wanted to get married. She was the college principal's daughter and a brahmin. No one could fault his choice and there was nothing anyone could say except perhaps—Don't you think you should wait for your elder sister to get married before you think of a wife and a family?

But who was to mouth this rebuke?

Akhila waited for Amma or Narayan to say something. To broach the subject of Akhila's marriage. When they didn't, Akhila swallowed the hurt she felt and let the anger that grew in her flare. She insisted that a suitable bride for Narayan be found. 'Let both the weddings take place together. Same wedding hall, same day, same time...Narayan has taken care of this family and it is not fair that he is sidelined simply because Mr College Professor is in a tearing hurry to get married.'

Even then, Amma and her brothers never asked, 'What about you? You've been the head of this family ever since Appa died. Don't you want a husband, children, a home of your own?'

In their minds Akhila had ceased to be a woman and had already metamorphosed into a spinster.

Besides, there was Padma. When she had her first period, Amma dressed her as a bride and had her photograph taken in the local studio with her back to a mirror, so that the intricate flower arrangement on her braid would be seen as well. She gave the photograph to Akhila to admire and stood looking at it from over her shoulder.

'My little one is a woman now,' she said quietly.

The message couldn't have been more explicit. Soon it would be time for her to be married and dowries don't accumulate by themselves like dust on a windowsill.

Padma was twenty-two by the time Akhila put together a dowry for her. Gold jewellery; a diamond nose-stud; a steel almirah, a cot and a mattress; stainless steel and bronze cookware; silver lamps; a gold ring and an expensive wrist watch for the groom; and twenty thousand rupees in cash. And even then, it wasn't easy. Prospective grooms worried that once they married her, there was little more they could expect from her family. Finally they found someone who was willing to believe Akhila when she said she wouldn't forsake her Padma.

Akhila was thirty-four. What does a single woman do next in life?

She took a train to work every morning from Ambattur. Her job didn't demand much from her; after all, she was just a clerk. In the evenings, she took the same route back and was home by seven. Her mother would wait for Akhila to arrive before she put the pressure cooker on. They ate, they listened to the radio, and by a quarter to ten were in their beds. They lived quiet, starched and ironed lives where there was no room for chiffon-like flourishes of feeling or heavy zari-lined silken excesses.

When they fell ill, they went to Steadford hospital. And for their souls, Akhila and her mother visited the Shiva temple at Thirumulavayil on Mondays. While Amma stood with her palms pressed together, her eyes closed and her lips moving in prayer, Akhila would stand entranced by the Nandi that guarded the entrance of the temple.

Akhila would touch the flanks of the stone bull that unlike all other Nandis rested with its back to the sanctum sanctorum. An aberration like me, she told herself with a wry smile every Monday.

If the Nandi's position had been correct, the temple would have been one of the holiest of Shiva shrines, rivalling even the Kailasa temple. For, in the Thirumulavayil temple yard grew the rare lingam and yoni flower. Manifestations of Shiva's and Shakthi's presence on every branch, scenting the air with the power of a divine consummation.

No matter how many times Akhila saw the Nandi, it still intrigued her. This Nandi that had turned its back on its lord and master to protect a devotee from being killed by his enemies. Had the Nandi ever wondered what came first—devotion or duty? Had the Nandi known that with this gesture it had de-sanctified the temple and turned Shiva's presence away? Had the Nandi known what it was doing?

Once a month, Akhila took her mother out to lunch at the Dasaprakash Hotel where they always chose the Special Meals. A thick, viciously red tomato soup; two puris and a bowl of vegetable korma; a helping of curd rice; a helping of sambar rice; a bowl of rasam; three kinds of vegetables; an appalum; two pickles; as much plain rice as one wanted; and finally a fruit salad that came with half a cherry on top and a cream wafer stuck into the melting ice cream.

Akhila would watch in concealed irritation as her mother ate. She pecked at the food as if she hated every crumb and yet when Akhila suggested that they try another restaurant, Amma was vehement in her protests. 'What is wrong with Dasaprakash? It is one place where brahmins can eat without worrying about who's doing the chopping and cooking or even the washing-up. Haven't you noticed that even the boys who serve us wear the sacred thread?'

To Amma, all waiters were boys and all brahmins above reproach. Which is why, even though they saw Sarasa Mami, Subramani Iyer's widow, standing with her oldest daughter Jaya at the bus stand, Amma simply gathered the folds of her sari tightly around her and pretended not to see them.

If it had been anyone else, Amma would have used her tongue like a scythe, chopping brutally at their reputation, their character, their lack of shame, and end with her favourite—'If I was in her place, I would have fed my children poison and killed myself. Anything is better than selling one's honour.'

But Sarasa Mami was a brahmin. And it was easier to forgive a brahmin, no matter how serious her crime, than the rest of the world that was made of flesh-eaters and gravediggers.

Perhaps I'm doing Amma an injustice, Akhila thought eyeing her mother. Maybe Amma found it easier to accept what Subramani Iyer's widow did because it could have happened to her.

When Subramani Iyer's eyes remained fixed on the ceiling one morning as if he had been stricken by some revelation at the crack of dawn, Sarasa Mami raised her eyes to the heavens for help. What am I going to do? she wept, beating her chest. How am I to cope? How do I look after three girls and a blind boy?

What was she expecting? Akhila watched Sarasa Mami beg and plead with the various gods her family had worshipped for generations. Did she seriously think that one of those gods would descend to earth and help her in her distress?

For a while Sarasa Mami coped. She sold all the little pieces of jewellery she owned. Finally, when there was nothing left to sell and hunger gnawed at their wilting honour and shook the respectability out of their bones, she sold her eldest daughter Jaya.

From the tin trunk, she took out the only Kancheepuram sari she owned and unfolded it gently. Sarasa had clung to it for that last journey of her life. She, like all good Hindu wives, had prayed every day that she be allowed to die before her husband did. She had wanted to climb the stairway to the heavens, lit by the radiance of the bright red circle of kumkum on her forehead. The strands of jasmine in her hair would scent her passageway and all those who saw her would think how blessed she was to die looking like a bride. And this sari was the one that would have put the world's nose out of joint when it flocked to pay its last respects to a woman it had ignored when alive. Now that this was no longer to be, Sarasa allowed her dreams to roll out of the folds of the sari. Mothballs that dissipated into nothingness when touched by air.

What did Sarasa Mami think of when she helped Jaya with the sari? A little lower around the hip. Let the curve of your waist show. Tighter over your bosom. Don't hide the tilt of your breasts. Let it fall over your shoulder and cascade down your back so that when you walk, it hints at the fullness of your hips. Maybe she felt she was helping dress a bride or maybe it was a corpse that swam into her mind as she teased and arranged the layers of woven cloth.

And Jaya? What did Jaya think when her mother asked her to bathe earlier than usual one evening? Did she feel a cloud of butterflies dance in her stomach when Sarasa lined her eyelids with the density of darkness and wound jasmine buds in her plait? Jaya must have thought that at least tonight she wouldn't go hungry. They never did after that night.

It wasn't as if Jaya stood on street corners soliciting lust. There was a thin veneer of respectability Sarasa concocted to disguise what was expected of Jaya. The men who lived in the bachelor quarters needed someone to cook for them, she said. That was all Jaya did, she claimed when someone asked. 'They treat her well and are generous,' she added.

It soon became a familiar sight; the blind Srini pretending to be a motor car as he jogged along by his sister's side every evening on their way to the barracks. Parp...parp...his mouth honked when they crossed the road. Vroom...vroom...his lips blubbered when she hurried to escape the knowing looks the neighbours threw at her like darts.

What do the dead think of the havoc wrought by their absence? Subramani Iyer? Appa? In some bubbled realm of no-return, do they twist and writhe in pain? Or is that what death is all about? To be able to leave. To cease to care. To be free.

At first, the whole neighbourhood watched in horrified silence. Then they talked in voices that quivered with righteous indignation of the slur Sarasa Mami was inflicting by this brazen behaviour. On Subramani Iyer's good name. On the brahmin community. On womanhood. Wasn't there a more honourable way to stay alive?

'You tell me how,' Sarasa told a neighbour who decided to confront her. 'I'm willing to work. Do any kind of work to earn a living. I went to each one of the houses in the neighbourhood and asked if anyone wanted a maid. And everyone behaved just like you did. Giving me a handful of rice as though I were a beggar woman and then shooing me away.'

'I didn't do that,' the neighbour defended herself.

'You didn't. What you did was even worse. You hid in a room inside and asked your daughter to tell me that you had gone out to the shops.'

'It was true. I had gone out to the shops,' the neighbour pressed.

Sarasa shrugged, unwilling to debate on what had transpired some months ago. Hoping that her silence would sweep away from her doorstep this woman and her vicious curiosity disguised as neighbourly concern.

'But even so, this?' the neighbour persisted, letting her distaste show with a curl of the lip, nostrils that tightened and an open-handed comprehensive gesture.

'If I was younger, I would have sold myself to keep my family fed and clothed. But this is tired flesh. No man has any use for it. And it isn't as if she is consorting with several males. There is just one man. A regular. And she is happy.'

'You are disgusting,' the neighbour spat as she walked away. 'And unnatural. What woman would talk of her daughter having a regular?'

By that evening, for the brahmin community of that neighbourhood, the inmates of House 21 had forever ceased to exist.

It was fortunate that they didn't live in an agraharam, Akhila thought. In the brahmin ghetto where even air is allowed entry only through narrow passages; where vermilion stripes anointing the lime-washed walls of the house exteriors suggest a rigidity of thought and a narrowness of acceptance; where the intricate rice powder kolam on the doorway prevents the arrival of any new thought, and all aberrant behaviour is exorcised by censure and complete isolation.

Often Akhila thought that if some wandering god were to pass that way, he would know an agraharam from the very sight of houses clinging to houses. Like an exotic species of caterpillar with a million red and white legs running into one another, emitting a curiously unique stench of asafoetida and soapnut.

But even though they didn't live in an agraharam, the brahmin community behaved as though they did. So Sarasa, her whore daughter, her blind son and soon-to-be whore daughters were excommunicated. To Amma, this was a fate worse than death. For what was a brahmin if not accepted by the brahmin world to be one?

'Look who is here,' Akhila said under her breath. But Amma refused to rise to the bait. She pretended not to hear her and stared ahead into the horizon, willing the bus to appear and ferry them away before Akhila did something embarrassing like going up to them and beginning a conversation.

'That is Jaya and her mother standing there,' Akhila persisted. 'Don't you want to talk to Sarasa Mami? She was once your best friend, wasn't she? Why don't you? No one will know. We are so far away from home. Or, is it that you don't want to have anything to do with a woman who's reputed to have sold her daughter into prostitution?'

Amma pursed her lips and frowned. 'Will you be quiet?'

'Don't be unkind,' she added as an afterthought.

'Who is being unkind?' Akhila snapped, angered by her mother's self-righteous tone. 'Are you accusing me of being unkind? Not me. It's you and your brahmin cronies who have ostracized that poor woman and her family.'

'I wish it weren't so. But when one lives in a society, one has to conform to its expectations. I am not one of those revolutionaries who can stand up to the world. I'm a simple woman. A widow. And I need to belong to the society we live in.'

'Do you realize it could have been us standing there, Amma?' Akhila asked softly.

'I know it could have been us. Which is why I don't ever say a word against her, no matter how much the others have slandered her.' And then Amma turned towards Akhila and put her hand on her shoulder. 'But I had you.'

Akhila felt the heaviness of her hand press down upon her. Amma had her to rescue her from the threat of penury and degradation. Amma had Akhila to replace her husband as the head of the household. Amma had her—Akhila. Akhilandeswari. Mistress of all worlds. Master of none.

What Akhila missed the most was that no one ever called her by her name any more. Her brothers and sister had always called her Akka. Elder Sister. At work, her colleagues called her Madam. All women were Madam and all men Sir. And Amma had taken to addressing her as Ammadi. As though to call Akhila by her name would be an affront to her head-of-the-household status.

So who was Akhilandeswari? Did she exist at all? If she did, what was her identity? Did her heart skip a beat when it saw a mango tree studded with blossoms? Did the feel of rain on her bare skin send a line of goose bumps down her spine? Did she sing? Did she dream? Did she weep for no reason?

Akhila often thought of a Tamil film she had seen some years before. Of a woman like her who was destined to be nothing more than a workhorse. A woman who gave up her life and love for her family.

When the film came to the cinema theatre near her home, Amma and she had gone to see it. Though they had read enough about the film to know what the plot was and the character of the heroine, the film took them both by surprise. Akhila could have been the heroine and her despair Akhila's. They had watched the film in silence and when the lights came on during the interval, Akhila saw her mother avoid her eyes. That night they didn't talk much and Amma went to bed early. Akhila couldn't sleep. She looked at Padma who lay curled into a ball by her side. Padma who was maturing into a woman. Her face had lost its babyish roundness and had begun to hint at what her adult face would look like. If I had a man who loved me madly and wanted to marry me, would I give him up for Padma, Akhila wondered. No, she wouldn't, she told herself. Akhila dismissed the film as silly sentimental sop and turned on her side. In those days, she was still young enough to think that this would not be the pattern of the rest of her life. One day, she too would have a home and family of her own.

But ten years later, when Akhila thought of the film, she felt darkness lick at her. Would her life end like the life of the woman in the film?

Akhila never let her mind dwell on these things. To do so would be entering dangerous territory. Instead, on her thirty-fifth birthday, she decided to get herself an education.

She enrolled in the open university for a Bachelor of Arts degree. Akhila chose history as her main subject. There is probably no one more suited to study history than a spinster, she thought. To trace the rise and fall of civilizations. To study the intricacies of what made a certain dynasty behave in a certain manner. To watch the unravelling of life from the sidelines. To read about monarchs and concubines; wars and heroes; to observe and no more.

✝

It was Katherine Webber who brought an egg into Akhila's life.

Katherine was the closest thing Akhila had for a friend. Though Akhila had worked in the same income-tax office for more than sixteen years, she still didn't have any friends there. Each one of them was a colleague she shared her working hours with and no more. It wasn't as if they didn't make any overtures but Akhila preferred to keep her distance from them and all that their individual lives revolved around. Akhila was the only unmarried person in that entire office of twenty-four people. And she had nothing in common with them. What would she understand of a father's anguish when his child was persistently ill? Or a mother's joy when her child took its first step? The world of the householder was not hers.

From the Gurukula stage of life, she had moved directly to the Vanaprastha. And she wanted no part of someone else's karmic flow.

In that office of husbands and wives, Katherine and Akhila were thrown together. Katherine Webber came on a transfer from Bangalore. Her family lived in Madras and she said she had managed to get the transfer with great difficulty. Akhila liked Katherine. She liked Katherine's calf-length dresses and the way her wispy brown hair framed her face. (The only time Amma saw her, she whispered darkly, 'Don't they have oil in her house? If I were her mother, I would oil her hair and comb it back into a nice tight plait. What is her mother thinking of, letting a young unmarried girl walk around with hair flowing down her back and her legs on display for the whole world!')

Akhila liked the way Katherine talked tirelessly, pausing only to giggle. But most of all, Akhila liked Katherine because she was perhaps the only other person she knew who was not preoccupied with the four corner stones of the grihasthashrama—husband, baby, home and mother-in-law.

'Why are you so friendly with that Anglo-Indian girl?' Sarala, the Upper Division Clerk, murmured one day as they went over a file together.

'Why? What's wrong?' Akhila asked quietly.

'Nothing is wrong. But you know what they say about Anglo-Indians. They eat beef and their flesh stinks. Both men and women smoke and drink. And they have no moral standards like us Hindus. If you wanted a friend, there are so many other women in this office. All from respectable families like yours,' Sarala said, pressing her index finger on the wet sponge and flicking a page.

'Don't be silly!' Akhila snapped. 'Katherine is a good girl and as respectable as you and me. Just because she is not a Hindu doesn't automatically make her an immoral person.'

Sarala's mouth twisted into a smirk, 'One of these days you will find out for yourself.'

Sarala's warning further cemented their relationship. Katherine and Akhila began to talk. Not the usual prattle that had tempered their earlier conversations. Instead they spoke about what really mattered to them. Katherine told Akhila about her Daddy; her piano teacher Daddy who was drunk on happiness when he was playing the piano and drunk on cheap alcohol at all other times. She told Akhila of her Mummy from whom she inherited her pale skin, brown hair, and a fondness for men with a cleft chin and moustache (Daddy had both). She told Akhila of her brothers and sister, who had escaped the fug compounded of Daddy's alcohol fumes and Mummy's unhappiness, to make a life for themselves. And then she told Akhila about Raymond, her boyfriend who had gone away to Melbourne and had forgotten all about her. In some strange way Akhila felt comforted. Here was a companion who knew what it was like to be her—single and lonely.

They shared confidences and lunch. Katherine liked Amma's cooking—the lemon rice and coconut rice; the idli and vada; the puri and korma. Akhila in turn enjoyed the bread-butter-jam sandwich that Katherine wrapped separately for her. And then one day Katherine opened her lunch box and brought out an egg.

Akhila watched Katherine tap the egg on the table and saw a crack run down the shell in zigzag lines. She watched as Katherine removed the fragments of the shell and it seemed to Akhila that it must be the most pleasurable thing anyone could do. Then, like a Russian doll, the shell gave way to yet another layer of white. What lay inside that? What did the inside smell of? What did it feel like to touch?

Akhila felt a great urge to know and before she could help it, she blurted out, 'Can I have a bite?'

At first, Katherine gaped at her in surprise. Then she said, 'Sure.'

'Here, take it,' she said, passing Akhila the egg.

She took it in her hand gingerly. It felt cold and smooth in her palm. The next time, she would crack the shell herself. But now that she held it in her hand, Akhila felt fear. What would Amma say if she knew? Akhila had never done anything like this before.

'Eat it with this,' Katherine said, thrusting a screw of paper with salt in it towards Akhila. Then she giggled. 'My mother always says that eating an egg without salt is like kissing a man without a moustache.'

'Really?'

Katherine giggled some more. 'Oh, I forgot. You have never been kissed.'

Akhila shrugged and bit into the egg. The first bite yielded nothing. Neither taste nor disgust.

'The white of an egg is tasteless,' Katherine said at the look of surprise on Akhila's face.

Then came the hint of yellow. The yolk crumbled in her mouth, coating her tongue, clinging to her palate even as it slid down her throat spreading a pure sensation of delight in its wake.

'I can see that you like it,' Katherine said, amused by what a mere egg was doing to Akhila. 'Maybe I should bring you an egg for lunch every now and then.'

Akhila nodded, still a little overwhelmed by what she had done. She had actually eaten an egg.

For a whole year, Akhila feasted secretly on hard-boiled eggs. In spite of what Katherine's Mummy believed, she needed neither salt nor pepper. Akhila liked it plain so that she could taste the translucent white of the albumen, the opaque yellow of the yolk, the composite joy of surreptitious pleasures.

Then Katherine's emigration papers arrived. She was going to Australia where she had fifty-two cousins, nine uncles and twelve aunts, she said. They would take care of her, help her settle down, introduce her to their friends and shape a new life for her there.

Akhila knew that things would never be the same again. She bought Katherine a narrow gold ring set with a pearl as a goodbye present. And Katherine bought her a pair of high-heeled sandals with slender straps and a lipstick. 'Akhila, you are a very good-looking woman. This is just to make you look smarter. You are only thirty-six years old. So stop pretending you are fifty,' she said, laying the gift-wrapped parcel on Akhila's table.

Akhila smiled her thanks, knowing that she would never use either of Katherine's gifts. Then Katherine placed a jute shopping bag on Akhila's table and murmured mischievously, 'Look inside.'

Akhila peered in and saw what seemed to be a green-coloured plastic egg case.

'There are four eggs in it,' Katherine continued to whisper. 'For you to take home. Maybe you can hide them in your home and cook them when your mother's asleep or something. Do you know how to boil an egg? Just fill a small vessel with enough water to cover the egg and boil it for about eight minutes. Then pour cold water on it and it'll be nice and firm. If you boil it for just five minutes, the white would have set and the yellow will be a little gooey. That's nice as well. Try a soft-boiled egg sometime. I think you'll like it.'

Akhila put the bag near hers and worried what she was going to do with it. Perhaps she could leave it behind on the train and that would be the end of it. But when it was time to get off the train, Akhila found herself taking the bag with her. As she walked home, she wondered if she could thrust it behind some bush and then suddenly, she was turning into her street and she knew that she was taking the eggs home. And she was going to tell her mother about it.

Amma accepted her taste for eggs like she had endured Akhila's father's fondness for snuff. It wasn't the done thing but it could have been worse. What if Akhila had taken to eating flesh? An egg in many ways could be considered akin to milk. All Amma asked was that Akhila buy the eggs in the city and that she dispose of the shells secretly and away from the home and neighbourhood.

Akhila cooked and ate her eggs in her mother's kitchen.

Amma gave her a saucepan, a long-handled spoon and a little bowl that were relegated to a far corner of the kitchen when not in use.

All of Akhila's wondrous explorations and magical discoveries were locked within the fragile shell of an egg. First there was the perfect eight-minute egg that she sliced and arranged on a slice of bread and butter. Then there was the five-minute egg. Akhila tapped a little hole on top and scooped out the almost set white and quivering, runny yellow insides with a spoon. But it was the three-minute egg that made Akhila feel the most adventurous. The three-minute egg was an almost raw egg that she tossed down her throat without gagging even once. But it had to be piping hot. Once Akhila tried beating a raw egg into a cup of milk. But she almost threw up. To Akhila, an egg was an egg only when it was surrounded by a shell and baptised by boiling water.

✝

Akhila—spinster, government employee, historian, eater of eggs, reminisced about the years that had gone past. How easily the memories tumbled tonight. How effortless it was to remember when the coupé cradled and rocked; a mother that stroked the brow and said: Child, think on. Child, dream on...

Akhila raised herself on her elbow and peered outside. The countryside swathed by the night sped by. Sheela had finally said she was ready to sleep. Together they had pulled up the middle berth and now Sheela lay on it, curled, still clutching her leather bag to her chest.

Sheela and Janaki. Two ends of a spectrum. Young girl, old woman, and yet how different were their lives from hers? They could be her, Akhila thought. She could be them. Each confronting life and trying to make some sense of its uncertain lines. If they could somehow do that, as well as they knew best, why can't I? With that thought, Akhila felt a slow gathering of joy. A thin stream that let loose tributaries of trickling hope. An anticipation that what she had set out to do might not all be in vain. That Akhila would triumph one way or the other.

Akhila settled back on the berth. The fiery, noisy mating of the wheel and track echoed through her head. She pulled the sheet to her chin and closed her eyes. For the first time, she felt protected. Sheltered from her own self. The train knew where it was headed. She didn't have to tell the train what to do. The train would stay awake while she slept.

Akhila, cherished, safeguarded, secure, felt sleep slither over her. Her eyes grew heavy. It was a respite from being Akhila. She dreamt:

Akhila is a little girl. She is in a railway compartment. A first-class coupé. They are all there—Appa, Amma, Narayan, Narsi and Padma. They are going to Vishakapatnam. Why Vishakapatnam, Akhila doesn't know. But she knows it is far away and by the sea. The landscape is unfamiliar—sand dunes and a sea that is an almost impossible navy blue. Appa is happy. He is laughing. Amma too. The boys are playing with a car and Padma is singing loudly. Akhila is so happy that her heart could almost burst.

Amma opens the huge lunch box that's been kept on the little table attached to the wall of the coupé. Tiers and tiers of her delicious food. Mysorepak dripping with ghee and round brown pebble-like cheeda. Coconut rice and puliyodhare. Curd rice studded with jewels of glistening pomegranate seeds, emerald slivers of chillies and curls of coriander.

They eat. Akhila can smell the oregano in the murukku. Its salt floods her mouth. A crumb clings to the corner of her mouth. She snakes her tongue out and licks it in.

Appa stands up and combs his hair looking into the mirror above the little table. He smiles at himself in the mirror and says, 'Let's all take a little nap.'

Akhila wonders at this new Appa who can't stop smiling.

They lie down. This is a first-class coupé. There are only four berths. Amma and Appa have a berth each. The boys share one berth and the girls another. Akhila puts her arm around

Padma's waist and croons her to sleep.

Akhila wakes up suddenly. The coupé is layered in darkness. There is no one there. She is alone. 'Amma, Appa,' she calls. But there is no response.

'Narayan, Narsi, Padma, where are you?' She is crying by now. She climbs down. The coupé is empty, she thinks. Then she sees the man seated by the window. She turns around wildly. The door has been latched.

'Who are you? What are you doing here?' she demands. The voice that comes out is a grown-up voice. Akhila is not a little girl any more.

'You don't know me,' he says. 'But I know you. I know all about you.'

'What...what do you mean?' she stutters in confusion.

'You are Akhila,' he says and comes to stand by her. 'You are Akhila the woman. Everyone else might have forgotten about the woman within you. But I see her. I see the desire in her eyes, the colours in her heart.'

His voice is low and husky. Akhila feels it wind around her. A python that gathers her within its grasping coils.

'Don't you know me, Akhila?' he asks. 'Don't you know me, really? Think. Think hard.'

But Akhila can't remember. All she knows is that suddenly she feels a strange elation. 'Yes,' she says. 'Yes, I remember,' she lies.

'Do you remember this?' he says and traces the outline of her lips with the forefinger of his right hand. She sucks in her breath. She should feel outraged, she knows. She doesn't. She feels electric shocks shoot through her.

His finger moves, along her jaw. She closes her eyes. He blows on her eyelids. She arches her throat. His finger slides down. He runs it down the length of her arm. Between her fingers. She moans.

'Do you remember this?' he says.

She doesn't. These sensations are new but she fears that to say so would make him stop. 'Yes, yes,' she pleads.

With the finger, he flicks her sari off. It is sheer chiffon. It falls easily. A pool of yellow chiffon lies at their feet. He touches her breasts. First one, then the other. She wants to rip open her blouse and bare her flesh to him. Her fingers rush to the buttons. He murmurs, 'Ssh, ssh, not yet.'

He circles her nipples through the cloth. An aching tautness grips her. She leans towards him.

Suddenly the door of the coupé opens. They stand there. Appa and Amma, her brothers and sister—except that they are children no more. 'You shameless creature. You brazen slut,' Appa thunders.

'How could you?' Amma cries.

'What are you doing?' her brothers shout and turn their faces away, ashamed by the lust that they can see dancing on her face.

Akhila feels blood rush up to her face. 'Here, cover yourself,' Padma says, a grown-up Padma who flings her sari at her.

'I...I...' Akhila tries to explain.

'Don't let them get to you,' his voice murmurs in her ear. And as they watch, he cups her breasts. Hefting them, rubbing her nipples between his thumb and forefinger. And Akhila doesn't care about anyone any more. She simply leans back against his body and closes her eyes. Nothing has ever felt so good before. She hears the coupé door slam.

Akhila woke up with a start. Where am I? she asked herself, looking around her wildly. Everything was unfamiliar...then slowly she remembered.

She thought of her dream and blushed. She ran her hand over her breasts. Her nipples were stiff. How can I dream such dreams?

She saw Margaret open the door of the coupé. 'I have to go to the bathroom,' the younger woman said.

The train was still. Akhila looked out of the window. It was an unscheduled stop in the middle of nowhere. Akhila glanced at her watch. It was quarter past three. Neither night nor day. The hour of reckoning when dreams tumble and fears surface.

Margaret came back. 'The train has been here for more than twenty minutes. I woke up to a crying sound.'

Akhila's hand rushed to her mouth. Had she been voicing the lust of her dream?

'It was that girl. She was crying in her sleep,' Margaret said.

'No one else seemed to have heard her,' she said. 'So I climbed down and woke her up. She is asleep now.'

Akhila glanced at the girl who was curled on her side.

'I don't think I can go back to sleep. The train gets in to Coimbatore at five in the morning and if I go back to sleep now, I won't wake up and I might miss the stop.'

Akhila nodded. What on earth did the younger woman plan to do?

Margaret leaned against the middle berth. 'It's such a pity we are not sleeping on the same side or we could have pulled down my berth and been more comfortable.'

'I heard the girl and you talk,' Margaret continued. She was whispering as if she didn't want anyone else to overhear her. 'I wasn't asleep yet.'

Akhila didn't say anything. Margaret, she thought, wasn't expecting a response anyway.

'I was thinking...of us, the women in this coupé. I don't mean the woman in the top berth or the young girl. They don't count...not really. I was thinking of Janaki and Prabha Devi. Women like you and me, and I couldn't stop thinking of how angry I felt, no, I don't know if anger is the word, it was more like vexation when I saw your face after Janaki told us about herself. I saw how unsure you felt. As though you felt you had made a mistake and...I thought, even if Prabha Devi talks to you, how different would her life be from Janaki's? That bothered me. Do you understand what I am trying to say?

'They are nice women but they are the kind who don't feel complete without a man. They might say otherwise but I know them and women like them. Deep in their hearts, they think the world has no use for a single woman.'

Margaret paused for a moment as if she was making up her mind on which direction her words should take. 'The truth as I know it and as I live it is that a woman needs a man but not to make her feel whole. Are you asking yourself—what does she know? A married woman talking of not needing a man...

'Which is why I am going to have to tell you about Ebe and me. And when I have, you'll understand why I say that a woman doesn't really need a man. That is a myth that men have tried to twist into reality.

'Do you know what I was doing in Bangalore?'

Akhila shook her head. She felt overwhelmed by the intensity of Margaret's words. What startling revelation was she about to hear?

'I came here to drop my husband off at a health clinic. A place where people go to get a hold on their weight; and on their lives. He goes to the health clinic every year. Ebe needs to. I don't know about the others but the effects of the regimen there don't last long with Ebe. For a few days, he is almost back to what he once was. Which makes him think that he has managed to wrest his life back. So I have to step right back in and wrench it back from him. Once I do that, Ebe becomes of no consequence.'

6

Oil of Vitriol

God didn't make Ebenezer Paulraj a fat man. I did.

I, Margaret Shanthi, did it with the sole desire for revenge. To erode his self-esteem and shake the very foundations of his being. To rid this world of a creature who if allowed to remain the way he was, slim, lithe and arrogant, would continue to harvest sorrow with a single-minded joy.

Among the five elements that constitute life, I classify myself as water. Water that moistens. Water that heals. Water that forgets. Water that accepts. Water that flows tirelessly. Water that also destroys. For the power to dissolve and destroy is as much a part of being water as wetness is.

In the world of chemicals, water is the universal solvent. Swayed by the character of all those who take it over. But just because I'm familiar, I'm not typical. That was the mistake Ebe made. He dismissed me as someone of no significance. So I had no other recourse but to show him what the true nature of water is and how magnificent its powers are. That it is water in its various forms that configures the earth, atmosphere, sky, mountains, gods and men, beasts and birds, grass and trees, and animals down to worms, flies and ants. That all these are only different forms of water. That water is to be weighed carefully or it will weigh upon you! That was the first lesson I had to teach him.

All these years, I was frozen in a solid state. In this form, my ability to make things happen remained low. I let myself float on the surface of time, impervious and oblivious to what my life had become.

In my frozen state, I had forgotten what it was to be water. Then something in me snapped. Something happened. A chemical change.

There is a technical name for the water that I turned into. Supercritical water. Capable of dissolving just about anything which as mere water, it wouldn't even dare aspire to. Raging with a vehemence that could burn and destroy poisons that if allowed to remain, would kill all that was natural and good.

†

When I woke up that morning, it seemed no different from any other day. I went through the morning chores and walked to the school as I usually did. When there were just a few minutes for the morning assembly bell to ring, I went to stand by the window of the chemistry lab. From there I could see most of the quadrangle where the assembly is held, the senior school classrooms and in the distance, the school gate. The usual number of stragglers wheeling their bicycles were trickling in.

The older children were seldom late. In fact, they came in earlier than they were required to. In those precious minutes before the watchful eyes of the coterie began their incessant beat through the hallways of the school, love notes were exchanged, exploratory caresses managed and juvenile dreams spun.

The younger children had no such hormones to prise their eyelids open at dawn. There would come a time when they too would feel the tug of their teens, outgrow their shorts and skirts and take to entering the school portals long before they were required to. But right now, late and breathless from running, they had to contend with the teacher and the boy prefect on duty.

Three minutes before the assembly bell rang, the gates were closed. And a prefect wrote down the names of the children who were stranded outside. The names were pinned up on the noticeboard and depending on the offenders' frequency of lapses, punishments were meted out.

I craned my neck to get a better look at the teacher in charge. The god of the school gates and pre-teen anguish for the day. The stance was both familiar and unmistakable. Legs slightly apart. Hands clasped at the back, a slim cane around which the long fingers of the right hand curled ever so daintily, authority in every fibre, priggish righteousness in every breath. The quintessential school principal. And my husband. Ebenezer Paulraj.

The sky was the colour of freshly cast zinc. A bluish silver surface that would slowly oxidize to form a greyish protective film as the day wore on. Swirls of dust rose from the vast acres of playing-fields. Where hundreds of feet trampled, even the hardiest of grass couldn't survive. The few shoots that dared show their effrontery by raising their green heads were ruthlessly pulled out and thrown into the compost heap as per the orders of Ebenezer Paulraj—the destroyer of blades, grass and human alike.

I stood there watching him as he surveyed his kingdom. The cane was his sceptre; a symbol of the power that he wielded. He waggled the cane and in my mind, I saw the curl of the upper lip, heard the voice that barely rose above a few decibels and could yet rip a child's self-esteem to shreds in a matter of seconds. And I realized that I hated him more than I had ever hated anyone.

I mouthed the words: I HATE HIM. I HATE MY HUSBAND. I HATE EBENEZER PAULRAJ. HATE HIM. HATE HIM. I waited for a clap of thunder, a hurling meteor, a whirlwind, a dust storm...for some super phenomenon that is usually meant to accompany such momentous and perhaps sacrilegious revelations.

The sky continued to shine a bluish silver and the breeze

settled to merely rustling the leaves of the ficus tree and I knew that the literature that spawned such hyperbole had proved itself to be false again.

I turned my back to the window. A faint smell of sulphur clung to the room. The counters were arranged with gleaming lab paraphernalia—test tubes, beakers and pipettes, for the morning experiments. This was my familiar world. A world that was neatly divided into solids, liquids and gases. Predictable and orderly, where the composition of an element determined its behaviour. Here, there was no room for excesses and chaos. In my domain, there was order and calm.

I felt relief course through me. Pure, colourless, odourless, dense relief.

I was no longer unsure. My feelings, that had until now refused to clarify their chemical structure, had revealed themselves.

For so long, I had wondered what it was I felt for him. How does one know if one loves, hates or is merely indifferent to a man? How does one measure what one feels? With a test tube or a pipette? With a spatula or a weighing balance?

But now I knew. Peace licked at my insides with a luminescence as I hurried down the stairs. Children filed past me in orderly lines. There were staircase prefects who stood vigil at both staircases to ensure that there was no pushing or jostling. This was a far greater crime in Ebenezer Paulraj's eyes and the punishments were so much more dreadful.

It wasn't as if he resorted to corporal punishment. He was the regent of the incorporeal world. He simply found out what a student liked to do best and then forbade the child from doing it for a week or for as long as he deemed fit. No library for one. No hockey for the other. No taking part in an inter-house football match. No representing the school at a quiz contest. I did try suggesting that there were probably other ways to instil discipline in a child, that there was really no need to take it to this extent. But he pretended not to hear me. Ebenezer Paulraj listens to no one but himself.

You would know that by looking at him. By the manner in which he stands on the dais surveying his charges as they fall into place. The smaller ones in front, the taller ones at the back. Middle school to senior school. Brothers, sisters, neighbours, friends. Grey old plodders, gay young friskers...It doesn't matter who they are, when in front of Ebenezer Paulraj, they are all reduced to tongue-tied, round-eyed sponge bags, absorbing every word, every nuance, every inflection that he greets them with every day. Ebenezer Paulraj rouses fear; I doubt whether he has ever been adored, loved or worshipped by the children as some other teachers were. As for the coterie, they thought of him as their captain: a good captain, and a fair captain.

The coterie stood two steps behind him on the dais. It was only I, Margaret Shanthi, who stood apart. Positioned behind the children, posted there to reprimand the shufflers, jokers and trickster aces of senior school. But from where I stood, head tilted, I saw only his face. I saw Ebenezer Paulraj for who he really was.

✝

There had been a time when he streaked my thoughts with jeweller's rouge. Finely powdered ferric oxide; rosy-red dust that polished precious metals, diamonds and dreams. But just as ferric oxide turns to rust, so it was with the hopes I had for our life together.

I met Ebenezer Paulraj when I was barely twenty-two years old. I was riding a wave of triumph then. The university results had been declared and I was the gold medallist for that year. 'A gold medal in M.Sc. chemistry. She was always a good student but this...' my parents took great pride in telling any one who asked. 'We'd like her to study further. Work towards a doctorate and perhaps go to America where brains like hers are highly prized,' they added, confident that their dreams were mine too.

I wasn't so sure if I wanted to study further or leave Kodaikanal where we lived. I liked being home. Pottering about in the garden, taking long lazy naps in the afternoon and then, there was Ebenezer Paulraj. He had already insinuated himself into my life, corroding academic ambitions and parental aspirations. Ebenezer Paulraj wanted me to be a teacher just like him.

All through my university years, I worked so hard to be ahead of everyone else that I had little time to spare, for boys or real-life romance. Occasionally I read a Mills & Boons romance and allowed myself to fantasize about the time I would meet someone who was all that a man ought to be. Someone who would be worthy of the pages of a romance novel.

I always thought that fine features spoke of sensitivity. Ebenezer Paulraj's features were finely chiselled and he was tall and well built, with a dark complexion. I fell in love with him the first time I saw him at the church youth group meeting. Who was this magnificent looking man? I wondered, eyeing him again and again. He was dressed plainly and affected none of the fashions the men of my generation did. He stood apart and in that aloofness I saw a dignity. He was someone my favourite Mills & Boons authors would have approved of and I wanted to know him better. And then when he began to sing, I knew I would give up anything to have him. Mid-way through the song, he looked into my eyes and smiled. He feels the same way about me, I gleamed.

I wore my happiness like a halo. Luminescent phosphor. Glowing in the dark. Shedding light and laughter.

Two months later, before there could be even a whiff of scandal, Ebenezer Paulraj did what was expected of him. He had his parents meet mine and our wedding date was set.

'What a wily creature you are! Why didn't you tell us about him?' my elder sister Sara teased as soon as Ebenezer Paulraj and his parents had left. We were sitting in the living room drinking a second cup of tea that winter afternoon.

I smiled in embarrassment. 'I didn't know how you would

react. If you would find him suitable...'

'Why did you think we wouldn't find him suitable? We couldn't have found a better match for you if we had looked ourselves,' my brother-in-law said with a guffaw.

'He'll look wonderful in a suit; such broad shoulders and a perfectly upright carriage,' my mother gushed. My mother was a great one for appearances. She lavished most of her energy on the house. My father often joked that we could eat off her floors. But he wasn't joking now when he said, 'And so intelligent and charming. But that's no surprise. Everyone knows that the Paulraj family of Trichy is an aristocratic one. So many lawyers, judges, academics, high ranking bureaucrats are all Paulrajs—they are a breed of thinking men!'

'If you ask me, he's a terrific catch. Only twenty-nine and already vice-principal of such a prestigious school,' my uncle said.

'You will look very good together. He, so tall and dark, and you so delicate and pretty. Like a knight and a lady,' my aunt, who cherished Walter Scott as much as she did my uncle, whispered in my ear.

How they adored him, my family. And I basked in the praise they chose to bestow on him. He was mine and I was the one who had brought this amazing man into their lives.

On the night before the wedding, my mother came to my room. My silly mother with her gay prattle was suddenly serious. She had come to fill in the gaps the priest had left while instructing me on the holy sacrament called marriage. She told me what it meant to be a wife. Of the loyalty that was demanded of me. Of being faithful. Of putting in more effort than a man ever would, to make a marriage a successful partnership. She told me how a divorce was very often the result when a woman didn't make that extra effort. Of sex, except that she called it the physical side of marriage. And how a good wife never says 'no' even if she isn't in the mood. I listened patiently, wondering if she really believed I knew nothing about marriage or sex. I was a virgin as all good girls of good families are before marriage, but Ebenezer Paulraj and I had managed a few furtive kisses and experimental caresses. Besides, unlike her, I was marrying the man I had fallen in love with and not someone picked for me simply because he was suitable.

A few minutes after my mother left, my father walked in. I wondered what he would have to say. My usually reticent father who left all the gushing, explaining and narrating to my voluble mother. He pushed aside the heap of ironed and folded saris that were to accompany me to my new home and sat on the bed. He looked at my face and smiled. 'Tomorrow's the big day,' he began.

I nodded.

My father took my hand in his. 'He's a good man. Ebenezer will make you very happy.'

Why was he trying to convince me about something I already knew for a fact? But I nodded and smiled, pleased by his words. I wanted everyone to love Ebe—as I called him those days—as much as I did.

'He looks so strong and capable. But he has a soft heart. He's a sensitive soul,' my father said in a quiet voice. 'Any man who is as passionate as he is about literature has to be sensitive,' my father, an engineer with the electricity department and a secret poet, added.

I stared at him bewildered.

'You have to take good care of him and take care never to hurt him. He won't be able to bear it if you hurt him.'

I nodded again. I hurt Ebe? What was my father talking about?

When I was alone in the room, I let my eyes linger on Ebe's photograph, which after our engagement was allowed resident status on my dressing table. My family loved him as much as I did. We were going to be so happy together.

✝

Love is a colourless, volatile liquid. Love ignites and burns. Love leaves no residue—neither smoke nor ash. Love is a poison masquerading as the spirit of wine.

In that first year, my love for Ebe worked like a solvent. It loosened the tenacity, weakened the purposefulness that had until then been a part of my mental make-up. I was so drunk on my feelings for him that all I wanted to do was be with him. Please him. Show him in a thousand ways how much I loved him. Everything else was unimportant.

It was as if someone had clamped a gas mask over my face and made me inhale chloroform. Count backwards. First day of marriage. Wedding night. Wedding day...Everything that came before was wrapped in many layers of cellophane paper and packed away.

Of that year, all I remember is the trade fair that came to Kodaikanal. We spent an evening there buying things for our house. Coir mats for the doorstep; a rag rug for the doorway to the kitchen; glass plates and a bedspread with two good sides. This way or that. Two for the price of one. We bit into our candyfloss and felt pinkness dissolve into sugar crystals in our mouths. We held hands and beamed at each other. Love was a liquid fuel propelling our lives forward.

Eighteen months after we were married, I discovered I was pregnant. When we came back from the maternity clinic, I was so excited that I didn't notice Ebe was quiet and withdrawn. I wanted to call my parents and tell them the news. I wanted to stand on the rooftop and holler, 'I'm going to have a baby!'

'Maragatham,' Ebe said in a voice that was softer than usual. Ebe called me Maragatham then. He said Margaret Shanthi was what everyone else called me. He said both Margaret and Shanthi were common sounding names and I deserved a more lyrical one. So this was his special name for me. Maragatham. Emerald in Tamil. 'Maragatham'. And I glowed. A fiery green inner flame.

'Maragatham, I'm not so sure if we should have a baby now,' he said.

Was it then that the first whiff of a fragrance akin to the oil of wintergreen sped up my nostrils? Toxic, destructive methanol when heated with salicylic acid and a few drops of concentrated sulphuric acid produces methyl salicate. A compound that has the fragrance of the oil of wintergreen. Ethanol, or what I thought love to be, produces no such fragrance. I should have known then. But I was so much in love that I wanted only what he wanted.

What's the point in working for a doctorate? Do your B.Ed. so you can become a teacher and then we will always be together.

Long hair doesn't suit you. Cut it off. You'll look nicer with your hair in a blunt bob.

Do we really have to go to church every Sunday?

I don't think it is wise to eat bhelpuri from these roadside stalls. We could always go to a restaurant...

Let's wait till we're both settled in our careers before we have our baby. We have each other. What more do we want?

So I agreed to an abortion.

'You won't feel a thing,' he said as we walked down the corridor of the semi-private wing at the hospital. He had made all the arrangements. All I had to do was go along.

'I've spoken to the doctor at length about this and she said there was nothing to fear. At seven weeks, that thing in your uterus is little more than a zygote.'

I looked up in surprise. Ebe rarely used scientific terms. He preferred the poetic and sometimes incorrect versions. And so it was because he used the word zygote that from some recess of my mind came the memory of a textbook: 'At conception the haploid sex cells, the sperm and the egg, each of which contains only part of the genetic material required to form a person, merge to form a new biological entity. Unlike the sperm or the egg, the diploid zygote possesses a unique human genotype and the power of full differentiation, without which no human life can be expressed. The haploid sperm and egg are only parts of the potential for human life. The zygote is biological human life.'

I stopped and pulled at his sleeve. 'Ebe, I'm not sure. I don't feel right about this.' When I saw his mouth thin, I added, 'I don't think the Church would approve of this either.'

He ran his fingers through his hair and sighed. 'First of all, the Bible never mentions the word abortion. Secondly, if you study Church history you will find that it prohibits abortion only after a certain point. After "ensoulment", which happens only eighty days after conception. Aristotle said that too. That the soul enters a human life only after it has survived eighty days of physical life. Right now that cell in you is just that: a cell with no soul or feelings. If you had a boil that turned septic, wouldn't you have it lanced? Just think of this as a tumour that has to be removed.'

I sought the clasp of his hand. I was afraid. I was uncertain. And I felt guilty.

The semi-private room could be divided into two cubicles by pulling a thick green cloth curtain across. I had the window; not that I was going to be there long enough to enjoy the view.

I lay there and stared at the sky. All of yesterday I had organized my home and our lives in preparation for the next three days. 'You can leave in the afternoon but try and get as much rest as you can,' the doctor had said.

All of yesterday, I had readied myself for this morning. I had the maid wash the windows and mop the floors. I changed the sheets on our bed. I cooked enough food to feed a score of starving Ebenezers and put it into the fridge. And still not content, I sent the maid out to buy a fish.

She brought back from the market a medium-sized mullet. I began to scale it. 'Let me do it,' Kasturi offered.

But I wasn't going to let her. I had to keep my hands and my mind occupied. 'No, I'll do this. Why don't you start washing the clothes? I've left them to soak in the bucket.'

I could hear Kasturi grumbling in the bathroom, 'Is she

planning to go on a holiday? Why has she emptied out the clothesbasket? It's going to take me forever to finish...'

I paused for a moment and wondered if I should tell her. Kasturi, who lived in a hut with her four children and a husband who was a drunk. What would Kasturi understand about being settled in one's life before one had a baby?

I went back to the fish. As I was gutting it, along with the entrails, roe slid out of the belly of the fish; golden roe oozing through my fingers...

I stared at the wetness and heard a voice that whispered in my ear. A faint voice that stemmed from the faith that had once been an intrinsic part of my life: Your hands shaped and made me. Will you now turn and destroy me?...You created my inmost being; you knit me together in your womb...My frame was not hidden from you when I was made in that secret place. When I was woven together in the depths of the earth, your eyes saw my unformed body. All the days ordained for me were written in your book before one of them came to be...

A slow tear slid.

The nurse didn't mean to be unkind. But she had little patience for such procedures. She helped me on with the hospital gown, braided my shoulder-length hair, rolled it and fastened it tightly at the nape. 'Please take off all your jewellery and give it to the bystander,' she said in an extra loud voice, darting what I thought was a scornful look at Ebe. Perhaps she had seen many such husbands stand at the foot of the hospital bed on which their wives sat, slowly removing their jewellery. Perhaps she had been a bystander for many such women—racked with anguish and guilt, while their husbands hovered unseeingly.

My wedding band. I hesitated. How could I take that off? It was with this that he had promised to love and cherish me through sickness and health, till death did us part. 'Take it off too,' she said, not bothering to hide the impatience in her voice. 'You can't have any jewellery on when you are in the operation theatre. No nail polish. No hair pins. Nothing...'

I pulled my wedding ring off and gave it to Ebe. He held it in the palm of his hand and shot me a look of reproach. What else could I do? Hadn't I done everything he wanted me to? I didn't know what it was he expected of me now. And suddenly, I felt much too weary to care.

'Please wait outside,' the nurse told Ebe, shooing him out of the cubicle and the room. 'We have to prepare the patient for surgery.'

I lay back on the pillows and waited for her to come back to me. To take my hand in hers and tell me that there was nothing wrong in what I had agreed to do. That there was plenty of time left for me to be a mother. I waited for her to reassure and comfort me; to prepare me.

She drew the green curtains so that I was shielded from all eyes and set a tray on the bedside locker.

'Have you taken your panties off?' she asked.

I gazed at her stupidly. What on earth did she mean? Where were the kind and compassionate words she was meant to speak?

'Madam, I asked you, have you taken your panties off?'

I nodded.

She rolled the hospital gown up, till it rested on my abdomen. Then she covered my thighs with a towel and said, 'Don't move. If you do, I might nick your skin.'

And so, as I stared at the pattern on the ceiling, she shaved my pubic hair off. So carefully and so coldly.

On the other side of the curtain, I heard a murmur of voices. Soothing. Comforting. The ministering angel had chosen to be with my neighbour. On the other side was an old woman and what was happening to her body was no fault of hers. Whereas I was solely responsible for this wanton destruction of life.

A slow tear burnt.

Through the blur of tears, I saw the nurse's face soften. 'It's still not too late. You can change your mind if you want. Why are you doing this anyway? It isn't as if you are not married, and this is the first one, after all,' the nurse said, patting my arm, mopping me up, splattering the room with words that had echoed in my head for the past few days.

Ebe came in when she left. 'I suppose she told you that what you are doing is wrong; a sin in God's eyes,' he murmured. But his eyes were fierce and his tone, though low, was scathing.

How did he know?

'Don't look so surprised! She's a Roman Catholic. Don't you know what they think of birth control and abortion? She has no business pumping her perverse beliefs into you. I have a good mind to complain about her.'

I was shaken by this new Ebenezer. A bigot? Or, was it that she had threatened his authority? No one had ever done that before.

But suddenly his voice changed and his eyes softened. He stroked my brow and said, 'Maragatham, darling, I hope you understand that this is for our good. For our future.'

As always, I let his voice smoothen away my fears. He was Ebe. My Ebe. He was right. He was always right.

Half an hour later, an entourage of hospital staff arrived with a stretcher on a trolley. 'Have you passed urine?' the nurse asked in her brusque manner.

As they wheeled me away, Ebe walked by my side to the end of the corridor where the elevator banks were. 'All the best!' he said.

For the first time, I felt angry. All the best! What did he mean by that? Was I going in to write an exam or recite a poem? Was I going to run a race or perform an experiment? All the best for what? I had nothing to do but lie there while they scraped my baby off the inside of my womb. Zygote off the inner membrane of my uterus, if you please, Ebe.

In the pre-operative room, the anger dissipated and nervousness took its place. Nurses and doctors dressed in green scrubs and caps bustled around. There were six others like me waiting their turn.

Voices floated around. Disjointed voices that penetrated my

closed eyelids like prodding lances. But I kept my eyes tightly shut.

'Whose patient is this?'

'It's a long procedure but nothing to worry.'

'Why isn't Sister Sheela here? Wasn't she supposed to come in this morning?'

'Relax. If you relax, it won't hurt.'

And always at the foot of my stretcher trolley, different voices came and paused. I would hear the flip of the chart as it was examined. Then a voice brimming with judgement and laced with scorn would dismiss my presence with an 'Oh, MTP!'

Medical Termination of Pregnancy. Read: wilful woman. Unnatural creature. Resister of motherhood and God's handiwork. I told myself it didn't matter what they thought. Ebe knew what was best for me, for us.

Then it was my turn to be wheeled in. A cold stillness. Tubes and monitors. A huge round lamp loomed over my body. It looked like a plate with many compartments; the kind small vegetarian hotels use to serve their meals.

'How are you feeling, Margaret Shanthi?'

Beneath the green cap, I recognized my doctor's face.

How do I feel? I don't know...the words formed on my tongue. Would she understand if I tried to explain? I looked at her face and realized that it was a routine question. Perhaps one they asked everyone who was brought into the operation theatre.

I smiled. 'Fine,' I said, knowing that was what she wanted to hear.

Another doctor inserted a needle into my vein and began a drip. A mask was placed over my face and someone said, 'Count backwards, Margaret.'

So I did. Today. Yesterday. The day we fixed to have an abortion. The day I knew I was pregnant...

Hours later, or was it years later, a voice, reedy and hurried, called from within the back of my skull, 'Margaret, Margaret, wake up!'

I did. Coming back to consciousness reluctantly. An emptiness. An ache. A sense of flatness. Low in my back, an angry fist drummed on my spine. Coils of pain. I felt the pad of cotton wool between my legs. A quiet bleeding.

A slow tear dripped.

Love beckons with a rare bouquet. Love demands you drink of it. And then love burns the tongue, the senses. Love blinds. Love maddens. Love separates reason from thought. Love kills. Love is methyl alcohol pretending to be ethyl alcohol.

A week later, around midnight, Ebe woke me up with his fumbling. 'What are you doing?' I murmured half asleep.

'Nothing. I just want to touch you.' There was a strange note in his voice.

His fingers touched and probed. 'My little girl!' his voice crooned. 'My darling child.'

I felt afraid. What had got into Ebe? 'Ebe, Ebe,' I whispered, unable to keep the panic out of my voice.

'I love it when you call me Ebe, Ebe, just like you did now. Like a little girl. I like you like this,' Ebe murmured. 'So untainted and clean. My little darling. My lovely girl. With no big bouncy breasts and horrible woman's bush. I never want you to change. I want you to remain like this all your life.'

Where was I in all this? Margaret Shanthi, the woman. In Ebe's eyes, had I ceased to be? What did he see me as? A little girl he could rule and mould, make love to and jolly around? It was as if he had negated all that was grown-up and womanly about me...What would happen to us when I changed? When time caught me and left its marks. When I was no longer Ebe's little girl with shorn hair, buds for breasts, naked vulva and delicate ankles...In the dark, a sob strangled me.

I had a pile of lab record books in front of me. End-of-term evaluation time. But for the first time in many years, I couldn't concentrate. I thought of him, of us, of what I had to do next. If I were to leave him, where would I go? Who would be there to reassure me that what I had done was right, that what I needed to do now was to put it behind me and start a new life of my own? Who would offer me a hand to hold and a shoulder to cry on?

Over the years, my family grew to love and admire him even more. They saw him as a successful man, a respectable member of the community, a good husband, and thought that I, with all my numerous faults, overweight and barren, and given to long morose silences and a melancholic disposition, ought to go down on my knees everyday and thank the heavens that he, my husband, had still stuck by me.

When I tried to talk to my mother about the unhappiness that swelled my flesh, shadowed my thoughts and tied my tongue, she dismissed it saying, 'It is normal to quarrel with one's husband. Every day won't be the same when you've been married to a man for years. There will be bad days and there will be good days. The trick is to remember the good days. And like I have said many times before, it is a woman's responsibility to keep the marriage happy. Men have so many preoccupations that they might not have the time or the inclination to keep the wheels of a marriage oiled. Ebenezer is a busy man. The principal of such a large and prestigious school. You must understand this and behave accordingly. Not greet him with your glum silences and bitter words when he returns home after a day's work.'

What about me? I wanted to ask. Don't I have a right to have any expectations of him? Don't I work as hard as he does and more because I run the house as well? Why do you think he is busy and I have all the time in the world? Shouldn't you as my mother be on my side? Shouldn't you listen to my point of view? What happened to this thing called unconditional love that parents are supposed to feel for their children?

My mother, like my father, I knew then, didn't want to hear anything that threatened the idyllic world they had created for themselves. Retired with a good-sized pension and living in their own comfortable home with a pretty garden; both daughters married to eminent men and well settled in life; eldest grandchild a board-exam topper...So how could I take into that house of order and calm, my bitterness, my anger, my hate, my unhappiness?

Besides, there was the stigma of divorce. No one had ever been divorced in my family. What God had put together, no man or woman had cast asunder. In respectable families such as ours, no one gave up on their marriage. They grit their teeth and worked harder to preserve it. If I left Ebenezer Paulraj, I would have to be prepared to lose my family as well.

What do I do? I asked myself again and again.

When the school bell rang, I hurried out. The school was only a few minutes away from the street we lived on and every evening I walked down the tree-lined avenue, stopping at the little vegetable shop at the corner. I bought just enough for each day. Ebenezer Paulraj didn't approve of vegetables that had been refrigerated. But that evening, I decided to make do with what was left over from the previous day. A restlessness seemed to urge me on. To break routines. To do things differently.

When I reached home, I put the kettle on and switched on the TV. The silence of the house unnerved me. With music, laughter and advertising jingles, I populated the empty rooms of my house. I changed my clothes and then I sipped my tea.

We never had a child. I never conceived. The doctors said there was nothing wrong with either of us. They said that one of these days it just might happen...I tried not to think about it. But sometimes a baby crawled into my head; a baby that tried to hold onto the walls of my mind and hoist itself up; a baby that reached for me...

I decided to begin cooking. It was the second Friday of the month, the day the coterie came for dinner. Ebenezer Paulraj always got rampageous on coterie nights. I tried very hard to merge with the walls or the curtains but it didn't take much to

set Ebenezer Paulraj off. The coterie was his audience and he
enjoyed enthralling them with his mellifluous voice and malice
disguised as humour.

When Ebenezer Paulraj was offered the post of Principal of
the S. R. P. Trust School four years ago, we left Kodaikanal to
come to Coimbatore. As his wife and a postgraduate in
chemistry with a degree in education and ample experience, I
was offered the post of Head of Department of chemistry. I was
expected to teach the senior school. 'But since this is the first
batch and there is only one class, you might have to handle
some junior classes too,' Ebenezer Paulraj said, as he described
the school, the teachers, the challenge his job posed, the
wonderful opportunity it was going to be for him. I listened
quietly, wondering why he bothered at all. He had already
made up his mind.

The coterie formed in the first year of Ebenezer Paulraj's
reign. It wasn't as if he set out to form a power group. Ebenezer
Paulraj in his new role of 'Father of the State', for that was how
he thought of himself in relation to the school, instituted a
monthly lunch to be held at our house. The teachers were asked
to bring their spouses and a dish each. We had a full house the
first few times. But slowly the numbers began to dwindle until
only the coterie was left. The lunch became dinner and
Ebenezer Paulraj's power became supreme.

Now that there were only six mouths to feed and six minds to
entertain (none of the coterie was married), I was expected to
provide dinner. The coterie couldn't be faulted. They always
brought something—a box of cakes, a packet of chips and
sometimes fruit. In Ebenezer Paulraj's eyes, they did their bit
and I had to do mine.

'I don't ever ask anything of you. So if this is such a chore, I'll
ask Premilla or Daphne to cook the food. Except, think of how
it's going to make you look,' he said when I complained the first
time after a few dinners.

'But why do we have to have them over every month? It isn't
as if you don't see them every day,' I said, irritated by the

thought of having to open my house to a group who I knew thought of me as the principal's misfortune.

'I don't have many friends. Do you have to grudge me even this?' he said quietly, walking out of the room.

Ebe never argued. Ebe never lost his temper. Ebe never raised his voice. He shut himself in and sat there in stoic silence till I weakened and grovelled and gave in to doing whatever it was that he wanted.

When we were first married, Ebe wanted to play Daddy. He wanted to do his share of the household chores. He insisted when I refused his offers of help. I had a maid to do the more laborious chores and he, like all men, as I had heard my mother tell my father, simply got in the way.

But after things began to sour between us, I realized that Ebe treated the house like a hotel. He expected everything to run by itself without having to do anything except pay for the services. Food on the table. Laundered and ironed clothes for him to wear. Beds made, shelves dusted, towels changed, bathrooms cleaned, errands run, all by invisible hands. I suppressed an occasional burst of irritation at his self-absorption and let it continue. But it rankled that he never bothered to appreciate how well everything was managed.

When we moved to Coimbatore, things changed. My teaching hours grew longer and my responsibilities heavier. But Ebe was impervious to how our lives had altered. I found I could no longer cope, as I had done earlier, without his help. The irritation that I could rein in once began to show, in my speech, in my tone of voice, in the way I ran our house.

He complained about the food when I warmed up leftovers. The maids were found unsatisfactory: he found their nails were dirty, their voices loud and raucous, their manner shifty and their hair everywhere. 'Get rid of her,' he would say after a few days of each maid's tenure.

'Kasturi was just like them. But you never complained then,' I tried to argue.

'Kasturi was never in the house when I was. She didn't get in my way. These ones do. Frankly, I don't think we need a maid at all. I'll buy us a washing machine and that'll take care of most of it,' he said, flinging a glance at the maid who was sweeping the floors.

What about the washing up? The sweeping and mopping? The numerous little things a maid takes care of? I thought wearily. Angrily.

As my fatigue increased, our quarrels became more and more petty. I stopped hiding my annoyance at his callousness. He retaliated with sarcasm. The more derisive he was, the more I nagged. We were little children competing to see who could be nastier.

We fought over the food I cooked, which he said was so basic that we might as well chomp on raw vegetables and boiled meat. 'Why don't you cook then?' I would retort. He would walk away from the table with his unfinished plate and I would find him scraping the remains into the bin.

We argued over spider's webs that I had failed to detect and the dirty clothes he left on the floor expecting them to walk by themselves to the washing machine. 'Oh, stop nagging, will you? I said I'll put the clothes in the machine. Why does it have to be done right this very minute?'

Then there were Ebe's certificates. Every competition that Ebe had ever won, from his nursery school days when he came first in the infants' class Frog Jump race to the inter-college debating competition where he was awarded the best interjector, was framed and hung.

The certificates occupied a whole wall and had encroached onto the other walls as well. Ebe complained that I didn't dust them often enough. That the glass looked filthy and when he took down a frame, he could see dust lining its top. 'Why don't you do it yourself?' I snapped. 'This is silly. Which grown man would hang up a certificate that says he came first in threading the needle when he was three and was second in the sack race when he was four? Don't you realize, Ebe, that even your own friends laugh at you?'

In the beginning, I would tell Ebe about every little thing I did, every thought that crossed my mind; I thought he would want to know the details of my day like I did his. One day I noticed that he wasn't listening. He was only pretending to. I saw a fog of disinterest settle over his eyes as I talked. I saw him reach for a magazine and flick through its pages. I stopped. I didn't know what else to do. That night I couldn't sleep. I kept asking myself: if I can't tell him, who else is there for me to talk to? The next day, I was quiet. I waited for him to notice the silence; to ask me if everything was alright; to find out what was bothering me. He didn't. I realized then that Ebe didn't care what I did with myself when he wasn't around. And slowly, I stopped talking to him. If he wasn't interested in knowing, I told myself, I wasn't going to tell him.

That we didn't have conversations any more didn't surprise me. But what did was how we snapped at each other and as always, our arguments ended in my carping about his not helping with any of the household chores.

'You never have any time to devote to the house,' I grumbled. 'You always have meetings with the trust board or your welfare committee. Why don't you spare a moment for the welfare of your wife? What is that thing you advocate with such emphasis in the school? SUPW—Socially Useful Productive Work. Ha! How about some SUPW in your own home?'

He squashed my rebellion sharply. 'Don't be ridiculous. My job is a very responsible one. There can be no half-measures. Unlike you, I take my responsibilities seriously and fulfil them.'

I felt my mouth fall open. What responsibilities didn't I take seriously?

'Besides, what are you complaining about? There are just the two of us in this house. How difficult can it be to manage a household of two people?'

After a while, I gave up. I didn't have the energy to try and thrash things out. Or, perhaps it was that I lost hope. That should have told me something. That when I knew I couldn't change him, I had no more expectations of this marriage or relationship...

I no longer protested. I smiled and joined in the laughter. I
became what he wanted me to be: a good sport and a team
player. The universal solvent.

✝

Every time I meet someone, after a few minutes, they cease to be
a person. To me, that person becomes a chemical. Someone
whose nature has been identified, recorded and reckoned with.
It helps me understand the person better; formulate my
behaviour in his or her company and therefore reduce any
chance of accidental explosions. It is a quirk; a peculiar but
harmless one. And it has always worked for me. For what is a
creature sans its chemical nature?

Ebenezer Paulraj smirked when I tried to explain my theory
to him. 'You think you are original? Let me tell you that
Virginia Woolf thought of it long before you were born. Except
that she used animals. Now, that is imagination for you. Who
would think of chemicals except someone completely lacking in
imagination? Nasty smelling horrible things!'

I don't care how Virginia Woolf came to terms with aspects
of human behaviour. To me, my chemicals were everything. My
friends, companions and guides who have been with me
through most of my thirty-five years. And it is they who wafted
to the top of my mind as I watched Ebenezer Paulraj and his
coterie display their unity and camaraderie.

I was not sure if each and every member of the teaching staff
felt the same adulation for Ebenezer Paulraj. I will never know.
For as his wife, they thought my allegiance rested with him.
They did not trust me either. So each time I walked into the
staff-room, an uneasy silence crawled on all fours, weaving its
way through the rows of tables and chairs.

For many years, I spent all my free hours in the chemistry lab.
Sometimes a member of the coterie came looking for me. But I
avoided them as deftly as I could. And if my silence didn't drive
them away, I made sure the smell of the chemistry lab did. All I

had to do was open the jar of hydrogen sulphide and the stink of rotten eggs would cloud the air. Why they sought me out, I don't know. Perhaps it was out of some misguided sense of loyalty they felt for their captain.

The coterie wasn't a large one. But it held the reins of the school.

There was Premilla Madhav, the Senior School economics teacher. The chemical element bromine. Heavy, with hair tinted a reddish brown. Volatile and giving off a strong and disagreeable body odour. Not very active by herself, but united readily with others. But she needed to be watched. For she was capable of causing much injury; inflicting wounds that almost never healed. And so maximum precaution had to be taken when handling her.

Next in line was Daphne, the English teacher. Light and silvery like the element lithium, she dazzled everyone with her charm and smile. When she was excited, crimson stained her cheeks, adding to her allure. Sometimes when he thought no one was watching him, Ebenezer Paulraj gazed at her, bewitched. She was special, that much was certain. More than her charm, more than her beauty, what made her so was her ability to make a person feel less unhappy. But she wasn't very popular with women; they felt dowdy in her presence.

Then there was Sankar Narayan, the Hindi master. There was only one element that could be him—cobalt. Goblin. Evil spirit. Short and dumpy. Hard and brittle, but posturing as the amiable iron and nickel. He could be counted upon to trace almost anything that happened in the school, from thefts to bathroom graffiti to romances. The children told me that they called him Tracer Gamma Ray and there was even a ribald limerick about him that made the rounds of the school, handed down from one class to the next:

Sankar Narayan Gamma
Went to a drama
Without his pyjama
Dangling his banana.

Not all of the coterie were elements. Some of them were so much more complex that they could be classified only as salts, acids or gases; derivatives displaying several characteristics. It was to this group that the last three members of Ebenezer Paulraj's coterie belonged. First of all, there was Xavier, the history master. Colourless, pleasant, sweet and completely undependable if one was in hot water. But one sip of alcohol and he was a different man. Droll and funny, he reduced everyone around him to uncontrollable laughter. Xavier, nitrous oxide, laughing gas. He was a great supporter of combustion, but by himself was incapable of igniting anything, let alone a child's mind.

Arsenic. Her name was Kalavati. With grey hair and a turmeric tinted face. Teacher of mathematics and poisoner of minds. Reeking of garlic and with a temperament that verged on the extreme, arsenic knew nothing of the middle path, the in-between stage. Either she was your best friend or your worst enemy.

And finally, tetrasulphur tetranide. The trickiest of the lot. Nawaz, the vice-principal. Second in command, trusted aide, he changed his colour with the temperature of the room. Vociferous when there was a general discussion; sitter on fences when opinion was divided, and almost invisible when an argument reached its climax. While he was stable enough, he could also explode in response to any sudden friction, so perhaps it was just as well that he stayed away from all controversial discussions and was simply a superconductor of Ebenezer Paulraj's theories.

And then there was him. Ebenezer Paulraj. Biting. Scathing. Colourless. Oily. Dense. Sour. Explosive. Given to extremes. Capable of wiping out all that was water, fluid and alive. Fortified to char almost anything that was organic—wood, paper, sugar, dreams. Concentrated sulphuric acid. H_2SO_4. Hydrogen sulphate. King of chemicals. Oil of vitriol.

There were shades to Ebenezer Paulraj. At times, he was blue vitriol, imbued with copper. Radiating goodness and positive energy; remedying deficiencies with his presence; helping, cleansing, healing. Other times, he was green vitriol, possessed by iron. Capable of reducing anything and anyone to insignificance by the sheer force of his personality. He did it unconsciously and naturally. When he was ruled by cobalt, he was rose vitriol. Protective of all that was weak and defenceless. Then there were times when zinc took over and he was white vitriol. Mordant and destructive of anything that he considered irrelevant. But nothing could change his core quality which determined who he was—oil of vitriol.

Ebenezer Paulraj liked to run. Ebe liked the image of himself running. When I first met Ebe, he took with him everywhere he went, a book called *The Loneliness of the Long-distance Runner*. 'This is one of the greatest books ever written,' Ebe said. 'Listen to this...'

I didn't know what the writer meant or why Ebe was so excited about it. But I was content to accept what Ebe claimed. That it was one of the greatest books ever written.

Only later, much later, when I read it, I realized that what Ebe liked about it more than anything else was its title. It was the kind of book he liked to be seen with. There was a copy on the book-shelf at home and another one that rested on his table in his office with its cover tantalizingly displayed, so that everyone who walked in could see it and draw their own inferences. It was unconventional. It was angry. And it was just the right age; too new to be called a classic in the true sense and too old to be thought of as avant-garde or modern. Ebe was like that: anyone who was his contemporary and an achiever, Ebe saw as a threat. Never mind that they probably lived in another country.

Ebe took the book with him everywhere he went. By now, he knew enough to recite a few passages from memory. But I doubted if Ebe ever really cared what the book was all about. It was simply his way of making a point about himself and his

running. Just as with the movie *Chariots of Fire*. Ebe loved it.
He arranged for a friend to bring him a video copy from the US
and he watched it again and again. All those supple young men,
running and racing against themselves. Ebe saw himself as one
of them. The runner. The lonely runner. The runner who kept
on running because that's what he did best.

Ebe would have liked to run by the sea. Or along a mountain
trail. But Ebe also liked an audience that would give him their
complete attention and so he chose the school. He stayed back
after school, waiting for the last bell to ring before he changed
his clothes and shoes. The children hovered in the playground
watching the school teams and the coaches as they went about
their evening practice of football and hockey. Ebe knew they
would all be there—waiting, watching. He would go to the
school playground, to the tracks, and run for the next forty-five
minutes. Some days he ran longer. When Ebe stopped, there
would be sweat dripping off him and his breath would come in
little gasps. The children and the coaches would watch him
admiringly. 'Running,' Ebe would claim to them, 'is the best
exercise. Nothing can match it, neither swimming nor
tennis—my other favourite sports.'

Running, Ebe claimed, helped him concentrate and focus.
Running was what had made him the man he was, he left
unsaid.

Ebenezer Paulraj was a man of routine and punctiliously
followed a timetable. Every evening, he came home by a quarter
to seven, if he wasn't attending a meeting or engaged elsewhere.
When I heard the car at the gate, I would put the kettle on. He
sipped his tea and walked around the house. Often he stood
before the gilt-edged mirror that hung near the door and
preened. He was still a magnificent looking man, with taut
muscles and skin like silk. Once, just looking at him had made
me desire him. Now all I felt was scorn for his vanity. Ageing
peacock!

When he had showered and changed into fresh clothes, Ebe

would switch on the stereo. His taste in music, like his appetite for food, was characterized by restraint.

If Ebe had a weakness, it was food. He loved eating; the richer the food, the better he liked it. Fatty bacon, roe-filled sardines, chicken liver, the globs of fat that butchers threw in to make up for the bones when selling mutton, double-yolked eggs, mangoes with cream and ripe sapodillas, puris, fritters, chips—heavy with oil, dense with calories. But Ebe loved his body even more. So he controlled his natural fondness for eating. He never took a second helping, fasted for a whole day once a week and had forbidden me to cook anything that would test his will and make him succumb.

I was the weak one. I allowed myself all that I shouldn't. Sometimes it was the only thing that comforted me. I bought the biggest bar of chocolate I could find and hid it. Each time I chose a different place. In the fridge; in the wardrobe; on top of the bookcase...Just knowing that it was somewhere in the house gave me a secret thrill that made me forget that I was dissatisfied with life. Ebe would get angry when he saw me snack. So I would wait for him to go out of the house and then I would take out my bar of chocolate. I allowed myself the pleasure of peeling the purple paper wrapping and then tearing open the gold foil little by little as I nibbled at my chocolate. Some days when I was not content with the chocolate alone, I opened a tin of condensed milk and dipped a spoon into it, eating till I felt nauseous. But my 'Milkmaid' days were not very frequent. Usually a bar of chocolate and a packet of chips to take the sweetness away from my mouth were all I needed to fulfil my cravings.

It showed on me: in the double chin, in the rolls of fat around my waist; in the thickness of my calves and the puffiness of my wrists. I hated to look at myself in the mirror. But at least I was no longer daddy's little girl.

Ebe liked Western classical music. I don't know if he really liked it or if he made himself like it because that's the kind of music principals of prestigious schools ought to listen to. To me, it sounded like the music they played in elevators and in the lobbies of luxury hotels.

Ebe worshipped the masters. But he was meticulous about categorizing his worship. So he chose a composer and then read everything he could find about him. While he read, he played the composer's music. He was forever getting tapes recorded or CDs sent to him. That night it was Bach.

Bah! Bah! Bah! I spat the name under my breath and felt like a defiant child.

Why couldn't we listen to music most people heard? Simon & Garfunkel, The Beatles, Madonna, Chicago, ghazals and Tamil songs...No, it had to be Bach or Beethoven, Chopin or Mozart. Sometimes the voice in my head raged and fumed so hard that it felt as if my skull would explode.

That night Ebe put aside his book and came to stand at the kitchen doorway. 'What have you cooked?' he asked.

'A vegetable pulao; curd vadas. A cauliflower curry and an egg masala. Then there are papads and pickles,' I said, lifting the lid off each dish and displaying it to him.

He made a face. I pretended not to see it.

'But that's exactly what you made the last time. Why didn't you think of something different? Everyone's going to think you have no imagination.'

I swallowed. Why did it hurt even now? And it was hurt that made me snap, 'If you don't like what I have cooked, you can order food from a restaurant. This is as much as I can do. And who are we trying to impress anyway? It's the same motley group that knows very well who we are. It isn't as if they are royalty...'

But Ebe had already left the room and I was left alone with my hurt and anger and a sense of shame. How could I be so petty? But a brief moment of remorse was all that I would allow myself.

That night my hate propelled me along. Oil of vitriol destroys water. It dehydrates all traces of water from any other compound. But that night I was Aqua Regia. Royal water. All acid and hate. Capable of dissolving even gold, as alchemists knew. Capable of dissolving shame and remorse and keeping my hate for him intact.

'Mmm...what a lovely aroma!' Daphne's silvery voice tinkled as she walked in through the door.

The lithium girl. Of the coterie, I liked her the best, even though I knew that Ebe was infatuated by her. I smiled at her.

The others—Bromine Premilla, Laughing Gas Xavier, Tetra Sulphur Nawaz and Gamma Ray Sankar Narayan smiled at me and sniffed the air appreciatively. Arsenic Kala alone pursed her mouth. On arrival, she had made it a point to tell me that she hoped that I hadn't made the pulao too spicy or oily or she would suffer from indigestion all night.

Daphne sat down next to me and said, 'I thought I'd never find an autorickshaw to come this way. You'll have to drop me back, Mr Principal.' Another peal of laughter.

Ebe smiled at her adoringly. I saw the approval in his eyes and felt a twisting pain inside. When was the last time he had looked at me so adoringly?

What had changed between us? Or was it I who had changed? And with it my expectations of him?

'You have completed the crossword again,' Daphne said, riffling through the newspapers that Ebe had just put down.

'How does he manage to get it right every day? Maggie, what is the secret?' Daphne pouted.

I smiled and shook my head. On the day the coterie dined with us, he woke up early in the morning, sat with a book of phrases and a dictionary and set about doing the crossword in preparation for the evening. So that when the coterie came in, they almost inevitably found him finishing the crossword with a flourish. I could tell them that, but instead I smiled and said, 'He doesn't tell me.'

'No secrets. I just have a natural aptitude for crosswords, I suppose,' Ebe said, wanting to deflect attention back to himself.

'Daphne, do you have anything new for us?' Sankar Narayan asked.

Daphne wrote poetry. Poems about trees shaped like hands, and clouds that winged their way through the skies like birds, and buds that were 'destined to die untouched, unplucked, unloved'. Daphne was quite sensible except when it came to her poetry and when suitably persuaded, would draw out her burgundy-coloured leather-jacketed notebook from her bag and read aloud her most recent effort.

Now, she paused in the middle of whatever it was she was saying and said, 'I actually do have a new one but I'm not very sure about it.'

'Come, come, don't be so modest. Let's hear it,' Ebe said.

Daphne, like she had a book set aside for poetry, had a voice reserved for reading poetry. A breathless husky voice. A sweet young thing's voice swayed by what it thought was the lyricism of phrases such as 'ungainly seas'. The voice embarrassed me. Her poetry embarrassed me. When Daphne did her little girl act, it made me want to squirm. But I held my breath and always tried to look very interested when she began to read. I worried that someone would burst into laughter and show her up for what she was.

When the poetry reading was over and done without mishap, the coterie began discussing school affairs. Gamma Ray cleared his throat. I could see that he was brimming with a new story.

'I don't know if any of you has been observing this, but I spotted the beginning of a new romance in the school corridors.'

Ebe frowned. He hated it when someone knew for a fact what he hadn't even suspected.

'Now which is this pair of love birds?'

Daphne giggled. Ebe cocked his eyebrow and repeated, 'So who are the love birds?'

'Nisha from IXD...'

Daphne gasped. Everyone knew that Daphne was very fond

of the girl and groomed her to represent the school in inter-school debates.

'...and Mansoor from XIA. I've been watching them for a while now. Ever since this term began they have been together at every recess, huddled in a corner, chatting about god knows what. So one morning I warned them. I told them that if I caught them talking in the corridors, I would send them to you. So Nisha began going to his classroom where a group always surrounds them. I called her and asked her what business she had in the XIA classroom and she had the audacity to tell me that she and some of the girls in that class are good friends and was there any rule against seniors and juniors mixing. We have to do something about this.'

'That one is a little snob anyway,' Arsenic Kala added. 'When I told her that she should spend more time concentrating on improving her mathematics, instead of participating in inter-school debates, she told me that she intends to have nothing to do with math once she's cleared her tenth standard public exams.'

'She is a good girl,' Daphne defended her protégé.

'That she might be,' Ebe said, 'but we can't have such goings-on. The next time,' he said turning to Sankar Narayan, 'you spot them together, let me know immediately. I'll sort this out once and for all.'

In an effort to change the subject, Daphne began to talk of an inter-school cultural festival that would begin next month. I listened to the voices as they rolled and cascaded and thought of molecules bonding and separating...

'Maggie, why are you so quiet?' No one called me Maggie except Daphne.

They all turned to look at me.

'She's not a great one for discussions. She doesn't have an opinion about anything. The only time I've ever seen her truly animated was many years ago in Kodaikanal. There was this student Alfred...' Ebe butted in and steered the attention away to a reminiscence; yet another piece of history that revealed what a brilliant man Ebenezer Paulraj was.

Alfred Arokiaswami. Nine years old with dimples in his cheeks and mischief in his eyes. He had springy, curly hair that his mother always left a little too long for Ebenezer Paulraj's taste.

Ebenezer Paulraj sent Alfred's mother a note. But she ignored it. So Ebenezer Paulraj had Alfred's soccer practice stopped and instead he was asked to join the SUPW group as they went about emptying wastepaper baskets from each classroom. And still Alfred's whorl of curls continued to flaunt themselves.

The next Monday, Ebenezer Paulraj had Alfred summoned to his room after morning assembly. And then, Ebenezer Paulraj gathered a handful of Alfred's hair and clasped a rubber band around it so that the tuft of curls resembled a pineapple.

'You will not take this off till the evening bell rings. Do you understand?' Ebenezer Paulraj told a snivelling Alfred. 'Since you like your hair so much you leave me with no other option but to do this. In my school, only girls are permitted to wear their hair long,' Ebenezer Paulraj said, and sent Alfred back to his class.

During lunch hour, I saw a giggling group huddled around a child in the 4B classroom. I could hear muffled sobs. 'What's going on here?' I demanded, going in.

There sat poor Alfred. Ridiculed and teased. The butt of many jibes and the cause of much merriment. I saw the humiliation in his eyes, the stricken look, the confusion, and I felt a great rage explode in me.

'Aren't you ashamed of yourselves?' I asked, and the group melted away.

I undid the rubber band which I recognized to be mine and smoothened Alfred's curls down. I wiped his eyes and told him that it didn't matter what the others said. He was a good little boy, I said again and again, emphasizing the word 'boy', for the other children had been calling him Alfreda when I walked in.

Then I took the rubber band and stormed into Ebenezer Paulraj's room.

'What is the meaning of this?' I demanded.

Ebenezer Paulraj looked up from his sheaf of papers and asked, 'What is the meaning of what?'

I flung the rubber band on the table and snapped, 'How could you do this to a child? How could you humiliate him so badly? Don't you realize what you could have done to him? You might have scarred him for life. And for what? An extra inch of hair?'

Ebenezer Paulraj touched the blue beads of the rubber band thoughtfully. 'I suppose you took this off Alfred's hair. That was very silly of you.'

'Answer me, Ebe. Don't tell me I'm silly. Why were you so cruel to a child?' Exasperation made my tone sharper than I meant it to be.

'Madam,' Ebenezer Paulraj said in a voice that I had never heard him use before, 'I would like to remind you that I'm in charge here and not you. I do not like anyone flouting my authority and the next time you do so, I will have to take strict action. I will not let who you are influence my decisions. Do you understand? This is my school and I know what's best for my students.'

He lowered his head and pretended to be absorbed in his papers and I knew I was dismissed.

Alfred had his mother take him to a barber and shave his hair off. Ebenezer Paulraj's wish had prevailed.

And Alfred. He took to tormenting the younger children; being rude in the class and accepting every dare from climbing the highest branch of a tree to sliding down the banisters of the staircase. But Ebenezer Paulraj would never accept responsibility for what he had done. When I pointed Alfred's behaviour out to him, all he said was, 'Boys will be boys.'

And I. Perhaps that was the first time I began to question my feelings for Ebenezer Paulraj. Suddenly Ebe was a stranger and a despicable one at that. A bully and a tyrant.

But Ebe didn't remember it the way I did. As a horrific episode. Instead, it was another example of the psychological warfare he waged against young rascals with too much sauce for their own good. 'You cane a child and in a week's time, he'll have forgotten it. But something like this will never be forgotten,' Ebe said, finishing his version of the tale and passing a plate of peanuts around.

'Only you would think of something so ingenious,' Kala gushed, taking a peanut and then dropping it back.

'I suppose one has to use one's imagination,' Xavier said through a mouthful of nuts.

'Imagination!' Ebenezer Paulraj slapped his thigh. 'That's the key word. No offence to any one of you here, but have you ever wondered why most school principals are English or history teachers? I have my own theory of course: it's only when you have taught subjects that require and even nurture imagination that you can employ it in running a school. You need imagination to be able to interest a child in poetry or understand the implications of a battle waged many hundreds of years ago...it's not the same as teaching algebra or biology. And if you ask me, there can't be a more dry or boring subject than chemistry. But the little imps like it because to them it's like a game. This plus this equals that! Frankly, if you want my opinion, when I think of chemistry, what comes to mind is the odour of rotten eggs...'

Laughter. Peanuts rustled. Chips crackled.

I looked at my hands clasped tightly in my lap. What did he know of chemistry or the poetry of the elements?

The magic of the litmus paper test: blue litmus when dipped in acid turns red and red litmus when dipped in an alkaline solution turns blue. The lyricism of phosphorous which when taken out of water self-ignites, burns and becomes a gas. The vigour of potassium nitrate, sulphur and charcoal coming together—explosions that rock the earth. The illusions that transparent calcite can create. The colours—brick red beryllium carbide; the brassy yellow of fool's gold, the silvery white of uranium...The words formed on my tongue.

I wanted to stand up and shout, 'He takes such pride in what he calls his imagination. Let me tell you all about the quality of his imagination. Go to the school library and take down the books that the senior school students are expected to read, or go to the Circle Library or the lending library in the next street, and you'll see for yourself the handiwork of the man with an imagination.'

Ebe was crafty. He chose the books with care and rotated his vandalism among the three libraries that he's a member of. So that no one would ever trace the ruined books back to him. Besides, who would suspect him of such obscenity? For Ebe, with great meticulousness, drew human genitalia—penises, testicles, anuses, vaginas bearing his signature, namely the stubble of pubic hair. Human genitalia attached to humans and genitalia by themselves. Delicate and explicit sketches of sexual organs created by Ebenezer Paulraj, the Da Vinci of book margins. Ebenezer Paulraj, the man with an imagination.

A hysterical laugh ran up my throat. But I swallowed it down as I had all these years swallowed my sense of pride. Suddenly I felt suffocated by my marriage.

That night after everyone had left and I had washed up, I lay on my side of the bed watching Ebe go through the rituals of the night. The anger in me bubbled but there was little I could do apart from letting it bubble. I thought of how he had turned the evening into another moment of triumph for himself. I thought of Alfred Arokiaswami and the poetry of chemicals. I thought of all that was good and noble about my life that he had destroyed. I thought of the baby that died even before it had a soul. I thought of how there was nothing left for me to dream of and the words rose to the surface again: I HATE HIM. I HATE HIM. What am I going to do?

By the window was the goldfish bowl in which Ebe kept his goldfish pair. Another theory he advocated: fifteen minutes of watching goldfish twice a day as they swam hopelessly in circles relaxed the nerves, reduced stress and revived the spirit. His. Not the goldfish's.

Ebe clucked in annoyance. What was wrong now? I wondered. Had the fish failed to swim in the mandatory circles?

'Poor James. He got too greedy. I knew he wasn't well. He'd slowed down for the past couple of days and seemed to be almost dragging himself. But this is unfortunate. Now I'll have to find another James.'

I raised myself on my elbow. A dead fish.

Ebe called the pair James and Joyce. A private joke, he said, but nevertheless he made sure that everyone knew about it and chuckled at the principal's sense of humour. And now James was dead. Of some fish-disease. Or perhaps of greed and over-eating.

James floated on top with his belly split open. I stared at the dead James and the living Joyce who seemed sleeker and friskier, frolicking happier than I had ever seen her. A tiny scale of suspicion tickled my throat. Had Joyce managed it so?

I felt a smile stretch my lips. An airiness. A sense of calm.

Am I being unfair? Am I letting my hate cloud my sense of shame? If so, let be it. There is nothing fair about love or war, Ebe often said. And this was war.

†

I am a good cook. When I want to be. I am a sensitive cook and when I wish it so, the ingredients heed my commands. But for long, I had cooked like my art inclined students did their chemistry experiments. It had to be done and so it got done. With neither a sense of joy nor any pride in what the results would be. Not any more, I thought. My cooking would have a sense of purpose now. But first, I had to persuade Ebe to let down his defences. To open his senses and taste buds to me.

When Ebe came to bed, I pretended to be asleep as usual. I did not remember when we last had sexual intercourse. I don't even remember who turned away first. Was it he, disgusted by my body; folds of flesh, unclear lines, sagging muscles and my woman's bush? Or was it I who wanted an equal in bed and decided that I could no longer keep up the pretence of being a little girl?

But that night when Ebe had settled into sleep, I turned to him and ran my tongue down the side of his neck. I let my fingers tease and pull the hair on his chest. Ever so gently, like a little girl would...I wooed him, as I knew how. With stealth and cunning. With butterfly kisses and bold caresses. With a child-like naïvete that made an 'O' of my lips and shaven skin. With steely resolve and parted legs.

In the morning, I rose at dawn and rushed into the kitchen. Your time begins now Ebe, I told a sleeping Ebe. Your time begins with this breakfast. Puris fried in ghee and a potato, peas and cauliflower korma. Two fried eggs sunny side up and a tall glass of cold creamy milk into which I stirred two big spoons of sugar.

Ebe stared at the array of dishes before him and said, 'What is all this? Do you expect me to eat it all? Take it away.'

'Oh come, come,' I teased. How easy it was to seem playful and little-girlish now that freedom was in sight. 'You're a big man. And you need to eat a big meal. And it isn't as if you don't exercise. Besides, you need your strength, don't you,' I smiled coyly.

It was easy to flatter Ebe. He never perceived it to be false. To him, flattery was merely the truth. And so Ebe ate the first of his many big breakfasts with gusto and relish.

Ebe ate. Breakfasts. Lunches. Dinners. An evening snack as soon as he came home from school. A late night snack as he worked on his files. I wasn't expecting a miracle, an overnight transformation. It wasn't going to be as easy or as simple as it had been for Joyce. But I was willing to wait.

Almost a year later, fat found its home. What was mine became his. The sleek lines began to blur. The breath shortened and the pace slowed. Folds appeared around the neck. A second chin. A belly that jiggled. Ebe no longer strutted. He waddled. When he climbed a staircase, he gasped. He no longer roamed the corridors of the school restlessly as and when the whim took him. Instead, he limited himself to two rounds, once in the morning and once in the afternoon.

Ebe slowly became a fat man. A quiet man. An easy man. A man who no longer needed the coterie or defaced books. A man whose fondness for eating blunted his razor edge. Since I was the one to appease his appetite, he sought me more and more. I tantalized his appetite for food and occasionally for sex, in every which way I knew. He needed me like he had never before. And Ebe became a man I could live with once again.

For the second time, I became pregnant and my baby was born. A girl. Then it became imperative that I keep Ebe from reverting to his earlier self. For if he did, I couldn't even begin to think of the evils that would be visited upon us. I had my little girl to think of.

While Ebe remained fat, there were no adrenaline surges; no power struggles. All was quiet and calm and watered down in our lives.

When you add water to sulphuric acid, it splutters at first. But soon it loses its strength; it loses its bite. The trick is to know when to add it, and how much.

7

I am a lamp without wicks. I am that which mothers of new-borns and brides fear. I am the one they ward against with a black dot on their child's left cheek. I am the reason why a father's eyes dim. I cause younger sisters to worry that I would put their life on pause. I make mothers weep. I fill the innards of a house with my presence and weigh its rafters down with my unshed sorrow.

I am the one who is long in the tooth. I am the cold dregs at the bottom of a cup. I am the merchandise no one wants. I am the untouched tin on the back shelf.

I turn milk sour with my breath. I can shrivel to ash all that is green and fecund. Marshes dry when I walk on them. Earth crumbles at my sigh. Rain clouds dissipate when I raise my eyes to them. Babies weep when I run a finger on their brow. I don't bleed; instead I store within me the spores of a million hates. I am the nightmare young wives wake up from. I am the rustle of skirts all women dread. I am a curse. I am the shadow of evil. I am the ghoul that dams gene pools and feasts on husbands.

I carry on my back every fear, every dark whisper, and every tormented thought that can cross the human mind. My skin is opaque. My eyes are painted-over mirrors. My voice is tinged with the acrid stench of bitterness. My fragrance is that of mothballs. My name when spelt aloud reads defeat.

Akhila lay on her back. Her eyes felt heavy and yet she couldn't sleep.

Margaret had got off at Coimbatore. Before leaving, she ran a comb through her hair and adjusted her sari pleats, then said, 'Akhila, if there is one virtue I have, it is immunity to what people think of me. Naturally this makes them dislike me even more. People don't like to think that their opinion of someone means nothing to that person. And when it is a woman . . . the thought is intolerable. But like I said, I don't care. I'm not saying that you ought to think like I do. But you'll discover that once you stop worrying what the world will think of you, your life will become that much easier to live.'

She said, 'Just remember that you have to look out for yourself. No one else will.'

Akhila had smiled, not trusting herself to speak. What could she say to this woman who she wasn't even sure she liked? Who, in fact, scared her a little. How could anyone be so impervious to what people thought of her? Did she really mean it? Or was it merely bravado to cover up the anguish she felt for being seen as a misfit?

Akhila was suddenly struck by the condition of individual lives. All these women, she thought, all these women, Janaki, Sheela and even Margaret who wears her self-sufficiency as a halo, are trying to make some sense of their own existence by talking about it to anyone who will listen. I am the same, she thought. I'm trying to define the reality of my life, justify my failures and my own sense of hopelessness by preying on the fabric of their lives, seeking in it a similar thread that in some way will connect their lives with mine, make me feel less guilty for who I am and what I have let myself become.

Akhila turned on her side and cradled her head on her arm. The metal wall of the coupé was cold to the touch. What was it that Margaret had said?

Love is a colourless, volatile liquid. Love ignites and burns. Love leaves no residue—neither smoke nor ash. Love is a poison masquerading as the spirit of wine.

How could love turn like this? Would she too have been consumed with bitterness, as Margaret was, if she had chosen to marry the man she had loved? Would she too have sought ways to negate his role in her life once she fell out of love? How did one know when you didn't love any more?

Margaret made love seem as if it were a wild beast she had domesticated. A docile creature that lay at her feet and could be reined in any time she chose. But is that what she wanted from life? A watered down love?

Suddenly Akhila turned her head and glanced at the woman asleep on the opposite berth. Here was Janaki who after pretending for most of her adult life that security was love, had grappled with her inner self and grabbed at her last chance to love and be truly loved. And that girl Sheela...even she had allowed her instincts to rule rather than do what was expected of her—the sober dictates of good conduct.

Then for the first time in many years, Akhila thought of Hari. Of the shaping of what had been her first chance...

†

In those first years of being an employed woman, when everything else seemed to be in a state of flux around her, Akhila sought comfort in routine. As long as she stuck to the habitual and the predictable, she knew that she still had some measure of control over the direction her days were taking.

Akhila took the 7.20 train every morning from Ambattur, which meant that she had to leave home exactly at seven. Something about that time of the morning filled her with delight. It was the hour of peace and new beginnings. Even the sun and the moon stared at each other from opposite sides of the horizon without willing the other away. A gentle breeze blew ruffling the tree tops with a father-like caress. The doorsteps were swept clean and the lines of the kolam gleamed.

At that time of the morning, the roads were empty. Akhila's companions were the newspaper boys and milk vendors, the kerosene man who pulled his cart and hailed her with an extra vigorous cry of 'Krishnoil' and the rock-salt seller who carried his load on his head and grunted 'uppu' as he went from street to street. And the man with a towel around his hips who stood by the water pipe at the street corner working a film of soapy lather into his hair and skin, while his wife furiously pumped water into a bucket. All of them knew her by sight and reserved a glance, a smile and a nod of the head, or a sound for her. They knew that she wasn't one of those early morning walkers who was out only for exercise. They knew that like them, if she didn't leave home early, a family would starve. That was their bond.

'Why do you have to leave so early?' Padma grumbled at being woken up at the crack of dawn. For when Akhila woke up at five in the morning, she insisted that the others get up too. Or, if not at five, they should wake up early enough to get a head start on their day. It bothered Akhila to leave home when they still hadn't rubbed the sleep out of their eyes.

'The 7.20 is not so crowded. The trains after that are packed and I'll have to stand all the way to Central,' she said.

In those first years, the train ride was part of the routine. Akhila knew every station, every landmark, every level crossing, every ditch they ran alongside. Even before the train sped through Korattur, she would take a deep breath and screw up her face to prevent the stench from the milk pasteurizing factory from riding up her nostrils. At Madras Central she would cross the road to the bus stop near Madras Medical College and catch a bus to Nungambakkam. By 8.45, she was at her desk. On time always.

Even after the boys and Padma left home, Akhila clung to her routine. She knew no other way to structure her day.

Later when Akhila thought about it, she couldn't remember what the reason was, but for the first time in almost sixteen years, she missed both the 7.20 and the 7.35 trains. She walked to the bus stop and had to force herself to squeeze into a bus. There was no time to wait for a less crowded bus. Akhila had to push her way in and that was how she found herself pressed against the steel pole. She clutched it to prevent herself from being propelled any further and then stood there trying not to let the sensation of being pressed against so many bodies bother her.

There were a few women in that mass of skin and scents. But what caught at her throat and filled her senses was the smell of hair cream and coconut oil, Lifebuoy soap and tobacco. After Appa died, Akhila hadn't smelt these masculine fragrances from so close. She closed her eyes and inhaled deeply.

At first, when the back of a hand brushed against her waist, she dismissed it as an accident. There were so many people packed into the bus and its motion threw them against each other.

Akhila felt it again. This time the hand, as if emboldened by its previous foray, let itself rest on her midriff. She sucked in her breath, as if by doing so she would repulse the marauder. The hand lifted, scared by the clenched muscle, the million pores that screamed: leave me alone. Only to return a few seconds later.

Akhila wore her sari like all women of her age did; an inch below the navel. Only old women and pregnant women wore their saris above the navel. Between the blouse and the skirt of the sari were almost eight inches of exposed skin veiled by a layer of the sari. And it was here, protected by the cover of the fabric, that the hand chose to gambol and play.

Five fingers. Slightly coarse skin. Closely cut nails except for the nail of the little finger which stretched about an inch long, slightly curved, a frisson of savagery on an otherwise gentle hand. It drew lines as it let itself dribble over the skin of her midriff. Akhila felt a warmth rush over her...She had never known anything like this before. An unfurling. Beads of sweat. A rasping edge to her muted breath. A quiet flowering.

Akhila stood there, willing enough, and let the hand send a thousand messages to her almost dead nerve ends: wake up, wake up.

For a fortnight, the hand and Akhila encountered. She began to take the bus, morning after morning. No matter where she stood, the hand would find her. Gentle at first. Then exploratory and finally demanding. So that she knew what it was to feel the ball of a thumb against her lower spine. The bony arc of knuckles as they traced the curve of her waist. The extended nail of the little finger as it skated in circles and figure eights. The tip of a forefinger as it circled her navel and then plunged into it fleetingly...

Sometimes Akhila allowed herself to lean against the body that stood behind her and the hand would pause in its wanderings and just lie there, supine, comforting, a presence that she had begun to seek.

When Akhila got out of the bus, she put aside the sensations the hand aroused in her and didn't think about what she was doing. She knew that she was behaving like no self-respecting woman would. But there was gratification for her as well. She felt desired. She felt as if she had fed a hunger. Akhila felt like a woman.

Sometimes she thought that she would like to know the owner of the hand. And then immediately, she would quell the thought.

One morning, as Akhila stood there with wide-open senses and downcast eyes and the hand loved her body, the bus jerked to a stop. She looked up and caught the eye of a man who was watching her. The conductor. She dropped her eyes when she saw disgust in his. He had seen the trespassing hand and he had seen her welcome the trespasser. What woman would let a stranger take such liberties?

'There is a vacant seat there. Why don't you sit down?' he said, pointing to the seats.

Akhila flushed and tried to pretend to be grateful to him for having rescued her from the hands of a vagrant creature.

As she moved towards the empty seat near a woman, he said, 'There is really no need for you to squeeze yourself between all these men when there are seats set aside for women. Try catching an earlier bus. It is never this crowded.'

Akhila pretended not to hear him and sat in her seat feeling the yellow, watery bile of mortification rush into her mouth. What am I doing? How could I let my wanton senses rule me? How can I forget who I am?

Akhila went back to the 7.20 train and because she could no longer bear the thought of the fortnight when the madness had taken over her, she bought a first-class pass and travelled in almost solitary splendour. There were no bodies to taunt or tempt.

At first, Akhila didn't even notice the man who always chose the window seat. In the evening, since the train started from Central station, they had the pick of the seats. She chose a window seat and he chose the one opposite her. But Akhila was oblivious to him or anyone else. All she could think of was the look on the bus conductor's face. When she saw a man, she wanted to hang her head and cover her face. She worried: would he too see what a wanton creature she was?

One evening, Akhila was a little late and she thought that her window seat would be gone. There were no reservations in the suburban trains but there was an unspoken understanding among the passengers that if a book or even a handkerchief had been placed upon the seat, it meant it was occupied and that the occupant would be there in a moment's time. Akhila saw a magazine and a handkerchief placed on her usual seat and as she turned to find another place, a voice called, 'Madam, your seat is here.'

Akhila turned in surprise. The man who sat by the window smiled, gesturing to the seat opposite. 'When I didn't see you in your usual place, I thought you must have been delayed and I put my things there so no one else would sit in your place,' he explained.

'Thank you,' Akhila said as she sat down. 'You needn't have bothered,' she added.

'I needn't have,' he said. 'But for many weeks now, I have seen you sit in the same place and I thought you probably had a

fondness for it. Besides, you can hardly call placing a
handkerchief on a seat a bother,' he grinned.

He was younger than she was. Many years younger.
Probably her younger brother Narsi's age. But there was an
honesty in his face which Narsi lacked. Narsi resembled a
jackal; with narrow eyes and a pointed face forever sniffing out
an opportunity to gain from. This boy had an open face with
widely spaced features and a pleasantness that was beguiling.
Akhila sighed in relief. It was men she was scared of, not boys.

'What is your name?' Akhila asked, putting on her older
sister voice.

'Hari,' he said.

'Just plain Hari. Not Hari Prasad or Hari Kumar?'

'Yes, just plain Hari,' he said. 'And what's yours?'

She wondered what she should tell him. Akhila?
Akhilandeswari? Easwari?

'Akhila,' she said, because that sounded the closest to Akka.
Akhila was defining the boundaries of their relationship
rightaway. Akka. Older sister. Treat me as one. That is how I
see myself. I do not want to be seen as a woman. To do so
would be to open a Pandora's box within me.

They became friends. It was as easy as that. An instant
camaraderie that they nurtured in the thirty-five minutes he and
she sat opposite each other. Soon they began taking the same
morning train too. She told him about herself and he drew a
word picture of his life for her.

Twenty-eight years old. He was a draftsman in the railway
engineering department. He was a north Indian from a small
town in Madhya Pradesh but he had lived in Avadi, the town
next to Ambattur, almost all of his life. His father had a sweet
shop and his sister was studying at Queen Mary's Collage. His
Tamil was as good as his Hindi, he said. His parents were keen
that he get married soon. Every once in a while they insisted
that he meet a prospective bride. But he found the whole
business repugnant. 'How can you decide to marry a woman by
just looking at her?' he asked Akhila.

She shrugged. 'That's how it's always been done. The only
other option you have is to fall in love with a girl, get to know
her and then tell your parents about her...'

Hari grimaced. 'If I ever do that, my parents will come up
with a hundred good reasons why she isn't suitable.'

'In that case, you should marry the girl they pick for you.
Thousands of people do it everyday and still manage to be
happy together.'

Akhila's day suddenly had a bright spot. Hari. Every
evening, they reached the station a few minutes before the train
came in. He introduced a ritual to the time they spent together.
Hari and she would walk to the railway vegetarian cafeteria on
the platform and buy a plate of samosas and coffee in plastic
cups. They would stand there side by side on the platform
thronged with people and share a plate that was dotted with
mint and tamarind chutney. Hari moistened his samosa in the
chutnies. Akhila preferred hers dry. They would bite into their
samosas and sip their coffee. Spice and heat. Flaky crust and
liquid prayers.

He talked to her; of his colleagues, the frustration he felt in
his job, a visiting aunt who kept thrusting a friend's niece at
him, a movie he had seen the night before...And in turn, he
drew her out. So that when her stop arrived, she got off the
train reluctantly. But there was the consolation that he would
be there the next day. That was enough, Akhila thought.

Slowly he began to fill Akhila's every thought and waking
moment. She would pause in the middle of what she was doing,
reminded of a silly joke he had made, and giggle. A hoarding
would make her think of a phrase he had used once. She would
watch her mother crack her knuckles and think of how that was
the first thing he did after he sat down in his seat. She would
flick through a magazine and a model's expression would
remind her of him. A stranger's smile would remind her of how
his eyes crinkled when he smiled...

The rare occasions when he missed the train and she had to
travel alone would put a blight on her day. In the evening, he

was usually there before she was and when she saw him, she would begin to feel a golden warmth creep around her.

Akhila told herself that she was being silly. He was much younger than her. And she should also remember that he probably saw her as an older sister and nothing more. Someone he could jolly around without worrying that she would pounce on him and claim him for her own.

One evening, most of the seats were empty in the compartment. They chatted for a few minutes and then Hari grew silent, which was completely unlike him.

'What is wrong?' Akhila asked.

'Nothing,' he said.

'No, I know something is the matter. Can't you tell me?'

'Akhila,' he said, 'you must stop treating me like I'm your younger brother.'

'You are younger than me,' she said.

'That's true. But that doesn't make me any less a man. How long can we go on like this?'

'What are you saying?' Akhila asked and she could hear the shrill note of panic in her voice.

'That you should start seeing me as a man. As a man who is interested in you and in love with you,' Hari said, speaking under his breath so that no one but she could hear him.

She should have been happy. This was what her fantasies had been all about.

Instead she heard herself say in a fierce voice, 'Stop it, Hari. Don't say anything more, you'll ruin everything.'

'Ruin what?' he demanded.

'Hari,' Akhila said quietly. 'Do you realize what you are saying?' From the corner of her eye, she could see the station approaching. 'Let us forget we had this conversation.'

'I can't,' he said and the bleakness in his voice made her want to cry.

When Akhila got off, he called out to her, 'Just think about it. That is all I ask.'

His voice rang through the platform, startling everyone.

Akhila pretended not to hear him and walked away as fast as she could.

The next morning, when she stepped out to go to work, the kerosene man stopped and hollered to her from across the road, 'Are you going to work this morning? Haven't you heard the news?'

'Haven't I heard what?' Akhila asked, suddenly struck by how silent the roads were even for this time of the day.

'Puraichi Thalaivar is dead. He died this morning. There is going to be trouble so you better stock up on provisions. I'm sure you don't remember this but when Anna Durai died, the city went mad. This is going to be as bad or perhaps worse. Buy whatever you can and go home quickly. I must be on my way too.' The kerosene man lifted the handles of his cart and moved on.

Akhila stood on the road unsure about what she should do. How could a man who wore a fur cap and a pair of dark glasses indoors, change the course of her life, she thought. Puraichi Thalaivar. The Revolutionary Leader. Chief Minister. He could be dead but she had to go to work. She had to see Hari. She had to tell him that he shouldn't see her as a woman; that she was a friend and no more.

A milk vendor wheeling his bicycle came into the street. He saw Akhila walking towards the station and called out, 'Don't go to work, madam. You'll be stranded in the city. Thousands of people will pour into the city by afternoon and there will be trouble.'

The rock-salt seller added his bit. 'Everyone knew he was dying but no one ever thought it would happen. Poor people like us have lost our only protector. There will never be another man like him.' Tears filled his eyes. He put his sack of salt down and sat on his haunches. He stared into the distance as if collecting all his sorrow and then began to weep openly. 'What is left for us in life? Thalaivar is dead. We have lost our father and guardian.'

The milk vendor, a young man who was studying at the

polytechnic institute to be a refrigeration engineer, met her eye. The message was clear: This is what you will encounter this morning and for many more days. A frenzied grief that will soon go out of control. Do you want to be stuck in the middle of it? Go home. Close the doors and wait for all this to pass.

Akhila walked back home and on the way bought some extra provisions and vegetables. Groups of men stood huddled in street corners and some of them were brandishing sticks. Who are all these men? Where did they come from? she wondered. Suddenly Akhila thought of Hari. Would Hari take a chance and get on the train? Would Hari wait for her in the train? Would Hari wonder what had happened to her? At times like these buried hates spring to the surface. Would the mob look at him and know he was a north Indian? Would they slash his face and beat him up?

Millions grieved for the dead man. A grief that soon turned into violence. Shops were broken into and looted. The opposition party members skulked, afraid the mob anger would soon turn towards them. A few people killed themselves, unable to bear the thought that their Thalaivar was dead.

The newspaper was full of reports on violence and arson. The radio played songs from the films the Thalaivar had acted in. Only, then he had been called Makkal Thilagam. The people's icon. It wasn't as if Akhila had admired him as an actor or as a politician but the grief encroached into her life and entwined with her feelings for Hari so that she didn't know if she was crying for the dead man or for the living one. Was he safe? Was he alright? Akhila worried. Why had she never thought of asking him for his address or for the telephone number of his uncle who lived next door to him and owned a textile shop? How was she going to get through these days till she saw her Hari again?

The year crumbled to an end. The days of grief passed, and her resolve diminished. Akhila wanted to see Hari, be with him. And nothing was more important than that.

A week after Thalaivar's death, life came back to what it

used to be and Akhila rushed through her morning chores, wanting to be at the station well ahead of time. When the train came in, she rushed to the first-class compartment. She searched its insides and there he was. When he saw her, he stood up with a broad grin and she had to stop herself from rushing into his arms.

Akhila walked towards him slowly. Her heart beat faster and all that she had meant to say jumbled into a heap of meaningless words on her tongue. So she did the only thing she could think of. Instead of sitting opposite him like she always did, she went to sit beside him.

'Does this mean you have changed your mind?' he asked.

Akhila nodded, still unwilling to put into words what she felt for him.

'So where do we go from here?' His breath fanned her ear.

Akhila looked at him. She had no answers to any of his questions. She really had no idea what they were going to do or where they were heading. His gaze met hers and held. That was enough, she thought. She had seen in his eyes everything a woman dared hope for from a man.

They sat there together in silence, the line of his body touching hers, their thoughts whirling around each other. A cloud of fireflies bound together by invisible threads.

Their relationship had moved on to another plane. Here silences weighed with unspoken feelings crushed them. A casual glance was striped with many meanings and even a mere brushing of hands ignited raging fires. Arousing and throwing little sparks that burnt all reason: touch me, hold me, make love to me...

Every evening he would come to her office and they would walk down Sterling Road. Slowly she let him take her hand in his. One evening, Hari had his arm around her waist as they strolled. She could feel the line of his body against hers; the pressure of his fingers on her skin. She wanted to turn towards him and press herself against him, to be aware of only him, everything else a haze. As they turned a corner, a policeman rode past them on his bicycle. He stopped and eyed them suspiciously. He crooked a finger and beckoned. 'Who is this?' he asked Hari.

Even in the darkness, Akhila could see Hari's Adam's apple bob as he swallowed. 'My wife,' he said.

The policeman peered at her. Akhila saw his eyes fall on the black bead and gold chain she wore. It could pass for a thali. For a long time that had been her defence; although it wasn't the traditional thali, it did stop people from speculating if she was married or not.

'She is your wife?'

Akhila heard the disbelief in the policeman's voice, the mockery in his eyes, and cringed. Why couldn't Hari have said she was his elder sister, his aunt, his neighbour.

'Well...' the policeman said, 'if you are husband and wife, then you should be doing what you were doing in the privacy of your home and not on the streets where people are.'

For a few days, they reverted to sitting pressed against each other in the electric train. But soon Hari and Akhila began to look for places they could be together without law and the world censuring them.

Like many others in the city, they sought the beach and tucked-away parks for their rendezvous. In the shadows of the evening, hushed by the boom of the waves, cradled by sand, hindered by clothing, they became lovers. Except that unlike their friendship, this was an uneasy relationship fraught with darkness.

Loving him came naturally and when he turned to her with longing, her body was there to please and delight. And in his rapture, Akhila revelled, knowing that even if she was older than him, her body was still firm and young and that she pleased him.

At first, it was enough. The slow forays, the tentative unearthings, but soon they wanted more and when they parted to return to their homes, it was always with a sense of having left something unfinished. Throwing a dark stain of purple on those stolen twilights, a dissatisfaction that made them even more frantic when they met the next morning.

Sometimes Akhila wished they could go away and spend a night together. She would have liked to sleep in his arms and wake up feeling his stubble scratch her cheek. There was so much she didn't know about him: Did he sleep favouring his right side or left? Did he brush his teeth before he bathed or after? How many spoons of sugar did he like in his coffee? Did he read the newspaper from back to front? Did he go to sleep as soon as he lay down or did sleep come to him after much deliberation?

They planned to marry one day but Hari said he would have to wait till his younger sister was married. She had just a few months left for graduation and they were already looking for grooms for her. Akhila could understand that. She knew how at the very breath of a scandal, prospective grooms would shy away. And yet.

'Are you sure? Are you sure?' Akhila would cry and then she would forget when his mouth and hands found ways to still the restless demons.

A week before Hari's twenty-ninth birthday, they were sitting in a quiet corner of Marina Beach Park. The sun had almost set and a stiff breeze blew lifting the ends of her sari.

Before they became lovers, their conversation had known no pauses. She had spoken all her thoughts. But now, she chose her words carefully. She worried that if she trod unwarily, she would stumble upon loss.

A few times Akhila tried to tell him what he meant to her; what the import of this love was. But Hari looked at her without comprehending. People fell in love; people got married; people lived together. His love was an uncomplicated feeling that needed no explanations nor reasoning. It was only Akhila who tried to dissect this feeling again and again and came up with no definite conclusions.

'You think too much,' he said as she stared into the horizon feeling a great sadness descend upon her. Akhila didn't know why she felt the way she did. She should be happy, she thought. But all she could feel was the weight of this love pressing down upon her.

'You haven't asked me what I want for my birthday,' he said with a sly grin.

'What do you want for your birthday?'

Hari inched a finger along her elbow and said, 'I know what I want but I don't think you'll give it to me.'

'Stop teasing. What is it?'

'I would like to see you naked.'

A hard fist slammed into her chest. Suddenly she was conscious of the years between them. This was a boy talking. A man wouldn't be so gauche...

'Will you come with me for a weekend? There is a nice beach resort on the way to Mahabalipuram. We can go there on Friday evening and come back by Sunday afternoon,' he said. 'That is all I want from you for my birthday.'

When Akhila didn't reply, his tone changed to a plaintive wheedle. 'Please, Akhila.' When she felt his eyes bore into hers, she gave in as she had always done. The weight of this love was such.

Two days later, Akhila told Amma that she was going away for the weekend with an office group. 'We are going to Mysore,' she said, thinking how easy it was to lie.

'I don't know why you want to go with all those strangers,' Amma said. 'Perhaps you should ask your brothers for permission first.'

'Amma, I'm their elder sister. Why should I ask them for permission to go on an office tour?'

'You might be older but you are a woman and they are the men of the family,' Amma said, making no effort to mask her disapproval.

'This is ridiculous. I'm not going to ask them for permission to go on a trip. I'd rather not go,' Akhila said, walking out of the room.

The next morning, she maintained a stony silence and Amma

capitulated like Akhila had known she would. 'If you are sure about the people you are going with, I guess there is no problem. But do be careful. You are a single woman, you know, and people need very little reason to put two and two together and come up with five.'

Amma, Akhila wanted to say, Amma, I'm in love with this boy. He must be our Narsi's age but he truly loves me. He does, Amma. Do you remember how it was with you and Appa? That is how it is with us, Amma. It is him I'm going with. We are going to a beach. He has chosen a night when the moon will be full and golden and he said we could sit by the sea and bathe in the moonlight. He is romantic, Amma, like Appa was. He makes me happy and no one has for a long time. I had forgotten what it was to be a woman and he makes me feel like one. Do you grudge me this love, Amma? Will you forbid me this love?

But how could Akhila tell Amma? Amma would never understand. In Amma's world, men married women younger than themselves. Women never offered their bodies to men before their union was sanctified by marriage. Women never went away with men who were not their husbands. Women never knew what it was to desire.

The moon shone for them. For Akhila and Hari. Full and golden, cresting the waves with a warm silvery edge. They sat on the beach and Akhila thought: this must be the happiest moment of my life.

A little later, they walked back to one of the huts that stood on stilts on the sand. Akhila could hear the clink of glasses and men laughing. 'I'm going to have a drink. Do you mind?' Hari asked.

She shook her head. All young men drank these days. Akhila knew that and besides, she was scared that if she asked him not to, he would think she was behaving like an older sister again.

In the confines of their room, Akhila felt an awkwardness. What am I doing here? Why am I doing this? The chant in her head wouldn't stop. Hari stood on the balcony smoking a cigarette. Akhila switched off the light and let the moonlight guide her through her ablutions. She crept into bed fully dressed. When Hari sat down next to her, she could smell the alcohol on his breath. It excited her, that strange fragrance, and she felt a tingling down her spine.

'This is not fair,' he said. 'Where is my birthday present?'

'What do you...mean?' Akhila stammered.

'You know what I mean,' he said and waited with glittering eyes while she slowly undressed.

That night they made love for the first time. Proper adult love and not all those tentative fumblings that had been the sum total of their lovemaking before. It hurt first and then the sheer rapture of being with him swamped her and the hurt dwindled to content.

In the morning, Akhila awoke before he did. The sunlight streamed in and bathed his face and hers. She stared down at their bodies, limbs tangled in the sheet, clothes strewn on the floor...His face was so young and unlined. In the clear light of day, the mirror told no lies. Akhila could see the age that marked her eyes. The lines that told the years. Akhila saw what they would be. A young man and an older woman. And how it would only get worse as time sped by.

Akhila thought of the stray comments that had floated in the air last night. Wafting in with the breeze to fill her ears.

'She must be his elder sister.'

'Don't be silly. Do men bring their sisters to places like this?'

'Just an older woman tired of her husband and looking for a stud to fill her day.'

'More than just filling her day, I'd think.'

Akhila cringed. The words had hurt then. They hurt even more now. She thought of the policeman on the bicycle. She thought of all the strange looks that had come their way as they sat in restaurants, in movie theatres, on the train. They were an anomaly, Hari and Akhila, and nothing he said would ever change that.

Is this what I want? Akhila asked herself. This constant hurt. This constant fear that she would age before he did and he would turn away from her. That someday he would regret their relationship, regret having spurned his family to be with her, regret being bound to her when he could have been with someone younger and more suitable. This constant weight of an unbearable love that would destroy everything and leave her with nothing, not even her self-respect.

Akhila watched him sleep, favouring his right side so that he lay cradled against her body. Akhila watched him wake up. How his eyes opened and how he turned on to his back and stretched. Akhila watched him as he brushed his teeth, and saw that he shaved his left cheek first and then the right cheek. That he bathed first before he drank his coffee which he sweetened with two spoons of sugar. And that he read the sports pages of the newspaper first. All day Akhila watched him and at night, and after each time they made love, he fell asleep, like a baby. Instantly.

In the train as they sped back, Akhila took his hands in hers and said, 'Hari, this is goodbye. I will never see you again.'

She saw the shock on his face. 'Why? What are you saying? Akhila, what is wrong? What did I do wrong?'

'Everything is wrong, Hari,' Akhila said. 'All these days, I tried to tell myself that it didn't matter. That we could bridge the years between us with love. But I don't think I can. Every time I look at someone watching us, I can see the question in their minds: what is he doing with an older woman? That bothers me very much, Hari. It bothers me that we are not suited. That I am older and look older, and I can't live with the thought that some day you might regret this relationship, that you might turn away and I would be left with nothing—neither you nor my family.'

'Are you done?' Hari asked. Akhila could see that he was angry. Hurt and upset too. But she was older than he was and it was up to her to sever the ties.

'Yes,' Akhila said. 'I'm done and I will never see you again. Please don't call me at my office or try and meet me. You will leave me with no option but to leave this city. I love you, Hari. I will perhaps never love anyone else but this is not meant to be.'

'Won't you even give me a chance?' His eyes pleaded. But Akhila turned away and walked to the door of the compartment.

That night, she wrote Katherine a letter. For a while, they had written to each other regularly. But Akhila had kept Hari a secret even from her. Now, she wrote to her about this love, this sadness that clamped her chest, and as she wrote Akhila tried to explain why she had to do what she did. Would Katherine understand? Akhila wondered. Would Katherine approve? Would Katherine have done the same?

In the morning, Akhila knew that she couldn't tell even Katherine about this love. She tore up the letter, called a colleague and said her mother was ill and she was going to be on leave for the next two weeks. She told Amma that she was due for some leave and stayed at home. For the next two weeks, she relived their every moment together and then she went back to work. She left by the 6.55 train and took a later train back. Their paths never crossed again.

Sometimes Akhila would see the curve of a cheek or the slope of a head in a crowd and her heart would race: Hari. But it was never Hari and even if it had been Hari, Akhila would have pretended not to have seen him.

✝

Akhila curled up on her side and pulled her knees towards her chest. She suddenly felt bereft and alone. Had she made a mistake when she gave up Hari? Or was it the right thing to have done? What was it that had held her back? How was she to shake off these crumbs of regret that still clung to her?

Perhaps if I let myself, I too will arrive at happiness. A wild warming, a magic content, an inner peace, all from knowing that the past years haven't been in vain and what lies ahead will bring forth more than what I have resigned myself to accepting as my lot. Perhaps it is not too late, Akhila thought. That while what she had lost might be irretrievable, life would toss forth a second chance. Like it had for Janaki. And for Margaret too in some convoluted way.

And then Akhila remembered that there had been the makings of a second chance, but she had not known it to be so at that time...

✝

Five years ago when Amma died, the rhythm of Akhila's life slipped again. What was she to do? How was she to live alone?

After much discussion, it was decided that Akhila would ask for a transfer to Trichy where Narsi was, or to Bangalore where Padma was. Narayan was often transferred so she couldn't make her home with him.

Akhila's section superintendent managed to arrange a transfer to Bangalore and that was the end of her life in Ambattur. All that had to be done was to pack the few things that were hers and give the keys to Narayan. The house was not their own and all they had to do was divide between Narayan and Narsi the few household things that they owned.

In the evening, Akhila cleaned out the steel cupboard that had always stood in the inner room. She remembered the day it had been brought in. Amma had wanted one badly for so long; every home in the neighbourhood had a steel cupboard. Every now and then she would throw a scathing look at the wooden cupboard that had been part of her dowry and say, 'It doesn't have to be a Godrej, even a less expensive one will do. All our clothes smell musty and your papers are being eaten up by insects. Now, if we had a steel cupboard everything would stay as it was...'

Appa had managed to find a furniture shop that would let him have a steel cupboard on monthly instalments and no deposit. All they asked was that he pay six months' instalments up front and then he could take the cupboard home and pay the rest in eighteen months.

When the steel cupboard came home, everyone had a

particular treasure that had to be put into it. Amma had shooed them away pretending to be angry. 'This is not a place to put your silly things. We will keep in it only what is important. Like my silk saris and Appa's shirts, do you understand?'

The locker inside it was exclusively for Appa and it was there he would keep all his important papers, he announced. When Appa died, the locker became Akhila's.

Akhila took out her service papers and underneath was a small brown envelope with five New Year cards in it. Akhila stared at it for a long while. Should she keep it or throw it away? Why had she kept it all this while anyway?

Akhila opened the card dated five years ago. Hari's signature was scrawled all over it. Hari and nothing else. Every year he sent her a card as if to remind her of his existence. But Akhila had never wanted to pursue that thought. What was over was over, she told herself.

In the last one was a phone number and an address. I don't stay at home any more, he had written. Akhila had been tempted to call when the card arrived. But she had resisted. Her life had a pattern now and she wanted nothing to disrupt it. Five years was a long time. But the chasm that lay between them still couldn't be bridged. Perhaps it would simply have widened.

Akhila began to tear the cards up. She would burn them, she decided. Then on a whim and because she couldn't sever herself from him completely, she took out the small address book she had bought to write down the names and addresses of her colleagues at work and carefully wrote out Hari's address and telephone number. That was his place in her life, she told herself. A name among several names. Suddenly Akhila thought of Sarasa Mami and Jaya.

Later that evening, she went to Sarasa Mami's house. I should have done this a long time ago, she told herself as she walked down the street. I shouldn't have abandoned Sarasa Mami and the children. Even though Amma would have been angry, I should have visited them, let them know that nothing had changed.

Outside Sarasa Mami's house, she paused. The door that always had a line of plastic mango leaves crowning it was bare and shut. The white kolam painted on the doorstep had been erased. What had happened to Sarasa Mami? Had she completely abandoned her former life? Through one of the open windows, Akhila saw the bluish glare of a TV screen. She stared in surprise. Then she pressed the doorbell, yet another oddity in a doorway that had never had any such adornment, for it had always been kept open.

A stranger opened the door. 'Yes?' he asked.

Akhila suddenly felt sweat break out on her forehead. Was this one of Jaya's men?

'Sarasa Mami...' she said. 'Is Sarasa Mami here?'

The man looked at her for a moment as if trying to fathom who she was. Then he sighed. 'There is no one called Sarasa Mami here. We moved to this house four years ago. It was empty for about six months before we shifted in. The owner couldn't find a good tenant. And after we began living here, we found out why. I came here on a transfer and knew nothing about the history of this house.'

'Do you know what happened to them?' Akhila asked, not knowing what else to say.

The man shrugged. 'No...someone told my wife that they were evicted and that they went away to—' he paused, 'Kodambakkam.'

Akhila bent her head, embarrassed. She realized what the meaning of the pause was. What do you have to do with a family that moved into an area famous for its whores? the pause demanded.

'But how do you know them?' the man asked, unable to hide his curiosity. You look too respectable to have had a connection with a family of ill repute, his expression said.

Akhila looked into his eyes, wondering what she should say. What would he think of her if she said that Sarasa Mami's family and hers were almost like a family once. Then feeling defiant, she said, 'They were family friends,' but suddenly she lost her courage and added, 'but we haven't seen them for many years.'

'That explains it. So you didn't know what had happened to them. Or that the daughter had become a, you know...' the man said, unable to mouth the word prostitute.

Akhila turned to go. Why did I wait so long? Why didn't I have the courage until now? And yet if I had, what could I have done?

The night before Akhila left the house, she lay awake. She was never going to come back here again. Was this how a bride felt on the eve of her marriage? Or a pregnant woman felt when the first wave of labour pains rocked her insides? Fear. Excitement. A manic swinging between a complete numbness of thought and an explosion of serrated nerve ends.

My life is going to change forever. My life will never be the same again—Akhila chanted this to herself as if it were a Devi mantra. To safeguard. To protect. To bless. To renew.

†

The flat was designed for a family. For a husband, wife and two children as per the government scheme of things.

Akhila thought of how hard the government tried to put a lid on the burgeoning population and began to giggle. First, there were the cute lines that encouraged family planning. From the back of trucks, around garbage bins and on top of bus shelters, a red inverted triangle with a single message beamed cheerily—We two, our two; small family, happy family. Then there was the matter of maternity leave. Women government employees could avail of maternity leave for only two pregnancies. Thereafter, the only leave they were eligible for was to have an MTP done. And now these flats. But at least it was saner than what they did some years ago: forcibly dragging men of all ages to family planning centres and performing vasectomies on them against their will. As reward or compensation for their inability to fill the world with more babies, they were given a plastic bucket and fifty rupees, she had heard.

The house had a main hall where a three-seater sofa, two armchairs and a low coffee table would fit in easily. And if one really wanted to, a small dining table could be squeezed in against the wall. It was a room where the family could spend time together, watch TV and entertain visitors. There were two rooms adjacent to each other that opened from the main hall. Two bedrooms with open cupboards and enormous windows. The kitchen, long and narrow, ran the full width of the house and was behind the main hall. There was a veranda, partly enclosed by grills, at the back of the flat and on one side of it were the bathroom and the toilet. A small patch of land surrounded three sides of the flat. The fourth side was taken up by a replica of this flat. Like Siamese twins joined at the hip, the inner wall that ran the length of the house linked the twin flats. Above were two identical flats but as they had no garden, it was understood that the terrace was theirs.

Maybe it made economical sense to build a block of flats. Or, maybe the government thought that to give a not-so-senior employee a separate house would encourage him or her to think beyond their station in life. Or, maybe they thought it fostered national integration to share a wall and cooking smells.

Akhila didn't care one way or the other. She was delighted by the sheer prospect of having a home to herself. She thought of how her life was finally beginning to acquire a dimension of its own. Then she heard Padma say, 'It's a little old-fashioned. And quite plain. Did you see the kitchen? I didn't expect a stainless steel sink but I thought it would at least be tiled. And the counters are plain cement slabs...not even mosaic.'

Akhila was silent. No matter what Padma said, Akhila loved her little quarters. Then Padma added, 'But it has a certain charm. And it is just perfect for us.'

What 'us'? Akhila wanted to demand. Isn't it time you left me alone to live my life?

'I can see we will be very happy here. I can walk the girls to school and back. The shops are just around the corner and the neighbours seem very nice.'

Akhila looked at her aghast. She had imagined Padma would be happy to have her home back. Akhila had been living with her for the past nine months till her quarters were sanctioned, and it hadn't been an easy time. Often Akhila had to remind herself that this woman who gnawed at her nerves like a relentless mouse was her sister. Her own flesh and blood. So she had to forgive Padma for becoming the overbearing callous creature that wifedom and motherhood had turned her into. And now here she was proposing to come and live with her.

Akhila thought of the toothpaste blobs and stray hair clinging to the wash basin in the bathroom, the grubby paw prints Padma's daughters would speckle her immaculate white walls and magazines with, the toys that she almost always tripped over, the messing up of her neat bed, the borrowing of her saris with not even a may-I-please, the continuous blaring of the TV, the smells, the noise, the disorder, the interference...and stifled the sob that clawed at her throat.

'Will Murthy like it? He will probably be offended by the very thought of living under my roof,' Akhila said, trying to control the panic in her voice. Murthy, Padma's husband, didn't have a single self-respecting bone in his body. But Akhila was desperate enough to clutch at any straw she could find.

'Oh, he won't mind at all. Once he is promoted, he will need to travel all over the south. One day in Madras. Two days later in Hyderabad. The next week in Hubli...and I don't like the thought of being alone with the girls. And why should we run two households when we can be together? Besides, how can you live all by yourself?' Padma said firmly and Akhila could see her already planning where to put what and choosing the material for the curtains.

'But...' Akhila began. And then Padma brought out the trump card that she knew would sweep all her objections away, 'I don't think I can cope alone, Akka.'

Akhila wished she had spoken then. Akhila wished she had admitted to herself this overwhelming desire and told Padma how much she preferred to be on her own. Instead, she retreated into silence.

An uneasy silence that often splintered, flinging slivers of glass all around. Cutting skin and drawing blood. Akhila almost always regretted the outburst afterwards. For she was to blame as much as Padma. She should have had the courage to speak up. Instead Akhila had allowed Padma to coax her into sharing her home with her. And let the churning ooze of regret suck at her feet with little suckling sounds: it would have been different if she were living alone. None of this need ever have happened.

Then came the matter of the egg. Perhaps that's when Padma began choosing the silken threads with which to embroider her reputation.

For nine months, Akhila had had to forgo the pleasure of an egg. After all, she had been living in Padma's house and she had no wish to take any liberties that would upset her. But now that she lived in what were her entitled living quarters, she decided to resurrect her everyday egg.

'What on earth is this doing here?' Padma's voice swirled around Akhila in waves of incredulity when she saw her bring out Katherine's egg case.

'What does it look like to you?' Akhila murmured, unable to keep the bite out of her words.

'I know what it is. I asked what an egg case is doing in this house, a brahmin household?' Padma retorted.

'Well, in this brahmin household, someone eats eggs.'

'Who?' Padma asked and then suddenly her jaw dropped. 'Are you telling me that you eat eggs?'

Akhila ignored her.

'How can you? Aren't you ashamed of yourself?' she began, stung by Akhila's silence.

'What do I have to be ashamed of? It's just an egg after all.'

'How can you?' Padma persisted. 'We are brahmins. We are

not supposed to. It is against the norms of our caste.'

'What about the time the doctor said your children's health needed building up and you fed them an egg beaten with milk? Weren't you committing sacrilege then?' Akhila said, allowing herself to be drawn into an argument.

'That was for health reasons. But you eat eggs because you like the taste. Have you thought of what Amma would have said if she knew?'

'Amma knew. And she didn't say anything.'

'Poor Amma. How she must have hated it. But she must have been too scared of your razor-edged tongue to try and stop you.' Padma's words tore through Akhila. Was that why Amma had never said a word? Had my mother come to fear me? Have I turned into some stone-faced scythe-tongued monster?

Akhila turned towards Padma blindly. Look at me, she wanted to cry. I'm your older sister. The one who gave up her life for you and for our family. Do you realize what you are saying? I thought it was your love for me that made you treat me with such esteem. Are you telling me it was just terror?

But all Akhila saw there was the gleam of victory. Padma knew that she had hurt her in the worst way possible. Akhila felt a great anger cloud her eyes and she snapped, 'This is my house and if I wish to eat eggs here or prance around naked, I will do so. If someone doesn't care for it, they are free to leave.'

Akhila heard Padma gasp and she knew that this time she had scored a point.

For the next four years, Akhila managed to barely survive many such skirmishes. Padma made friends with the women in the neighbourhood. Most of them, like her, were housewives and they often met in each other's homes. One of the first things that Padma did was to tell the other women what a misfit Akhila was as a woman. Her next-door neighbour Mr Dharmappa's wife was a broad-faced beaming woman who took special pride in telling the whole world that her husband, who was extremely efficient at work, was no better than a baby on its back when he got home, and just about as useless. 'He can't even make himself a cup of tea,' she announced and then added, 'I have to take care of every single thing. If I were to place the dishes on the dining table, he wouldn't serve himself. I have to do even that for him.'

Padma made a sound to pronounce agreement. Akhila was in her bedroom eavesdropping. She waited in amusement to hear what Padma would offer in turn about Murthy's misdemeanours. And Akhila heard her say, 'Akka is just the same. She is so smart when it comes to office duties, but at home...' she paused. 'Why, my seven-year-old Madhavi is a better housekeeper than she is. I have to do everything for my sister. Cook for her. Iron her clothes, even sew on the missing buttons on her blouses!'

What is it with women who are wedded to the kitchen counters? Why is it that they can't endure the thought of a woman being capable both at home and in the outside world? Akhila fumed in disgust.

At first, Akhila consoled herself with the thought that perhaps Padma resented her being able to escape the periphery of the home. Maybe she longed for wider horizons, the financial independence that Akhila possessed. But Akhila soon realized that Padma's feelings for her had acquired a complexity that Akhila no longer knew how to decipher or handle. Padma needed to make Akhila look inadequate to feel complete herself.

Another afternoon. Akhila was in the bedroom with the blankets pulled up to her chin. She had the flu. She could hear the murmur of voices from the front room. Padma had found a group of five other brahmin women. They took turns to meet in each other's homes every Tuesday to practice singing Meera bhajans. This afternoon, it was Padma's turn to host the singing party. Akhila heard a voice ask, 'Would your sister like to join us?'

'Don't be foolish. She is ill. How can she?' another voice retorted.

'Anyway, she doesn't like all this. She is a different kind of person.' Akhila recognized that voice. Padma's.

'What do you mean she is different?' the first voice asked. Akhila began to feel a certain kinship with that unknown voice.

'She is not like us. She is not interested in any of the things that give us or any normal person pleasure. She likes to be left alone. And she can be very scathing if someone tries to draw her out of her shell. I have no intention of asking her to join us. So put that thought out of your mind.' Padma's voice bore just the right inflection to suggest misery at the hands of a callous older sister.

'But doesn't she believe in God?' an incredulous voice asked. 'These are bhajans, after all. Songs praising Krishna.'

'I don't know. Sometimes I think she isn't even a practising Hindu. She won't light the lamp in the puja room or go to the temple or observe any of the rituals we brahmins do. When she has her periods, she continues to water the plants and if I object, she bites my head off.'

'Why do you live with her then? Why don't you move and leave her?' the first voice said.

Padma sighed, 'I would love to do just that. But she is my older sister and a spinster. If we abandon her, she will be all alone.'

'But there is a limit to how much you can tolerate.'

'My husband says the same. But no matter how badly she behaves, I have to do my duty. That is what our scriptures teach us.' As a martyr, no one could be more convincing than Padma.

By evening these women, Akhila knew, would have spread the story further. Of how much poor Padma endured. Of Akhila's eccentricities. Of her godless state. Of how lucky she was to have a sister like Padma living with her and putting up with what she dished out to her day after day.

Akhila tolerated the invasion of space and privacy that took many forms. But the worst were the nights when Padma's husband Murthy was at home. The two girls Priya and Madhavi were shunted off to Akhila's room to share her bed. And when the lights had been switched off—because the two girls couldn't sleep if there was even a tiny flicker of light in the room and they needed their sleep or they would doze off in class the next day—muffled noises crept in through the crack between the bedroom door and the floor.

A reined in breath. A caressing sigh. The rustle of clothes. Feverish excitement. And sometimes a whisper—Ssh...she'll hear us...

Akhila would turn towards the window and pull the sheet over her ears. Those nights she felt a crippling longing for Hari. Had she made a mistake by letting him go? Where was Hari now? If she were to meet him again, would he feel the same way about her? Hari, Hari, she cried...If only I hadn't been such a coward.

With the longing came a bitter resentment. A rancour she couldn't stop from curdling within her and crawling down the sides of her mouth in narrow lines.

It wasn't that Akhila grudged Padma the happiness her life seemed to be speckled with. Akhila didn't grudge her anything. The entwining of limbs; an arm thrown around her waist; a chest to rest her head upon; the blossoming of her womb; the engorging of her breasts with milk; the sound of her babies, and laughter; the waiting for her husband to come home; the sharing of an ordinary moment...

What she resented was being thrust into the middle of all this change, this expanding of horizon, while her life continued in its sedate, dull, spinsterish, constant way. No highs. No lows. Just seamless travel from day to day.

✝

The train wheezed to a halt. Voices crowded. Strange sounds that made no sense. Akhila opened her eyes. For a moment, she didn't know where she was. She panicked. Then she remembered and a slow smile bloomed. She turned onto her stomach and propped herself up on her elbows.

How strange, she thought. All railway platforms look alike.

The puddles of water near the occasional dripping tap. The passengers with clenched faces and feverish eyes. The piled up suitcases. The occupied benches. The porters. The vendors with coffee and tea urns, packets of biscuits and glossy magazines. The garbage bins stuffed with litter. The cigarette butts. A crumpled plastic coffee cup. A chocolate wrapper. A banana peel. The pink and green plastic bags caught between the railway tracks, ballooning with the breeze, deflating in stillness. The once white but now silvery grey stakes fencing the station in.

PALAKKAD. Akhila saw the name of the station. The pass in the mountains that allowed the world entry through the Western Ghats. This was a major junction and the stop would be a long one.

She turned her head and looked at the other passengers. All the others were asleep except Prabha Devi who was climbing down from her berth. 'Good morning,' she said. 'So did you sleep well?'

Akhila nodded and sat up. 'I'm going to buy a cup of tea. Would you like one?' Then, pointing to Janaki, she asked, 'Should we wake her up? She has to get off at Ernakulam. So does the girl, and they seem to be fast asleep.'

'There is still time. We'll wake them up after a while. Do you want to eat breakfast? This is the stop for it. The food will be warm and fresh.'

'How can I? I haven't brushed my teeth.' Akhila shook her head.

'Do you plan to go hungry all day? Just rinse your mouth well and that should do,' Prabha Devi said impatiently.

When they had washed their faces, rinsed their mouths, combed their hair and re-pleated their saris, they set about buying breakfast. 'What are you going to have?' Akhila asked.

'I'm going to eat an appam with vegetable korma, and a banana fritter. I make everything else in my kitchen and besides, what is the point in coming to a new place if we do everything the way we do it at home? We might as well stay there,' Prabha Devi said, sticking her hand out of the window and waggling it to catch the attention of a nearby vendor.

Akhila thought for a second. 'Alright, I'll have the same,' she said.

'That's more like it,' Prabha Devi said with a smile.

The white fluffy appam came wrapped in a banana leaf that was covered with a sheet of newspaper. 'I love the aroma of food wrapped in banana leaf,' Prabha Devi said breathing in deeply. 'Do you?'

Do I? Akhila wondered. She had never thought about it. She inhaled the aromas and said, 'Yes, I do too. But I never knew. How strange it is that someone has to tell us what we like and what we don't.'

'There is nothing strange about that. Most of us are like that.'

'I find it hard to believe that of you,' Akhila said. 'You seem completely assured of who you are, what you want, what you like and what you don't.'

Prabha Devi swallowed her mouthful and said thoughtfully, 'Is that how I seem to you?'

'You are one of the most confident and content persons I have met,' Akhila said, gingerly placing a piece of appam in her mouth.

'There, it wasn't all that bad, was it?' Prabha Devi teased.

'You know what,' Prabha Devi said when they had eaten and washed their hands, 'I used to be very much like you. Quiet and timid and afraid to try anything new. Then one day, I discovered I didn't like the person I had become and so I changed.'

'Just like that?' Akhila asked disbelievingly.

'Of course, it wasn't just like that. There was a cause and effect like there always is. Except that in my case, I was both the cause and the effect.'

8

Afloat

During the course of an afternoon in September, a week after her fortieth birthday, it occurred to Prabha Devi that she had forgotten the sound of her own voice. What do I sound like? Is my voice shrill or harsh? Does it pitch low or high? Does it float like the wind or fall like bricks? She opened her mouth and spoke her name: Pra-bhaa-de-vi. A sound emerged that was a little like a bleat and more like a mewl. So this is my voice, she thought. Between an irate sheep and a kitten being strangled.

Prabha Devi rose from the spring mattress-fitted bed covered with a satin spread and switched off the air-conditioning. She pushed aside the heavy drapes that turned the room into an embryo the waking world had no entry into, and flung open the French windows. The terraced lawn beamed, flushed with sunshine and moisture. Prabha Devi walked on to the grass. The blades tickled her toes. She raised her head to the evening sun and parted her lips. Sunshine dribbled down her throat. She licked her lips and tried saying her name again. This time, the ghost of a former life drifted out of her mouth. And Prabha Devi felt a gradual awakening of life. Where have I been all this while? she asked herself. At first quietly, tremulously and then furiously. What was I doing all this while?

When Prabha Devi was born, her father sighed. He had hoped it would be a boy. He had planned to open a fifth jewellery store in the city. Madras was big enough to provide ample business for five stores and if Prabha Devi had been a boy, he could have settled everything so tidily. Five stores, five boys, everyone happy. Now he'd have to shelve the idea of the fifth store.

Prabha Devi's mother, though, was pleased with her daughter. 'I have someone to leave my recipes to. Someone who'll treasure my jewellery. Someone who'll want to be like me. Someone who'll say—in my mother's house, this is how we did it...'

Prabha Devi's father stared down at her disapprovingly and muttered, 'Has this baby, apart from ruining my business plans, addled your brains as well? If you ask me, a daughter is a bloody nuisance.'

Prabha Devi's mother sighed. It was foolish of her to have bared her soul to him. What he would give in to was flesh. Creamy globules, pert and plump, all signs of having nourished four lusty sons erased now that they were engorged with milk for this new one. Her daughter. Prabha Devi's mother snapped open the buttons of her blouse and cradled the baby against her breast. A fleeting glimpse was enough to ensure that her husband's disagreeable mood dissipated. 'We have four sons. A daughter can do no harm. Besides, when it is time for her to be married, you can choose a family that will aid your business interests,' she said to her husband in a low voice.

He looked at her thoughtfully, then smiled. Things seemed better now that they had been put into perspective. He touched the baby's cheek, stroked the curve of his wife's breast and went out of the room quite satisfied with life.

Prabha Devi grew up. Her mother saw to it that she had a near perfect childhood. Expensive dolls were ordered from Singapore, with blonde hair and eyes that shut when you lay them down on their back. Old saris were cut up for Prabha Devi to dress up in and play schoolteacher. A kitchen was set up for her to play house and mother games. Sometimes Prabha Devi's mother joined in her daughter's games, pretending to be an adult-child while her daughter tried hard to be a child-adult. This one daughter of hers gave her more pleasure than all her four sons put together. But she kept quiet about it. Long ago she had discovered that a woman with an opinion was treated like a bad smell. To be shunned. And so Prabha Devi's mother swallowed the thought as she had done all her life.

When Prabha Devi was fifteen years old, her father moved her from the family-owned school to a convent school. The nuns were as strict and as fastidious as Prabha Devi's father expected them to be. 'The nuns will groom her well. Besides, if we have to find a good alliance for her, she should be able to speak proper English and look a little fashionable,' her father told her mother who was all for Prabha Devi leaving school now that she had passed her tenth standard.

When Prabha Devi asked her mother for permission to go with a friend to a matinée show at a nearby cinema theatre, she shook her head nervously. 'I don't think your father will like it.'

But to her surprise, he said she could go. 'No roaming around the city from the theatre to ice-cream parlours. But she can go out every Saturday morning for two hours. These days, boys prefer girls who are friendly and can hold their own in a conversation. But the word is friendly, not brazen or wanton, do you understand?'

In all other aspects, Prabha Devi turned out to be the kind of woman her mother had envisioned she would be when she was born. A replica of herself.

Her embroidery was done with stitches so fine that you could barely see them. Just shadows and shapes. Her idlies were light and soft. But the true test of a woman lies in the curd she makes and even there Prabha Devi excelled. Sweet and tart with a faint taste of mangoes. In the stone dish that her mother used to set her curd, it wobbled with delicious excitement every time Prabha Devi was responsible for its making. Her voice rose pleasingly full when she was asked to join in the singing at a puja. She walked with small mincing steps, her head forever bowed, suppliant, womanly.

Prabha Devi's skin remained fair, dewy and spotless; other girls of her age had acne. The result of over-indulgence and negligence, Prabha Devi knew. She avoided chocolates, she didn't like them anyway. And she gave herself a face pack every two weeks. Green gram flour, orange peel and sandal dust mixed with sour curds. When she had washed the muck off her face, she ran a half-slice of lime over her skin. Around the mouth. On the cheeks. Over the nose and forehead and then all around her neck. Just the way her mother had taught her to.

Prabha Devi was eighteen when her father came home beaming one evening. He had found her a husband. Prabha Devi's brothers and their wives beamed as well. An unwed younger sister, even though she was docile and well mannered, was a concern. Why their father had waited this long was beyond their comprehension. But Prabha Devi's father was not given to explaining why he did what. So in the same spirit, they accepted his decision to wed Prabha Devi to Jagdeesh. The only son and heir of a prosperous diamond merchant. Besides, they could expand the diamond section in their four jewellery stores.

Only Prabha Devi's mother was saddened by the news. She should be happy, she knew. Jagdeesh was good-looking and smart; his family pedigree was excellent and her daughter was lucky to marry into such a fine family. Besides, Prabha Devi would be moving to Bangalore, which was only a few hundred kilometres away and not to some far-flung place like Delhi or Bombay.

But once Prabha Devi left, there would be nothing for her to do. Bringing up a daughter was a full-time occupation. One never stopped being a mother with a daughter. Sons were different. Their allegiances were constantly shifting. From mother to father to friends to wives to their own vested interests. But a daughter's loyalty was constant as long as she lived under your roof. Prabha Devi's mother already felt bereft. Soon there would be a vacuum nothing in this world could fill. And yet, she knew she was an oddity. Other women couldn't wait to get rid of their daughters. 'What do you want to do?

Keep her with you for life? Have you ever heard anything so sacrilegious? You were always a strange one,' they would say if she tried to explain her feelings to any of her friends or sisters. So Prabha Devi's mother wept quietly into the scallop-edged hanky Prabha Devi had embroidered for her and let everyone believe that they were tears of happiness.

Prabha Devi outlined her lips with pale pink lipstick and filled in the colour with a few deft strokes. She stuck a bindi in the middle of her forehead, a precise two centimetres above the meeting point of her eyebrows, and rained a reddish trickle of kumkum in the parting of her hair. She patted her heavy gold earrings, pushed back a strand of hair that was already in place, and pulled the end of her sari over her head so that it framed her face becomingly. She glanced at her new gold watch. It was half past five in the morning. The household was still asleep. Her husband turned on his side and pulled the sheet to his chin. He smacked his lips and chewed on saliva. His Adam's Apple bobbed in his throat. She felt a huge swell of emotion—love, fear, hope, expectations...she had been a wife for less than a day. Then she waited.

For the next many years that was all Prabha Devi did. Wait. For Jagdeesh to come home. For the babies to be born. For their first step, their first word, their first triumph...Waiting for something to happen while her life swished past in a blur of insignificant days.

There were stray moments that parted themselves from the morass of nothingness and clung to the walls of her mind. Cobwebs of fleeting happiness; a ripeness of joy that overwhelmed Prabha Devi with a single thought in its wispy wake: How lucky I am to be me!

A couple of months after her marriage, there was a death in Jagdeesh's family. It was decided that Jagdeesh's parents would attend the funeral while the younger couple stayed behind at home. 'The servants will take care of everything. You just have to keep an eye on them,' Jagdeesh's mother said, thrusting the filigree silver key ring into Prabha Devi's hands.

Prabha Devi fixed it to the waist of her sari where it hung, pressing on her lower abdomen, brushing against her inner thigh, through the layers of the sari, with the weight of responsibility and the gleam of power.

Jagdeesh's mother smiled approvingly. 'Be careful. Don't trust anyone and see that Jagdeesh eats all his meals on time.' Her parting words sailed through Prabha Devi's ears and sank with a gentle plop into the lily pond in the garden.

Prabha Devi unhooked the key ring from her waist and laid it carefully in the top drawer of the dressing table. Then she went into the kitchen and checked on the servants. They were busy rearranging the kitchen shelves. Prabha Devi closed the door behind her and walked to the pond in which white lilies bloomed, goldfish swam and frogs lived, all in perennial wetness of content. She pulled up her sari to above her knees and stepped into the pond. The water moved, splashed, rippled and lapped against the boulders heaped to one side of the pond behind which a concealed motor slumbered. One flick of the switch and it would begin to hum and a waterfall would be born. But Prabha Devi was oblivious to everything but the delight of the water that crept between her toes and pressed itself against her with a reckless abandon. The flat pads of the lily leaves nudged her and the goldfish came to examine and experimentally nibble at the flesh that had dropped so suddenly into their realm.

Prabha Devi smiled. Then she felt a giggle escape her. It was, she thought, as if all of them had conspired to add to the fun. The breeze lifted a strand of her hair and tickled her nose. The lily stems ran ghost fingers on the back of her knees and the fish wriggled their bellies on her toes. Prabha Devi lifted her face to the skies and laughed loud and clear.

In the evening, when Jagdeesh came home, she waited for him to shower and change his clothes. Then she took his hand in hers and led him to the lily pond. 'What is all this?' he asked, bashful and surprised.

'Sssh...' she whispered. 'Just do as I ask you to.'

They sat at the edge of the pond with feet dangling in the water, now a greenish black in the gloom of the evening. Jagdeesh lifted his foot and watched the droplets drip from his toes. 'My father will be very angry if he knows that we have been wading in his precious lily pond,' he said with a sly grin.

'We won't tell him what we did. Just this once. Let's pretend that we are in a beautiful garden like you see in the movies. Where the hero and heroine hold hands and sing songs about their love for each other,' she said, slipping her hand into his.

He gazed into her eyes, uncertain. Was her suggestion tinged with treachery? 'Wives often lead their husbands down the wrong path. Away from their family and responsibilities. We're not suggesting that your wife will...' his mother had said a few days before he was married. 'But it is up to a good husband to accept or discard what his wife suggests. And not be smitten by a slavish love that makes him agree to her every demand.'

Was Prabha Devi's whim to be accepted or discarded? Jagdeesh's twenty-three-year-old body and still boyish sense of adventure goaded him. What the hell, it was just this once...

He stretched towards the boulder and clicked the switch on. Underwater lights came on, and a waterfall that cascaded. The waters turned a greenish gold; the plump fish danced; the lilies unfurled their petals; the frogs set up a chorus. Jagdeesh touched Prabha Devi's face with his index finger and ran the tip of his tongue over her lips. She shivered: How lucky I am to be me.

A month later. Prabha Devi was radiant with excitement. Jagdeesh was taking her with him on a business trip to New York and on the way back, they would stop over at London. Prabha Devi felt as if her life had just begun. At the international airport in Bombay, she sat in the lounge trying to read a magazine. Jagdeesh was making a last minute phone call. She felt fingers curl around her forearm. 'Prabha Devi,' a voice probed, nervous and hesitant, 'excuse me, are you Prabha Devi?'

Prabha Devi turned around perplexed. The voice belonged to

a girl she had gone to school with. Sharmila. The most brilliant student the school had ever had. She was destined for great things, everyone had said. She would be either a doctor or an IAS officer or someone noteworthy. But here she was. Sweat dotting her brow, in spite of the air-conditioning; lank hair, droopy mouth; chained to a fractious toddler in a stroller and a mother-in-law who darted suspicious glances at everyone and everything.

'This is my mother-in-law,' Sharmila said with a sweep of her arm. In that gesture, Prabha Devi read the story of Sharmila's life. Mostly unspoken complaints: This is the woman whose son now rules my destiny and dreams. My thoughts have been reduced to whether I should cook rice or chapattis for lunch, fry okras or aubergine; load the washing machine with cotton whites or cotton coloured...

Prabha Devi smiled at the older woman. She didn't know what else she could do.

'Are you going to New York?' she asked. A silly question. After all, they were boarding the same flight.

'New York. And then across the river to New Jersey,' Sharmila sighed. 'Give me a minute. Let me settle them in a seat and I'll be back.'

Prabha Devi watched Sharmila. The mother-in-law was led to a corner seat. The stroller was wedged between the bags arranged near the seat. And then it seemed to Prabha Devi that her schoolmate winged her way back before mother-in-law or baby could whimper in protest at being left alone.

'You look very nice,' Sharmila said, eyeing Prabha Devi's peach-coloured trouser suit. 'Doesn't your husband mind you wearing Western clothes?'

'His parents are just a teeny bit conservative. Not him though,' Prabha Devi said, thinking of how she'd to cajole Jagdeesh into buying her a new wardrobe for her first visit abroad. What had clinched the argument in her favour was the plea—No one will know who I am or where we are going. So what does it matter what I wear or don't wear?

'What about you? I didn't even know you were married,' Prabha Devi began. 'All of us thought that you were studying to be a doctor in America.'

Sharmila stared at the floor. 'My family tricked me. I was sent there to my uncle's house and he was supposed to have arranged for everything. I actually had admission for an undergraduate degree with a fully paid scholarship. Then Naresh was introduced into the scene. He was someone my uncle knew very well. Very good husband material, my uncle claimed. Naresh said he didn't mind me studying even after we were married.'

'So are you at some university now?' Prabha Devi asked, wondering how she managed to combine studying for a degree with household chores and a baby.

'Are you kidding?' A faint trace of an American accent crept into Sharmila's voice. 'With a baby and a mother-in-law? Do you know, she's lived in the US for ten years and yet doesn't speak one word of English. How can I leave the baby with her and go away...'

As if on cue the baby set up a wail. Sharmila wrote her telephone number on a piece of paper and slipped it into Prabha Devi's hand. 'Give me a call when you have the time. You and your husband must come over for a meal.'

Prabha Devi nodded. They both knew that it was one of those gestures that would never bear fruition. And yet the effort had to be made.

In the aircraft, Prabha Devi followed Jagdeesh down the aisle. He was in charge, brandishing boarding passes and hand baggage. All she had to do was clutch her purse and the stack of magazines he had bought for her to read during the flight. She spotted a harassed looking Sharmila trying to calm the baby, settle the mother-in-law, find a place for the hand baggage that wouldn't fit into the overhead cabinet and not lose her temper, all at the same time.

How could it be that what was an adventure for her was for Sharmila yet another hardship to add to her list of grievances?

Prabha Devi felt relief flood her.

Jagdeesh had picked seats right at the back. Just as the plane was about to take off, Prabha Devi felt Jagdeesh take her hand in his. 'Don't be scared,' he said. 'At first, it'll feel like you are going up in a swing, then everything will be fine...'

She smiled. His touch reassured her even though she wasn't scared, just excited. How lucky I am to be me.

But there was one memory that Prabha Devi had to force herself not to dwell upon. She had tried very hard to erase it from her mind, but like a splinter under the skin, an almost invisible fish bone in the throat, it refused to be dislodged. And there it stayed, eating into the flesh, causing an occasional spasm of pain, oozing discomfort and a perennial sense of shame.

It owed its origins to the American adventure. Prabha Devi came back from the holiday with a whole set of acquisitions. There was the unbreakable dinner service in apple green; the vials of perfume; a make-up kit; lingerie frothy with artificial lace and the dreams of Taiwanese women. Knick-knacks for the home and gifts for everyone. But she had acquired something more, which she packed into her body with the careful dexterity she applied when packing her suitcase.

Prabha Devi wanted to be like the women she had seen in New York. With swinging hair and a confident stride. They seemed to know exactly where they were going and once they got there, what they had to do. Their lives were ruled by themselves and no one else. Such poise, such confidence, such celebration of life and beauty. Prabha Devi wanted that for herself.

So she practised the walk: an upright stance with squared shoulders, pulled in belly and a gentle but provocative swing of the hips. Then Prabha Devi discovered that a three-inch pointed heel made this whole process much easier. There was no way one could slouch wearing footwear with stiletto heels.

Then came the face. Prabha Devi made three trips to Macy's, to the cosmetic counters, to learn how to apply make-up. Her eyes became dreamier and her lips looked as if a bee had stung them and injected them with the hues of a rose.

Prabha Devi watched talk shows and soap operas till she had perfected the lazy shake of the head, the slow widening of her eyes that accompanied the dramatic exhaling of breath when she wished to effect a meaningful pause in the middle of a sentence.

The last thing that Prabha Devi acquired to complete the transformation was clothes. She packed away her saris and began to wear silky caftans with ornately embroidered designs around the neck and sleeves. At first, she worried her mother-in-law would disapprove. But the older woman simply fingered the embroidery and said, 'They tell me a machine does all this. It's very pretty. I suppose this is what all young women wear these days. I must say it makes sense. No need to worry about matching blouses and petticoats. But when you go before the men, do remember to drape a towel or some piece of cloth over your bosom.'

With that Prabha Devi felt she was finally a woman of the world sans the slouch, the downcast eyes and the sari pallu weighing down her youth.

Jagdeesh chewed on his bottom lip and worried at the change. What, he wondered, did his parents think about all this? And how would it all end? He soon knew.

Prabha Devi told him that she didn't want a baby. 'Not just yet,' she added when she saw the look of alarm on his face.

'What do you mean?' he asked, shaken by her words into a purely rhetorical question.

Prabha Devi stared at the corner of the sheet. For the first time, she missed wearing a sari. There was much to be said for its pallu. An ill-fitting blouse or a missing button was camouflaged by simply pulling the pallu over one's shoulder like a shawl. It served as a scarf for the head when the sun burned. A hood when caught in a drizzle. A fringe of decorum when one wanted to avoid someone's penetrating gaze. Then there were its ends. To wipe tears; to mop the sweat off one's brow; to pleat and gather or crumple into a ball, something for the hands to cling to in awkward moments. All that she had now were the ends of the sheet. She pleated and gathered them as she tried to frame an answer to her husband's question.

'There are ways in which pregnancy can be avoided,' she began.

'Like what?' he croaked.

'Couldn't you wear a condom?'

Jagdeesh stiffened in shame and embarrassment. What kind of a woman was she? Sex was something a man and a woman did beneath the covers of the night and a thin sheet. It was not a topic of conversation. Did she think that he was going to sit there and discuss it? For the hundredth time, he wished he had never taken her with him on that trip abroad. She had come back a completely changed person.

He looked at her. At the spaghetti-strap nightie that bared her shoulders and most of her bosom. Desire was replaced by dislike. He turned on his side and pretended to go to sleep.

Not for long, though. Her breath fanned the back of his neck. They nestled against each other. Two spoons in a tray of bedclothes.

He groaned and turned to her. He felt her slide towards him and throw an arm around his waist. His leg planted itself on hers. 'My parents are getting impatient. They talk of a grandchild all the time. We have been married for almost a year now,' he said, caressing the side of her neck.

'I want a baby too. But not just yet. Once a baby comes, nothing will be the same.' She pushed the hair back from his brow and rocked him in her arms. 'Tonight we'll sleep, and tomorrow when you are prepared, we will love each other,' she murmured, kissing his eyelids shut.

For the next three months, Prabha Devi winged her way through the days. When people shot her admiring looks, she pretended not to notice. But she knew that wherever she went, she attracted attention. And she revelled in it. I am young. I am beautiful. I am desirable. How lucky I am to be me.

So when Pramod remained indifferent to her presence, she saw it as a slight to the person she had become. She saw him every weekend at the club where Jagdeesh played his weekly game of tennis. As she sat in the lawns sipping iced lemon juice and flipping through a magazine, Prabha Devi began to wait for Pramod. He often stopped by to chat if Jagdeesh was present. If she was by herself, he merely tilted his head in greeting and ignored her. Prabha Devi didn't like it. How dare he? she thought. Am I not a person by myself? Am I to be treated as a mere extension of someone else's personality? Jagdeesh's Mrs and no more.

When Pramod continued to remain immune to her presence, unconsciously she began to practise her wiles on him. With a tilt of her head and a widening of her eyes; with meaningful pauses and secret smiles.

If someone had accused her of flirting, she would have been horrified. 'All I do is talk. Is there anything wrong in that? Besides, I'm married, aren't I?'

But no one did. Particularly not Jagdeesh who flopped into a chair after a game, rivulets of sweat running down his back, too exhausted to notice what was going on.

As for Pramod, he was a mere mortal who succumbed to Prabha Devi's attentions, turning from terse stranger to fawning slave. And Prabha Devi, triumphant at yet another conquest, lapped up the admiration. Until the afternoon he came calling on her.

It was quarter past three. The time when Prabha Devi woke up from her afternoon nap. She had a bath, sluicing the sleep off her skin with brimming mugs of tepid water. Fresh clothes. Daytime make-up. When Pramod saw her come down the stairs, she seemed to him fresh and inviting and so very desirable.

Prabha Devi felt a tiny tremor of fear when she saw Pramod. The maid had come up to her bedroom and said, 'You have guests. A man and a child.'

'For me? I'm not expecting anyone this afternoon,' Prabha

Devi said, examining herself in the mirror. 'Do you know who they are?' she asked, wondering if her clothes were appropriate for receiving guests.

The maid shook her head. 'They look respectable enough. The man said he knows you,' she added, justifying her seating them in the living room.

He stood up when he saw her and went towards her with extended arms. Prabha Devi stepped sideways and evaded them. She put on a bright smile and looked around the room searchingly, 'What a surprise to see you here! I was told there was a child. Where is she?'

'My niece. She's outside. She is sitting on the swing reading a comic. She won't bother us,' he murmured, taking her hands in his.

She withdrew her hands from his clasp and sank into a chair. Her legs were trembling so badly that she didn't know if they would hold her up much longer.

He stared at her and then sat down in a chair opposite hers. 'You don't look very pleased to see me,' he accused in a low voice.

'Friends are always welcome,' she said in a mock-bright voice, trying to still the panic in her.

'How welcome?'

'Would you like a cup of tea or some fresh juice?' she asked, trying to infuse a sense of normalcy to the visit. 'There are some delicious grapes in the fridge. It'll take me just a minute to make the juice. What about the child? Would she like some biscuits?'

'I don't want tea or grape juice. I wanted to see you...be with you. Do you know how long I have waited for this day?' Pramod said quietly, gazing into her face. Prabha Devi refused to meet his eyes. He sighed.

'Yesterday when I saw your parents-in-law at the railway station, I knew that the day had come. That finally I could meet you alone. That what I have wanted for so long would be mine.'

'What do you want?' she asked. Pause. Sidelong glance. A hint of a smile.

'Don't do this to me,' he groaned. 'Don't you know that I want you? That I'm in love with you?'

Prabha Devi suddenly realized with a sinking of her heart that she had ignited something she had no idea how to extinguish. Her mind whirled. A series of thoughts drawn by a single thread of disbelief: Why on earth did he think that she would welcome his advances? Didn't he know she was married? What kind of a woman did he think she was?

And then there he was. In one swift motion he was kneeling at her feet with his arms around her waist. 'You are so lovely—' words that she barely heard. All she could think of was the feel of his touch through the silk of the caftan. His fingers splayed on her skin, seeking, moving, a spider hunting for its prey. When his hands cupped her breasts, she gasped.

Prabha Devi wanted to scream, shriek, rake her fingernails down his face, bunch her fingers into a fist and smash his nose, knee him in the groin, kick his shins...But the shock of what was happening to her froze her into saying nothing, doing nothing. His hands continued to knead her flesh. His mouth murmured words that she no longer comprehended. This is not happening to me. This violation of my body is not happening to me. This is just a nightmare. I'm asleep in my bed and I will wake up any moment now...

The clock struck the hour. And suddenly Prabha Devi came alive. 'How dare you?' she screamed, thrusting his hands away fiercely. 'How dare you come to my house and take such...' she fumbled for a word '...liberties with me? Don't you have any sense of decency? Get out of my house. Get out before I have you thrown out.'

'Oh, come now,' Pramod said, circling her wrists with his fingers, pulling her towards him. 'Quit playing the good wife, will you? Remember you chased me first. You enticed me with your smiles and coy looks. And now you are accusing me of making indecent advances. Prabha, you want me as much as I want you. You can deny it as long and as loudly as you want, but I know.'

Prabha Devi pulled her wrists out of his grasp, raised her arm and slapped him on the cheek. 'Get out, I said. I never want to see you again.'

He moved towards her to retaliate. But from the veranda the child called. He stopped mid-stride, stared at her for a moment and said, 'There's a name for women like you. I don't have to say it. I think you know it.' Then he turned on his heel and walked out.

And then the enormity of the incident struck Prabha Devi. A sledgehammer that slammed into her and had her crouching in the chair hugging her knees to her chest. What if the servants had come in at the wrong moment and seen her in his arms? What if they had overheard the whole sordid encounter between Pramod and her? What if one of them took it upon herself to inform Jagdeesh or his parents of what had happened? What if they didn't believe her version? What if she was condemned as a brazen woman and thrown out of the house and family?

She wept into her hands, ashamed and afraid. Maybe she really was to blame. Maybe she had led him on. Maybe her body had sent him all the wrong signals. The what-ifs and maybes twisted and turned; puncturing dreams and expectations she had of life and swiftly draining away her confidence. When there were no more tears to shed, Prabha Devi made a decision. She would camouflage this body that had sent such reckless messages to the world. She would lock away that gay spirited woman who had caused her such anguish, and unlearn every single mannerism she had worked so hard to acquire. She would never again ask for anything and would be content with what was offered to her. She would withdraw herself from life. She would revert to being who she was when she first married Jagdeesh. A woman beyond reproach and above all suspicion.

Prabha Devi became the woman her mother had hoped she would be. With eyes forever downcast and busy hands;

embroidering, pickling, dusting, birthing babies, preserving order and bliss in the confines of her home and all the while chanting to herself: this is who I ought to be, this is the way to be happy.

Some nights Jagdeesh would lie awake as she slept. He would turn towards her and gaze at her sleeping face. What had happened to the woman who had wrapped her legs around his body and teased his senses with her lips? She had been right after all. Once the first child arrived, everything had changed. In fact, it changed the moment he realized that she wanted him to make her pregnant. One day she was a confident girl with desires and needs that she demanded be met. The next day she was the cringing shy girl he had married, who asked for little and gave all of herself.

He was glad even though he missed the passion she had fuelled their lives with. She was a good wife and an excellent mother. What more could a man ask for?

What more could a woman need apart from a happy marriage and healthy children? he thought as sleep curled into his eyes.

†

That September afternoon, Prabha Devi stood before the full-length mirror in her room. Unbidden, an echo of a nursery rhyme popped into her thoughts.

'Prabha Devi, Prabha Devi, where have you been?'

'I became a woman, neither heard nor seen,' the mirror retorted, rhyming grimly.

'Prabha Devi, Prabha Devi, what did you do there?' the parody continued.

'I waited and waited till ash speckled my hair.'

Prabha Devi smiled. A narrow humourless smile. Women dwindled to faded specks as the years went by. And cats tormented mice even under the queen's chair. That was the rule of life, her life, she told herself as salt rimmed her eyes. Tears for herself. For the woman she had become. For ceasing to want more for herself.

When she had dried her eyes, Prabha Devi realized it was time to pick up her son from his tennis lessons. The children had been born in quick succession. A girl came first and then a boy. Children who even from birth seemed to have an in-built sense of decorum and Jagdeesh's equable temperament. So when friends and relatives remarked, 'How lucky you are to have such delightful children,' Prabha Devi didn't know whether she ought to be sad or glad that neither of the children had inherited any of the quirks that had surfaced in her so briefly.

Nitya was in college and had a schedule so hectic that it left her with little time to spend with Prabha Devi. Nitya doesn't need me, not like she had needed her mother when she was eighteen, Prabha Devi often thought when she saw her daughter rush out of the house to go to a friend's home or to college or for a film or a music lesson. But at least there was Vikram. Fifteen-year-old Vikram, not sure whether he was man or boy, and still available for his mother to love and cherish.

Vikram hadn't finished his game and so Prabha Devi decided to stroll through the club grounds while she waited for him. For a long time she had avoided the club, afraid that she would run into Pramod there. Once the children were born, she no longer needed to make any excuses. The children required her attention. Her hours and thoughts were filled from seam to seam with vests and knickers, geometry kits and drawing books, school uniforms and vitamin tablets, homework and vacations...

This afternoon, Prabha Devi found that it was possible to put aside the corollary that hinged itself to her mind when a child's mealtime was delayed: He must be hungry, he must be tired. I ought to take him home right away and feed him till the fatigue is pushed out of his bones and smoothened out of his features. Prabha Devi discovered that it didn't matter so much any more. So she didn't hover by the tennis courts willing the tennis coach to finish as she usually did. Instead she walked.

The sprinklers were on. By dusk, the lawns would be green and moist; the crackle in every blade of grass dampened with a relentless spray of water. Prabha Devi skirted the sprinklers and walked down the path till it ended abruptly at a wall covered with cascades of pink and white bougainvillaea. A little gate in the wall beckoned. Another schoolgirl memory tumbled into her mind. Was this how Alice felt when she saw the little door in the wall? What wonderland lay beyond it?

Prabha Devi opened the gate and went in. A pool gurgled, its blueness mirroring the skies. Touch me, it said.

Prabha Devi crouched by the poolside and let her fingers slide through the water. There was no one around. On one side was a bamboo clump. Its feathery leaves created an arc of shade. Prabha Devi moved to the shaded spot and sat down by the side of the pool, her feet dangling in the water. The pool made little cooing noises. The water tugged at her ankles. Come in, it said.

Prabha Devi felt a great desire possess her. She had never known anything like this before. She would, she decided, learn to swim.

Prabha Devi wished she could tell someone how she felt. The excitement, the tingling of her toes, the surge of blood into her head at the mere thought of entering the shrugging waters of the rectangular pool, of being able to swim. But it would have to remain a secret. Jagdeesh would neither approve nor commend her decision. In fact, she knew it would horrify him. Perhaps even more than the time she had suggested he use a condom, she thought with a giggle. Already she felt like a girl again.

So, with subterfuge and stealth that is as much a good housewifely virtue as pickling onions, bottling mango chutney, selling old newspapers or converting worn-out towels into bath mats by merely folding them and stitching together the edges, Prabha Devi plotted and schemed.

She bought her swimsuit from the shop where she bought her lingerie. Navy blue with a little frill around the hip.

'Would you like a pair of bicycling shorts? Most ladies wear one and pull the swimsuit over it,' the saleswoman said, fingering a row of lycra shorts. Then lowering her voice, she added, 'They tell me that way their thighs are covered and they needn't worry about catching any infectious diseases from the water.'

Prabha Devi nodded. Every time she shopped for underwear this happened. An instant camaraderie seemed to spring up between her and the saleswoman. A bonding so familiar that for a moment, she thought, this is how it must be with a sister or a best friend. Beneath what their clothes made them out to be, they were the same. Their problems were the same. Bra straps that cut into the skin. Thickening of the waist. Mottled thighs. A heart that ached to be needed. A mind that longed to soar.

Prabha Devi tried on the swimsuit. The mirror told no lies. She ran her palms down her flanks, feeling the fabric slide under her skin. 'At least you don't have hips like pumpkins or a paunch that sticks out farther than your bosom. And even if it did, it shouldn't matter. You are doing this for yourself. For the first time in many years, you are doing what you want and not what everyone else thinks you ought to want,' she told herself sternly.

When it was time to draw up the bill, she asked them to write down the items as mere numbers. Jagdeesh gave her as much money as she wanted. But he liked every rupee to be accounted for. 'Bills! Don't forget to pick up the bill when you buy something,' he said each time he gave her a stack of notes.

Discreet enquiries at the club house revealed that there was a swimming coach but he came in the afternoon and the class was only for children below fourteen.

'He conducts special camps for ladies in the summer. Perhaps you can enrol then,' the clerk suggested.

Prabha Devi felt her excitement drain away. But only for a minute. It surged back when the clerk suggested, 'Why don't you just observe what the coach does for a few days? Swimming is not all that easy. Last year, many of our lady members stopped halfway through the camp. They said it was much too difficult and tiring.'

Prabha Devi decided that she would learn to swim by herself. No one had taught her how to welcome her husband into her body. Nor had anyone shown her how to nurse her children at her breast. An instinct had worked then. She would have to call that instinct to the fore again. After all, she had spent nine months in her mother's womb swimming.

For the next three weeks, Prabha Devi went an hour earlier than usual to pick Vikram up from his tennis lessons.

'What is the need for you to go there so early?' Jagdeesh asked one morning.

'If I don't go there, he fools around instead of playing,' she lied. How did I get to be a woman who has to account for her every hour besides every rupee spent? Jagdeesh had never been such a domineering man. I let him rule me and now he knows no other way to treat me, Prabha Devi realized with a pang. There is a lesson here. Someday I will have to tell my daughter all about it. How women set the tone of a marriage.

'Daughter,' I'll have to say, 'show him you are incapable of doing anything beyond the periphery of your home and he will manage your life, from sending postal orders to balancing cheque books to booking railway tickets to managing household expenses. He will pet you and cosset you at first, for after all, you are appealing to the male in him to protect and safeguard. But it will be only a matter of days before he turns into a tyrant who will want to control your every thought.

'There is an alternative. You could choose to demonstrate how independent you are and show him how well you manage by yourself. Except that when you need a pair of arms around you, someone to hold you and cherish you, he might not be there because you have always let him know that you don't need him. Where is the middle path, the golden mean? Daughter, I wish I knew. I wish my mother had told me what was the right thing to do. Or, perhaps the truth is, she didn't know either.'

Prabha Devi stood by the swimming pool trying to sort the

chaos within her.

'Which one is yours?' the swimming coach floated towards her and asked with a sweep of his arm.

'None,' she smiled.

'So what are you doing here?' he prodded, not that he particularly cared. But it was a relief to talk to someone who wasn't snivelling or screaming for their mother—and was not fourteen years old. Besides, it broke the monotony of trying to teach children who hated water how to swim.

'Trying to learn to swim,' Prabha Devi said, not taking her eyes off the children who held the steel bar at the shallow end and kept kicking at the water furiously, desperately, trying to hold their breath, stay afloat, conquer their fear of water and not draw the attention of the coach to themselves, all at the same time.

'So, have you learned to swim yet?' the coach mocked a few days later.

'I will,' she said, quietly brushing aside his scorn with dignity.

Prabha Devi watched the children. She saw how they kicked the surface of the water raising glittering rainbows. How they stretched their arms. How they moved their arms. How their legs propelled them forward. And how they did all this with borrowed air held so desperately in lungs that strained to hold it in. Air that demanded to be let out. Prabha Devi took a deep breath and held on. One of these days, it would be time.

For a while Prabha Devi despaired. It seemed the time would never come. October spent itself out in storms. The monsoon descended on the city and wrung everything and everyone out into a state of tiredness. Then came the festivals, Dussera and Deepavali, for which Prabha Devi had much to organize. The hours of the days were dictated and monitored by Jagdeesh. There was the puja; the sweet boxes for employees, associates and clients to be ordered; fire crackers and new clothes to be shopped for; visits to various homes; playing hostess...Prabha Devi thought of the swimming pool longingly and forced herself to go on with her chores.

'What's wrong with you?' Jagdeesh demanded. 'Are you unwell? You don't seem very interested in anything.'

Prabha Devi shook her head mutely. 'Nothing is wrong. I'm just a little tired,' she said.

He gave her a piercing glance and went away to make a telephone call. Prabha Devi stared at his back, dejected.

For so many years now, this has been the tone of voice he uses when he talks to me. Halfway between a reprimand and a lesson...why does it rankle now when it never did before? Prabha Devi asked herself. Perhaps it is his disappointment speaking. For the woman I have become. A meek, mean spirited shadow of who I was. How could any man not be irritable when faced with the thought of spending a lifetime with such a woman? And yet, I do not know how to change; how to restore the balance of our relationship...It seems to me more and more that I know nothing.

A week after Deepavali, Prabha Devi decided that the day had arrived. She told Jagdeesh that she had enrolled in a baking class for three weeks.

'Why?' he asked curiously.

'Why not?' she retorted.

Jagdeesh looked at her in surprise. For a second, he thought he saw the woman she had once been. The spirited sensual creature who had whetted his senses with her dazzling smiles, mercurial disposition and exacting body. This Prabha Devi was the keeper of his home and the mother of his children. She listened. She obeyed. She lived on the outposts of his life. And frankly, he found himself getting a little irked by her complete lack of self-worth. What was this sudden fascination to learn to bake, to do something more with her time, he wondered.

Prabha Devi was oblivious to the gyrations of Jagdeesh's mind. All she could think of was the moment when she would feel the waters of the pool surround her.

Prabha Devi walked to the swimming pool with a hollow feeling in the pit of her stomach. Part fear, part excitement. With a little girlish giggle, she thought how it reminded her of her wedding night when she was led to the flower-bedecked bedroom. Jagdeesh had waited for her there. The pool waited for her here.

Prabha Devi stood in the changing room, uncertain. Should she keep her bra and panties on? Or should she strip completely before she pulled the swimming things on? In the end, she took off her underclothes, smeared herself with sunscreen lotion and put on the swimsuit-bicycling shorts combination. She wrapped a bath towel around her, put on the cap to keep her hair dry, left her stick-on bindi on her forehead and holding the float walked to the pool.

The pool attendant gave her a curious look. She hesitated. How could she take her towel off when he was around? 'What are you doing here gawking at the pool? Don't you have anything else to do?' she demanded in her most imperious manner.

'I'm on lifeguard duty, madam,' he stuttered.

There was nothing she could do but pretend that he wasn't there. She began to walk towards the pool.

'Excuse me, madam,' he mumbled, 'you have to take a shower before you enter the pool. It's the rule,' he said, pointing to a wall where the pool rules were clearly written in red paint. Dictates about long hair and swimming caps; showering; eatables and drinks; proper swimming attire and behaviour; diving and unaccompanied children below twelve; and the club authorities not being responsible for any accidents...

'Of course I was going to shower,' Prabha Devi said, anxiety adding a scythe-like edge to her voice. 'Do you think this is my first time at a swimming pool?' Prabha Devi walked to the open-air shower area at the side of the pool. She took a deep breath and removed the towel. The shower came on, spouting jets of piercingly cold water. It took her breath away, and made her forget her embarrassment at being near naked in front of a strange man.

She stood by the pool rim at the shallow end. There was a little metal ladder leading into the water. Which way now? Do I climb down with my back to the water? Or facing it? Everything I do now is at my own risk. I won't even have the club authorities to blame, Prabha Devi told herself as she climbed down the ladder.

The water was cold. It nibbled at her skin, raising her flesh into bumps and sending little electric shocks to her brain. Then she remembered the coach hollering at the children, 'Duck down, go on, hold your breath and go under water. You won't feel so cold any more...'

Prabha Devi did just that and the water gathered over her head. When she surfaced, spluttering and swallowing as the air rushed out of her mouth, she felt completely unprepared for what lay ahead. What am I going to do next?

Prabha Devi held the bar, put her face in the water and tried kicking. When it was time to leave, her legs felt like sacks of sand, heavy and rooted. Muscles she had never known she had announced their presence with little spasms of soreness. It was a struggle to climb up the ladder without falling back into the water.

For three days, she did nothing but kick the water into arcs of misty spray and fill the air with the flat thwack-thwack sound of limbs slapping water. When she tired, she ducked under water trying to keep her eyes open. The chlorine waters stung, causing her eyes to redden, but she would get used to it, she told herself as she held onto the bar and raised her back so that it seemed as if she was almost floating on her back.

On the fourth day, Prabha Devi discovered that she didn't need to cling to the bar. She held it with just the tips of her fingers, and she could still stay afloat, as long as she kept her head in the water and held her breath.

Fifth day. Prabha Devi decided it was time she weaned herself away from the steel bar. She rested a leg on the pool's sidewall, gathered as much air as she could in her lungs, and propelled herself forward, hanging onto the rubber ring the pool attendant had given her. She moved. She tried to let go of the rubber ring. She sank. For a second, panic swirled. I'm drowning, I'm dying, a voice shrieked in her head. Then she surfaced. Prabha Devi reached for the bobbing ring and went back to the steel bar. She wasn't ready yet, she decided.

Sixth day. Prabha Devi tried to explore the breadth of the pool at the shallow end. When she ran out of air, she sank. When she surfaced, she saw the swimming coach watching her with amusement. 'Throw that ring away,' he said.

'How can I stay afloat without it?' she asked.

'You are already doing that,' he said with a grin.

'Oh,' Prabha Devi said, pleased by his words. Then realization dawned. It was all very well for him to say so. What if she drowned? 'I could drown. With the ring, I have something to cling to,' she tried to explain.

The coach squatted by the side of the pool and asked her, 'How tall are you?'

'Five foot, two inches,' Prabha Devi said, wondering what that had to do with the rubber ring. In tennis, she had heard Vikram mention that the weight of the racquet depended on the weight of the player. Was there a similar equation she didn't know about in swimming?

'So what do you have to worry about?' the coach retorted. 'Look, you are in four feet of water. How can you drown? Even if you ran out of air and sank, your feet would touch the bottom instantly. And you'll surface,' he said, holding out his hand. 'Here, give me that useless thing.'

Prabha Devi gave him the ring wordlessly. What he said made perfect sense. She smiled. 'Thank you,' she said.

'I'll come by in a couple of days and see how you are doing,' he said on his way out.

For the rest of the hour, Prabha Devi tried to float. As long as she trapped air in her lungs, the water gave her right of way. When the air escaped, like irate prison guards, the water closed in on her. At the end of the hour, she had floated across the pool's breadth in three consecutive attempts.

On the seventh day, Prabha Devi rested. That night she felt a tiny fist of desire unfurl. A flowering of senses. A singing of nerve ends. A passion tinged with recklessness that made her press the line of her body against her husband's. Jagdeesh, half asleep, felt the warmth of her body against his. A sensuality ripe and about to explode. For so long, there had been none of that between them. When Jagdeesh wanted to, they coupled quickly and quietly. For him, a mere satiation of a bodily need. For her, a dutiful acceptance of her role in his life.

Jagdeesh stirred. A slow excitement crawled through him.

In his arms, she felt different. The slackness gone. A new tautness. A hint of muscle. Tensile sinews. Electric shocks.

'What have you been doing?' he asked, his hands seeking with a boyish fervour this almost strange body.

'Nothing. Just floating around,' she murmured truthfully, revelling in the awakening of what she had thought were forever entombed desires.

When had she last known such a plethora of sensations?

Skin against skin. Fingers. Mouth. The arc of eyelids. The curve of the ear. The bristles of his moustache. The coil of her hair. His breath hers.

Taut nipples drew patterns. A clenching within: not yet, not yet. Toes that explored. A tingling down the spine; now all over...The rustle of desire. Floods that raged. A rush of wetness. Bodies arched. Clung. Parted. Only to melt together again.

The roar in the eardrums as water gathered over the head suddenly. I'm drowning. I'm dying. When there was no more air to draw upon, cut through the waters to the surface and the feet touched ground.

Jagdeesh went to sleep with a smile. God was just. Life was good. And Prabha Devi made him feel like a boy of twenty-one.

But Prabha Devi lay awake. When would this body that had spun and whirled through corridors of pure feeling learn to stay afloat?

The next morning, Prabha Devi stood in the pool deep in thought. Last night had taught her many lessons. All of her married life, she had wondered what would happen if she let Jagdeesh know that she wanted to make love. Would he be repelled by the nakedness of her hunger? Would he turn away? Would he lose his respect for her?

But she had discovered that desire spawns desire; fulfilment begets fulfilment. A kiss for a kiss. A caress for a caress. What one gives comes back manifold. Ever since Pramod, ever since the souring of life, she had held back. Crippled by the fear of what would happen if things didn't work out the way she wanted them to. Prabha Devi looked at the stretch of water. She took a deep breath and pushed herself forward. Beneath her the floor tiles gleamed with dancing reflections. The water was like silk, curling around her with a quiet swish.

She felt the years slip away from her. This body that had been the cause of much unhappiness, first with its excessive demands for gratification and then with an abrupt deadening of nerve ends, now melted. She was the blue of the pool and the water was she.

Time ceased. A weightlessness. A haze of memories. A cloud of unconnected thoughts. Of being and not being. From the tips of her toes to the tips of her fingers, a straight line, a slow triumph. I am afloat. I am afloat. My body no longer matters. I have this. I have conquered fear.

When Prabha Devi's fingertips touched the other end of the pool wall, she straightened. And Prabha Devi knew that life would never be the same again. That nothing else that happened would ever measure up to that moment of supreme content when she realized that she had stayed afloat.

9

Akhila gazed at the landscape that whizzed past her. The lushness made her eyes smart. She had never seen so many shades of green. The train ran alongside paddy fields fringed with coconut palms. It was harvest time. Yellow stacks of paddy lay supine on the brown thirsty earth. Yellow and brown, green and gold...how restful the landscape seemed even though change was so much a part of it. Why is it only we humans who resist change? Why do we fight it? Why couldn't her family accept her decision?

✝

Some weeks ago Akhila was filling a raffle coupon in a supermarket and when she came to the box against which was written 'age', she wrote mechanically the number 45. All of a sudden, Akhila paused. She was forty-five years old and she had nothing to show for it. Not even memories.

Akhila looked around her at the other women shoppers, their baskets brimming like their lives. She glanced down at the basket she held. Its sparseness was pitiful. A face cream that promised to defy age; a shampoo that offered to put the bounce back in her lank hair, and a packet of instant starch. She could have bought any of these from the corner shop near the railway quarters but Akhila didn't like the thought of Padma standing beside her at the shop counter, unscrewing jar lids and sniffing at their contents. Nor did she want to be present when Padma announced to anyone who cared to listen: when I get to be in my forties, I intend to age gracefully. None of these creams and hair dyes for me. Let me tell you, nothing can match the glow of contentment on a woman's face.

An opinion that she was perfectly entitled to, but nevertheless it wounded Akhila's feelings as it was meant to. These days she thought two steps ahead of Padma to protect herself from hurt. But it wasn't fear that old age would increase her dependence on Padma and with it bring pain that prompted Akhila's decision to make a life for herself.

First of all, it was the realization that at forty-five, she was still living life from the sidelines. But mostly it was because of Karpagam.

Karpagam who squeezed herself into the aisle and back into Akhila's life with the ease of a veteran queue jumper. 'Akhilandeswari, is that you?' she shrieked, her breath fanning down the back of Akhila's neck.

A voice from the past. From a time when life had been a series of boxes drawn in the dust beneath a mango tree. All one had to do was hop, skip and jump to triumph.

The measure of the familiarity in that voice was born of a bonding sprung within the arc of a skipping rope. As it slid beneath their feet, swept the dust and swung into the air, binding them together by a single rhythm and an obsessive need to go on and on till they could jump no more.

A friendship that flourished while walking to school and back, sharing secrets and five-paise coconut toffee. A relationship that ran itself out when they left childhood behind and Karpagam became a wife and Akhila, the head of her family.

Akhila stiffened. No one had called her by her full name for almost twenty-five years now. She felt afraid. Her mouth dried up and her tongue felt like that of an old shoe. Unwieldy and brittle.

'Who? How?' Akhila stuttered.

'Have you forgotten me?' she cried jostling her arm. 'I'm Karpagam. Don't you remember me?'

Akhila took a deep breath and let the air cushion her nerve ends. 'This is a surprise. A real surprise!'

Karpagam gave Akhila an amazed look and put her basket down on the counter with a thud. 'It should be. I haven't seen you for more than twenty years. You look the same, though.'

'What is this? Is that all you are buying?' she asked, looking at Akhila's basket.

Akhila felt Karpagam's eyes sweep over her. What did she see?

In the mirror, a stranger accosted Akhila. A pale ghost of a former self. A woman with sallow cheeks and a droop to her mouth. Lines on her throat. Concentric circles on the trunk of a teak tree. Either way they determine age.

Akhila touched her hair. During the day she coiled her hair into a little bun and let it lie on the nape of her neck. Only in the night, only when she was alone did she let her hair flow down her back. Akhila pulled her hair to either side of her face and sometimes, perhaps it was a trick of the light or it was a flowering of a secret desire, but she saw Akhilandeswari. The girl who talked in soft rounded sounds. This stranger had a voice with the rasping hoarseness of responsibility.

When Akhila stepped two feet back, the stranger in the mirror disappeared. She knew this body: Akhilandeswari's body. Akhila wedged a pencil beneath the curve of her breast. It rolled off. Her stomach was flat and smooth. No silvery fish sailed across it. She slid her hands over her body.

Akhila paused. Who was this creature in whose thighs age crawled in green-blue bands? How could time have stilled and been laid to rest in a nest of blue veins on her calves? This was not her. The real her. Akhilandeswari.

In Karpagam's eyes, Akhila saw the stranger. A quiet creature with little life or spirit. Barren of all the marks that proclaimed she was a wife—no thali sparkling on her bosom, no kumkum bleeding in the parting of her hair, no glistening toe rings bonding her to connubial bliss. A colourless insignificant woman who had nothing better to do than drift aimlessly through the aisles of a supermarket pretending to shop for things she didn't need.

'Let's sit down somewhere,' Karpagam said, taking Akhila's arm and leading her to the supermarket café.

Akhila sat at a table and watched Karpagam as she piled the tray with jam rolls, a plate of samosas and two steaming cups of coffee. She radiated content. It was there in the roll of flesh around her midriff; in the hint of a double chin; in the padding of fat around her wrist. It was in the colours she wore: the chrome yellow of the blouse; the green and yellow Bengal cotton sari; the gold of her jewellery, the vibrant maroon of her kumkum. Her eyes sparkled. Her cheeks dimpled. Her hair was streaked with an occasional line of grey. Ripeness in all.

'I couldn't resist it,' she smiled, pointing with her chin to the loaded tray. 'I don't understand how people can ever go on a diet. My daughter is always on a diet. One week, she exists on juices—have you heard of anything more ludicrous than that? The next week, it is just raw chopped vegetables. All nonsense. If you ask me, you only live once. So you might as well live well.'

Akhila smiled uncertainly, wondering if there was a reproach hidden in there for her.

Karpagam bit into her samosa and brushed the crumbs off her chin. 'All of us admired the way you took charge of your family when your father died. My mother would often talk of you almost with awe and then bring up Jaya's name. Do you remember her?'

Akhila nodded, unable to speak.

'I wonder what's happened to Jaya. Where she is now and what happened to Sarasa Mami and the other children. When the head of a family dies, the family dies with him, my mother would say, unless there is a daughter like Akhila.'

Akhila smiled. She didn't know what else to do. She hadn't

thought of Jaya for a very long time now.

'So tell me, what have you been doing with yourself? I know that you left Ambattur after your mother died. Have you decided to live in Bangalore for good?' Karpagam asked.

'I haven't been doing anything. Just the usual. Office, home, office...Padma—you remember her, don't you, my younger sister—and her family live with me, so she takes care of the house.' Akhila dismissed questions for which she had no answers anyway.

Karpagam reached across the table and squeezed Akhila's hand. 'I thought you would have a life of your own by now. I can see that you don't. Doesn't your selfish family realize that you deserve some happiness of your own?'

The samosa lodged in Akhila's throat. 'What can they do? I'm past the age for all that.'

'Past the age for what?' she asked. Akhila saw Karpagam's eyes narrow. For a moment, she gazed at Akhila appraisingly. Then she asked softly, 'Define happiness for me. What will make you happy?'

Akhila drew patterns on the formica table-top with her forefinger. How would she define happiness? Would she even know what happiness was if it stared her in the face?

She thought of the New Year greeting cards that she and Katherine sent each other every year. 'Happiness is,' Akhila said, parroting the greeting card messages, 'being allowed to choose one's own life; to live it the way one wants. Happiness is knowing one is loved and having someone to love. Happiness is being able to hope for tomorrow.'

Karpagam sighed. 'Akhi,' she began, reverting to her childhood name for Akhila, 'are you happy?'

'I don't know.' For once, Akhila could answer truthfully.

'Why? Is it because you don't have a husband or children?'

'No, no,' Akhila whispered, wondering if any one in the café was eavesdropping. 'It isn't that.'

Sometimes Akhila thought what she hated the most was not having an identity of her own. She was always an extension of someone else's identity. Chandra's daughter; Narayan's Akka; Priya's aunt; Murthy's sister-in-law...Akhila wished for once someone would see her as a whole being.

But would Karpagam understand? Would she who wore marriage as if it were a Kancheepuram silk understand that what Akhila most desired in the world was to be her own person? In a place that was her own. To do as she pleased. To live as she chose with neither restraint nor fear of censure.

That while Akhila did ache to be with a man and yearned to allow her senses to explore and seek fulfilment, that while she wished to be loved by a man who would fill her silences and share all of himself with her, she didn't want a husband. Akhila didn't want to be a mere extension again.

Karpagam listened as Akhila tried to explain what she had never dared to voice even to herself.

'So why don't you live alone? Your sister is old enough to look after herself. And it isn't as if she doesn't have a husband and family. Akhi, you are educated. Employed. Get a life for yourself,' Karpagam said, pushing a hairpin into place with the same determined attention she was giving Akhila's life. 'And,' she added, 'stop looking around every few minutes. What are you afraid of—what the world will say? Akhi, ask your sister and family to leave your home. That's the first thing you need to do.'

Akhila looked at all the other people in the café. Cups of coffee being drunk, pastries being eaten; everyone was with someone.

'How can I live alone? How can any woman live alone?' she asked hopelessly.

'Look at me,' Karpagam's voice tore through the dense layers of self-pity. 'If I can live alone, why can't you?'

'But you are married. You don't live alone,' Akhila said in exasperation. How could Karpagam compare herself to her?

'I was married,' Karpagam said, meeting Akhila's gaze steadily. 'My husband died some years ago.'

'I'm sorry to hear that. But...' Akhila mumbled.

'I know what you are thinking. You are wondering how is it I still wear the kumkum and these colourful clothes? Would you rather that I dressed in white and went about looking like a corpse ready for the funeral pyre?'

'No, of course not,' Akhila murmured. 'But what does your family have to say about all this?'

Karpagam took a deep breath and said, 'I don't care what my family or anyone thinks. I am who I am. And I have as much right as anyone else to live as I choose. Tell me, didn't we as young girls wear colourful clothes and jewellery and a bottu? It isn't a privilege that marriage sanctions. The way I look at it, it is natural for a woman to want to be feminine. It has nothing to do with whether she is married or not and whether her husband is alive or dead. Who made these laws anyway? Some man who couldn't bear the thought that in spite of his death, his wife continued to be attractive to other men.'

The words cascaded out of her mouth with the ease of one who has mouthed them several times before. And Akhila realized with shame that while she had in the manner of a docile water-buffalo wallowed in a pond of self-pity, allowing parasites to feast on her, Karpagam had gone ahead and learnt to survive.

'I live alone. I have for many years now. My daughter who is just twenty-three does as well. We are strong, Akhi. We are if we want to be.'

'So what do you suggest I do?' Akhila asked.

'Whatever you think you want to. Live alone. Build a life for yourself where your needs come first. Tell your family to go to hell or wherever.' Karpagam smiled and scribbled her address on the back of the bill. 'Write to me. Let's stay in touch.'

Akhila put the piece of paper in her purse. Outside, she touched Karpagam's arm. 'Karpagam, are you real or are you some goddess who has come here to lead me out of this...' Akhila stopped, thinking of the dark and dismal hues of the world she had lived in for so long now.

'Don't be silly,' Karpagam laughed. And it was the memory

of that laugh, a cock-a-thumb-at-the-world laugh that became Akhila's totem for what she intended to do with her life.

✝

On Sundays Padma oiled her daughters' hair. She warmed sesame oil and rubbed it into their scalps till the hair glistened and lay heavily against the scalp. Then she washed their heads with soap nut powder. Padma should have been the older one and not I, Akhila thought.

A month had passed since she met Karpagam. A month of frenzied planning, frantic activity and furtive thoughts. A month in which she examined every single thought and her service files with close attention. A month in which Akhila took the many skeins of her life and began to braid them into a future. A month later, she was ready.

'Padma,' she said, watching Padma's fingers treat her daughter's scalp as if it were a ball of dough. Knead it till it becomes malleable. Knead it till you drive out every single thought of resistance. Knead it so that it does your bidding when the time comes. 'I'm thinking of buying a house.'

Padma looked up, interested. 'I have also been thinking about it for some time now. Soon these girls will be of marriageable age and how can we find them decent husbands if we don't even have a house of our own.'

'Padma,' Akhila said, trying to be as gentle as she could, 'I am buying a flat; a one-bedroom flat.'

'But how can we all fit in a flat that size? Can't you afford anything bigger?'

'Padma,' Akhila repeated her name and she could feel steel coat the words forming in her mouth. 'How much room does one person need?'

'What do you mean?' Suspicion rasped.

'I wish to be by myself. It is time I did this—lived alone. And it is time you did as well,' Akhila said, meeting her eyes. Their gaze locked and Akhila noted with a tremendous sense of satisfaction that it was Padma who faltered first.

'Are you feeling alright?' Padma asked, wiping the oil on her palms on to her feet. 'At your age, women go through a difficult time. It's something to do with hormones. I was reading about it in a magazine the other day. Menopause, it said, can play havoc with a woman's mind.'

'Shut up, Padma,' Akhila snapped. 'I'm sick and tired of your know-it-all tone of voice when you talk to me. If you want the truth, I've had enough of you. The noise your children fill my home with. The way your husband and you have been sponging off me for years.'

Akhila stopped when she saw the look of horror on Padma's face. And then she wished she hadn't, for the words began to spill out of Padma's mouth. Words with forked tongues spewing venom.

'All these years that I cooked and cleaned for you…you repay me by telling me that you are sick and tired of us. You are a jealous old woman. That's what you are. Full of envy and spite because I have a husband and children and you have nothing.'

'All the more reason why you and I should go our separate ways,' Akhila retorted icily.

'Do you think the brothers will consent to this? Do you think they'll let you live alone?' Padma asked, smug in the knowledge that Narayan and Narsi would think the same way she did.

'For heaven's sake, I don't need anyone's consent. Look at me, I'm forty-five years old. And older than all of you. I will do exactly as I please and I don't give a damn about what you or anyone else thinks…'

'That's what you think. They are the men of the family,' Padma's voice mocked.

Why am I standing here listening to her? Akhila asked herself. She began to walk away. She felt calm and even more certain about what she intended to do.

For the next few days, an uneasy quiet prevailed. The children were admonished loudly and often in Akhila's presence. 'Priya,' Padma would hiss, 'do you have to recite that poem aloud to memorize it? Shut the book and set it aside. After all, what is the worst that can happen... you might just fail in the monthly test. But I don't want you disturbing Akka.'

'Madhavi,' she would snarl, 'why do you have to slam down that plate? Don't you know the noise we make irritates Akka?'

Food was left in covered dishes for Akhila on the dining table. The clothes that she hung out to dry were stacked in neatly ironed piles on her bed. Padma was punishing her with her silence. And making sure at the same time that she understood exactly how well she ran the household for Akhila. And how without her, there would be chaos and confusion. All it did was make Akhila angry. How dare Padma subject her to her silences and reproach, her palpable anger and bitterness, and that too in a house Akhila paid the rent for?

Why does she grudge me my freedom? Akhila wondered again and again.

'Why have you come to this decision, Akka?' Narayan's question was pitched in his usual low tones. Love for this younger brother washed over Akhila. Of the lot, he alone was non-judgemental and unconditional in his affection. The others—Narsi and Padma—had been impetuous children, untouched by the tragedy in their lives, and they had grown up to become impetuous adults. Self-centred and definite that the world existed only to provide for them.

They had each finished their individual tirades.

Narsi—It's improper for a woman to live alone. What will society say? That your family has abandoned you. Besides, there will be a whole lot of questions that will pop up about your reputation. You know how people put two and two together and come up with six. Nalini's family will be scandalized if they hear about this. Have you thought of how embarrassing my position will be?

Padma—Why do you have to live alone? Haven't I taken care of your house for you? Apart from everything that Narsi Anna has said, have you thought of the expense? I have two girls and my husband doesn't have a very well paying job. I was counting on your help to get my girls married and settled in their lives.'

'You heard them, didn't you, Narayan?' Akhila sheathed her voice with control; with a calmness she didn't feel. 'For twenty-six years, I gave all of myself to this family. I asked for nothing in return. And now when I wish to make a life of my own, do any one of you come forward and say—It's time you did this, Akka. You deserve to have a life of your own. Instead you worry about what it will do to your individual lives.

'Now tell me Narayan, why shouldn't I live alone? I'm of able body and mind. I can look after myself. I earn reasonably well.' Akhila paused when her voice choked with tears, and began again.

'Has any one of you ever asked me what my desires were or what my dreams are? Did any one of you ever think of me as a woman? Someone who has needs and longings just like you do?'

'So, that's what it is!' Padma broke in. 'She's having a love affair. And she doesn't want us to find out. That's why she wants to go away by herself. Who is he? And how did you find him?'

Akhila reached out and did what she had wanted to for a very long time. She slapped Padma across her mouth. A tight hard slap that echoed all the contempt and resentment she carried in her.

There was silence. A hard silence that reverberated with the resonance of that slap.

'I don't have to explain my actions to any one of you. I don't owe you anything. I hope I have made myself clear to you.'

'You don't owe us anything. Instead we owe you our lives,' Narayan said, seeking to soothe, console and heal the bruises that festered. 'Which is why I'm afraid for you. How will you cope? This is not a reflection on who you are. How can any woman cope alone?'

His concern touched Akhila but she had her answers ready. 'I know I can. I did once before when you were children. Now I can for me, for Akhilandeswari. Nobody's daughter. Nobody's sister. Nobody's wife. Nobody's mother.'

'Akka, please listen to me,' he cajoled. The others had already turned their heads away. They didn't care any more now that they knew her mind was made up.

'Akka, please talk to a few others and you'll hear for yourself how difficult it is for a woman to live alone,' he held her hand between his and beseeched.

Akhila saw the fear in his eyes. She saw how scared he was for her. She knew he thought that she would fall easy prey to the first man who came bearing false hopes and empty promises. In his mind, her future would be striated with disappointment. Perhaps debasement and desolation. She felt a faint twinge of fear: Am I being stubborn? Am I being unwise?

'Fine, I will do as you say and talk to a few people. And only then will I make up my mind.'

One by one, they left the room convinced that she would see reason. Any woman she talked to would tell her the universal truth that everyone but she seemed to know—how utterly awful it was for a woman to be by herself. She would revert to being their gentle, timid elder sister and all this could be forgotten as a time when Akka went temporarily and inexplicably insane.

Only the laugh remained with her. Karpagam's cock-a-thumb-at-the-world laugh.

✝

Opposite Akhila sat the last of the passengers who had boarded the train with her the previous night. All the others had got off. One by one, bidding her farewell, offering her advice.

Janaki at Ernakulam. 'Whatever you do, think well and do it. And once you have, don't think of the past and yearn for it,' she said, patting Akhila's head.

Prabha Devi had scribbled her telephone number on a piece of paper and taken down Akhila's address. 'Let's meet one of these days. After all, we stay in the same city. So don't forget to stay in touch.' Even the girl Sheela had smiled her goodbye and said, 'Thank you for listening to me!'

Now there was only this woman. The sixth passenger. Akhila wondered who she was. She watched her pull out a magazine from her bag and read it. It was a Tamil magazine. Akhila went back to looking out of the window.

The train was crowded. Even the reservation compartments were not spared. People banged on the doors if they were locked from the inside or pushed their way in when someone opened the door to step out. Daytime passengers filled the aisles and insisted that three-seaters could hold four. Through the packed compartment, beggars and vendors wove their way with practised ease. Orange peel, biscuit wrappers and groundnut shells littered the floors. When the train stopped and the breeze ceased, the faint stench of urine wafted through the compartment from the toilets. Akhila heaved a sigh of relief. The coupé was full but at least it was clean. An oasis of calm.

Akhila opened the packet of cashewnuts she had bought at Kottayam station. She felt their sweetish meatiness flood her mouth. I am not the Akhila who boarded this train last night, she thought. The other Akhila would have settled for peanuts. Cashewnuts suggested an excess, a grander scheme of things which she wouldn't dare tempt herself with. But this Akhila would. She could feel a slow loosening within; a certain feeling that she was right; a heady anticipation that was the aftermath of Prabha Devi's revelation. Perhaps more than any of the other women, Prabha Devi was the closest to her in age and manner, too. So if Prabha Devi could triumph over her innate timidity and rise above traditions to float, she could do the same, Akhila thought. I too must learn to move on with the tide of life rather than be cast on its banks.

Some time later, Akhila turned from the window and caught the woman's eye. Her magazine lay on her lap. Akhila smiled. 'Where are you going?' she asked in Tamil.

'Nagercoil,' the woman said.

'I'm going to Kanyakumari,' Akhila said, even though the

woman hadn't asked. 'Do your parents live in Nagercoil?' she asked.

The woman shook her head. 'I work for a foreigner. An Englishwoman who is a doctor. She has been posted to Nagercoil and I'm going ahead to set up the house before she arrives. The household articles are already on their way. The doctor and my son are driving down and will start tomorrow morning.'

'How old is your son?'

'Thirteen years,' the woman said.

'What about your husband? What does he do?' Akhila asked.

The woman's face stilled for a moment. 'You are very curious,' she said.

Akhila flushed. The other women had been so forthcoming with their lives that she had imagined everyone would be the same.

'I'm sorry,' the woman said. 'That was rude of me. But last night, all of you shut me out from your conversation simply because you thought I didn't belong. You looked at my clothes, my face, and decided that I was not your kind.'

Akhila flushed. 'I'm sorry. We didn't mean to...' she began.

The woman gazed at her unflinchingly. 'Don't apologize. You were right to think that I am not your kind. It is true. I don't belong with you. Not because I am poor or uneducated. But because you have all led such sheltered lives, yes, even you. I heard each one of them tell you the story of their lives and I thought, these women are making such a fuss about little things. What would they ever do if real tragedy confronted them? What do they know of life and the toll it takes? What do they know of how cruel the world can be to women?'

Akhila stared at the stranger. Who was this woman from whom anger poured forth like a stream of lava?

The sixth passenger rolled her magazine and said, 'I'm not telling you that women are weak. Women are strong. Women can do everything as well as men. Women can do much more.

But a woman has to seek that vein of strength in herself. It does not show itself naturally.'

10

Sister to the Real Thing

My name is Marikolanthu. I am thirty-one years old. I was born in a little village called Palur near Kancheepuram. I have a son and no husband. My parents have been dead a long time and I have severed all ties with my brothers. I work as a helper in a mission hospital.

My father was a farmer. He was an only child, so when my grandfather died, he inherited both the land and the house. My mother belonged to another village; she was an orphan and was brought up by her aunt. We didn't have any relatives or much money, but we were happy. My two brothers, Easwaran and Sivakumar, and I. But a few days after my ninth birthday my father died. He had a disease that even the doctors at Vellore Hospital couldn't cure.

There was no one we could turn to for help and so Amma turned her face to the lime-washed walls of the Chettiar Kottai and pleaded. The house was enormous, with countless rooms and annexes. It stood three floors high and from the outside it seemed impregnable. Though its real name was Raj Vilas, everyone in the village and the nearby villages referred to it as the Chettiar Kottai—the Chettiar Fort.

The Chettiar was a rich man; they are still the richest family in the district. The Chettiar made his fortune from silkworms. He bred them, stuffing them with mulberry leaves till they grew so fat that they burst out of their skins. To hide their shame the poor naked worms spun silk and wrapped it around themselves. But the Chettiar wouldn't let them be even then. He boiled them and stripped their silk off them. Skeins of silk, ounces of silk. None of us in the village saw any of it for the Chettiar's silkworm farm was somewhere else, but the ones who had seen it told us all about it.

I often thought of the silkworms, though, and felt sorry for them. 'You are lucky to be you,' I told every earthworm that wriggled on my palm.

I was still a child then. I talked to worms, trees and rocks. I believed the schoolmaster when he drew a circle on the blackboard and said, 'This is the world. Half of it is lit by the sun and the other half remains in darkness. It is the same with life. There is good and bad and it's our duty to remain in the light, be good.'

I nodded my head as did all the others and resolved to never step into the dark. Like I said, I was still a child then.

The Chettiar owned many looms on which men wove silk saris with real gold zari and these were sold in shops in Madras, Coimbatore, Salem, Madurai and in far-away cities like Delhi.

Our house was small; one among a line of houses that flanked either side of the temple street. Two streets away was the mango orchard and beyond it the Chettiar Kottai. My mother's culinary skills were well known in the village and on special occasions she was often called in to help at the Chettiar Kottai. But now this became our sole means of livelihood.

Every morning, she left home by seven and returned only after six in the evening. So I did most of the chores. I didn't mind that at all; it was like playing house.

I liked drawing water from the village well and carrying it home in the big brass pots balanced on the curve of my hip. I swept and mopped the floors and washed the dirty dishes. When we came home from school, my brothers and I would go around the village picking pats of cow-dung. I liked making balls of them and flattening them with my palms. I slapped rows and rows of them onto the back walls of our house.

Greenish-black circles like a packet of stick-on bottus that turned grey-green when they were dry. As long as we had them drying on our walls, the fire beneath the cooking pots would never cease to burn.

Amma sometimes held me to her bosom and wept, 'What have I reduced my child to? I have stolen her childhood from her.'

But I didn't understand what she was fussing about. Why did she grieve for what I delighted in?

...When Brahma writes our destiny, they say, he allots a specific number of years to each one of us to experience all aspects of living. My time as housewife was spent long before I became an adult. In my mother's house, I did all that a woman with her own house does. Perhaps that was the way it was meant to be. Even after I left the house, each time I returned, I took over its running until my mother died and my brothers staked their claim and I had no house to call my own...But here I am telling you of things that came much later. Before all that was the time when I went to work at the Chettiar Kottai...

My father the farmer didn't approve of the Chettiar. 'What a way to make money!' he often said as he lit a beedi and inhaled the smoke.

'To kill God's creatures day after day and profit from their death. I'm glad I'm a farmer. The only creatures that die because of me are the ones that my plough cuts into and even those I kill unknowingly.'

The farmland was a long way from the village, but he never complained or tired of working on it. In the village, the people spoke of my father with an amazement that is usually reserved for the foolhardy. 'Only Shanmugam would expend so much energy on that piece of rock.'

The rest of them worked for the Chettiar one way or the other. The Chettiar was God, they said, generous and benevolent. But to my father, he was a slave king. 'And I have no wish to be one of his grateful slaves,' he told Amma when she complained that the fields yielded just about enough to make ends meet.

My father had a small piece of land on which he grew various crops by rotation. Groundnuts, chillies and rice once a year. But one field was always reserved for the kanakambaram flower. And this, my mother and I tended. In the light of the dawn, we were greeted by a riot of blooms that seemed to have gathered into their petals the hues of the rising sun. Before the sun sucked the moisture away and reduced the flowers to pale replicas of themselves, we plucked them. For every two flowers we picked, we left the third on the plant for seed. We kept some of the flowers for ourselves and sold the rest to the flower-seller by the temple.

Did my father, I wondered, grow kanakambaram because that was Amma's name? 'I wish you had called me Roja or Chempakam,' I cried one day, vexed by the thought that a whole field of delicate orange blooms paid homage to my mother day after day while there was nothing for me.

'Then I would have had a field of roses like Amma has a field of flowers. Marikolanthu? What's a marikolanthu except a spike of green leaves?'

My father laughed aloud and drew me to his knee. 'You silly girl,' he cajoled. 'What is a marikolanthu, you ask me? Haven't you seen how a few marikolanthu leaves are always woven into kanakambaram garlands? Without the fragrance of the marikolanthu, the kanakambaram is a dead flower. But if it makes you happy, next season we'll plant a patch of marikolanthu.'

Father worked the rock, making it green and fragrant, till the disease planted its roots in his body. He clung to his land as long as he could, but the bills for medicines and X-rays, specialists and special foods, grew longer. So he sold the land to the Chettiar and then crumpled up and died.

Two years later, my mother decided that she needed me in the Chettiar household. Besides, I would have to go to the town if I wished to study any further. The village school had classes only till the fifth standard.

'We'll send your brothers to the town school when the time comes but we can't afford it on my salary alone,' Amma said. 'You do understand, don't you, that it would be impossible for me to send you to the school by bus everyday. It's not just the money but how can I send a young girl by herself...there is too much at risk.'

I didn't understand what was at risk. But I nodded anyway. In the black and white films that I saw in the village cinema tent, good girls always listened to their mothers. My favourite heroines did—Savitri and B. Saroja Devi, Vijayakumari and even Jayalalitha.

'As you wish, Amma. It's my duty to do everything for you and my brothers,' I said, parroting the film heroines and enjoying the sensation of being able to mouth a film dialogue.

'The Chettiar is a good man,' Amma often said. But I could only think of how he boiled worms to rob them of their clothes.

'Don't be silly,' Amma scolded when I pulled back at the gate of the Chettiar Kottai. 'Your father liked to exaggerate.'

The Chettiar Kottai was huge. It had many rooms and many things I had never seen before except in films. A fridge that hummed as though a swarm of bees was trapped in it; ceiling fans that whirled round and round; chairs that looked like thrones and beds that seemed to be stuffed with all the flowers in the world.

On my first day, I realized why my mother had begun to hate the smell of cooking. All she did in that house was cook. She cooked breakfast, lunch and dinner for twelve people everyday. And extra for guests who turned up for just about every meal. 'Let me keep her with me today so that she gets used to the routine of this household and tomorrow she can begin her duties,' Amma said, washing her hands before cooking the first meal of the day. By the time breakfast was finished, it would be time to begin lunch.

'If it was anyone else but your mother, they would have left

long ago,' Amma's helper, another widow, grumbled. 'Even if
they see the milk begin to boil over, they won't come and take it
off the stove. Your mother or I have to rush to do it.'

'They' figured a great deal in Rukmini Akka's conversation.

'Do you think they gave us this job because they felt sorry for
us? They think because we are widows, we know well enough
not to pander to our taste buds. No chillies, no tamarind, no
spices...our nerve ends, they think, are as dead as our husbands.
So we won't taste their food or hunger for it, and will be
content with a bowl of gruel and a pinch of salt.'

'Ssh,' Amma hissed. But Rukmini Akka had only just begun
on her list of grievances that grew by the day. As if to make up
for it, Amma never complained.

I watched my mother chop and sliver, sauté and fry, grind
and pound...I saw how she went about her chores expending
not even an iota of feeling. What did these wondrous foods my
mother created taste of? Tears and bitterness; rage at an unfair
destiny and fear?

But I liked my job. I liked the baby Prabhu-papa, and I liked
Sujata Akka. Sometimes when I couldn't stop talking about
Sujata Akka, Amma would snap, 'You give your heart too
easily, child. They'll break it into a thousand pieces and leave it
on the ground for others to trample into the dust.'

'Is the heart a glass bangle?' I giggled, amused by my own
sauciness. B. Saroja Devi would have been proud of me.
Easwaran and Sivakumar giggled too.

My mother sighed.

But from that day on, the boys greeted me every evening
with, 'So how's the glass bangle? Broken or intact?'

And we'd giggle some more.

...But you know what, the heart is a glass bangle. One careless
moment and it's shattered...we know that, don't we? And yet we
continue to wear glass bangles. Each time they break, we buy
new ones hoping that these will last longer than the others did.

How silly we women are. We should wear bangles made of

granite and turn our hearts into the same. But they wouldn't catch the light so prettily or sing so gaily...

Sujata Akka made me her slave with her cast-off glass bangles. She wore them for a few days and then either tired of them or broke so many that she had to buy a dozen new bangles. But to me they were precious possessions—red, blue and green, with purple flecks and silver dust.

'Don't you feel bad when you break a bangle?' I asked Sujata Akka as I gathered the shards of one to take home. My brothers and I had created a game we could play with them.

'Of course not. It's only a glass bangle. I can always buy more,' she said, opening her bangle-box to take out a new set of bangles.

No one grudged Sujata Akka anything. Whether it was her fondness for glass bangles or her greed for special Mysorepak, so rich with ghee that it dissolved as soon as you put it into your mouth. Sujata Akka often gave me a piece and though I knew I should take it home so that my brothers could taste it, I never did.

The Chettiar had said that Sujata Akka's every whim and desire was to be fulfilled. She was special. She was a city girl; she'd come from Coimbatore and she had even gone to college for two years. And Sujata Akka had given birth to a son. Next to the Chettiar, Sujata Akka was the most important person in that house.

The Chettiar had three sons. Rajendran Anna who looked after the silk looms. His wife Rani Akka was a timid woman made even more timid by the fact that she had failed to bear sons. She was the Chettiar's niece and came from a rather impoverished family. How could she even consider competing against Sujata Akka? So she let Sujata Akka reign, content to remain in the shadows on the premise that out of sight was out of scorn.

Sridhar Anna was the Chettiar's second son and his favourite. It was he who had added to the Chettiar's extensive fortunes by bringing orders from far-flung places. So when the Chettiar chose a bride for Sridhar Anna, he made sure the girl would bring with her more than a fat dowry. She had to be beautiful and educated and from a family that had a predilection for bearing sons. Sridhar Anna was rewarded with Sujata Akka.

Then there was Ranganathan Anna who was studying to be a doctor in Vellore.

There was one more person. Chettiar Amma. She lived by herself on the top floor of the west wing and was never seen outside.

'After the last son was born, something went wrong with her. She screamed each time she saw the Chettiar and refused to feed the baby. A wet nurse was brought in and she fed the baby and looked after Chettiar Amma. That is who Vadivu is. She is not a member of this family and yet the Chettiar treats her like one for after all, she takes good care of Chettiar Amma. Only she can control Chettiar Amma when the demons enter her and take over,' Rukmini Akka told my mother.

'On full moon nights, Vadivu closes the doors and windows of the west wing and no one is allowed in. Chettiar Amma, they say, scratches the walls till they shriek and then she howls and tears her clothes off...thud, thud, thud, you can hear her feet stamp the floor as she paces up and down the room as far as the iron bracelet and chain attached to her ankle will let her go,' Rukmini Akka shuddered.

'What about the others? Are they also scared of Chettiar Amma?' Amma asked.

'The Chettiar and his sons visit her once in a while. Rani Akka used to, until one day when she took her baby daughter there, the Chettiar Amma grabbed the baby from her arms and almost threw it down from the top floor. After that, Rani Akka's visits ceased,' Rukmini Akka replied.

At first, Sujata Akka was sorry for Chettiar Amma. She sent her little treats to eat and visited her often. But once she had her baby, all she could think of was what Chettiar Amma had almost done with Rani Akka's little girl and she began to fear her. So she told the Chettiar that she needed someone to watch over the baby while she was busy. And that was how I came to be there.

'Though busy doing what, I'd like to know,' Rukmini Akka had said on my first day there. 'She,' she said pointing to my mother with her chin, 'does all the cooking and I do the rest of the work. There are others who sweep and mop, wash the clothes and do all the other chores. But the Chettiar didn't realize that. Or even if he did, he said: "Yes, yes, find a young girl. Ask Kanakambaram, she has a young daughter."'

'He was on his way to that Seethalakshmi's house and was in a great hurry. So that's how your name came up,' Rukmini Akka told me a little later as she and I cleaned the rice.

'Who is Seethalakshmi?' I asked.

'A relative,' my mother hastened to say.

'The Chettiar's concubine,' Rukmini Akka corrected. I looked from Amma's face to Rukmini Akka.

'Don't fill the girl's head with nonsense,' my mother said, chopping the brinjals with extra vigour, letting her anger show for once.

Rukmini Akka popped a rice grain into her mouth and said, 'She's not a baby. She's bound to find out sooner or later.'

The Chettiar has a concubine. Some say it's because of her that Chettiar Amma went insane. Others say that it was because she went mad that the Chettiar began to seek consolation in Seethalakshmi's arms.

'If a man's appetite is not fed at home, he'll find another place where it will be,' Rukmini Akka began, but I was no longer listening.

I had heard a baby wail and I went looking for it.

The first time I saw Sujata Akka, I lost my heart to her. Sujata Akka was fairer than anyone I had ever seen. She had long black hair and she wore an orange and green sari. Her blouse had sleeves that ended halfway down her upper arms. A diamond nose-stud sparkled and on her wrists were gold and green glass bangles. There were flowers in her hair and talcum powder on her face. And she wore spectacles. She looked like a film star and all I wanted to do was worship her.

Sujata Akka was sitting on the bed feeding the baby. I stood in the doorway, too scared to go in until invited to do so.

'Come here,' Sujata Akka said. 'Aren't you Kanakambaram Amma's daughter?'

I smiled.

She eased the baby's mouth off the nipple and gave him to me. 'Here, you hold him. He's full, so don't rock him. Just pat his back gently till he burps.'

I did as she asked me to and when the baby burped and a mouthful of milk dribbled down my back, I felt a great love swamp me—for the baby, for Sujata Akka, for everyone in the Chettiar household including Chettiar Amma in the west wing.

...Yet when my son was born, all I felt was revulsion for the child. My mother would bring him to me and ask me to let him feed at my breast, and a tremendous loathing would fill me. I would thrust him away screaming, 'Take him away. I don't want him near me.'

My mother would heat cow's milk, dilute it with water and feed this to my son who drank it greedily. Even then he was a quiet child who demanded nothing.

I have been a bad mother. That much I know. I spent all my maternal love on Sujata Akka's baby and had none left for my own. Perhaps that too was Brahma's doing.

But I am digressing. Where was I? The Chettiar household...

For the next three years my world revolved around Sujata Akka and Prabhu-papa. Nothing was more important than them.

When Prabhu-papa turned on his stomach for the first time, I rushed to the kitchen for a coconut and a brand new moram, and laid the baby on it. I broke the coconut on a doorstep and offered a prayer to Bhoomidevi, 'Amma, goddess of the earth, I entrust this baby to you. Forgive him for wanting to tread on you. Don't punish him with bruises and broken bones. When he misses his footing, take him into your arms that are as soft as flowers and break the fall with your blessings.'

Sujata Akka watched, amusement crinkling her eyes. 'You are a strange girl. Who taught you all this?'

I tugged at a strand of hair behind my ear and said, 'When Easwaran turned on his stomach, I watched Amma do this and when it was Sivakumar's turn, Amma let me perform the puja.'

Sujata Akka patted my cheek and gave me a dozen of her new glass bangles. Purple with silver and blue flecks. I ran into the kitchen to show my mother my new treasure. Amma looked at it and said, 'Keep them away carefully. You can wear them for Deepavali.'

Rukmini Akka snorted, 'Glass bangles! How mean of her. It isn't as if she can't afford anything better. A blouse piece! Or some money. That's what she should have given you. Glass bangles, I tell you...'

'Rukmini Akka,' my mother interrupted in a worried voice, afraid that the tones of rebellion and scorn would seep beyond the kitchen walls. 'Hush.'

'Listen, Marikolanthu,' Amma said, turning to me and wiping her hands with the end of her sari pallu, 'we shouldn't expect anything from anyone. That way there will be no disappointment.'

'You are filling the girl's head with nonsense.' Rukmini Akka made a face. 'What do you want her to become? A silkworm? To be made use of through life and death?'

I giggled at the thought, but Amma's words had found a firm niche in my mind.

When Prabhu-papa took his first step, I did what I had to do, expecting nothing in return.

'Can I have a coconut with its beard intact,' I asked Rukmini Akka. She opened her mouth to spew scorn, when she spotted Sujata Akka by the kitchen door.

'Here, here,' she gushed as she rummaged among the

coconuts placed in the corner. 'Will this do? Isn't it much too small?'

I took an enormous coconut and went with it to the main door of the house. When I shook the coconut, I could hear the water slapping against the cool white flesh. My mouth watered.

Outside the gate, I saw a little boy playing with a stick. 'Here Pichu,' I called out to him, 'go fetch a few of your friends. I'm going to break a coconut and you can take the pieces.'

When the boys had gathered, I asked Sujata Akka to help Prabhu-papa take his first step over the threshold.

'Vinayaka, Vigneshwara, Ganesha, Ganapati,' I prayed, repeating all the names of Pulayar who alone can remove all the obstacles in one's path. 'Let his every step be an easy one. Let his every step lead him to happiness.'

I circled the coconut three times around Prabhu-papa's face to remove the evil eye and hurled it onto the rock by the side of the dust road.

The coconut smashed into many pieces and the boys fell on it, fighting for the larger share.

'You should have kept the coconut for yourself,' Sujata Akka said, gesturing to me to carry Prabhu-papa in.

'How could I? The evil eye would have settled within my body then,' I said, wondering how someone as educated as Sujata Akka could be so ignorant.

Later she gave me a crisp ten-rupee note. 'Keep this,' she said, pressing the money into my palm. 'To spend as you please.'

'What do you have to say now?' I taunted Rukmini Akka.

But Rukmini Akka simply made another face. 'Ten rupees? What is ten rupees to her? Now if she'd given you fifteen or twenty rupees, that would have meant something!'

But Amma had already snapped the note from between my fingers. 'You'll lose it. This will come in useful at the end of the month.'

I stared at my mother. That was my money, I wanted to say. She gave it to me to spend as I please. But I didn't say anything and walked away holding back the tears. I wouldn't expect anything from anyone, not even from my mother, I told myself. But if some one ever wanted to give me a reward, I would say—buy me something I want, but no money please. That way there would be no disappointments.

Sujata Akka understood. So for Deepavali, she gave me a rolled gold chain with a blue stone pendant. For Pongal, she gave me a new cotton pavadai. I wore the pavadai and the chain and went to show them off to Sujata Akka.

'Look at me, Akka.' I turned on my heel and almost tripped. The skirt was too long.

'Very pretty, but you need to raise the hem.'

I said nothing, too ashamed to admit that I didn't know how to sew. Sujata Akka sighed and rummaged in the chest-of-drawers on which a round mirror rested. Sujata Akka's talcum powder tin, the powder puff box, snow bottle and kumkum, comb and hair pins, spectacles and bangle-box were all kept on top of the chest and everyday it was my job to carefully dust them.

'Watch me as I pass the thread through the needle's eye and then knot it at the end,' Sujata Akka murmured, snapping the thread with her teeth. She made me sit on the floor and raising the hem just a little bit, she showed me how to fold it in and make tiny stitches.

'Now what do I do?' I asked when the hem was raised in the front.

'Use your brains and turn your skirt around.'

When the pavadai was two inches above my ankles, Sujata Akka said, 'That's better. All you need now is a golasu and you'll be the prettiest girl in the village.' And she drew out a pair of silver anklets.

I recognized them. They were her old ones and a few of the silver beads were missing. But what did it matter? They were the most beautiful anklets I had seen and they were mine. I put them on and took a step. The tinkly notes filled the room...

I ran to the kitchen, the silver bells echoing my steps, the red pavadai with white flowers swirling around my legs, the blue stone in the pendant shooting arcs of light.

'Amma, see what Akka gave me,' I said, doing a little dance so that the anklets leapt and sang their resonant song.

Rukmini Akka stared. 'Kanakambaram Amma, she's growing up. Has she...?' she stopped abruptly, catching my eye, but my mother obviously knew what she was talking about.

'Not yet.'

I couldn't understand what they were talking about then. But a few months later I did.

One day I was simply Marikolanthu—wearing the fragrance of naïvete with a single-minded joy. And then came womanhood...

I was sitting on the floor one evening with a heap of jasmine buds. Sujata Akka didn't know how to string flowers using a long piece of plantain fibre. Instead she used a needle and thread to string the flowers as if they were beads. But plantain fibre is the best; the flowers don't die that quickly and it doesn't snag the hair like a regular thread. I tried to teach Sujata Akka the right way to do it; how to thread the fibre around two fingers, place the stalk of one bud—to put more than one bud at a time would cause the flowers to decay faster—and briskly knot it. But she just couldn't do it right. The knots were loose and the flowers would slip out. So every evening, I wove a jasmine garland for her to wear in her hair.

But that evening, I felt a pain shoot through my middle. For a couple of days, I had felt some discomfort in my tummy and Amma had told me to crush ginger and salt and chew on it. The pain came in spasms, unfurled and clenched in turns. My legs began to feel weak and my lower back began to hurt.

'What's wrong?' Sujata Akka asked.

'Nothing,' I said standing up. Something trickled down my leg. Had I been holding my pee in too long? It had happened to me a couple of times before.

'Stay here,' Sujata Akka said. She returned with my mother and Rukmini Akka. The women stood around, smiling and sighing and smiling again.

'You're a woman now. No more running around like a little girl,' Rukmini Akka said.

'You'll have to wear a davani to hide your bosom,' Sujata Akka offered as consolation.

'Why?' There were a hundred other questions that rattled in my head but all I could ask was why.

'Because you are a woman and a good woman is one who safeguards her virtue.' Sujata Akka mouthed words I had heard so many times in the films. Virtue. Modesty. Words that slithered and crept through my nerves as the redness oozed between my legs.

During the course of the next few days, I learnt that my life had changed forever. I was not to hug my brothers or cuddle up to them when we slept; I was not to light the lamp, or touch the pickle jars or the curry leaf plant in the courtyard or the stove, or even enter the kitchen on the days the blood came calling; I was to always cover my bosom with the davani; I was to wash my hair every Friday and smear my face with green turmeric paste to prevent pimples and any ungainly hair from growing; I was to avoid being in the company of men—young and old alike—as men couldn't be trusted; I was to never sit with my legs wide open or fill my lungs with air—the bodice my mother had the tailor stitch constricted my chest so tightly that it hurt me to take a deep breath. I was a woman and nothing was the same again.

...But why am I telling you all this? You are a woman and it must have been the same for you. Except that I had Sujata Akka ...

She gave me her old cotton drawers; she was too fat to fit into them but they were as good as new. She'd had them specially made for her wedding trousseau, with lace edging. She gave me her frayed brassieres so that I didn't have to wear the hated bodice that squashed my breasts and ate up my breath. I began to breathe again.

She let me forget this business of being a woman and if the

davani slipped from my shoulders, she didn't hiss angrily at my brazen manner as my mother did. She didn't moan about finding me a dowry or plague me to walk with my head bent like all modest women did. She saw me as Marikolanthu—a person, neither girl nor woman.

One day Sujata Akka saw that the hems of my skirts had to be let down and that my breasts filled her cast-off bras. She caught her younger brother-in-law stripping me with his eyes and saw how her husband looked up from his files each time I walked past. And Sujata Akka could no longer accept that I was just Marikolanthu. Suddenly I had become a woman to her as well.

Sujata Akka's aunt lived in Vellore. She had a tenant—two in fact. Two lady doctors from across the seas. And they were looking for a young girl to be their housemaid.

Sujata Akka pressed a hundred-rupee note into my hand when no one was looking and said in a voice thick with tears, 'I wouldn't do this if it wasn't necessary. But there are young men in this house...'

'But I don't ever talk to them,' I pleaded, hoping she would change her mind and let me stay.

'I know you are a good girl, but it is unwise to leave cotton and a matchstick side by side. One wrong move and everything could go up in flames.'

I stared at the floor hopelessly. I knew Sujata Akka well enough to know that she sought proverbs only when she wanted to sort out a difficult situation and that she had already made up her mind. I was a difficult situation.

Amma said little. I knew she didn't like me leaving the village. But to Rukmini Akka, it was a great big adventure. 'Lucky girl! To be able to live in a town and that too in a house with doctors. You'll be able to see all kinds of diseases. Don't forget to wash your hands before you eat or you might catch a disease. They are foreigners, I hear, with white skin and blue eyes. You must observe them carefully and tell me everything. I have heard that their skin has a stench from all the meat they devour. And that they don't wash their backsides after they shit and instead use paper. Now don't you start behaving like them, and watch out that you don't eat beef mistaking it for mutton. And tell me how they eat, whether they bathe as regularly as us and if they ever oil their hair.' .

'Oh, shut up,' Sujata Akka snapped. 'You make them sound like a travelling circus.'

'They are women just like you and me,' Sujata Akka said, turning to me, seeing my eyes widen in fear. 'One of them has lived in Vellore for more than five years and she can speak Tamil well enough. So you have nothing to worry about. They'll take good care of you.'

Vellore town was congested. The houses crowded, one upon the other. And there were so many people. Not all of them lived there. Some of them were relatives of the patients in Vellore Hospital. I began to feel hot and sweaty and a little claustrophobic. After the wide-open spaces of the village, how could I thrive in this town where there was too much of everything—houses, shops, roads, people and noise.

The doctors' house was in a little lane off Barbara Street. Periaswamy, the old gardener, told me that more than a hundred years ago, in an adjacent street, there was a young bride who was suddenly taken ill and as she lay dying, she asked for a bowl of rasam to be brought to her. But lunch was long past over and the rasam pot was empty. The bride died with her last wish unfulfilled. And so, to make amends, her father-in-law ordered that a cauldron of simmering rasam be kept near the doorstep all day and night so that anyone in Vellore town who ever felt a craving for rasam at any time of the day or night could appease their desire.

'When I was a young boy, I would go there everyday and fill the yawning hole in my belly with bowls of rasam. It was the best I have ever tasted in my life,' Periaswamy said and I saw his Adam's apple bob as saliva filled his mouth and gushed down his throat. Wait till you taste mine, I thought. 'One day, I'll take you there and you can taste it yourself, but it's not as good as it used to be.'

Periaswamy was only as tall as I was. His hair was a grey stubble and his skin was like old leather, crinkly and ashen. His eyes shone like pebbles behind his thick glasses and often he burst into a rasping cough that sucked in his cheeks and turned his breath into a whistle. He looked frail and ill and I wondered how good a gardener he could be. One tug at a firmly rooted weed and he would fall back, I thought with a giggle.

On my first day, I couldn't take my eyes off the two lady doctors. Sujata Akka had arranged for me to be dropped off at their house. 'No. 24, Doctors Villa, off Barbara Street; ask anyone and they'll show you the place. Everyone knows that house,' she told Muniandi the driver who escorted me to Vellore.

'Don't talk to him or to anyone else on the bus. Do your work well and be a good girl.' Those were my mother's parting words.

I was to call them Missy V and Missy K, they said. Missy V was young, with green eyes and hair that seemed spun of gold-coloured silk. She wore it in a plait and only in the evening did she leave it loose and then it fell to her waist. Like a jamandi field in full blossom, the blooms swaying their golden heads when the breeze blew. She had come to Vellore only six months ago and could speak only a few words of Tamil. But Missy K's Tamil was very good, even if the way she spoke it made it sound harsh. There was an edge to everything about Missy K. Her eyes were like slivers of brown rock, her hair that was a dark brown was chopped off at ear level, and she had big hands and feet like a man's, with nails cut very close.

'What's your name?' Missy K asked when Muniandi had left.

'Marikolanthu,' I whispered, overwhelmed by the strange-ness of all I saw and felt around me.

'What does that mean, Kate?' Missy V's voice bore the

inflection of a little girl's.

Missy K drew out a white handkerchief from her skirt pocket and mopped her brow. The rains had begun, but even then it was very warm. I could feel the sweat run down my back as well. In our village, the rains would have stirred the cool winds to blow. The leaves of the trees would be dripping, the earth would be damp and fragrant...Suddenly I wished I could roll on the grass and cup the fragrance in my palms and drink deep of that wetness.

'Marikolanthu is the name of a plant,' Missy K explained, breaking into my thoughts. 'It's rather like the lavender.'

That evening when the flower-seller went by the gate, I asked for a sprig of marikolanthu. I took it to Missy V.

'Marikolanthu,' I said, giving it to her.

Missy V sniffed at it. 'Kate, look what she's brought me. You were right. It is rather like the lavender, but it's not lavender. So Marikolanthu, is that what you are? Sister to the real thing?'

Missy K explained what Missy V had said and I smiled, not letting them see how rankled I was. Who wants to be sister to the real thing?

'But we can't call her that. Her name is such a mouthful. I think we'll call her Mari. What do you think, Kate?'

Missy K grunted and my name changed to Mari with the 'eee' echoing long after my name was said. But I liked it and it had none of that sister-to-the-real-thing allusion.

'Have they turned you into a Christian? What is this Mari nonsense?' Periaswamy alone took umbrage to my new name.

'Of course not. Have they turned you into a Christian? I hear them calling you Perry,' I giggled and bent to pick a weed that had escaped his notice.

Periaswamy was old and cranky, but he was the only friend I had ever had. We had nothing in common but we were equals in each other's eyes and that was enough to nurture our friendship.

They didn't really need him but they liked having him—a

man around the house, they said, and looked at each other giggling.

They called him the gardener, but he was more an odd-job man whose only business in the garden was to weed and water the potted plants.

Missy K did the real gardening. My father would have approved of her. She had the same primitive power to speak to the earth and tame it to do her bidding. Her roses were the darkest red and when they bloomed, they scented the air, subduing the jasmine to a pale whiff.

'She must have magic in her fingers,' I told Periaswamy, burying my nose in a blossom.

Missy K didn't like either of us tampering with her rose patch. But during the day I had the house and garden to myself and did as I pleased. I examined their rooms, taking care to put everything back the way it was. Not that they had too many possessions. Compared to what Sujata Akka had in her room and wardrobes, their rooms were bare. I tasted the strange foods they stored in the fridge and often dipped a spoon into the condensed milk tin and licked it off. Someday when I had the money, I would buy a whole tin of condensed milk and eat it up all by myself. Once I used a bit of Missy V's shampoo to see if it would make my hair wave like hers did. But mine stayed straight as always.

'I've never seen roses as beautiful as these,' I repeated loudly. Periaswamy was hard of hearing, but he hid his deafness behind feigned surliness.

Periaswamy snorted. 'You'll never see roses like these, anywhere in the world. Do you know why?' He lowered his voice and drew close to me. 'She brings afterbirth from the hospital, chops it up like liver and feeds it to the earth. The roses thrive on blood, human blood. So tell me, why won't they be unique?'

I felt bile rush up to my mouth. Periaswamy stared at me, defying me to disbelieve him. For the first time, I wondered if he was a little mad. Only someone deranged could come up with such a preposterous story.

'I don't believe you,' I said.

'No one does. But I don't care. I only say what I have seen.
What do you know of this world? You are knee high to a
jasmine bush and you think you know everything. Stupid girl!'
Periaswamy went back to digging the soil around the coconut
tree.

For the rest of the morning, we didn't talk to each other, but
by lunchtime I forgot to be angry with him. We always ate our
lunch together. After the first few days I began to cook a little
extra food for Periaswamy. I had seen how meagre his lunch
packet was and decided to risk the Missies' displeasure. Except
when they did find out, all they did was look at each other and
say, 'Quite a bleeding heart!'

What on earth is a bleeding heart?

Every morning Periaswamy came in, dressed in a white shirt
and veshti. He took them off as soon as he closed the gate, and
hung them on the crook of a branch. Then in a pair of khaki
shorts that came to his knees and an old vest with more holes
than cloth, he went about his chores. In the evening, he would
sluice himself clean at the garden pipe, don his clothes and
leave, for all purposes like a man who had done nothing but fan
himself all day.

We ate lunch in the backyard. Rice, kara kozambhu or vatha
kozambhu or mor kozambhu, one poriyal and pickle, and
buttermilk. Sometimes there would be leftovers from the fish or
mutton I had cooked for the Missies and these I kept aside for
him.

'I haven't eaten a tastier kara kozambhu,' he said that
afternoon as he dribbled the curry over the mound of rice. I
accepted his apology and we never talked about the roses again.

I didn't know how much truth there was in what he claimed,
but I knew that the more he needed the Missies, the more he
resented it. He knew that no one else would employ him and
that what he was paid was merely charity disguised as wages.
He was never rude or surly, but when they were not looking, he
shot them malevolent looks and muttered under his breath

about their strangeness.

In spite of everything I was very fond of Periaswamy. He taught me about plants and how to change a light bulb. He showed me how to fix a leaking tap and clean windowpanes with newspapers. And without knowing it, he taught me to observe.

Every night, I watched Missy K leave her room and walk past me where I lay curled on a mat in the corridor between their rooms, and go to Missy V's room. In the early hours, she crept back to her bed. Why this secrecy, I wondered. If Missy K was afraid to sleep alone, the sensible thing to do would be for them to share a bed. I would have thought nothing of two women sharing a bed. It was the most obvious thing to do when there wasn't a man around. For the women to stick together. Perhaps these foreigners are different, I told myself. They do not like to admit their fears and would rather pretend they are just as strong and self-sufficient as men. How silly, I thought.

For three years, we all lived content in our lives—three women and a decrepit old man. I visited my mother every few months, but seldom stayed long. I was always in a hurry to get back to Vellore where there was so much more happening. The fields and the villagers bored me. I felt stifled by the narrowness of the streets and the boundaries that were everywhere. Between field and field; home and field; man and woman; woman and life; living and dignity...

The Missies taught me the English alphabet and bought me books to read in both English and Tamil. I didn't understand everything I read. I had to read aloud the English books, which were meant for very young children, so that they made some sense to my confused brain. But the Missies were happy with my progress. Instead of glass bangles, I began to collect words and these would always be with me, I told myself with some degree of satisfaction...

When I turned eighteen, they said, they'd help me find a job in the hospital as a helper.

'You should try and finish your SSLC privately and then we'll pay for you to do a nursing assistant's course,' Missy K said one morning.

'Ask her if that's what she wants, Kate. Not everyone wants to tend to patients,' Missy V said, spooning uppma into her mouth.

Missy V liked uppma and vada, idli and sambar, dosai and onion chutney. Not Missy K. She preferred her toast; two slices. One she smeared with butter that she said was more like ghee, and the other with jam, which she complained was too sweet to be real fruit. Missy K ate two plantains every morning. Not Missy V. She wanted guavas and papaya, sapodillas and mangoes, and in the summer she ate the palm fruit, scooping its quivering transparent flesh into her mouth with great relish.

They were so different from each other. Missy V smiled. Missy K stretched her lips into a grimace. Missy V liked change. Missy K hated it if anything disrupted our lives. Missy V preferred gay colours and wore lots of beads and chains. Missy K dressed in sombre colours and left her neck and wrists and earlobes bare. Missy K talked to Missy V as if she were the husband and Missy V the wife. Sometimes I caught Missy K caressing Missy V's face with her eyes. It sent a line of goose bumps down my back.

'Of course she'd like to work with patients. She has the aptitude and most importantly, the makings of a good nurse.' Missy K crunched her toast.

'I do,' I agreed. I told myself I did. I wasn't squeamish about blood or pee or shit. I didn't think I was. 'I'd like to start as a helper when I'm eighteen and I'll try and pass the SSLC privately.' And when I had said it, I felt as if I were on the threshold of a whole new world.

'Well then, that's settled,' Missy K said, sounding pleased.

Missy V shrugged. That was the other thing. Missy V became petulant if she didn't get her way. But not Missy K. She never bore a grudge or sulked.

When I look back, I wonder if the fabric of my life would

have been woven on a different loom if I had done as the Missies had expected me to. Would everything have been different? This is the one question that punctuated my early morning thoughts during those terrible days...

My mother fell down and cracked a bone. Her leg was put in a cast and she was advised to rest for a few weeks. My brothers came to fetch me. They seemed to have grown up all of a sudden. Four months ago they were little boys, but now they stood a head taller than me and when they spoke, their voices cracked with the effort of becoming men.

'How tall you've become,' I said, unable to reconcile myself to the idea that these lanky boys were my little brothers.

'You can't call us Kulla Kathrika and Odachu Kadala any more,' they grinned.

Little aubergine. And split pea. My names for them.

'That's true,' I sighed. 'Perhaps I should call you Easwaran Sir and Sivakumar Sir now.'

I giggled. Suddenly, going back to the Chettiar household didn't seem so bad.

Amma was afraid that her place in the household would be usurped if she left it vacant. Rukmini Akka would be asked to step in, and though she had tried very hard to keep her recipes a secret, Rukmini Akka and she had spent many hours together and there was little Rukmini Akka didn't know. 'And where will that leave us?' Amma said, her eyes resting on the boys' faces.

I understood. I was to take Amma's place. I may not be Amma. But I was Marikolanthu. Sister to the real thing. Daughter of the cook.

'But Amma, how can I manage? I'm not used to cooking such large quantities,' I said, wondering if I could cope at all.

'I'm here to advise you. What you have to remember is that Rukmini does most of the work. In spite of her tongue that wags all the time like a dog's tail, she's a good worker. She can very easily do all that I do in that kitchen. Which is why it is important that you don't let her. The Chettiar family has to think that in our hands, and in our hands alone, lie the culinary secrets that have whetted and appeased their taste buds for so long,' Amma said, dispelling my fears as if they were an errant fly to be slapped and squashed out of existence.

I managed just as Amma had said I would. But I hated every minute of it. In Vellore, I had enjoyed cooking. I cooked to please. Here I cooked to feed. And such rapacious mouths that chewed, chomped, swallowed, belched and demanded more...

The smell of smoking oil clung to my hair; my fingertips stank of garlic; the pores of my skin oozed the odour of asafoetida. Every night I scrubbed myself hard to erase the embrace of the kitchen. For a few brief minutes I would smell Lux soap and then again the kitchen smells would ride my body.

Each night I crossed the date on the calendar that hung on the wall. My house didn't feel like a home any more. I was busy all day; my hands and feet toiled. But my mind felt empty. At Vellore, the Missies and Periaswamy had nurtured my mind. I would have felt less lonely if I could have spent time with Sujata Akka. But once the chores of the day were done, all I wanted to do was rush home and bathe.

Sometimes it occurred to me that my mother and brothers had unconsciously severed ties with me. I was the daughter whose tenure in the household would soon end. My rights in the house would cease the day I was wed.

Each night I told myself that six weeks later, I could return to Vellore where the Missies would help shape my future. Each night I dreamt of independence and dignity.

When just a week more was left, Amma began to insist that I stay on. 'Go back after Pongal,' she said. 'God knows where you will be for your next Pongal.'

'I want you to wear that new sari Sujata Akka gave you,' she said, one evening. 'She wanted to know if you liked it.'

I have always wanted to own a Kancheepuram silk sari. With a parrot green body and a chilli red border; with real gold zari drawn into the shape of mangoes and peacocks, dots and triangles. A few days after I returned from Vellore, Sujata Akka had given me a new Dharmavaram silk sari. I had stuck a smile on my face and my eyes reflected the glitter of the fake zari because that was what she expected. But I didn't want it. Everyone knows what a Dharmavaram silk sari is compared to the Kancheepuram—a sister to the real thing, and I wanted none of that.

Instead I confided in Amma about the Missies' plans for me.

'All that is very well but I have already started looking for a husband for you. The Chettiar has promised to help with the dowry,' Amma said, weaving jasmine buds into my plait.

Ever since my father died, Amma saw to it that my plait was adorned with flowers. Jasmine or kadambam, chrysanthemum or marigolds...And if there wasn't a single flower available, Amma brought out a pink plastic rose she had bought at a village fair long ago and nagged until I wore it in my hair. It was as if she were making up for not being able to wear flowers herself.

'You've become careless of your appearance since you began staying with the Missies. Do you want to end up looking like them? Plain and hag-like with hair like coconut fibre and skin like old leather.

'Girls of your age should be seen with flowers in their hair, collyrium rimming their eyes, bangles on their wrists, and the tinkle of anklets should echo every step that they take. Look at you...you look like a widow even before you are married,' my mother's words fell like tiny darts.

There was no room for fripperies in the Missies' home. Flowers were frowned upon unless they were on bushes, and anklets irritated Missy K. At first, Periaswamy teased me that I was beginning to resemble a nun. But soon he too got used to the drab Mari, with tightly braided plaits and bare wrists; naked eyes and sallow face.

More than anything else the Missies hated the turmeric paste I smeared on my face after oiling my hair and washing it every Friday morning. The first time I did it in the Vellore house, Missy V took one look at me and shrieked, 'Kate, do you think she has hepatitis? I've never seen anyone turn this yellow overnight. Do you think this is some particularly vicious strain?'

Missy K glanced at my face and said in a scathing voice, 'Mari, wash that muck off your face. She thinks you have jaundice.'

In Vellore, where I was Mari, they liked me plain and bare. But Amma would have none of that. So I reverted to being the daughter she wanted. Blooming and pretty; with a merry laugh and the coquettish wiles of an eighteen-year-old seeking the world's admiration and willing it to fall at her feet. I tossed my head when I talked. I developed a sidelong glance. I swayed my hips when I walked.

Perhaps it was the incandescence that Amma lit within me that plunged the rest of my life into darkness.

When Amma returned to the Chettiar kitchen, I went back to being Sujata Akka's handmaiden. I was in and out of the rooms all day and I guess that was how Rani Akka's brother spotted me.

His name was Murugesan. I often try to remember what he looked like. It isn't as if I hadn't seen him enough times. But all I can come up with is a face wiped clean of all features. A ghost face. When I think of him, what comes to mind are his hands. His big hands with meaty fingers...

...I don't know if I should be telling you all this. You may be older than I am but you are unmarried. I don't want to embarrass you...You smile. I understand that smile...

On the day before Pongal, it was customary to light a big bonfire in the Chettiar's courtyard. Everyone in the village would come there with their old things to fling into the fire and scream: Bogi! Bogi! Out with the old! Burn the past! Throw out the debris of the year! Bogi! Bogi!

I had to go back home to wash and change into fresh clothes. I looked at the wristwatch Sujata Akka had given me a few days ago and asked, 'Amma, can I leave now? Sujata Akka wants me to spend the night here, at the Chettiar House.'

'Don't be long,' Amma said as I left the Chettiar Kottai. 'Take one of the boys with you.'

'Stop fussing,' I said. 'I'm only going home, two streets away, and not to Vellore.'

'Is this any way to talk to your mother?' Rukmini Akka snapped. 'You are a grown-up girl and not a young child any more. Don't you know that there are dangers lurking in every corner, hiding behind every tree and bush?'

'Like what?' I said in my head.

'Ever since she came back from Vellore, she thinks she knows everything. When I say something, she says, "I'm old enough to look after myself." When something does happen to her, she'll understand...' Amma's voice was harsh with anger. It is the fatigue that's making her irritable, I told myself and agreed to take Sivakumar with me. Except that he wouldn't come. He wanted to be there when they lit the bonfire.

In January, the village was at its beautiful best. Every bull, ox and cow in the village had its horns freshly painted. Children chewed on sugarcane and the sticky sap ran down their chins... The trees were dense with leaves and there was grass growing everywhere. A cool breeze winnowed through the fields and hair left loose. Flowers bloomed; thousands of them. This was the season of the jasmine—plump, rounded gundu- mallis, the fragile narrow-petalled mullai...The houses newly whitewashed gleamed in the moonlight; a row of jasmines strung with the thread of darkness.

In January it was so easy to forget the toll the summer would take, baking the earth and drying up the abundance in the village.

In January, the night came early and the shadows loomed everywhere, threatening, menacing...

I hurried through the mango orchard, the grass beneath my feet wet with dew. I never liked the mango orchard. It was flanked on one side by a giant tamarind tree. When I was a child, the orchard keeper who guarded the mangoes as they ripened enticingly on the trees had frightened me and the other children with stories of a female ghoul who lived on the tamarind tree and chose to capture her victims in the mango orchard. When I grew up, I understood that it was merely a ploy to keep us from stealing the mangoes, but the orchard still made me uneasy each time I walked through it alone.

And then, like it had in my childhood nightmares, a hand grabbed me from behind a tree. Did I scream? I must have. How could I not have? But the whole village was echoing with the cries of Bogi! Bogi!

A hand clamped around my mouth and another hand gathered me into a clinch. Fleshy meaty hands that robbed me of my voice and tore at my body.

'Please, please,' I cried when I saw that it was Murugesan. 'Please let me go.'

'Oh, I can't let you go.' His eyes glittered. 'You should have thought of that when you set out to tease me with your body.' I smelt alcohol on his breath.

I wriggled and pleaded, but he clamped his palm across my mouth to silence me and then he dragged me deeper into the orchard and there in the shadows, he ripped at my clothes. 'Why are you pretending to be a guileless virgin? I know all about women like you. If the Chettiar sons can feast on this body of yours...remember I'm a relative, even if only a poor one, and I'm entitled to their pickings before anyone else...' he snarled.

I held onto his shoulders and began to beg, 'Let me go...don't ruin my life.'

He stared at me and slapped my face. 'Shut up. Who do you think you are? A little princess?'

Then his eye caught the glint of metal on my wrist and he sneered. 'They have spoilt you in that house...do you hear that? What is a servant like you doing wearing a watch? Do you know that my sister was sent back home for many months because on her wedding night, in all innocence, she asked her husband if he would teach her to read the time? They said she was ignorant and unfit to be a daughter-in-law of the house. But look at you. You have more rights in that house than my sister. It's time someone reminded you of who you are.'

He snapped the watch bracelet and flung it into the darkness.

I didn't understand what he was talking about or why he was so angry with me but I knew that if I didn't try and escape, it would be too late. I scratched at his face and hands. And then spurred by rage I kicked at his shins and shrieked, 'Do you think you can get away with this? I'll tell the Chettiar. I'll tell the village elders. I'll tell everyone that you raped me.'

His fingers dug into the flesh of my upper arms. 'No one will believe you. You might think you are our equal, but you are not. I'm the Chettiar's nephew, his daughter-in-law's brother, and you are only the cook's daughter. No one will dare question me.'

For a moment I paused, struck by the truth of his words. What was I going to do? Murugesan seized his opportunity in the stillness of that moment. He threw me on the ground and flung himself upon me, grinding his hips against mine. His hands reached beneath my skirt and ripped my drawers off. 'Just like a town girl, are you? With drawers and a bra? You like this, don't you, you little whore?'

I felt him weigh me down with his hot breath, his lust and the complete disregard of what he was doing to me...this is not happening to me, I told myself...as his mouth feasted on my breasts, his hands squeezed my buttocks, and he savagely kneed my legs apart, I closed my eyes and thought—this is a bad dream, I will wake up soon and none of it would have happened...and then I felt him tear into me, filling me with a great anguish, and the tears began to rain. Thick viscous tears that slid into me. Pale transparent tears that squeezed themselves out from my tightly scrunched up eyes.

In the distance, I heard the calls. Bogi! Bogi! The sparks would fly as the bonfire was set alight and the night would crackle with the sound of dried logs and twigs waking up. With my past, my future too had been torched alive.

...What should I have done? What would you have done? Now I know...I should have rushed to the Chettiar's courtyard the way I was, with torn clothes, mussed up hair, his fluids and mine trickling down my legs, and terror in my eyes. I should have threatened suicide and demanded justice. I should have wept and stormed and let the world and the Chettiar see me as a victim...

I went home. All I could think of was what Amma would say if she found out: I told you so...you never listen to me and now your life is ruined forever...who will marry you...I pleaded with you to take care, not to wander through the village alone, but you wouldn't listen...

I bathed. A whole bar of soap and a handful of coconut fibre that turned into a soggy mess...I scrubbed myself relentlessly, trying to erase what had happened to me, trying to muffle the drumming in my head...If I pretended nothing had happened, nothing had changed, I presumed everything would remain the way it was...

In the Chettiar Kottai, the bonfire was ebbing. The villagers still clung to the courtyard, unwilling to relinquish the excitement of being there. I spotted my brothers and a mouthful of bile curdled my insides. If only they had been with me. If only Amma had insisted they go with me.

I watched the fire die. An acrid smell of burning hung over the courtyard. Nothing has changed, I told myself fiercely...nothing has changed. Once I went back to Vellore, I would be able to dismiss the mango orchard and its meaty-pawed ghoul from my thoughts. One week was all that was left. I would never set foot in this village again, I swore.

But a week later, I was still at the Chettiar Kottai. Sujata Akka had begun to throw up; she refused to eat and said that the smell of food made her want to retch. Her eyes took on a turmeric hue and finally when she scattered a few grains of boiled rice in her urine, they turned yellow. Sujata Akka had jaundice. And someone had to look after Prabhu-papa.

A message was despatched to Vellore and the boys came back saying that Missy K was annoyed about the further delay. The stand-in maid was not satisfactory and Missy K had said that I should return as quickly as I could.

I sighed in relief. At least they still wanted me back. I had worried that they wouldn't keep my job for me.

'How is Periaswamy? Did you see him?'

'How should we know?'

'But didn't you see him? He's the gardener. An old man with glasses and sunken cheeks,' I said, anxious at the thought that something must have happened to Periaswamy.

'We know who he is. He wasn't there. Maybe he's ill. Maybe he's gone to visit someone,' the boys said. 'Maybe he's dead,' their faces suggested.

I stared at them. I didn't like the thought of Periaswamy not being there. I didn't like the thought of the stand-in maid. I didn't want anything to change. When I went back to Vellore, I wanted everything to be the way it had been. That way my life would remain untouched too.

A few weeks later, as Sujata Akka began to recover, I began to feel ill. A queer malaise that clung to me all day. The sight of food made me nauseous. I felt listless and tired. 'I think I've got jaundice too,' I told Amma.

'I told you to be careful. But you wouldn't listen,' Amma said pulling my face closer to hers. 'Is your urine yellow? Your eyeballs are still white. If it's jaundice, I think it must be in its very early stages. I'll ask the boys to go look for some kizharnelli leaves and make you a brew. Drink it for a few days and you'll begin to feel better.'

Two mornings later, I woke with churning insides and watery bile in my mouth. When my mother saw me pounding ginger with salt, she paused on her way to work. 'What's wrong?'

'I feel nauseous,' I said, sucking on the ball of crushed ginger.

Amma gave me a strange look and went on her way.

I didn't get any better. My face grew wan and pale. My hair lost its shine and the smell of Amma sautéeing mustard made me want to throw up. Amma confronted me one morning. 'Tell me the truth,' she demanded. 'When did you have your last period?'

I thought for a moment and said, 'About seven weeks ago.'

Amma sat down on the floor and covered her face with her hands. 'What have you done, you wicked girl?'

'I didn't do anything, Amma,' I said, frightened by the look on her face.

'What do you mean by saying you haven't done anything? Don't you realize that you are pregnant? Who is he? Tell me, who was it?'

'Amma, I didn't do anything wrong.'

'Stop pretending. How could you be so shameless? Tell me, who is he?'

I sat down on the floor. I knew that I could no longer pretend that nothing had happened. I was no longer who I once was. The night in the mango orchard had returned to haunt me.

'Amma,' I said, willing my tongue to form the words. 'Amma, it's not what you think.'

So I told her my story. Of every scream and shriek. Of a little stone that had pressed against my spine when he fell upon me. Of the wetness of the dew beneath my feet and his wetness that had flooded me. Of my fervent pleas and the mad fervour with which his hands and mouth had roamed my body. Of how he left me lying in a dishevelled heap and stumbled away into the darkness. When I finished, I saw only suspicion in her eyes. And disbelief. He was right, I knew with a bitterness that made me want to walk away from that room, from her gaze. No one would believe me, he had said, and he was right.

'Amma, everything I have told you is the truth,' I tried again.

'You were raped and you kept quiet about it. A man steals your virginity and you think nothing is going to change...You expect me to believe that?'

Amma wept. Amma stormed. Amma ranted and raved. Amma had a fainting fit. Amma threatened to kill herself. Amma did all that I should have done on the night I was raped.

'Tell me, tell me, you slut! Who was it really? You think I'm a fool to believe Murugesan would do something like this...'

But I had nothing more to offer her. No consoling fact that the man whose imprint I bore within me was someone from the village. Someone the village elders could coerce into marrying me. Not even the village elders would dare point a finger at Murugesan and that was the truth Amma was reluctant to accept.

Distraught, Amma confided in Sujata Akka. 'What am I to do? Will you speak to her and find out whom she is shielding? He must be someone unsuitable, perhaps some Christian or Muslim boy.'

And so for Sujata Akka's benefit, I repeated the events of the night I was raped. She listened to me quietly, not interrupting once, and then turned to my mother. 'I think she's speaking the truth. Murugesan is a sly beast; when he looks at me I see only lust in his eyes. So what is to prevent him from doing this? Besides, he knew very well that no one would believe her, and it happened just as he thought it would. Not even you believe her!'

I began to cry then. Amma's face crinkled up as well and drawing me close to her, she too began to weep. 'What do we do now?'

'Why did you hide it from us?' Sujata Akka asked. 'If only you had made a hue and cry right then, something could have been done...'

'I don't know. I didn't think of the consequences. All I wanted to do was not think about it and that way I thought I could go on like nothing had happened,' I tried to explain.

'But don't you see, no one will believe your story. Not now. If only you had told me on the night you were raped, I would have brought it up with the Chettiar and insisted that Murugesan marry you.'

'Akka, I don't want to have anything to do with that filthy animal,' I said. 'I'd rather die than marry him.'

Amma's head snapped up in rage. 'Do you hear her? Have you heard such arrogance? Her reputation, her life is in tatters and she isn't the least bothered about it.'

Her eyes blazed, seeking to burn my wilfulness that she thought had eroded all sense of shame and self-preservation.

'Who will marry you? Your life is over and you'll end up in the gutter like a street dog with its litter...you have nothing left in your life.'

I knew that. I knew that my life had paused on its path. But I didn't want him to put it back on its course. 'I'll leave home, Amma,' I said. 'I'll leave so that you won't be disgraced. I'll go away, someplace where no one will recognize me and kill myself,' the words tripped from my mouth so effortlessly. I had heard them a hundred times before, mouthed by my favourite film heroines.

'What are you saying?' Amma cried, horrified by the vision of a daughter bloated and washed ashore; a child pulverized beyond recognition by a train. I began to cry. I was sorry for myself, for my mother who deserved better, and sorry for the mess our lives were in.

'Stop this,' Sujata Akka butted in, anxious to prevent our wailing from echoing through the house. 'Stop tormenting yourselves. We'll find a way.'

But there was nothing that even Sujata Akka could do to remedy the situation. At first, Sujata Akka's husband refused to believe that I wasn't at fault. 'The girl must have led him on and now that she is pregnant she's making up a story about rape. All nonsense, if you ask me.'

But when she insisted, he lost his temper and said, 'All right, I believe you. Murugesan raped her. But do you realize what you are asking of me? Do you expect me to sever relations with my brother for the sake of a servant, no matter how precious she is to you? I want you to steer clear of this...do you understand? No more involving yourself in this mess. Let them find a solution themselves.'

In the end Sujata Akka did nothing. She called my mother and explained her helplessness. 'My husband won't let me bring it up. He's ordered me to keep out of this. I know the truth, but what can I do?'

Amma began to cry. No loud sobs. No scrunching up of features, but a relentless stream of salted defeat.

'Now don't start this. All I said is, we can't bring up Murugesan's name. But there are other things we can do,' Sujata Akka said softly. 'No one knows about this except my husband and he won't talk about it to anyone. You must send her away and have the pregnancy aborted. When she returns, send her back to Vellore. She was talking about the doctors offering to train her. Let her do that training. Arranging a marriage for her is going to be very difficult. No man will be willing to marry a woman who's lost her virginity and even if we kept it a secret, what if he finds out later? He'll forsake her then. But if she has a job, that will replace a husband's protection.'

...Husband's protection! The phrase made me cringe. Neither Sujata Akka nor my mother ever had their husbands look out for them. The Chettiar took care of Sujata Akka's needs. And Amma had to look after herself. The men in their lives had done nothing and yet to them a fulfilled woman was one who was married. Everything else was secondary. But I was so young then that these thoughts were like strands of a cobweb floating through the air. I didn't know enough to think them through and even if I had, they would have dismissed it as arrogance...

Periamma. My mother's aunt was old with giant gold earrings that dragged her earlobes down nearly to her shoulders, and a mouth tainted red with her incessant chewing of betel leaves. She had silver hair pulled back in a knot and she wore a white sari the old way, stretched to cover her sagging breasts so that it didn't matter that she didn't wear a blouse.

Periamma lived in a little village called Arsikuppam, near Salem. She was a widow and lived alone. Her two sons were soldiers and were stationed in some northern land. After four years of continuous drought, they had to forsake their lands and find another way to earn a living. For young men like them, with only a high school education, the sole recourse was the army, where well-developed muscles and a willingness to toil were enough to secure them a place. Periamma's daughters were married and lived elsewhere. Amma turned to Periamma because she had no one else to go to. Besides, Periamma always knew what needed to be done.

We travelled together, my mother and I, to Arsikuppam. In hushed tones, Amma explained while I sat with my head hung in embarrassment. Everyone expected me to be ashamed. I didn't feel shame; anger, humiliation but not shame...

I saw Periamma sneak glances at me. Once I caught her eye and I saw sympathy. Or was it pity?

Periamma was capable and strong. She was the mother of many children. Periamma didn't believe in doctors and hospitals. She would take care of everything, she said. Besides, the outside world was not known for its discretion. A thousand tongues and a million renderings of the same story—that is what happened if one sought the outside world for help.

Amma went back reassured. The boys were alone at home and they would wonder what had happened if Amma stayed away too long. Periamma will deal with it, Amma said.

Periamma did. With slices of golden yellow papaya, and toasted sesame seeds rolled in jaggery syrup ladoos. With green jackfruit cooked and sautéed with mustard and curry leaves. With the sap of a wild plant that grew in clumps. 'Look at this one,' Periamma said, pointing to the plant that grew everywhere, in my village and hers, and any odd piece of 'poromboke' land. An innocuous-looking thing with fleshy leaves and a star-shaped flower cluster the colour of a faded ink spot.

Periamma snapped the fleshy, rubbery stalk of the plant and

a milky fluid oozed out. 'This will finish off the weevil growing inside you,' she said.

Every day we waited for the cramps to begin. For hate to drip out of me. For pain to take root and cleanse. Every day we waited. Six weeks later, I was still pregnant.

'What do we do now?' Amma asked on her next visit, worry creasing her face into an old woman's.

'It will be born dead. No foetus can survive all this and be alive,' Periamma offered.

'It's still alive. That much we know. Maybe we should take her to a clinic and get it aborted there.'

'Are you mad? Do you want the whole world to know about this?'

'If the child is born alive, the whole world will know anyway,' I said, vexed by Periamma's insistence that we not go to a clinic.

'If the child is born alive, you can leave it with me. I'll take care of it. It will keep me company in my old age. But trust me, this one won't be born alive,' Periamma said, stuffing her mouth with betel leaves and cutting further conversation off.

Amma went back home and I returned to waiting for it to die.

Periamma wasn't worried when I began to show. Right from the beginning she had made it known that I was an abandoned wife. My husband, she told everyone, had forsaken me for another woman. 'Which is the truth,' she said when she saw me grimace. 'He did forsake you, didn't he?'

'This way, no one will think any less of you,' she added.

'But can't we say the same at the hospital,' I asked. 'I'm still only four months gone.'

'We could, but at the hospital, they'll ask for names and details. Your name. Your husband's name. Your address. Your next of kin. Do you want to let everyone know who you are? Let me do it my way. No one will be hurt.' Periamma fanned herself briskly.

The heat ate into our skins and oozed out of our pores. It was

May. The fiercest month of the year. The heat parched the earth and stilled the breeze. 'This summer is the worst I have ever known,' Periamma said as I sluiced the floors with water, hoping that would cool the rooms. 'Maybe the heat will accomplish what the others didn't,' she said.

A month later, we gave up. The child still lived within me. What next, I wondered.

I pressed my palm on my belly. Go away. Leave me. I don't want you, I told this child of mine. The creature kicked. My belly rippled gently. Die, die, I prayed.

I delivered a month early. The pains began, two iron fists that crept out of my lower spine and pulled at my hip bones, trying to wrench them apart while a giant foot pressed on my insides, squeezing, pushing, making me bite on my inner cheek to quell the pain...Periamma narrowed her eyes and shook her head knowingly. 'I told you,' she said. 'It's going to be born dead.'

Periamma stood vigil as with a giant heave I thrust it out of me. Through the pain, and the relief of knowing there was to be no more pain, I heard a cry. A lusty wail.

Through a haze, I saw the delight in Periamma's eyes and knew that she had planned for this to happen. And so all those cures Periamma had wrought to piece my life together had been a kind of sham. The less vicious ones she had administered, and the more powerful ones she had pretended to.

'Why? Why?' I cried.

Holding the baby close to her bosom, she said, 'It didn't ask to be created, but once it is here, who are we to play God and take its life?'

The sight of one's own baby; the feeling of holding your own baby in your arms—Periamma thought all of it would make me want the child. But she didn't know me well enough, nor the power of hate.

'Put the baby to your breast. Let him suckle. That's how you'll bond with the baby even though the umbilicus is severed,' Periamma said, offering me the child.

I turned away. 'No,' I said. 'I told you I want nothing to do with him. It's still not too late. Shove a grain of paddy into his throat. Wring his neck. Kill him.'

Periamma gathered the baby to her bosom and stared at me, unable to believe her ears. 'You are a wicked girl and you don't deserve to have him,' she said and walked away.

I stared at the ceiling and felt tears wet the corners of my eyes and trickle into my hair. Why didn't anyone understand how I felt?

Amma arrived. Amma would be more realistic. I would tell Amma that we should leave the child with Periamma. After all, she had offered to keep him with her if it was born alive.

'Take him with you,' Periamma said. 'In time, she will learn to love him. Some day when you are no more and she has no one to call her own in the world, he will be there for her...'

'Amma, I don't want him. You should have taken me to a clinic for an abortion. It is all her fault. She was cheating us,' I said, pointing my finger at Periamma. I heard Amma gasp in shock. No one ever did that to an older person. Point a finger literally or figuratively.

'She knew that this baby would be born alive, but she let us believe that she had taken care of everything. Let her keep it. Or give it away or do as she pleases. I don't want it near me.'

Nothing of what I said registered with Amma. Periamma knew how to convince her and so they decided to pass the baby off as a relative's child. An orphan whose parents had died in an accident and for whom no one else could be responsible but Amma.

I watched the women as they petted him. To them, he was a baby to be cherished and cosseted. To them, he was blameless. To them, he was my crutch for tomorrow.

What of now? My life...how could I forget what had happened as he grew before me, a reminder of what my life had turned out to be...

I went back to Vellore. The stand-in maid was found another place and I moved in as if nothing had changed. I waited for the

Missies to broach the subject of my training. They didn't.

The Missies' lives too had changed. Missy V didn't look very happy and I sensed a tension between them. Some nights Missy V kept her door locked and Missy K would knock on it softly, calling, 'Viv, it's me, Viv, open the door...'

But Missy V either pretended to be asleep or was really sleeping. Missy K would go back to her room and sometimes I would feel her glance at me. Now I knew what it was they sought each other for: loving—mouths, fingers, arching toes, curving tongues...

I thought of how the monster had forced himself on me in the mango orchard and told myself that what these women did was not wrong. Nothing could be worse than what had happened to me. Nothing could be more wrong than a man raping a woman.

I was nineteen years old. My dreams were ashes and the overriding taste in my mouth was bitterness. My eyes were blinkered with self-pity and it showed. In my walk, manner, on my face...

My nights were swamped with the most frightening dreams. Almost every night, I woke up screaming. Missy V gave me some tablets. 'Take one every night, before you go to sleep,' she said.

Missy K didn't approve. 'You are starting her on something she's going to need hereafter to sleep well.'

'Don't be so sanctimonious,' Missy V snapped. 'I know what I'm doing. She needs help. Haven't you heard her screaming in her sleep every night? Do you think that's normal?'

'I'm not denying she needs help. But this,' Missy K said, pointing to the little white tablets, 'is not help. This is going to create more trouble than you think.'

I didn't care what Missy K said or thought. I took one tablet every night and slept as if I were dead. No dreams prodded my mind; nothing touched me. In the mornings when I woke up, my arms and legs felt heavy, as if they were filled with iron rods. My eyelids drooped and lethargy clung to me all day. All I wanted to do was lie down and sleep. Perhaps that was why I failed to notice the signs that all was not well in the household.

Missy V was going back to England and Missy K was unhappy about it. I heard them quarrel all the time and Missy K would storm out stone-faced while Missy V sat in her room shredding paper.

Periaswamy had disappeared and not even the Missies knew what had happened to him. The garden was wild and overgrown and while I waited for him to come back, I weeded and watered and tried to take his place.

'Missy K, the roses need to be tended,' I said one day.

She rose from her chair and went into the garden with a pair of garden scissors. And quietly she set about snipping the rose plants till they stood just about six inches high. Then she took a hoe and dug up the bed till all the rose plants lay with their roots exposed and shivering...

'Kate, what's wrong with you?' Missy V screamed from the window.

'You,' she said. 'These were for you. I don't want them here reminding me of you.'

Missy V turned away from the window. When the rose bed was wrecked beyond redemption, Missy K went back in.

A few months after Missy V left, Missy K called me and said, 'Mari, I'm leaving Vellore. I'm going away to Bangalore to join a hospital there. Would you like me to find you another place here in Vellore?'

'Missy K, what about the training in the hospital? I was hoping you would recommend my name for that.'

Missy K looked at the floor and made a complicated gesture with her arms. Oh that, it seemed to say. She sighed, 'I won't be able to help you with that. I don't think you are right for it.'

'Why? Is it because I'm an unwed mother?'

'You have changed, Mari. At first when you came here, I thought you would suit the job. You had so much joy in you; a willingness to please. There was a kind of glow that came from you that made me think you would bring light into those dreadful hospital wards. Not any more.

'A helper's job is difficult and thankless. You need to be at peace with yourself to be able to do your job well. More than anything else, you need to have compassion. And you...' Missy K's face was pale with the effort of having to speak those hateful words.

'Do you blame me for what I have become?'

'I don't, but...'

'Not everyone in the hospital wards is a nice and noble soul,' I snapped.

'I know that. Compassion is a very underrated virtue, Mari, but only where there is compassion can there be healing.

'I'd like to persuade myself that this is just a phase. That someday you will become again who you once were; that you will seek your son out and accept him as your own. All these days I waited for you to tell me about your child. I thought you would want to go and see him. But I see a woman who pretends that her life hasn't changed. How can I turn a blind eye to what you have become? What happened to you, Mari?'

I grimaced. What happened to me? Ask God. Ask that Brahma who wrote my destiny.

...I have been trained in despair. Despair came easily to us, my mother and me. And we accepted it because we told ourselves that what was meted out to us was what we deserved. But Amma set a limit to how much despair could take its toll. It was I who erected no such defences. Sometimes I think I was so used to despair that even if it shied away from me, I beckoned it back. And when it drew close, instead of pulling a basket over myself and hiding from it, I welcomed it with arms flung wide...

The Chettiar died, and the household fell apart. Rajendran Anna moved to Kancheepuram and Ranganathan Anna stayed on in Madras. Sridhar Anna and Sujata Akka inherited the Chettiar Kottai. With its turrets, long corridors, creaking doors, bottomless wells and the mad woman in the west wing.

'If only she could be freed from this illness,' Sujata Akka

moaned. If only she would die, I knew she thought.

'She might be old but the demons in her are only getting fiercer with age. Vadivu can't handle her any more. She says she wants to leave. What do I do? I can't lock her up in a mental asylum. We have to look after her and we need someone young and strong.' Sujata Akka's eyes descended on mine. 'Will you come back, Marikolanthu?'

I nodded. I didn't want to live at home where the child was. I didn't want to see the contempt in my brothers' eyes—or hear their self-righteous polemics. Since my brothers were earning, my mother had given up her job and she devoted her time to raising the child. If I went to live at home, Amma would expect me to do all that she did for the boy. Amma hadn't ceased to hope that I would accept him.

I stared at my feet. Missy K was right, I thought. I must seem stern and uncompromising; incapable of compassion and gentleness; the perfect keeper for a mad woman.

'You will have to live in the house. Someone has to be there to keep an eye on her all the time,' Sujata Akka added.

Amma was furious with me. She thumped her palm on her forehead and hissed, 'Why couldn't you have stayed on in Vellore? It is better to wash someone's dirty underwear than be a mad woman's maid even if you don't have much to do. She is dangerous, do you understand that?'

I shrugged. 'I'm not frightened. And the pay is good.'

Amma peered at me closely, 'Come on, admit it, you want to be near Muthu. That's why you are taking this job. Isn't that right?'

Amma would never give up. She thought that someday I would learn to love this child whose very sight made me feel ill. She called him Muthu, her rare pearl. I called him 'it'. But Amma never ceased to hope.

'Please Amma,' I said, rising from the floor where we were sitting. 'This has nothing to do with "it". Sometimes I think I'm going mad myself and if I'm with a mad woman all day, perhaps I will learn to curb my own madness.'

Amma slumped. She raised her eyes to heaven and mumbled, 'When will you show me some mercy?'

The next few years passed in a haze, aided by the tablets Missy V had prescribed for me. I increased the dosage to two a night and with that I kept at arm's length all that happened around me.

Every day was just like the day before. There were no surprises. No events that shook me out of the trance-like state I had drifted into. Sometimes the thick veil-like mist that shrouded my mind parted and I glimpsed the passing of time on my brothers' faces. I saw that my brothers were married. That their moustaches quivered with indignation when they saw me in their house. That they didn't like their wives to have anything to do with me. I saw the seasons come and go. I learnt the child had begun to attend the village school. I saw how age spared no one when my mother began to walk with a stoop and complained of a persistent backache. But all I had to do was blink and I would be back where I had wandered from. The quiet grey world where nothing changed and I knew who I was. The mad woman's keeper.

Every morning I woke Chettiar Amma and persuaded her to enter the bathroom. Some days she brushed her teeth quietly. Other days she refused to do so or kept at it relentlessly till I feared that her few remaining teeth would fall out. Then I would bathe her. Ten buckets of cold water had to be emptied over her head; to keep her system cool, the herbal doctor had said. Then I dried her and helped her into her clothes. Sujata Akka had decided that saris were impractical and Chettiar Amma, who had worn only the finest of silk and cotton saris, now dressed like an old Anglo-Indian woman in long drab gowns.

Some days Chettiar Amma was coy and girlish, demanding flowers be braided into her hair, which was cropped to ear length. Some days she refused to wear any clothes and walked around naked. A baby with sagging breasts and a puckered stomach, and a wrinkled bottom, she crawled around, played with her faeces and spat food into my face. I let her be whatever she chose to be.

We were not all that different. In her madness, she escaped from the long iron chain that manacled her to this world. In my sleep, I escaped from the child that grew in my mother's house.

On a damp October afternoon, Chettiar Amma finally escaped her madness and the chain.

When I had cleaned out the west wing, I went to Sujata Akka. 'What do I do now?' I asked.

'Don't go away. I want you to stay here. I'll find you something to do,' she said.

'I will not replace my mother in your kitchen. I will not be another Rukmini Akka. I will not sweep your yards or clean the cowsheds. And now that Prabhu-papa is at boarding school, he doesn't need an ayah chasing after him. What is there left for me to do?' I asked.

Sujata Akka looked at me thoughtfully. I sensed that she was reluctant to let me go. In many ways, I was the only tie she had with the past. Of the times when all she had to be was the daughter-in-law of the house and no more was expected of her. 'You will be my assistant—my eyes and ears. Your hands will reach where mine don't. Your feet will tread where mine can't. Do you understand?'

I stared at her in disbelief. Did she mean what I thought she meant? She wanted me to take her place. She wanted me to be her in proxy.

'Are you sure?' I asked. She looked at me for a long moment and said, 'Yes.'

So I nodded my acceptance.

Amma didn't approve. I'd known she wouldn't. 'Who does she think she is? A queen? What kind of a job is this? What sane woman would give up her house for another woman to run? Her assistant!' Amma snorted. 'If you ask me, the trick is to find a position where you are indispensable ...what is this? All of it will end in grief.'

Then Amma wiped her face and with it her manner. Her

voice softened as she cajoled, 'Don't you want to see Muthu? He'll be back from school in a few minutes. He is very good and the school master says when the time comes, we should send him to a good school in Kancheepuram.'

'No,' I said. 'I don't want to see him. As far as I'm concerned, my duty ends with the money I provide for his care. Don't expect more than that from me.'

'But this is unnatural,' Amma cried. 'He is your son, no matter how often you deny it. I see you with the Chettiar's grandson and I get angry. How can you love someone else's child and not your own?'

I walked away. I had a job to do. To be someone else's eyes, ears, hands and feet. Amma could keep her advice and her Muthu. I wanted no part of it.

My life was the way I determined it to be. I continued to sleep in the west wing. I preferred its isolation to the hum of the main house. My days had no fixed pattern; I did everything Sujata Akka wanted me to do. I wasn't unhappy. In the night, the tablets swept me away into a dark hole that I crouched in till the morning came with its long-handled broom and prodded my eyelids open.

...A year later I discovered how thin the walls of this quiet content were. A year later, I was caught in a churning whirlpool of emotions.

Aren't you bored? Do you really wish me to go on? If you do, I must warn you that you will not approve of what happened next.

I'm not ashamed. I'm not sorry. I am not ridden with guilt. I did what I thought I had to do. If at all any emotion rocks me, it is anger. For valuing myself so little...

Sujata Akka was thirty-seven years old. I had known her for seventeen years. Which meant she had been married for at least nineteen years. But she had only one child. Like everyone else, I too wondered why. Until the day she let me read her eyes and I was reminded of the Missies in Vellore...

Every afternoon, Sujata Akka and I watched TV together for a while. There was a dish antenna on the roof, which offered a choice of seven channels. To me, it was like having a private movie hall.

The Chettiar household had acquired a TV many years ago. But it was placed in the hall and seldom switched on except three times a week. For the Sunday movie, for a film-songs programme on Friday night and for another programme on Wednesday nights.

But once Chettiar Amma died and Sujata Akka became the new Chettiar Amma, she changed everything. The heavy old furniture was replaced; curtains were hung over windows and the old TV was exchanged for a new one.

Sujata Akka placed it in the hall upstairs and she watched it any time she felt like it, and she let me watch it with her.

I reduced the dosage of my sleeping tablets. I no longer had to go through the day in a haze. The TV kept my mind occupied. I only needed to sleep at night. I began to put on weight and the dark circles around my eyes disappeared. I don't know what the other servants thought of me but I didn't care. It wasn't as if I fraternized with them. Once again, just as when I had first come here seventeen years ago, my world was built around Sujata Akka and that was all I needed.

Around two in the afternoon Sujata Akka would begin to look sleepy and I knew what I had to do. I went into the bedroom, pulled the curtains shut, switched the fan on and folded the bedspread so that all she had to do was lie down. While she slept, I turned the volume of the TV down and watched a film. At quarter past four, I would wake her up and she would bathe and wear the sari that I had laid out for her. Sujata Akka was no longer the fresh-faced beauty she was when she first came to the Chettiar Kottai, but she was still very beautiful.

One afternoon as I prepared the room for her, she said, 'Bring a mat and lie down here. Let's talk a bit.'

Sujata Akka was lonely. I knew that. Sridhar Anna was

always busy or travelling and Prabhu-papa had been sent to a boarding school in Ooty. There was hardly anyone she could talk to. If she became friendly with the other women, she knew that they would take advantage and start making demands on her. She had no one but me. I didn't mind that she turned to me only because she didn't have an alternative.

One afternoon, she lay on her side facing me and she said in a faltering voice, 'Tell me about the Missies again. Tell me what you saw.'

I was silent for a moment and then I told her about their strange love for each other and how they seemed to need no one else when they were together. And the joy they found in each others' bodies.

Sujata Akka stared at the ceiling and asked, 'Do you ever wonder what it must be like to be with a man?'

'I've been with a man. Which is why I'm here and there is a child growing in my mother's house.'

'That's not what I meant. In all the films that we see they make such a fuss about love. All those dialogues they speak, the songs they sing, if only those heroines knew what came after.'

'What comes after?' I turned on my side so that I could see her face.

'What comes after is revulsion. When he comes near me, I feel as though a lizard is crawling up my skin. But I close my eyes and let him do whatever he wants to. I know he goes to other women, but if I don't let him do it once in a while, he'll find a mistress like his father did, and flaunt her beneath my nose. Every night when I go to bed, I wait for his touch. Only when he turns on his side and goes to sleep do I fall asleep.

'Marikolanthu, I worry that something is wrong with me. What if I go mad like his mother did? Was it this revulsion for the physical part of marriage that turned her into a mad woman? Is it some sort of a curse on this house?'

'Sujata Akka,' I said, rising to sit by the bed, 'don't be silly. Nothing is wrong with you.'

I placed my palm on her belly. 'Here...do you feel as if a

lizard is crawling over you?'

'No, but...'

And then, her eyes met mine and I saw a hunger there. Such forlorn eyes. Such frustrated desires. Such need...I thought of how Missy K's eyes had followed Missy V. I began to comprehend that Sujata Akka too was filled with the same longings that had made Missy K seek Missy V. But where was she to find someone like Missy V?

Thereafter, every afternoon when Sujata Akka and I talked, we came back to the same subject and I knew for certain that what Sujata Akka felt repelled by was not touch but a man's touch. Was I the same? I wondered.

I didn't know. It was as if I had retrenched all sensation to a point just below my scalp so that the only time I felt alive was when someone ran their fingertips through my hair. So one afternoon when Sujata Akka slid her fingers through my hair I felt a slow unwinding of sensation.

I didn't know what I was doing. All I knew was that it came to me unbidden, the manner in which I could erase that pain, fulfil those desires in her...With the back of my palm, I caressed the side of her breast. With my other hand, I turned her around and very gently let my fingers slide down her spine...

Her voice crept up to greet my touch. 'You have such magic in your fingers.'

I increased the pressure a tiny bit and felt her squirm beneath my fingers. 'I like it when you touch me,' she said and I knew that this was all she would ever say about how she felt.

How easy it is to pleasure a woman. She asks for little except that she be treated as a desirable woman; that she be wooed with abandon and loved gently. With my fingers and mouth, my eyes and soul, I wet that parched body; I rained a million raindrops of sensual pleasure that she gathered with the thirst of one who is condemned to a desert for life and has lost all hope of ever chancing upon an oasis.

I cupped, caressed and contoured. I licked, mouthed and nibbled. Nipples bloomed into garnets. Tongue grazed against hair. Cheek against cheek. Her hair coiled with mine. Our breaths met.

Her fingers slid through my palm. That was all she would do for me. It was I who had sought to give her pleasure and in her pleasure lay my reward. There was to be no more. But I didn't care. I had loved her with my heart for so long; it seemed natural that I love her now with my body; my thwarted dreams and unfulfilled desires.

We never spoke about it. Of what had suddenly happened between us. But every afternoon when the house slumbered, I invented new ways to tease her nerve ends. To slake her thirst. To make her cry softly, 'Enough, enough.'

Nothing had changed between us. There was no room for change in our relationship anyway. I was happy being what I was to her and I needed no more. All my capacity for loving and giving had found a vent in Sujata Akka.

So it was to preserve her happiness, her position in the household, her hold over Sridhar Anna that I welcomed Sridhar Anna into my body.

As long as I fed his appetites, he would never seek another woman. As long as I was available, he would never trouble Sujata Akka on the days he was at home. As long as it was me, I would ask no more of him than what I already had. I was sister to the real thing and I desired no more.

How easy it is to bring a man to your bed. What is perhaps difficult is to keep him happy there. I didn't know who I should be with him: the naïve girl or the brazen whore. So I was both and he seemed to revel in it. I must confess though that from those moments of his ecstasy, I managed to drain a few dregs for myself. I hadn't sought it and so when it happened, I treated it as it was meant to be—as a windfall.

Sometimes I thought of the irony of it all and smiled to myself. By day I gathered with Sujata Akka lilies by a giant lake where herons fished and a gentle breeze blew, ruffling the brown heads of the bulrushes. And by night, Sridhar Anna drove me to the centre of the earth, where molten lava clutched at my feet as I heaved, panted and burnt in the crush of his embrace.

Neither of them loved me. But they needed me. Those who can't have love have to settle for need. What is love if not a need disguised?

When my mother died, my charmed life fell apart. After the funeral, my brothers said, 'Akka, it's time you took Muthu away. All these years you shied away from what was your responsibility. When Amma was alive, she let you do as you wished. But we don't want to be responsible for him any more. It isn't as if you are not alive and earning.'

I heard them out silently. They were bonded in a brotherhood of respectability. I was the outsider who had trespassed into a land of shame. No matter how hard I tried to distance myself from it, they saw only what they wanted to see. I no longer had room or rights in that house.

'Keep him here for a few more days,' I said. 'I have to make arrangements. I have to tell Sujata Akka about this.'

What was I going to do with the boy? Would Sujata Akka let me keep him there? Over the past few months, I had noticed how she grudged my spending time on anything or anyone but herself. She even disliked me watching TV by myself. Only my nights she left alone. Sridhar Anna, no matter how long he was with me, slept in their bed and by her side.

But when I returned to the Chettiar Kottai, it was to discover that once again the seams of my life had been ripped apart.

Sujata Akka was cold and distant. In the afternoon when I went to her room, the door was shut and latched from within. Was she angry with me for having stayed away so long?

I sighed. I couldn't help it. Sometimes Sujata Akka was unreasonable. In my head, I pieced together words of apology, messages of love. Once I explained, she would revert back to my beloved Sujata Akka.

I returned to my room and waited. She would come looking for me soon. In the evening, just as I had expected her to, Sujata

Akka marched into the west wing. 'I want you to pack up and leave right now,' she said.

'What are you saying?' I asked, suddenly frightened by her quivering nostrils, the anger in her eyes, the contempt in her voice.

'How could you do this to me?' she demanded. 'How could you steal my husband away from me? Did you think I would never find out?

'And I never would have, the silly trusting fool that I am...if I hadn't come in here yesterday to have this room cleaned out. I said to myself: it's been shut up for so long, let me get it cleaned and ready for Marikolanthu...I saw his things in here. And suddenly I realized why he has stopped pestering me for some time now. He has you, his whore, right under my roof, that's why.

'How could you forget all that I have done for you? You repay me with treachery...'

Her words squeezed my breath and choked my reply. 'I did it for you,' I tried to explain. 'I know how much you hated it when he came near you and at the same time I didn't want you to lose him to another woman.'

'You are another woman,' she stood stiff, impervious to my pleas.

'But not in the way you think. I wanted nothing more than for you to be happy.' I touched her arm.

She shook my hand off. 'I should have known. I should have guessed this about you. You are unnatural. Do you know that? You turn away from your own child. You prefer a mad woman's company to your mother's. In the daytime, you pretend to be my friend, at night you feed on my husband's lust. What kind of fiend are you?'

'You should know,' I retorted, angry myself. 'We share more than your husband. What will you do once you send me away? Who will love you the way I do?'

'Shut up, shut up, will you?' Sujata Akka's voice rose to a scream. 'You are a wicked creature. I know you used black magic to make me your slave...make me do things no woman would...but not any more, it won't work any more. Get out of this house before I have you thrown out.'

I left the Chettiar Kottai. I didn't collect the money she owed me as salary. I wanted to have nothing more to do with her. She had distorted my love for her with an ugliness I couldn't bear to see.

In my brothers' home, I pleaded for a reprieve. 'I need a few more days,' I said. 'Sujata Akka is making arrangements to send him away to a school in Kancheepuram,' I lied, not knowing what else to do. All I wanted to do was lie down and sleep. 'The child and I will have to stay here for a few more days. Is that too much for a sister to ask of her brothers?'

I saw their faces blanch. But they agreed reluctantly.

I lay on the mat and stared at the ceiling. The dull ache lower down in my belly began. At first, when Sridhar Anna began to sleep with me, I was afraid I would become pregnant. But he said I shouldn't worry and that he'd be careful. As if to reassure me, my periods became longer and heavier. Then the pain began. A dull pain that frequently turned into a throbbing one; a heaviness. That night, the pains were so bad that in the morning, I knew I could no longer put it off and I would have to go to the doctor.

I had a growth in my womb. Many of them, in fact. Flesh within my flesh that fed on my body and grew. A hundred tiny children devouring me alive. I had to have the womb, their home, removed. Where was I going to find the money for the operation?

I had four hundred rupees. I had never thought to put aside even a single paisa. I had kept a little money for myself and handed over the rest of my earnings to my mother. I could ask Sridhar Anna and he would give me the money. But that would make me a whore. Someone who accepted money for letting a man use her body. I thought of Sujata Akka's face. I didn't want anything that belonged to her. Neither her husband nor his money.

In the bus back to the village, I made up my mind. It was time the boy paid his dues. It was time Murugesan paid for what he did to me.

I took the boy to Kancheepuram, where the looms were. To Murugesan's looms. Murugesan wasn't there. He had become a busy man, a rich man, they told me. He travelled a great deal. He went by plane to foreign countries. Orders for his silk came from far-away places. But I didn't want to see Murugesan. His manager would do. His manager knew what I wanted. Others like me had been there before. It was a matter of mere routine for him. Every day they took on boys to stretch the warps of the loom and feed the threads to form the intricate patterns of the silk saris they wove. So I mortgaged the boy to Murugesan's looms for the next two years in return for five thousand rupees. He would be paid ten rupees a day. Thirty days made three hundred rupees; twelve months would fetch three thousand six hundred rupees. All I needed was five thousand rupees. The rest of the money would pay for the boy's keep.

A perverse satisfaction flared within me. Murugesan might not know it but I had sold him his own son. I had finally collected rent for nine months of housing the boy. With the rent money raised from the boy's sweat and blood, I would destroy the house and the bond that wove our lives together.

'Is this the new school that Sujata Akka has sent me to? It doesn't look like a school,' the boy said. He was only eight years old, but he understood more than he had been told.

I nodded and then decided that I would tell him the truth. 'This isn't a school. This is a silk loom. They will teach you a trade here; how to weave. In that sense, it is like a school.'

The boy didn't say anything. He looked at his feet. I gave him the small cloth bag with his clothes and things. 'I have to go,' I said.

'When will you come to take me back home?' he asked.

'There is no home any more. But I will come back one of these days,' I said and walked away.

After the surgery, the pain disappeared but the heaviness

remained. It dragged my feet and numbed my mind. I decided to stay on in Kancheepuram. The village with its mango orchard and Chettiar Kottai carried too many memories. I found a job as a cook. A series of jobs. As soon as the smells of a household began to permeate my pores, I left. I was a restless spirit, warped and bitter. Sometimes I would think of the past and I would feel a quickening in the vacuum that existed within me now.

✝

A year later, Murugesan died. I read about it in the Tamil newspaper they bought in the house I was working in. He had gone to Singapore on business and while there, he had a heart attack. His body would reach his home, the paper said, in three or four days.

The road to the cremation ground was two streets away from the house I worked in. I waited with my ears cocked. The moment I heard a funeral procession go past, I rushed to the terrace from where I could see the goings-on quite clearly. On the fourth day after the news item appeared, his funeral procession went past. He was laid out on a byre, dressed in sparkling white clothes. If he had died here, they would have seated him in a chair as though he were alive. But his body must have stiffened and they would have had to break his back and limbs to fit him into a chair.

Drumbeats rang through the air and his sons, his legitimate sons, walked holding a pot of water in their hands. Flowers rained and I was glad that the green sprigs of marikolanthu would never grace the body of that creature. Rose petals and marigolds, chrysanthemum strands and lilies of the valley—the air was heavy with the fragrance of flowers and incense. Urchins danced as they always did at funerals, twisting and wriggling their bodies with a manic joy, light on their feet, whistling through their teeth to the rhythm of the drum beat. Among the urchins, I spotted the boy.

Dance, dance, I told the boy. Dance at your own father's funeral and let his spirit watch you with sorrow. That you celebrate his passing with such glorious abandon.

The cremation ground was bathed in the evening light. It was the month of January. The night would come early. How strange, I thought, struck by the coincidence. It was in January that he had destroyed my life and now in another January, his life had come to an end.

From behind a clump of trees that fringed the ground, I watched the pyre being built. A woodpile that would smear the skies with the stench of death. I waited. When he was reduced to ashes and when everyone had left, I would stand on his ashes and spit on them.

Murugesan's son, his legitimate son, lit the pyre while the boy stood on the side watching. What was he doing here, I wondered.

The flames blazed. Voices carried: The body isn't burning. Must be because of all the chemicals they used to preserve it. Heap some more wood on it. Here boy, put this onto the pyre.

The flames died down. A horrified whisper: the body is untouched. It's charred in a few places and the skin has peeled off. But it's still there. Don't let his sons see it. Leave someone here to ensure that the men do the rest. There is nothing more for us here...Here boy, aren't you from Murugesan's loom? Stay here and keep an eye on the men while they try burning the body again...

Finally, it was the boy who had to assist his father's passage to the other world. The cremation ground was deserted except for the men who worked there, the boy, and I.

Hidden by the night, I stood there and watched the boy gather wood to light the pyre again. I saw him walking through the grounds foraging for leftover kindling from other pyres, twigs, branches, dried grass...anything that would break into flame. The boy's face was clenched in sorrow; or was it pity?

I crept closer and saw the half-charred and half-intact corpse. Grown-up men, Murugesan's relatives, had walked away unable to bear the thought of being confronted by such a horrifying creature. What was the boy thinking as he lit the second heap of logs? I felt a great sadness wash over me. I had reduced the boy to this. A chandala. A keeper of graves, the overseer of the dead. He didn't deserve this. Or any of what had happened to him.

As the flames leapt, my hate burnt with them. What was left in this world for me to hate, I thought. Murugesan was a smouldering heap of ashes. There was Muthu. But what could I hate him for? The bitterness unravelled. 'Muthu,' I called softly.

He turned towards where I stood. I saw his face fill with joy. I had expected hostility, anger, but not this unsullied joy. For the first time, I felt shame. Not remorse for having rejected him as a baby, you must understand. That was destined to be. But I felt shame for having used him. How was I any different from that long line of people who had used me and then discarded me when their need was over? I knew that I would have to make up to him for that.

There was so much work to be done before I could claim him for my own. I had to find the money to buy him back. Missy K, I thought. Missy K would understand and help. Perhaps she would even help me find a job in the city she lived in.

Once again, I felt a quickening in my phantom womb. My child was about to be born.

...Remember what I told you about the roles in my life having no chronology; no sense of rightness. What happened then was that for the first time, I wrested control of my destiny. I wasn't going to wage wars or rule kingdoms. All I wanted was a measure of happiness. All I wanted to be was Muthu's mother.

For so long now, I had been content to remain a sister to the real thing. Surrogate housewife. Surrogate mother. Surrogate lover. But now I wanted more. I wanted to be the real thing.

11

Akhila Speaks

Akhila is sitting on a bench by the sea. She will sit here till the streetlights come on and then she will walk back to the hotel, she decides. A short distance away, between her and the sea, is a young man leaning against his motorbike. He is trying to light a cigarette with his back to the sea. The breeze lifts his hair and flops it down on his brow. His face is chubby and boyish in spite of the thick moustache. His eyes are not a child's; his tight blue jeans and rust-coloured T-shirt swathe a body that is swaggeringly male, she thinks. When he lifts his head from his cupped palms, their eyes lock. She matches his scrutiny with hers. His eyes drop. A little later Akhila sees him leave. She smiles. She has never known such power before.

For two days now, Akhila has been living in a hotel at Kanyakumari. The hotel is by the beach and is called Sea Breeze. The porch leads to a small lobby. Along one wall is a sofa with paisley-patterned upholstery. On the opposite wall is a huge mural. The receptionist in a white shirt and black trousers smiles at her and calls her 'Madam'.

There is a restaurant attached to the hotel. The food is plain and vegetarian. Akhila sits at a table by herself three times a day and each day, she tries a new dish. She has already sampled everything there is on the menu.

Families stay here and old couples. Tourists and pilgrims.

Akhila doesn't know to which category she belongs. But it doesn't matter. She listens to the conversation that swirls around her.

Akhila has a room that faces the sea. From her balcony, she can watch the sun rise and set. Below the horizon the water rests, a calm sheet of copper. Every morning and evening, she goes out for a walk. Sometimes people stare at her. They are not used to the sight of a single woman all by herself. A foreigner they can understand, but an Indian woman...She walks past them slowly, not increasing her pace or letting them know that she can read their looks. It doesn't matter. She doesn't care any more.

Forty-five-year-old spinsters have a reputation. For primness; for a meanness around their mouths; for the drying up of pores, crevices and ducts; for a self-absorption that borders on the obsessive and for an unfailing ability to detect a flaw in everything that is fair and unsullied.

And so it was with Akhila. Elderly spinster. Older sister. Once the breadwinner of the family. Still the cash cow.

But Akhila is certain that she won't let her family use her any more. Look at me, she would tell them. Look at me: I'm the woman you think you know. I am the sister you have wondered about. There is more to this Akka. For within me is a woman I have discovered.

The next evening, he is waiting for her. In blue jeans and an olive green T-shirt, lounging against his bike. She pretends not to see him and sits in her usual place. He clears his throat. She turns towards him and smiles. 'Hello,' she says.

She sees confusion mark his face. The women of his world don't speak unless spoken to first and even then they would have nothing to do with a stranger.

'What's your name?' she asks. Then she changes her mind and says, 'Actually, don't tell me. I don't want to know your name.'

'Vinod. My name is Vinod,' he says quickly. She looks at

him. He must be in his mid-twenties, she decides.

She gets up to leave and feels his eyes follow her down the road.

Akhila discovers that she likes being alone. She has no more doubts about what her life will be like if she lives alone. It may not be what she dreamt it to be, but at least she would have made the effort to find out. And perhaps that is all she needs to ask of life now. That she be allowed to try and experience it...

Akhila is sitting by the sea. The young man isn't there. For a moment, only for a moment, Akhila feels a small stab of disappointment. She closes her eyes and feels the breeze caress her eyelids. For the first time in her life, Akhila knows what it is to woo the moment.

A motorbike roars past her and then shudders to a halt. She keeps her eyes shut. She hears a throat clear to announce a presence. Akhila opens her eyes. It is the young man.

'Hello,' she says. She sees his eyes light up in relief.

'I wasn't sure...you...would be here. I thought you would try to avoid me.' The words tumble out haltingly.

'Why would you think that?' Akhila asks.

'I don't know...because I spoke to you yesterday,' he says, running his hands through his hair.

'You didn't. I spoke to you first,' she corrects.

'Where are you from?' he asks suddenly.

Akhila smiles. He is a boy pretending to be a man, she thinks. 'Why do you want to know?'

She sees his eyes drop.

'Why don't you sit down?' she says, pointing to a place on the bench, and when he smiles and hastens to sit beside her, Akhila knows what it feels like to be the cat in a cat and mouse game.

At night, Akhila's dreams take on a pattern of a ceaseless searching. She wakes up with her mouth tasting of chalk and a spiralling helplessness. I know what I want to do. So why do my dreams leave me so despondent, she asks herself one morning. That is the day Akhila decides to seduce the young man. One final act to consummate her decision. Where the body goes, the mind will follow, she tells herself, repudiating all that has been instilled in her. One feat of courage, to tread where she has never gone before. If there was a mountain, Akhila would try and climb it. She feels lust crouch in her temples and demand that she do its bidding.

Akhila sets herself a little game: if he makes the first move, I'll go no further. I don't want a man trying to broaden his horizon with my body. I don't want to be another experience.

She walks to the bench. He is waiting there for her. A grin tugs at her lips. She bends her head to hide it. When she lifts her face, he sees an Akhila who wears the ghost of a smile.

'Hello,' he says. 'You are late today.'

She shrugs and sits down. He waits for her to invite him to join him on the bench. Akhila begins to enjoy her little game.

She looks at the sea.

'Aren't you going to sit down?' she asks.

'Where are you from?' he repeats his question of the day before.

She smiles and shakes her head. 'I don't like questions,' she says. Why am I so reluctant to talk about myself, Akhila asks herself. This is for now. This has to end here. That's why, she tells herself.

He doesn't know whether he should feel rebuffed and leave. He can't determine what she wants and yet he is reluctant to depart. To fill the silence, to prolong his stay, he begins to tell her about himself. Akhila lets his words wash over her. She sees that the people on the road are watching them. She thinks of what they will see: a middle-aged woman and a young man. She thinks of the speculation that will cross their minds. She thinks that what they see or will say is of no importance to her.

She turns and looks at him. Tomorrow she will play the game once more and then she will do what she has to do. The day after, it will be time to leave.

In the morning Akhila is drawn to a newspaper item about a suicide pact. A whole family in a small town in Kerala. The father of the family administered poison to his wife and four children and then hung himself from a hook in the ceiling. In the note he left behind, he talked of hopelessness. He had AIDS and he didn't want his family ostracized because of him. He knew of no other way to protect them from disgrace and unhappiness, he wrote.

Did his wife want to die with him? What about his children? Akhila thinks. How dare he take their lives as if it was his right to decide whether they lived or died?

Akhila turns the page in disgust. She thinks how a fortnight ago, she would have read the news item without worrying about the wife or children.

For the first time, Akhila remembers Sarasa Mami not with pity but with admiration. The difference as Akhila knows it now is that Sarasa Mami lived in the best way she knew; while she, Akhila, hadn't.

Akhila stares at her young man as if to inscribe his features in her mind. He is there, faithful, fawning, and still unable to hold her gaze. He will not make the move, she knows. Has she won her game or lost it? Akhila wonders. Don't be a coward now, she tells herself sternly. You want this. You need this. You have to be able to do this.

She takes his hand in hers and says, 'I'm staying at the hotel Sea Breeze. Why don't you come by later in the evening?'

A couple of hours later, the phone rings. The receptionist's voice is curious and disapproving. 'A Mr Vinod is here. He says he is your relative. Shall I send him up to your room?'

Akhila smiles into the receiver, 'Yes.'

She opens the door and goes to stand on the balcony. She hears him close the door. She waits for him to latch it. When he does, she smiles again. She knows what it is he wants. She wants the same.

He comes to stand by her.

'I love the sea at night. At night, it feasts upon each one of our senses,' Akhila says. He moves closer. She thinks she can hear his heart beat. Why, he is afraid, she laughs. He is looking to me to help him out.

'Do you have a condom?' she asks. He hasn't thought about it, she knows. He turns on his heel to leave. Just for a second, she thinks that she has dampened his ardour. Then she realizes that he will be back.

When he returns, she lets him love her with the windows and the balcony door flung open to the night and the lights on. When he reaches to switch off the light, she stills his hand. 'What are you ashamed of?' she asks.

He is impatient to enter her. She wriggles on her back and guides his hands to her breasts. 'Slowly, slowly,' she says. 'I'm not going anywhere.'

But he can't hold himself back and parts her legs. A spasm of hurt grabs at Akhila. It's been so long since Hari. But lust parts flesh easily and Akhila is swamped by lust. A lust which evolves, sustains and withdraws into itself. A lust that radiates the heat of fire. The energy that defines life. Akhila is lust. Akhila is Sakthi. Akhila is Akhilandeswari decimated into ten entities.

Kali. Ready to destroy all that comes between her and the flow of time.

Tara. With the golden embryo from which a new universe will evolve. She will be her own void and infinity.

Sodasi. Fullness at sixteen. Nurturing dreams and hopes. Even now, at forty-five.

Bhuvaneshwari. The forces of the material world surge within her.

Bhairavi. Seeking to find ways and means to fulfil her desires before all is null and void.

Chinnamasta. The naked one continuing the state of

self-sustenance in the created world; making possible destruction and renewal in a cyclic order.

Dhumathi. Misfortune personified. An old hag riding an ass with a broom in one hand and a crow on her banner.

Bagala. The crane-headed one, the ugly side of all living creatures. Jealousy, hatred, cruelty, she is all this and more.

Matangi. Seeking to dominate.

And then there is Kamala. Pure consciousness of the self, bestowing boons and allaying fears...The Akhila her family knew.

This is who Akhila is. Together and separate. Akhila knows this as her body moves through a catacomb of sensations. One wave after another hurling her through an underground stream that had remained dammed for so many years. Akhila has no more fears. Why then should she walk with a downcast head?

She throws her head back and voices her triumph.

The young man stands by the door and asks, 'Shall I come back tomorrow?'

Akhila smiles. He hasn't even asked her what her name is. Which is exactly how she wants it. A need satiated. Her past purged. A point proven to herself. An older man would want to know much more. An older man would want to lead the way. So Akhila smiles again because she discovers it is so easy to smile now that she has her life where she wants it to be.

In the morning, Akhila wakes up with Hari on her mind. Is she being foolish, she wonders? Hari must have made a life for himself and here she is, behaving like a heroine in a romance novel. Once she had thought that she couldn't love another man like she had loved Hari. Giving him all of her body and soul. This morning, she thinks anything is possible. That she will have the courage to pick up from where she left off and begin again. That as much as she desired Hari, she desires life more.

And so it is that Akhila opens her handbag and draws out the address book where Hari's name is one among several names.

She picks up the phone and places a person-to-person call to Madras. Will he be there? she wonders. Would he want to know about the years that have gone by? Or of why she had chosen to walk away from him?

She wonders if she is being foolish. Hari could be married. Hari could have left Madras. But there is the dream and so she waits...

She will wait one more hour and then she will have to leave for the railway station. To wrest the reins of her life back, she thinks, looking at her return train ticket.

The telephone on the table near the bed rings. Akhila walks towards it. Her heart races. She wonders: could it be him?

Hari's voice is low and cautious; incredulous, too.

'Hello,' she says. 'This is Akhila. Akhilandeswari.'

Author's Note

Until early 1998, there was a special counter for ladies, senior citizens and handicapped persons in the Bangalore Cantonment railway station. And there were ladies coupés in most overnight trains with second-class reservation compartments.

Since then, the ladies queue has been abolished in all railway stations. I have also been informed by various railway authorities, primarily stationmasters and ticket checkers, that the ladies coupé doesn't exist any more and that the new coaches are built without the coupé.